SHAPE OF A WARRIOR

SHAPE OF A WARRIOR

PEGGY CARR

Emmanuel Publishing House

Shape of a Warrior Published by:
Emmanuel Publishing House
Roseau, Commonwealth of Dominica

ISBN: 978-976-95888-9-9

Emmanuel Publishing House
www.emmanuelpublishinghouse.com
emmanuelpublications99@gmail.com

Cover art by Veronica Peace
Design by James Tampa

CONTENTS

Map of Hiroon I		IX
Map of Hiroon II		X
Glossary of Kalina Words		XI
CHAPTER 1	On the Banks of the River	1
CHAPTER 2	Five Hurricane Seasons Later	15
CHAPTER 3	Triumphant Return	27
CHAPTER 4	Night of Fire	34
CHAPTER 5	Finding Shelter	43
CHAPTER 6	Friends on the Plain	45
CHAPTER 7	Under the the Ash	54
CHAPTER 8	Morning Mirage	60
CHAPTER 9	Water Woes	65
CHAPTER 10	Chiefs' Meeting	71
CHAPTER 11	Boats in the Woods	74
CHAPTER 12	Girls in the Gorge	82
CHAPTER 13	Going Home	89
CHAPTER 14	Finding the Mark	105
CHAPTER 15	When Night Falls	111
CHAPTER 16	Sea Training	117
CHAPTER 17	Final Challenge	126
CHAPTER 18	Under the Shaman's Eye	130
CHAPTER 19	Initiation Ceremony	135
CHAPTER 20	Firelight on the Beach	142

CHAPTER 21	Unwelcome Visitor	148
CHAPTER 22	In the Heart of the Forest	155
CHAPTER 23	Cooking Practice	160
CHAPTER 24	Aloo Gets a Gift	165
CHAPTER 25	The Path of a Battle	169
CHAPTER 26	Learning from the Earth	172
CHAPTER 27	Above and Below	180
CHAPTER 28	A Deeply Hidden Secret	183
CHAPTER 29	Cracks in the Cover	189
CHAPTER 30	On a Rock	197
CHAPTER 31	The Launch of a Boat	201
CHAPTER 32	A Tough Task	212
CHAPTER 33	Early Morning Quest	218
CHAPTER 34	Out in the Open	224
CHAPTER 35	The Fist of the Storm	234
CHAPTER 36	Fighting to Rise Again	241
CHAPTER 37	A Strange Encounter	248
CHAPTER 38	Tough Choices	253
CHAPTER 39	Behind the Clouds	258
CHAPTER 40	A String of Isles	266
CHAPTER 41	A Sultry Night	282
CHAPTER 42	Two Warriors	289
CHAPTER 43	Three Moons Later	303
Author's Note		306
Acknowledgements		308
About the Author		310

To Nya and Reka,
so that you can roam the great outdoors,
even when you have to stay indoors.

Africans were navigating the Atlantic before Christ.... Paired men and women were being chosen for the new expedition, and fears were expressed that the king [Abubakari the Second, 14th century ruler of the Mali Empire in West Africa] in his madness would sacrifice hundreds of his subjects to the dark sea. ... Then one day, dressed in a flowing white robe and a jeweled turban, he took leave of Mali and set out with his fleet down the Senegal, heading west across the Atlantic, never to return. He took his griot and half his history with him.

—IVAN VAN SERTIMA, *They Came Before Columbus*

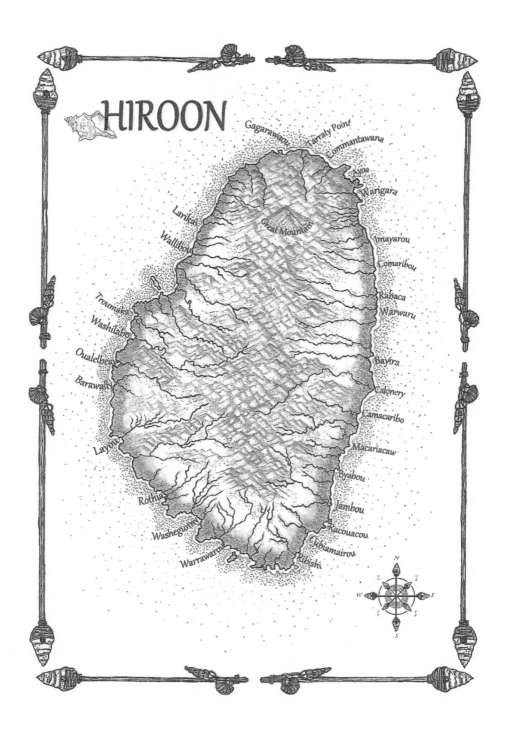

HIROON

Gagarawou
Tarraly Point
Commantawana
Ayoa
Warigara
Larikai
Wallibou
Imayarou
Great Mountain
Comaribou
Rabaca
Troumaka
Warwaru
Washilabo
Oualelbeu
Bayfra
Barawalli
Calonery
Camacaribo
Macariacaw
Layou
Byabou
Rothia
Jambou
Washegunno
Racouacou
Clibiamairou
Warrawarou
Ribishi

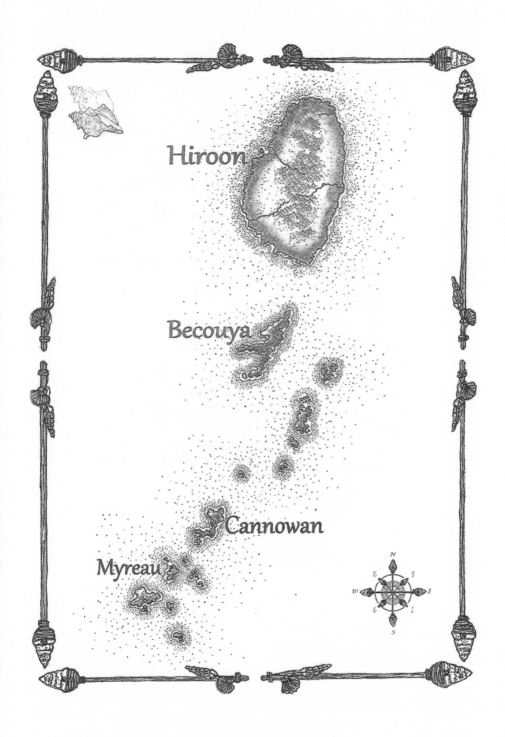

Hiroon

Becouya

Cannowan

Myreau

GLOSSARY OF KALINA WORDS

ajoupa   A shed or lean-to

bouleua   A multipurpose reed

coylaya   Black stone

mahoe   Any plant that can be used to make rope

manicou   Opossum

maybouya   Evil spirit

piragua   War canoe

taboui   Men's communal hut

woku   Cassava beer

ON THE BANKS OF THE RIVER

Yurubi knew she was in trouble.

The shadow of the almond tree was stretching toward the big sloping rock, which meant Ma was about to come looking for her. Yurubi grabbed her gourd from where she had wedged it between two stones. She waded a little further into the river and dipped the gourd just below the surface to avoid getting sand or leaves in the water. When the gourd was full, she hoisted it onto her head and hurried up the path to the village.

"Yuruuuubiiii!"

The voice reached her as she crested the hill.

"Coming, Ma!"

A few drops of water sloshed out of the gourd and down Yurubi's bare back as she reached the top of the slope and began to half-run across the dirt yard to her family's hut.

"You've been playing in the river by yourself again," Ma said, her forehead creased in a frown.

She lifted the gourd off Yurubi's head and in one motion poured the water into a huge pot of boiling yams. Ma set down the gourd and put her hands on her wide hips, her usual smile tucked away.

"How many times do I have to tell you not to linger down there, child? How many times?"

Yurubi bent her head. Out of the corner of her eye, she saw some of the other children on the far side of the yard stopping their game of leapfrog to stare as Ma scolded her. If she hadn't gotten into trouble for staying too long at the river, she could've been joining the game now.

She tilted her head a little to look up at Ma, trying to tell whether it would be a quick scolding or one of those that went on and on.

Ma's lips were still drawn in a hard, straight line. Yurubi's heart sank. She really was in trouble. She didn't mind the scolding so much as making Ma angry.

"You're a worry, child. A real worry."

Ma reached down and ran her hands over Yurubi's wet hair.

"Look at this," she said, squeezing water from the hair ends at Yurubi's waist. "You're supposed to go down to the river, fill up the gourd and come straight back here, like all the other little girls do."

"Yes, Ma."

"You say 'yes, Ma, yes, Ma,' and the next day you do the same thing again."

"No, Ma."

Ma rolled her eyes and turned back to the steaming pot of yams. "Go fetch me the stick to try these," she said, her voice sounding weary.

Yurubi ran over to a small *ajoupa* in the corner of the yard and where the cooking utensils were stored in baskets. She found the two-pronged stick for prodding the yams and took it over to Ma then darted back to the stack of baskets and rummaged around in one of them to find some limes. She took them to Grandma Lulou, who was crouched over a small fire, stirring a thick red sauce in a wide pot. The sharp smell of peppers rose on the steam that curled around Grandma Lulou's lined face.

"You never listen," said Grandma Lulou, her voice quavering. Her gnarled hand shook as she pointed her stirring stick at Yurubi. "If you don't pay heed, one of these days that river will take you. Like it took—"

"Like it took Carika's first boy," said Waasha from the knoll where she was kneeling, grinding cassava on a big flat rock.

Sweat beaded Waasha's lean face. Her hair, held back from her forehead by a red and yellow cotton band, swung back and forth over her shoulders. The muscles in her slender arms moved in live rhythm to the crunch of the cassava under the long oblong rock in her hands. The rustle of her shell necklace against her breasts was part of the music that was Waasha.

Yurubi ran over and set down a clay mug of water next to her. Waasha stopped grinding for a moment and took a long drink, her head thrown back, her hair brushing the back of her waist.

Waasha was like Yurubi's big sister. But she was really Ma's little sister. Yurubi hoped she'd grow up to be strong and beautiful like Waasha but didn't think she'd want to spend that much time grinding cassava and corn. She'd much prefer to roam along the cliffs and over the hills, finding hidden nooks, climbing trees and rolling about in fields of flowers.

"You dream too much, even in broad daylight, that's the trouble," said Waasha, almost as if she had heard Yurubi.

The scolding continued as Yurubi scampered back and forth across the yard, carrying things that Ma, Grandma Lulou and Waasha needed to do their work. But Yurubi had stopped listening.

She was thinking about her little play boat that she hadn't yet had a chance to try on the water. She had found the small piece of light bafflow wood on the riverbank and used a sharp stone to scoop out the soft core and shape the ends. She had rubbed it smooth, first with a flattish stone and then with a handful of dried coconut fibre. It looked like it would float well.

"… you listening, girl?" Waasha was looking at her with raised eyebrows.

"Yes, Waasha." Yurubi ran over with a wide shallow basket for the ground cassava.

"Little girls who don't know when to leave the river might never leave the river."

Yurubi nodded and squatted near Waasha to help scoop the ground cassava into the basket. She had heard over and over the stories of children who had been swept away by the river, never to be seen again. In some of the stories, the river had crept up the bank steadily and snatched the child playing on its banks. Or it had reared up suddenly, roaring around the bend and swallowing the child in one gulp.

But none of those stories scared Yurubi. What Ma and the others didn't know was that the river was Yurubi's playmate and would never harm her. If they knew, perhaps they wouldn't scold her so much. But if she tried to tell them, they'd only call her a dreamer. Again.

There was a time when Ma didn't mind so much if Yurubi wandered off after a hummingbird or got lost watching the clouds change shape. After all, Yurubi was not a baby. She'd been born seven whole hurricane seasons ago.

But since that day when the boats had returned without Ma's mate, she'd been different. Ma had cried a lot that day.

You've lost your father, little one, she'd said, clutching Yurubi tightly to her.

M-my father? Yurubi was shocked. Until then, she hadn't even known that girls had fathers. Since that day, something had changed about Ma. She didn't joke as much with Yurubi and often twisted her mouth when she was looking out over the ocean. And she got upset if she lost sight of Yurubi for too long.

Yurubi sighed softly as she tamped down the wet cassava in the basket. Right now, she so much wanted to go back to the river to try floating her boat. Perhaps she could slip back down there when the sun leaned away from the village, and Ma would be chatting drowsily with the other women under the flame tree in the yard.

Yurubi's world was bounded by the seashore and an expanse of blue ocean to the east, the river and folds of densely forested hills to the west, a steep drop into a valley to the south, and a hillside plot to the north where the women grew corn, cassava, sweet potatoes and yams in the shadow of a tall mountain.

In the hilltop village, she had the run of a wide yard half-ringed by round grass huts. A little distance away, on the open side of the half circle, stood the big four-cornered *taboui* that was out of bounds for her. That was where the men and boys lived, slept, and talked in secret about things they didn't want girls to hear. Yurubi was not even allowed to go near the wide platform on which the taboui stood, except if there was a celebration or some other kind of gathering for the whole village. She also knew, without being told, to stay away from the tightly woven hut far out on the edge of the village where the shaman lived.

Within those boundaries, Yurubi had a huge playground stretching from the black sand beach way below, up the hill to the village and down the other side to the river.

And over all of it, there was magic.

For a long time, Yurubi had thought that everyone could see and hear the magic.

Look, Ma, she'd say, pointing at the ocean as it breathed white foam like a huge restless blue-green animal.

Yes, child, it's rough out there today. It's this wind. Ma would tug Yurubi away from the cliffside and back to the ajoupa.

Looking over her shoulder as she trailed after Ma, Yurubi could see herself riding the heaving back of the ocean to those lands the men often talked about with such excitement.

Even when Yurubi was sitting under the ajoupa stacking bowls or eating cassava bread, she could find magic. On the far side of the village, the forest was busy all day, trying on shade after shade of green with jewellery of yellow, purple, brown and red. After sundown, the forest would complain raucously when it had to settle for only black.

When Yurubi was at the river, it would giggle with her about gossip it had heard in the forests, mountains and valleys. Sometimes when Ma was there doing the washing, Yurubi would lie flat on her back in the shallows, listening to the whispers of the river and watching flocks of parrots smudging the white clouds with their brilliant green, yellow and blue feathers.

Whether the river was laughing, whispering or roaring, Yurubi loved its voice. Like her, all the creatures on the island were drawn to it. Sharp-nosed agoutis, long green iguanas, shy *manicous*, blunt-nosed pigs and even snakes came to chat with the river.

Now, as Yurubi sped down the path, her hair flying behind her, she could hear the river singing along to the cawing of birds and the swish of the breeze through the trees on its banks.

Yurubi ran to the tall sloping rock on the riverbank and edged around the bushes to its sheer side. Standing on tiptoe, she felt for the crevice behind a clump of rock ferns. Her heart tripped as her fingers closed over the play boat she'd hidden there.

She splashed into the river and set the boat gently on the water. She bit her lip as the boat rocked wildly on the current, but it soon steadied and began to float downstream.

Yurubi waded in the shallows alongside the tiny craft, laughing as it picked up speed and began bouncing on a slightly stronger current. After a while, she grabbed the boat and filled it with a handful of gravel from the riverbed. When she released the little boat again, it was sitting lower in the water and was listing somewhat but was still floating well.

Yurubi chuckled. She stirred the water under the boat with one hand, creating some ripples. It rocked from side to side but rode easily on the little waves.

Using both hands now, Yurubi churned up the water, laughing in delight as the boat spun about and rocked crazily on the rough waves. Suddenly, it keeled over, tipping the stones into the water. Yurubi lurched forward and grabbed the boat before the current could carry it away.

She waded into a small pool where she and the other children usually bathed. Humming under her breath, she floated the boat gently, careful not to let it drift too far. The water was shallow and placid here, but it became deep and swift further out. She would lose her boat if it got caught on a faster current.

It was almost time to go, but she stood still for a moment, giggling at the tickle of fine riverbed gravel between her toes, the trickle of water from her bangs onto her eyelashes and nose, the tug of the river on the ends of her hair. On the bank, the bamboo fronds and reeds leaned over to whisper something to the river but reared back as the wind rattled the seed bushes behind them.

Yurubi waded to the bank and turned for one last look at the river. It was tossing up a laughing white spray as it splashed over smooth stones and rough rocks, playing with fingers of sunlight, stealing the dark green of the overhanging trees as it sneaked around the bend.

With a grin, Yurubi turned toward the big rock to hide her little boat again. Out of the corner of her eye, she caught a slight movement in the trees above the opposite bank. She stood still, waiting to see if it was an agouti coming down to the water to drink. They usually scampered away from the river at the slightest sound or movement.

Squatting slowly, Yurubi kept her eyes on the spot in the heavily shaded clump of trees where she had caught the movement. If it was one of those mean black pigs that roamed the forest, she wouldn't want to face it alone, even across the river.

There it was again. More like a shifting shadow. But now Yurubi could see the glint of what looked like a pair of eyes. The droplets of water on her back suddenly felt cold. If those were eyes, the creature in the forest was way bigger than anything Yurubi had ever seen. She should run home now, as fast as she could. But she stayed crouched there, heart pounding, waiting to see what would come out of the trees. She strained her ears for any strange sounds, but all she could hear was the rush of the river and the call of birds.

The shadow shifted again, and the eyes disappeared. But now something round and black was edging into view from behind one of the big trees.

Yurubi could not move even if she wanted to. The dark shape slowly grew bigger. Yurubi's eyes stretched wide. The movement stopped. Yurubi leaned forward on her haunches, her body trembling. Her mouth fell open. Staring back at her from the shadow of the tree was the face of a child.

Yurubi stood slowly. The face drew back behind the tree, but Yurubi could still see one eye peeking out. She couldn't tell whether it was a boy or a girl, but the child looked about her size.

"How did you get over there?" Yurubi called out, cupping her hands around her mouth.

No answer.

Perhaps the child had been swept away by the river from a village higher up. But why was he or she hiding?

Yurubi waded into the water and climbed up on the broad flat rock the women used for washing.

"Don't be frightened!" she shouted. "I'm going to get someone to bring you over!"

Still no answer, but now the child was coming out from behind the tree and stumbling toward the river. Yurubi's mouth dropped open again. A little boy, painted black from head to toe, stood swaying in the afternoon sunlight. He took another step forward then toppled over. Like a sack of cassava, he rolled down the riverbank and came to rest against a log on the edge of the water.

Yurubi let out a small cry. Was he wounded? Dead?

From her perch on the rock, she looked around to see if anyone else was in sight. There was no one. At this time of day, the women would be chatting or oiling each other's hair in the shade of the trees while the children played nearby. The boys and men would be sharpening their knives, axes, and arrows in the cool of the taboui and making plans for the next day's hunting and fishing.

With one last look at the unmoving body lying at the water's edge, Yurubi turned, slid down the rock and splashed to the shore. She ran along the river, going upstream to a point where a row of rocks formed an uneven line from one bank of the river to the other. She'd seen the men crossing the river here, leaping from one rock to another, as agile as agoutis.

Yurubi waded into the shallows, past the first two rocks, and when she was chest deep, she climbed onto the third rock. With a pounding heart, she looked at the huge gap to the next one. She couldn't leap that far. She would fall, for sure.

Like all the children in the village, she could swim like a fish, but this part of the river was not for swimming. The current was too strong, and there were too many sharp rocks.

She looked downstream at the boy, whose head was almost in the water. She should go get one of the men. But what if the river took the boy before they got back? Or a pig found him?

A shiver ran down Yurubi's back.

What if this boy was a captive who'd run away from another village? She had heard often enough the warriors' stories about their raids on other islands and how they dealt with captives. Men and boys in particular.

Yurubi braced her legs and leapt. She landed on the very edge of the next rock, her wet feet slipping a little, but she clung hard with both hands and pulled herself onto the sloping surface.

Drawing a deep breath, Yurubi stood and looked at the line of rocks ahead of her. Her heart sank. The gaps between the rocks were much wider here, too wide for her to leap. And she couldn't get back into the water because it was deep and swift out here, almost in the middle of the river.

On the far bank, the boy still had not moved. Yurubi couldn't tell if he was breathing.

Lying on her stomach, Yurubi leaned over the edge of the rock and stretched both hands toward the water. The stiff current pulled at her fingers.

"I've got to reach him," she whispered.

She felt dried twigs and leaves brushing her hands, bits of gravel running through her fingers. Above the gushing of the river, she heard a slight thump. Yurubi's head shot up. A little way upstream, a small log was bumping its way among the rocks, turning this way and that as if to find a clear path. Yurubi jumped to her feet, her heart racing. The log brushed against a boulder and spun around, floating crossways toward the rock on which she was standing.

She fixed her eyes on the log and waited. It hit a faster current and flipped around again. No time to ponder. Yurubi squatted and slid into the churning water as the log sailed past. The water picked her up like a twig and tossed her downstream. Kicking as hard as she could, she grabbed at the log. It rolled under her hands and bounced away. She paddled her arms and legs furiously, riding the powerful current as best she could. The log spun crossways again, and Yurubi crashed into it, her breath knocked out of her as she was folded almost in two against the wood.

She clung to the log, gasping for breath. It rolled a bit and she twisted her legs around it, trying to straddle it like she'd seen the big boys doing at the beach when they were riding lengths of driftwood.

The current was taking her closer to the far bank of the river, but it didn't look like she would make it to where the boy was lying. As she swept past a smooth rock, Yurubi kicked out with her left leg and pushed hard against the rock, trying to steer the log toward the riverbank.

A rough current caught the log, and Yurubi could feel it bouncing and rolling. She wrapped both arms around it and held on tight.

It turned a little, picking up speed. Yurubi tightened her grip and gritted her teeth as another rock loomed suddenly. The front end of the log crashed into the rock and Yurubi found herself underwater. She held her breath as she grappled with the log, fighting to hang on.

Pitching, bouncing and rolling, the log swept downstream with Yurubi wrapped around it like an octopus. There was a big jolt and a scraping sound as it hit another boulder and slowly swung to a stop. Yurubi sucked in a breath, clinging to the log with all her might. With a shaky laugh, she realized she was sitting on the riverbed, hugging the log. It was stuck on a mud bank close to the shore.

Yurubi was bedraggled, her hair all over her face, but she was unhurt except for a few bruises. The river might play rough at times, but it would never harm her.

She stood up in the knee-deep water and dragged the log closer to the shore. She jammed it with two small rocks and looked around. She was a little way downstream from where the boy lay. She pushed the hair out of her eyes, scrambled out of the water and ran toward him.

He was hurting all over. He wanted to crawl closer to the water for a drink, but he couldn't lift his head. It hurt to try to open his eyes. He was drifting in and out of a dream. Mother was hugging him close to her bosom and stroking his head. He wrapped his arms around her neck and breathed in her special scent of cinnamon and wild berries. She leaned her cheek against the top of his head, and he could feel her smile.

What should we eat today, my little one?

He leaned back to look at her. Mother stroked his cheek, her strong face alight with love.

I want plantain porridge. He jumped off her lap and tugged her toward the door of the mud hut to the fireplace outside.

Alright, alright. Her eyes crinkled with laugher.

He was very hungry, and his mouth was almost watering at the thought of the thick sweet porridge made from grated green plantains and sweetened with molasses.

He gasped as a splash of water hit his face. His eyes flew open.

Leaning over him was a naked brown-skinned little girl, her face half hidden by her long, straight hair. She was holding a huge green leaf filled with water and was about to splash him again.

"No," he croaked, lifting his arm weakly.

She knelt swiftly beside him, babbling something in an insistent voice. A shaft of sunlight broke through the trees, touching her like a wand and radiating off her serious face.

She must be one of the water spirits from Mother's many stories. His eyes fluttered shut again.

He could rest now. The water spirit would take him safely back home.

He felt something nudging at his lips. He opened his mouth and drank thirstily from the leaf spout then slipped back into the darkness.

Yurubi gasped in dismay as the boy passed out again. The water she was pouring into his mouth from the leaf trickled down his chin onto his chest, leaving a muddy trail.

She had no idea what to do next. She had slipped away during a game of hide-and-seek with the other children while Ma was napping. It would be a while before anyone noticed she was missing, but Yurubi knew she would be scolded again if she didn't get back soon. And she'd be in a lot more trouble if she was caught here on this side of the river.

Squatting in the mud, she glanced across the water and then looked down at the boy. He was as limp as a wilted tobacco leaf. His head, face, and the rest of him were covered in mud from his tumble down the riverbank. Yurubi rubbed a finger over his cheek. Under the mud, it was a smooth black. Yurubi's gaze moved over his wide cheekbones, full lips, slightly curling eyelashes, and tight black hair, down his body to his toes, which also looked black under the mud.

Yurubi had never seen anyone painted like this, black all over. Everyone in the village smeared their bodies with a reddish-brown juice from the roucou plant to keep off insects and protect themselves from the fierce heat of the midday sun. And sometimes the warriors would paint their faces and parts of their bodies black. But not like this.

Perhaps this boy was trying to hide himself really well. He must've run away days ago and gotten lost in the forest. He had old and new scratches and bruises on his round forehead, his chest, his arms and legs.

"How did you get here?" Yurubi shook his shoulder, but he didn't stir again.

She stood and looked back across the river. If she waited here long enough, Ma would come find her and would know what to do about the boy. But what if the men didn't want him?

Her mind racing, she looked up at the thick line of trees above the riverbank. She ran up the slope to a tangle of low-hanging branches and pulled two long pieces of a thick supple vine she and the other children often used to make skipping ropes. With a furtive glance into the green dimness of the forest, she slid back down the river-bank to where she'd left the log. She tied one of the vines around the log and dragged it to where the boy lay.

Yurubi rolled the log close to the boy and turned him half on his side. She pushed the log right up against his stomach, wrapped his arms and legs around it, then wound the length of vine around him and the log several times. She'd once seen a hunter do this to bring a huge pig carcass across the river. Her knots were not very tight, but she hoped they would hold.

Pushing and pulling, she eased the boy and the log into the water. With the other piece of vine, she also tied herself to the log, knotting one end around her waist. She pushed the log with the boy strapped to it into the deeper water and held onto them with both hands, kicking her legs hard.

Aloo's arms flailed weakly as the panic rose inside him again. He was back in the water. He tried to scream but no sound came from his raw throat. He struggled feebly as he felt himself spiralling down, down, down, into the darkness. A roaring sound filled his ears. Mother was there, trying frantically to reach him, but her terrified face kept sinking below the raging waves. Each time she surfaced, she was further away from him. A scream ripped from his belly as a giant wave reared up, swallowing Mother.

Then the wave was upon him. The scream snagged in his throat, the roaring died away, and a great silence engulfed him. The wave slammed into him, burying him, rolling him over and over in its blackness. He clutched at a tumbling piece of wood, trying to hold his breath. But it was no use. The water seared into his nose, throat and chest. His whole body felt on fire.

Against his will, his chest heaved again, but this time he sucked in a mouthful of damp salty air. He gasped, spluttered, coughed and vomited. Again, and again, he screamed for Mother as the huge waves tossed him about and the blinding rain whipped his face.

She was gone.

His arms fastened themselves around the broken piece of wood as darkness closed down on him.

At times, he could feel fire in his throat. Scorching heat on his face, arms and back. Big waves. Small waves. Darkness again. Cool rain. Always the fire in his throat. The wood bumping against things, rolling about. A big wave picking him up, folding him into the watery darkness once more. A crunch. More rolling. The wood torn from his arms.

Then the tumult stopped. The wave disappeared with a huge sucking sound, came back once to lick at him, and slunk away again.

He lay still in the coal-black darkness, waiting. He could hear the hiss and suck of the waves. But they did not pick him up again.

His eyes flew open. He was on a strip of sand. Not the black beach where he'd washed up. It was bright daylight. The water spirit with the long hair was tugging his arm, saying something in an urgent voice.

"Wake up, wake up! Come with me!" Yurubi shook the boy's shoulder and pulled him by the arm. "We must go quickly before anyone sees us!"

She helped him to his feet and half-pulled half-carried him up a steep rocky slope that rose above the river, downstream from the path to the village.

He stumbled along behind her, his hand gripping hers tightly as she climbed the slope. Halfway up the bluff, his legs seemed to give out. He wobbled, and his feet slid from under him. He fell forward onto his stomach, seeming to be hardly breathing. Yurubi quickly helped him up again. She changed places with him then, putting him ahead of her so she could push him up the slope. He pulled himself along sometimes, grabbing onto the scrub that covered the hillside.

Just when it seemed like the boy would collapse, they came to the spot where the bluff rose vertically. Yurubi let go of the boy and he slumped to the ground. Panting hard, Yurubi edged around him and parted the tangle of bushes and vines on the face of the cliff.

"Come on," she said, tugging the boy to his feet. She pulled him into the bushes and heaved him over the lip of a small cave. He rolled a little way down a slight incline inside the mouth of the cave and landed on a bed of fine sand.

"Stay here, I'll be back," she said softly.

He was lying on his back, looking at her with dazed eyes, his mouth quivering as if he was trying to say something.

She put a finger to her lips, signalling him to be quiet, then swung the vines back in place and sped down the hill.

She had stumbled on the small cave late one evening about two moons ago while she was chasing some little green lizards along the bluff. Below, in the river, Ma had been skinning a pair of iguanas on a rock. Holding the slender spine of a coconut leaf with a noose on the end, Yurubi had been trying to snare one of the lizards, but it had scampered up a thick hanging vine on the face of the cliff and disappeared.

Poking around in the bushes to flush out the lizard, Yurubi had been intrigued to find that her arm could go through the foliage at full stretch. She'd burrowed behind the scrub and vines and to her delight had found a cave there. She was about to crawl inside when Ma had called, saying it was time to go.

Yurubi had not told anyone about the hollow in the bluff and had been planning to go back to explore it on her own sometime. Now that she had hidden the boy in there, she'd have to be more careful than ever not to let anyone else find it.

FIVE HURRICANE SEASONS LATER

The sun nudged the horizon, promising an abundance of silver and gold. The tall mountains in the north of Hiroon Island waited their turn. With the first brush of light across the peak of the Great Mountain, the village of Warigara began stirring.

Ikupo sat up in his hammock and shook his head, trying to dispel the remnants of a bewildering dream. He yawned and pushed back his hair from his face. This was not a day to ponder the meaning of his strange recurring dream. He had work to do.

His necklaces, bracelets and anklets jangled in a familiar cadence as he swung out of his hammock and reached down one of the small reed bags hanging from the roof. He slung the bag over his back and walked briskly to the village centre.

Chief Oudou strode out of the taboui, his necklace of agouti teeth bouncing against his smooth chest.

"Almost ready," Oudou said when he saw Ikupo.

He turned and reentered the taboui, gesturing to Ikupo to follow him inside.

Like the other warriors who were milling about, Oudou's leanly muscled body was painted a reddish brown with wide streaks of black running across his cheekbones, his chest and limbs. His long hair, freshly oiled, was tied back from his face in a sleek black tail that hung halfway down his back.

Ikupo followed him into the taboui, past the rows of hammocks hanging along the sides, to the big open space in the middle and sat crossed legged on the floor. Ikupo closed his eyes, shutting out the chatter of the women and children on the other side of the village, the low voices of the warriors and the clunking sounds of their weapons as the men got ready. He knew, without looking, that the men were strapping some of the weapons to their bodies and packing others in their bags. When they were done, they'd be fully armed with bows, poison-tipped arrows, fire arrows, knives, clubs, spears, axes, ropes and slingshots.

Ikupo reached into his bag and felt around for a small wad of dried leaves. He stuffed the wad into his cheek and chewed slowly.

Gradually, the sounds around him receded. When all was still and quiet, Ikupo opened his eyes and stood.

"It's time," he said.

Gripping their spears, the men formed a circle around him. From his bag, Ikupo withdrew an intricately painted clay vessel and placed it in the centre of the circle.

Chief Oudou stepped forward and handed Ikupo a firestick. Ikupo touched the glowing tip of the stick to the dried leaves inside the vessel and blew gently. A wisp of smoke curled up from the bird-shaped jar. Ikupo remained bent over the vessel, waiting for the smoke to thicken. When it started pouring out of the open eyes and beak of the bird, he sucked in a deep breath. The acrid smoke burned its way down his throat, bringing tears to his eyes. He stood upright, arms outstretched, silently summoning the spirits and waiting for his eyes to stop watering.

When he could see clearly again, Ikupo began dancing slowly around the vessel, fanning the smoke outward with both hands toward the tight circle of warriors.

"Breathe the spirit of the bird, go with the spirit of the wind," he chanted.

Eyes closed, the men inhaled the wisps of smoke wafting under their noses. A few of the young men seemed on edge, their eyes flickering like a parrot's, trying hard to contain their excitement. But like the more seasoned warriors, they stood still, shoulders back, fingers tight around the shaft of their spears.

The men had all stripped bare of any ornaments and were wearing just a strip of dark cotton around their loins. Their bodies glistened in the early morning light that was creeping into the taboui.

"Breeeathe the spirit of the biiirrrd, goooo with the spirit of the wiiiind."

On his last turn inside the circle, Ikupo stopped in front of Oudou and touched the chief lightly on the forehead. Oudou opened his eyes and stared at Ikupo, waiting for the signal.

Ikupo met Oudou's resolute black eyes, nodded at him and stepped back.

Oudou reached back, picked up a long stick and held it aloft in his left hand. Then he raised his right arm and began pounding out a slow rhythm on the dirt floor with the butt of his spear.

Eyes fixed on the stick the chief was holding aloft, the warriors joined in, gradually speeding up the rhythm.

Ikupo waited quietly in the centre of the circle. His work was done here for the day. Now it was Oudou's turn.

The chief drew his knife and with a flourish cut away a notch on the end of the stick. The men cheered loudly and pounded their spears in an even more rapid beat. Oudou had made several notches in the stick many days ago and had been cutting them away, one each day, to reach the last one this morning. This was the day of the expedition.

The chief tossed the stick over his shoulder, raised his arm in farewell to Ikupo and led his men out of the taboui.

"Go with the spirit of the wind," Ikupo called after them as they snatched up their weapons and ran across the village.

Ikupo repacked his bag and joined the children lining the hillside to watch the warriors go. At the top of the steep path to the beach, the men slowed down briefly to grab their food bags from a group of women clustered there. Then, like one of the streams that flowed from the rocks in the surrounding mountains, the warriors poured down the hillside.

Below, on the beach, their *piraguas* waited.

As soon as the warriors started down the path, Yurubi slipped away from the crowd and turned in the other direction. When she got to the river, she looked around quickly to make sure no one was watching, then she climbed quickly up the cliffside.

From high up on the bluff, she could see a long way in three directions. To her left was a stack of rocky ridges that ended on the beach far below. To her right was the path from the village and a winding swathe of river. Straight ahead was the massive forest that stretched all the way from the far bank of the river to the Great Mountain, where a fierce and powerful spirit lived. Well, that's what the elders said anyway. Yurubi thought the Great Mountain almost always seemed aloof or sleepy, wearing its fluffy headdress of clouds.

Yurubi turned and gave a warbler whistle before slipping behind the thick foliage on the face of the cliff.

"Aloo, let's go," she called softly into the dimness of the cave.

No answer. They were supposed to leave before sunrise to search for some wood to make new spears, but Aloo seemed to be playing one of his games again. Yurubi grinned and climbed over the lip of the cave, her eyes searching for Aloo in the semi-dark.

"We've got to get to the forest and back before broad daylight," she said in a low teasing voice, as she edged into the cave. "The sun's coming up."

She had never gotten the better of Aloo in one of these games of camouflage. He could make himself practically invisible by melting into the smallest shadow and remaining as motionless as a piece of rock.

Yurubi sidled toward a little outcrop to her left, her eyes flicking from the cluster of baskets in the corner where Aloo kept his supplies, to the darker spot further back where he sometimes cooked, and the rocky ledge high up on the right where he usually slept.

A bat swooped past Yurubi's ear and she ducked, stumbling a little. A pair of arms grabbed her from behind and a hand clamped over her mouth. Aloo's warm breath brushed her ear. Yurubi's shoulders slumped. It was impossible to beat him at this game. But she had some tricks of her own. Aloo was taller than her now, although she reckoned he had not yet reached the twelve hurricane seasons by which she counted her own age. He held her tight, his chin resting on her head. Yurubi tensed her legs, preparing to knock him back by quickly bending and straightening her knees, but he swung her toward the opening of the cave and pointed over her shoulder. His hand dropped from her mouth.

Yurubi leaned forward and peered through the drape of vines. Far below, a figure was hurrying along the riverbank toward the men's bathing pool. Yurubi could not see the face, but she knew that slightly off-balance gait.

"Buaba," she whispered.

Aloo nodded against her shoulder. She had warned him long ago that of all the men in the village, Buaba was the one he should fear most. She had told Aloo the story of how Buaba had returned from an expedition with a deep cut on his shoulder and had never been able to lift his left arm again, although the wound had healed. He was now the headman, in charge of the village whenever the chief was away, and he was often as irate as a wasp with one wing. Now that Buaba could no longer go on expeditions, he probably couldn't bear to watch the warriors leaving today.

With Buaba down there at the river, there was no way Yurubi and Aloo could go into the forest now.

"It's too late," Yurubi whispered. "Soon, others would be down there too."

Aloo released Yurubi and moved back to the little outcrop, resting his forehead against the rock, his face drawn, his lips pressed tightly together.

Yurubi felt a sadness rising in her chest. She knew how much Aloo had been looking forward to their early morning trek into the forest. They had planned it carefully after she'd learned that the men were going on an expedition today. She and Aloo were going to cross the river and run into the forest, find some good straight branches to make spears and carry them back to the cave, all before the boats had cleared the headland and people started wandering down to the river. Now they would have to wait for another chance.

"We can go another day before the warriors return," Yurubi whispered.

But Aloo turned away, one fist gripping the locks hanging over his forehead.

In the five hurricane seasons since Yurubi had pulled Aloo half-dead from the riverbank, she had never seen him cry. Not even that time when she had startled him by climbing into the cave without giving their bird call signal, and he had fallen off his sleeping ledge, hurting his shoulder as he hit the ground. But he looked close to tears now.

Yurubi bit her lip. She ran over and gave him a playful punch in the chest. His head shot up, and he stared at her, his eyes wide, his nostrils flaring. Yurubi smiled and punched him again, this time a bit harder. He closed his eyes and raised his chin, his neck taut as a bowstring. Then his shoulders dropped, and he doubled over, clutching his chest. Yurubi pummelled his head with her fists. He collapsed silently onto the sandy floor of the cave and lay there motionless.

Yurubi grinned and flipped him over with her foot. He lay on his back, his neck twisted sideways, playing dead. As she stepped away, his right leg shot out and twisted between hers, bringing her down. He reached up with both arms and broke her fall just before she hit the sand. They lay in a pile on the soft sand, laughing silently. Most of their games were like this. Rough sometimes but always quiet.

Yurubi disentangled herself from Aloo and scowled at him in mock fury. He crossed his arms in front of his face, grinning at her. Relieved to see him in a playful mood again, she swatted at his arms then turned and crawled to the lip of the cave, peering through the vines to see what Buaba was doing. He had emerged from the bathing pool and was walking along the riverbank, shaking water from his hair.

"He's leaving," said Yurubi softly.

Aloo appeared next to her, his face tense again as he watched Buaba climb the path to the village and disappear behind a bamboo clump.

Yurubi sat back on her heels. The morning light was just touching the tops of the trees on the far side of the river.

"Want to play birds?" she said, nudging Aloo with her elbow.

It was a silly game they had been playing since they were little, before Aloo had learned the Kalina language well. They still found it hilarious even now.

"There's one," said Yurubi, pointing to a blackbird sitting on a shrub near the cave. "I'll go first."

Yurubi folded her hands under her armpits, stretched her neck forward and balanced on one leg, mimicking the bird. She giggled as she pretended to peck at something in front of her.

"Look, that one's yours," she said, gesturing with her chin. "It's a bananaquit."

"No, I'm going down."

Aloo stepped past her and in one fluid motion, vaulted from the cave and began running down the side of the cliff.

"Al—" Yurubi clapped a hand over her mouth.

Her eyes widened in alarm as Aloo zigzagged down the cliff at full speed, heading for the water. What if someone came down from the village?

Heart pounding, Yurubi jumped from the cave and ran after Aloo. She wanted to shout to him to come back but was afraid someone would hear her. She was only halfway down the bluff when Aloo got to the river. By habit, he was avoiding the soft sand on the riverbank, leaping lightly from rock to rock, the sleek line of his body broken only by his black breechcloth.

With hardly a pause, he jumped from a little rock on the shore to one in the water and with the ease of an egret crossed to the other side, his feet seeming to hardly touch the uneven line of small boulders in the river.

Yurubi's mouth went dry as she dashed to the edge of the water. Jumping up and down, she waved her arms frantically above her head, trying to attract Aloo's attention. But he ran up the riverbank toward the tree line on the opposite side without once looking back.

Yurubi crossed her arms on top of her head and turned away in frustration. She wanted to follow Aloo into the forest but knew her family would start calling for her soon. She took two steps along the river then stopped in her tracks. Someone was coming down the path from the village. Yurubi's eyes flicked from Aloo's fleeing figure to the man hurrying down the path.

It was Buaba again. He must have forgotten something.

Buaba stopped, his body going taut as he gazed across the river. His head whipped around, his eyes fastening on Yurubi. Her heart was thumping so hard, Buaba could probably see her chest pulsing. With a curl of his lips, he turned and ran back up the path, letting out a long hunting cry. It was a signal to the boys in the village that he'd spotted some game.

Yurubi bent almost double, clutching her stomach. There was no telling if Buaba had actually seen Aloo or had spotted the movement in the trees and thought it was an animal. But either way, he was going after Aloo.

Yurubi dashed a hand across her face, wiping away the dripping sweat. She strained forward, her eyes boring into the trees across the river. Aloo must have heard the hunting cry and was now running for his life. But even with a head start, he'd be in great danger.

Buaba was a skilled and experienced hunter. And he was mean. So were some of the boys who came hurtling down the hillside now, armed with bows and arrows, clubs, spears, knives, and anything else that could be used as a weapon.

Garu was brandishing a long hunting knife his father had given him. Just a few days ago Garu had been running around the village with that knife, chasing the little girls, until Chief Oudou had threatened to take it back.

"Whooo, hoooo," Garu shouted, his coarse hair flying behind him as he raced to the river. The other boys followed him, whooping and shouting. Yurubi counted nine of them.

Her stomach clenched when she saw Buaba carrying the long heavy spear that he used for hunting pigs. He hardly glanced at Yurubi as he herded his young hunters upstream. Strung out behind Buaba, the boys crossed the river in swift leaps across the rocks, growing silent as they swarmed up the far bank and into the forest.

Yurubi watched them melt into the dim green light, her chest tightening at the thought of them capturing Aloo, or worse. She folded her lips, fighting back the tears she could feel starting behind her eyes. She couldn't just crouch here and wait to see if Aloo would be dragged out of the forest. She got to her feet and ran a little way up the path to see if anyone else was coming down from the village. There was no one. She stood for a moment, her head cocked. All was quiet except for the shrill call of birds above the crisp early morning voice of the river.

Yurubi sped back down the path and ran along the river toward the line of rocks she had tried so hard to cross long ago. She had no trouble getting across now. Her feet were light and sure as she leapt from one rock to another, crossing swiftly to the other side. With one last look over her shoulder, she scrambled up the riverbank and ran into the forest. It was still and quiet in here except for the cawing of birds and the low buzzing of insects.

It was Yurubi's first time venturing alone into the forest. Girls usually didn't come over here unless they were with a group of women gathering food. But Yurubi had sneaked into the forest several times at dawn with Aloo to look for pieces of wood, help him dig for wild yams or find fruit and edible herbs.

This time was different, though. There were people in here, going after Aloo.

Aloo, who was—

Yurubi went still. Something was rustling in the undergrowth near her. Bending slowly, she picked up a stick and fixed her eyes on the clump of bushes near a big mapou tree. If a snake slithered out of that undergrowth, she'd have to try to chase it off like the women usually did. Yurubi wet her lips and gripped the stick tightly. She stifled a cry and jumped back as something darted toward her. A big brown lizard leapt from the bushes and scuttled through the dry leaves on the forest floor, chased by two others. Yurubi drew a shaky breath and dropped the stick. If she was going to help Aloo, she'd have to stop worrying about every little sound and try instead to listen for Buaba and the boys.

Although the sun was now up, the light under the dense canopy of trees was still dull.

Yurubi slipped through the forest, trying to walk the way Aloo usually did so as not to make a sound. No matter how dark it was or how fast he was walking, he seemed to be able to avoid stepping on dried twigs, brushing against dead branches, or stumbling over logs. He had learned to live in these hills as wily as a forest creature. But now he had ten people after him, one of them a seasoned hunter with a deadly spear.

Yurubi stopped and leaned against a tree, trying to swallow the sickness that was rising in her throat again. She looked around at the dense cluster of trees, bushes, vines and ferns. What chance did she have of finding Aloo or the hunters in here? She was more likely to get hit by an arrow or some other weapon if she continued to wander around.

But she had to find a way to help Aloo.

She straightened up from the rough tree trunk and looked around again, this time more carefully. Ahead of her was an upward slope, to her left a tangle of lightning scorched tree trunks and logs draped in green and yellow vines, to her right a flat stretch of trees. Behind her was the path she had taken from the river. She'd go right. Perhaps there was a chance.

Heart pounding, Yurubi untied her white loincloth and wadded it up in one hand. She drew a deep breath, crouched a little and began running, making no effort this time to be quiet. As she swerved through the trees, she kicked up piles of dried leaves, jumped on dead branches, ripped at low vines.

Up ahead, she saw a lush clump of ferns. Yurubi dived into them and crouched there, panting. Her hair clung to her face and naked body, which were slick with sweat.

She tilted her head, straining her ears above the forest sounds.

They were coming. They weren't making a lot of noise, but she could hear them, the snap of a twig underfoot, the thump of a body against a branch.

Yurubi squeezed her eyes shut for a moment. She was scared but somewhere deep down she could feel a swell of excitement. She could do this. It was not much different from playing agoutis with Aloo. She jumped to her feet and sped off again.

The sounds of the boys giving chase widened. They were spreading out now, preparing to trap their prey.

Yurubi didn't think they could see her yet but knew they could hear her crashing through the forest. She veered sharply to her right as she heard a crashing sound behind her. A tiny sob of relief escaped her at the rushing sound of the river. Crouching low, she scuttled toward the tree line. She burst out of the forest, hurling herself forward and catapulting head over heels down the bank into the water. With shaking hands, she hastily tied the loincloth around her hips then flopped on her back in the shallow water near the riverbank, her chest heaving. Above her, a few strands of clouds stretched themselves thin across the sky as if nothing had happened since dawn. As from a far distance, she heard the shouts of the boys. Yurubi turned her head and looked at them through her mesh of wet, muddy hair.

They were running back and forth along the riverbank, still looking for their prey.

"Yurubi, did you see anything run by here?" Garu shouted at her. He was gripping his knife by the blade, in the throwing position.

Yurubi opened her mouth but gulped back her answer as Buaba appeared on the bank directly above her. Ignoring the boys, he stuck the shaft of his spear in the soft dirt and stood there, glaring at Yurubi.

"What were you doing in there?" he said, his face hard, his eyes narrowed to slits.

Yurubi sat up, pushing her hair away from her face.

The boys came running and clustered around him.

"Answer me, girl." Buaba's fierce eyes were fixed on her.

"Yurubi, was that you?" said Garu, staring at her with his mouth open.

Yurubi hung her head.

"I-I'm sorry," she said. "I wanted to go with you, but I couldn't find you, and I got scared in the forest."

There was silence. Then the boys burst out laughing. Yurubi peered up at them from under her brows. Some of them were staggering about, slapping their chests and pointing at her.

"She wanted to hunt!"

"You're a girl!"

"Girls don't hunt!"

"You could've been killed!"

"You ruined our hunt!" said Garu, his lips curling.

Yurubi bent her head even further and brushed her hand across her face as if to wipe away tears. When she glanced up again, Buaba was still staring at her. He had not said another word.

The boys began chattering about their hunt in the forest.

"Think I spotted it before Yurubi began making that racket."

"Her fault it got away."

"Did you see what it was?"

"Seemed like a pig."

"Pigs make more noise."

"Enough for today," said Buaba.

He twisted around and glanced back into the forest then grabbed his spear and loped downstream toward the crossing. The boys hurried after Buaba, bumping into each other as he stopped abruptly and looked over his shoulder.

"Come on, girl," Buaba said, his voice rough.

Yurubi scrambled to her feet and clambered up the bank, sneaking a quick look into the trees. There was no movement in there. She ran after Buaba and the boys but really was not trying very hard to catch up with them. By the time she reached the crossing, Buaba was already halfway across the river. When he got to the other side, he stopped and turned around. Yurubi could feel his eyes on her as she started crossing. She took her time, pausing on each rock and pretending to brace herself before jumping to another. She didn't want Buaba or the boys to know that this was something she did all the time.

Buaba gave her a hard look when she finally stepped onto the sand. Then he turned and led the way up the hill to the village. Yurubi followed slowly, forcing herself not to look over her shoulder.

TRIUMPHANT RETURN

Ikupo sucked on his roll of tobacco leaves and blew the smoke out in slow puffs, squinting to see what shape it would take. He tilted his head this way and that but could see nothing other than puffs of smoke being quickly pulled apart by a stiff breeze. Not that he was expecting to see anything significant. His eyes were following the tendrils of smoke more out of habit than anything else. It was too early in the day to start looking for signs from the spirits. All he wanted right now was to enjoy a quiet smoke here under the trees before the horde of young boys descended on the beach.

They'd been coming down every day at dawn to look for the boats. Never mind it was a grey morning with angry looking clouds frowning at the ocean, and huge waves slamming to the shore. The boys would be here soon, prancing about and hollering, pretending to be warriors.

It wasn't that he disliked them. He still remembered what it was like to be a young boy, to wake up with all that energy and excitement every day. But he needed some peace and quiet to think about the strange fleeting dream that had been plaguing him for many nights. He didn't know what was more perplexing—the dream itself or the idea that the spirits were now attempting to send him a direct message. After all the baffling and obscure signals they'd sent him over his lifetime.

Ikupo scratched his head and drew on his tobacco roll.

"What do you think?" he muttered at a weather-beaten booby that had landed in front of him.

The booby folded its wings, shook its scrawny neck and turned its head to look out at the ocean.

Ikupo laughed softly. "Me neither," he said.

The bird tottered in the steady wind that was blowing in from the sea.

"What are you, my spirit bird?" Ikupo said, laughing again. "Why don't you just flap those old wings and fly off into the horizon, huh?"

Ignoring him, the bird ran a little way down the beach and pecked at something on the sand.

Ikupo sighed. "That's the trouble, isn't it? There's always something in front of you, distracting you from the serenity of the horizon."

He squished the stub of his tobacco roll and buried it in the sand as he heard the shrieks of the boys on the hill behind him. They sounded more boisterous than usual this morning.

"Enjoy your distractions while you can, my friend," he called to the bird, which was hopping further down the beach. "I'm off to find some quiet."

He was about to get to his feet when the boys came flying down the hill, shrieking at the top of their voices.

"They're back!"

"They're coming in!"

Ikupo leaned forward and squinted against the gritty wind, trying to spot the boats. The ocean looked the same as it did a moment ago. Big rolling waves and flocks of diving seabirds. That didn't mean the boats weren't indeed coming in. He wouldn't bet on his eyesight against a pack of young bloods.

With the warriors returning, his chance of a quiet day had disappeared. He might as well sit here and watch the boats come in. Ikupo rummaged around in his bag for a small wad of tobacco, stuffed it in his mouth and leaned back against the trunk of the almond tree.

The boys swarmed across the beach like ants, running this way and that, trying to keep the canoes in sight.

Ikupo smiled wryly, recalling his days of swimming out to the piraguas, racing with his friends to be the first to reach the returning boats. These boys would have a hard time doing that today because of the huge rollers breaking out there. As excited as the boys were, they weren't frolicking in the surf like they usually did. They were prancing about on the sand, the frothy edges of the waves sucking at their ankles.

"There!" said Garu, jumping up and down and pointing. "There's one. Bet it's my father's."

"How can you tell? It's too far away," Ranan said.

Ikupo rubbed his gravelly eyes and followed Garu's pointing finger.

Way out past the northern point of the bay, something that looked like a piece of driftwood was tossing about on the water. Ikupo lost sight of it as a massive wave crashed into the black headland and a plume of spray spewed skyward. A shout went up from the boys again, and Ikupo saw another boat staggering around the point.

"Here they come!" said Garu. "Let's go!"

He dived into a wave, and most of the other boys followed. Siwako and Tueke stayed on the shore, hopping about as they eyed the huge curling waves and the distance to the piraguas.

Ikupo grinned. Smart little boys. Kalina children learned to swim almost from birth, but they also learned to have great respect for the sea. Garu, as usual, was trying to show off. He so much wanted to be like his father, he often veered toward foolish recklessness. He and his little friends were out there now battling not just the waves, but a strong tide that seemed to be tugging them to the right of the canoes. Pitching and rolling, the piraguas were coming in almost sideways, as the warriors quartered the waves breaking across the bows.

Ikupo turned his good right ear as snatches of a song floated across the water. Ah, it was a victory song. The men were bringing captives.

He spat a mouthful of tobacco juice on the sand and got to his feet. It was going to be a long day and an even longer night. No use sticking around here to see the warriors land their spoils. He'd hear all about it tonight. Over and over.

Yurubi weaved through the cluster of women who were sweating over huge pots of yams, cassava and sweet potatoes. She strolled past the huts to the edge of the village, beyond the bright orange glow of the many fires. The beat of drums followed her, flowed through her and over the hills, chased by bursts of laughter, snatches of banter and playful squeals.

Somewhere out there, Aloo was either watching the celebrations or was hunting in the deep blackness of the forest. If he was close by, he was probably drooling at the smell of barbeque meat and fish wafting on the breeze. Wherever he was and whatever he was doing, he was alone. Yurubi wished she could talk with him the way the shaman talked with the spirits. Maybe if she concentrated hard enough …

She scrunched her eyes shut. She could hear nothing except the chirp of insects and the sounds of revelry behind her.

Yurubi sighed and turned away, walking slowly toward the village clearing. She dodged between the cooking fires until she came to where Grandma Lulou was bent over a big pot.

"Let me help with that, Grandma Lulou," said Yurubi.

Grandma Lulou peered at her in the firelight.

"What? You? Since when do you care about cooking?"

"I can do it, I can do it. I promise."

"Stop jumping about like a grasshopper. You're making me dizzy."

Yurubi giggled. She was sure Grandma Lulou's dizziness had more to do with the mug of *woku* she was holding in one hand.

"You should sit for a while, Grandma Lulou."

Yurubi ran around the fire to Grandma Lulou's side and reached for the stirring stick.

"Here, let me help."

"Be careful now, child. Stay still and stir it slowly and gently."

"Like this?" Yurubi said, moving the stirring stick through the thick stew of cassava and crabs.

Grandma Lulou nodded then shuffled off with her mug to sit on a patch of grass away from the heat of the fires.

Yurubi stirred the pot, slowly as Grandma Lulou had instructed. The smell of the stew rose on the steam that was swirling about her face, tempting her to taste the food. But she resisted. She didn't want Grandma Lulou to come back and take over. This cooking fire was the one closest to where the men were sitting. Yurubi shifted around a little so she could see them better.

Chief Oudou and some of his warriors were sitting near the biggest of the fires, sipping bamboo mugs of woku. The firelight glinted off their sleek back hair, their freshly painted skins and the war medals hanging from their necks.

Yurubi strained her ears to hear what they were saying. She

desperately wanted to be able to tell Aloo at least one story of the men being kind to strangers.

"… wave rolled right over our boat and before you knew it, everyone was in the water," Oudou was saying, moving his hands quickly to demonstrate.

Garu and a group of other young boys who were sitting nearby edged closer, their faces alight with excitement. Yurubi wished she could do the same.

"But our canoes never sink, right?" Garu said.

"… little danger of the boat sinking."

"… wild sea out there …"

The drumming stopped. The players were having a drink while they waited for the main part of the celebrations. Yurubi could hear the warriors more clearly now.

"By the time we managed to flip the piragua over, the three women had been carried off quite a way by the tide and were floundering in those big waves," said Chief Oudou.

"We rowed over to them, but they were too weak to get back on the canoe," said Maruku.

"Kuriji and Maruku had to jump back into the water, fish out the women and toss them back in the boat," Chief Oudou said with a laugh.

"Meanwhile, our food bags and all the stone weapons we were carrying had sunk out of sight," Maruku said.

"But we didn't lose the women," Kuriji said, with a broad smile.

The men roared with laughter.

Yurubi had stopped stirring. Her stomach felt like she'd swallowed mud. She peered at the sticky stew, hoping it wasn't burning. Grandma Lulou hated burnt food. Yurubi moved the stirring stick around in the pot, glancing at Grandma Lulou to see if she was watching. No need to worry. Grandma Lulou was sitting bent over her mug of woku, her head dipping like a sleepy owl.

"When can I go on a raid?" Garu's voice drew Yurubi's attention back to the men.

Oudou threw back his head and laughed.

"When you're old enough to have a woman," he said. "Besides, you have to learn how to fight."

Garu scowled as his friends joined in the laughter.

"I can fight," he said. "I've been practicing with my knife and my bow."

Yurubi cut her eyes at him. Oh yes, he'd been practicing to fight little girls.

"Look, son," said Oudou, gesturing in the direction of the taboui. "Look at what it means to fight."

Yurubi turned to follow the chief's pointing finger.

Several young warriors, armed with various types of weapons, were lining up just inside the opening of the taboui. Yurubi shifted around so she could see them better. They ran into the square, their bright hair feathers, white face paint, breechcloths and armbands changing colour in the firelight. Their fishbone earrings and nose rings, and necklaces, bracelets and anklets of agouti teeth jangled as they pranced around the big fire.

"Ayyyheeeee! Ayyyheeeee!" The warriors' cry bounced across the hills.

The women drew closer, and the smaller children came running, jostling with each other for a good spot near the big fire.

The drumming started up again at nothing more than a whisper. The warriors raised their arms and began playing out the story of the raid.

The canoes slid up and down the waves like eels, gliding to the shore under a black sky. The island loomed suddenly, tall and dark. As the boats neared the rocky shore, the men slipped overboard, leaving just a couple of rowers behind.

The warriors rode the surf and swarmed up the beach clutching their weapons. The sound of the waves crashing to the shore drowned out the crunch of the pebbles under their feet. They raced toward a steep narrow path leading up through the bushes.

Fireflies danced in and out of the trees, trying to light the way.

The warriors climbed the path with the speed and stealth of a serpent. As they neared the top of the slope, they could see a cluster of huts in a clearing that levelled off into a plateau overlooking the sea.

The men quickly spread out and surrounded the small village. Chief Oudou gave a signal. He struck a spark with two small fire stones, lit the sap-soaked padding on the tip of an arrow, and shot the arrow into the thatched roof of the largest hut. The fire arrow seemed to spawn others even before it hit, and a deadly shower rained down on the village.

Screams and shouts erupted inside the huts. Some of the warriors swiftly switched weapons, from bows and arrows to clubs.

The Taino villagers spilled out of the huts, the women clutching their children, the men and boys gripping spears, clubs, knives, bows and arrows. The flames shot higher, lighting the clearing. The warriors surged forward. The air grew thick. with spears, rocks, knives, arrows, smoke. The women and children ran for the stand of trees behind the village.

Kuriji broke away from the fighting to chase after a slender young woman who had caught his eye. A Taino man leapt in front of him with a raised club, but Kuriji's knife hand was quick and deadly. He jumped over the fallen man and bounded into the trees after his quarry. She screamed as Kuriji snatched her off her feet and tossed her over his shoulder. He turned and ran toward the path with his prize. His left hand lashed out, bringing down another Taino man who was trying to tackle him.

In front of him, Maruku was speeding down the hill with a writhing, screaming woman hanging over his left shoulder. Her long hair bounced against the back of Maruku's thighs and her fists pounded his back.

The woman Kuriji was carrying was deadweight on his shoulder. She had fainted.

The other warriors trickled down the hill to the beach, some of them with slight injuries. They were laden with food, tools and weapons looted from the village. Behind them, the smoke curled around the ruins of the huts and bodies of the Taino men and boys who had stayed to fight. A smudge of light was touching the sky as the warriors loaded their piraguas and slipped away.

The drumming picked up and the warriors started to dance again, brandishing their weapons, as they pranced around the fire.

Yurubi dropped the stirring stick and edged away.

"Come back here, girl," Grandma Lulou's voice called after her.

But Yurubi kept going.

"Can't stay still long enough to catch a fly," she heard Grandma Lulou muttering.

Yurubi skirted the cluster of women who had started filling calabashes of food for the men. She didn't think she could eat right now. Her stomach felt as if she'd eaten berries from the sumac tree. Sick and bitter.

NIGHT OF FIRE

A few dried leaves fluttered onto the dying embers of the fire and ignited with a slight hiss. An iguana stretched out high up on an overhanging branch cocked its head as if to listen better above the medley of snores rising from the ground. Two small brown lizards darted over a twitching foot. The smell of woku and fish clung like a fog to the snoring men sprawled around the dying fire. A deep voice grumbled in the distance.

Ikupo jerked awake, his arms flailing. He was in his hammock. He had made it back to his hut. His arms went slack again. Just a dream that he was still in the village clearing. Rainstorm coming.

He drifted off again.

A shiver ran down the spine of the mountain all the way to the sea. A family of owls swooped down from the hills, screeching at the iguana, which had climbed higher up the tree and was sniffing the air.

A crack of thunder split open Ikupo's dream. He struggled upright. The hut was swaying. Ikupo held his head. Too much woku. A flash of lightning lit up the hut, and it shook as the thunder roared. Thunder before rain. A bad storm coming. With a groan, Ikupo lowered his feet to the floor and tottered outside. There were no clouds over the half-moon hanging in the sky. Ikupo rubbed a hand over his face.

Something was—

A streak of lightning sizzled over the mountains behind him. Ikupo swung around, almost losing his balance as a massive crack of thunder shook the earth.

"No, no, no," he croaked. "Noooo!"

He turned and lurched toward the taboui.

"That's all the warning you give me?" he cried as he careened along the path. "A flock of owls and an iguana? Just before you go berserk?"

The mountain spirit answered with a deep angry roar and furious darts of lightning.

"Run! Run!" Ikupo screamed as he neared the village clearing. "Run! The mountain's blowing!"

He could hear a few grunts, but no one seemed to be moving.

Ikupo's head was pounding and his heart was fluttering against his ribs. Must find Oudou. Ikupo staggered into the clearing and grabbed the first upright jar he spotted. He splashed the contents over the two men closest to him. They sprang up, their eyes wild.

"Wha—"

"Find Oudou," Ikupo gasped.

He pointed at the Great Mountain. There was no need for words. With a roar, the mountain spewed a huge cloud into the air, blotting out the moon.

"You could've sent me a warning signal," Ikupo screamed, shaking his fists at the mountain. "A wisp of smoke, a whiff of your angry breath, anything!"

The mountain belched loudly, and a foul smell seeped through the village.

Tears streamed down Ikupo's face. The spirits were taunting him. Well, they did send the owls and iguana to warn him.

"But only a few moments before," he shouted at the Great Mountain.

Around him, pandemonium broke out as men, women and children spilled from the huts.

"To the boats!"

"No, the sea might boil!"

"Run, run, run!"

Above the shrieks and babble, Oudou's voice began bellowing orders.

"We run south!"

"Leave everything!"

"Men, take the elders and children!"

The ground under Ikupo's feet trembled as the mountain roared again.

"I'm done," he cried, throwing his arms wide. "You hear me? I'm not listening anymore. From now on, you can talk to someone else."

A streak of lightning hissed overhead, showing the angry face of the growling mountain.

Ikupo sank to his knees. "I'm done," he said, his voice breaking. "Done."

Yurubi dodged through the melee of shrieking women and children, her head down.

Lightning arced overhead, lighting the frantic faces around her.

"Yurubi, this way!" Ma's voice yelled.

"Go ahead, Ma," Yurubi called over her shoulder. "I just need to grab something quickly. I'll catch up. I can run fast."

"Don't be foolish, child," Ma shouted. "Come on, come now!"

"Go, Ma. I'll be right behind you."

Yurubi slipped behind one of the huts and crouched down, her heart racing as she glanced up at the snarling mountain. When she peeked out again, Ma had gone. Yurubi turned and sped down the path to the river.

"Aloooo! Aloooooo!" she screamed at the top of her voice.

He appeared at her side, almost out of nowhere.

"Aloo!"

She grabbed him in a quick hug of relief.

Come, we must run!" she said, tugging his hand as she turned back up the path.

But Aloo refused to move.

"Wh-what's ha-happening?" he whispered.

Yurubi swung around. Aloo was standing rigidly, his eyes wide and confused.

"The Great Mountain spirit is having a huge fit," said Yurubi, her words tumbling over each other. "We have to flee or we'll all die."

Aloo's lips moved as if to whisper something, but a crack of thunder drowned him out.

"Let's go!" said Yurubi, turning and running up the hill.

She dashed through the village, glancing behind her once to make sure Aloo was following. Almost everyone had gone. A broad-shouldered warrior was running toward the beach path, carrying someone that looked like the shaman on his back.

Yurubi and Aloo raced behind them down the path and onto a narrow trail along the shoreline.

Ahead of them, the villagers were fleeing as fast as they could, some of them carrying small children or elderly people on their backs.

Yurubi ducked as she heard a huge thump. A quick glance at the sky showed a massive sinister cloud unfurling slowly over the mountains. The elders had been right all along. The Great Mountain that looked so sleepy and unconcerned most days was indeed a fearful monster.

"Yurubiiiii, where are you?" Ma's voice rang out over the din of panicking voices.

"Right behind you, Ma," shouted Yurubi. "Don't stop."

She was running at full speed, Aloo close on her heels.

A drizzle was starting, and Yurubi could see some of the people ahead of her craning their necks to look up at the sky. She felt Aloo's hand brush her shoulder, flicking at the drops.

"Not rain," he said softly.

Yurubi passed a hand over her head. Her fingers came away slick with something that felt like warm bird droppings.

"Ash from the fire in the mountain's belly," someone shouted.

"We must go faster." Chief Oudou's voice called out. "We have to cross the Rabaca River before it turns to fire."

The drizzle was becoming a shower. Fat droplets plunked onto Yurubi's head, shoulders and arms. It was such a strange sensation, she couldn't help giggling. She turned around to look at Aloo. He was so splattered in grey, he looked like one of those rocks on which seabirds nested. She laughed as he made a face at her. Despite the great danger at this moment, Yurubi felt a mix of excitement and wonder that Aloo was here with her and everyone else. Never mind that he was hanging back at the end of the line and not saying a word. That was just Aloo. He probably would disappear into the bushes on the side of the path at the least sign of anyone noticing him. But that was becoming less likely as the air thickened with ash.

As they approached a headland, the path began to slant uphill, away from the shoreline. The woman in front of Yurubi leaned into the slope, her breath coming in gasps, her feet slipping on the mat of ash on the path. She seemed to be carrying a child.

Yurubi ran closer.

"Minda?"

"Yes, can't ... keep ... my ... footing."

"Here, let me take him," said Yurubi, reaching for the little boy strapped to Minda's chest.

Minda handed over the child, who stared at Yurubi silently, his eyes wide.

"He's ... heavy," Minda said. "I'll ... take ... him ... back ... at the ... top."

She placed both hands on her hips and started climbing again.

Yurubi stopped and set down the little boy, turning quickly to hoist him onto her back, but when she reached behind her, he wasn't there.

She spun around to see Aloo smiling at her, the child straddling his shoulders.

Overhead, a streak of fire ripped into the sky. The smile dropped off Aloo's face as he glanced up.

"Go," he whispered to Yurubi, his eyes wide.

Yurubi turned and raced up the slippery hill behind Minda.

Some new sporadic showers were starting. Coarse gravel rattled in the bushes on both sides of the path and bounced off Yurubi's head and shoulders as she ran.

She faltered as something thudded into the ground to her right.

"What's that?" a quavering young voice asked.

"The mountain's spitting hot rocks now," a man's voice said. "Be careful, they could knock you flat or set you on fire."

Yurubi shivered. Ma would start calling her again soon. She couldn't stay back here with Aloo. She looked back at him through the dense fog. Like everyone else, he was covered from head to toe in a slick coat of ash and sweat. There was no way anyone would even notice him.

"Let's move up," she said. "I want to find Ma."

But Aloo shook his head and signalled to her to go ahead. Yurubi hesitated. What if something happened to Aloo back here? As if he'd read her thoughts, he hooted softly like an owl, once, twice. Yurubi smiled. It was their special nighttime signal they had worked out long ago. She raised her hand in a quick wave to let Aloo know that she understood, then she edged past the people in front of her and ran ahead, trying to spot Ma.

Most of the women she passed were breathing hard in the foul air, tears cutting tracks through the ash on their cheeks. Yurubi's throat was dry, but she didn't stop to drink from the rock spring on the right of the path, where several women and children were clustered.

As Yurubi rounded a deep bend, she saw that the line had slowed to a crawl and people were staring at something on the seaward side. She rubbed her gritty eyes and tried to see what they were looking at. She could barely make out two limp forms on the rocks.

"Hurry, don't stop," one of the men up ahead called out. "They're dead. Knocked off the bluff above."

Yurubi shuddered and slipped past the panting women. Above the constant snarling of the mountain, the sea pounded out a familiar rhythm against the rocky shore.

Yurubi cupped her hands around her mouth. "Ma, Ma Erona!"

Her call was deadened by the thick air, but Ma's voice came back at her almost immediately.

"Yurubi, come on. Come, child."

The tight feeling in Yurubi's chest eased a little. Kicking up puffs of ash, she sped toward Ma's voice, her eyes searching the jumble of grey figures for her mother's easy swinging walk. There she was! Ma was hurrying along steadily, but her head kept twisting back.

Yurubi sprinted forward and grabbed Ma around the waist. "What—"

Yurubi laughed and clung tighter.

Ma gripped Yurubi's arms and pulled her around to the front.

"Stay near," was all she said, but Yurubi could hear the relief in her voice.

"Where's Grandma Lulou and Waasha?" said Yurubi.

"Waasha's up ahead and someone's carrying Grandma Lulou."

"How much farther do we have to go?"

"A long way still," said Ma. "A long way. Don't stray again."

The throng of grey figures swarmed toward the Rabaca River, some running, some shuffling, some walking swiftly. Yurubi could hardly recognize anyone, but she knew they were not all from Warigara. Along the way, the crowd had grown as the people from her village mingled with others fleeing the wrath of the mountain spirit.

Under her feet, Yurubi could feel the hard dirt of the path giving way to coarse loose gravel. They were close to the mouth of the Rabaca River, the place the elders said was most dangerous when the Great Mountain was raging. Yurubi looked over her shoulder to see if she could spot Aloo, but the ash cloud was too thick. A faint light was struggling through the fog on her left. It was dawn. Too late for owl cries. She tilted her head back and whistled like a pewee. She counted to five then whistled again.

From somewhere far back came an answering bird whistle. And then another.

Yurubi smiled. He was still there.

"Hurry, we must cross the river before it turns to fire!" Chief Oudou called out up ahead.

The bushes on both sides of the trail thinned out and the path soon became wide enough for Yurubi to run alongside Ma.

"Faster, faster," the men at the front shouted.

Yurubi slipped her hand into Ma's as they hurried across a broad stretch of gravel toward the river. Around them, other grey figures panted as they crunched over the gravelly riverbank. They had crossed several rivers and streams along the way, but this one was the most dangerous. This was the one that ran with fire spilled from the guts of the mountain.

Yurubi had heard many times the legend of the powerful mountain spirit that was provoked to anger once every three or four generations. For moons on end, the infuriated mountain spirit would pelt the villages with hot rocks and pebbles as it belched steam, ash, and a foul smell that made people sick. But worst of all, the legend said, the enraged mountain would spew thick, deadly streams of fire that spilled down its flanks to the sea, consuming everything along the way. Then the ocean spirit would rise up in a rage so terrible that the sea would boil like a huge cooking pot.

Yurubi had once asked Grandma Lulou if that meant people could pull cooked fish, manatees and lobsters from the sea, but Grandma had told her to stop being foolish.

As Yurubi neared the big river, she could see people stretching from one bank to the other. The river was swift but not very deep.

Most people were wading rather than swimming, many of them carrying small children and elders on their shoulders. Some of them appeared not to be moving but rather were just standing in the water.

"Hold onto me now," Ma said, as she stepped into the water. "Hold fast."

Yurubi waded into the river and locked her arms around Ma's waist from behind.

"The water's so warm," said Yurubi.

Ma gripped Yurubi's arms and surged forward.

"That's because the fire's coming," said Ma, her voice grim.

She planted her feet firmly one after the next on the gravelly riverbed, wading through the stiff current. Yurubi clung to her mother's solid form, following her movements. She probably could cross this river on her own, if she had to, but she was glad she didn't have to do that today.

Ahead of them, a slender young woman cried out as she lost her footing and was dragged downstream on the current, but she was steadied by a man standing up to his shoulders in the water.

Through the haze, Yurubi could see now that the people who were not moving were men from the various villages. They had formed a line across the river, downstream from where the women and children were crossing, to make sure that no one got swept away. Yurubi knew Aloo would not want to be rescued in that way, but she was relieved to see the catch line. Although he was stronger than her, Aloo was also slight in frame. The current tugging at her legs, laden with abrasive gravel, was much more challenging than it seemed.

A cry went up from the struggling villagers as the mountain rumbled and hissed.

"Hurry, hurry!"

"The fire's coming!"

"Run!"

Yurubi tightened her arms around Ma's middle and twisted her head back, looking for Aloo, but it was impossible to recognize anyone in the frenzied crowd surging through the thick fog of ash.

Ma strained forward, her feet scrabbling in the loose gravel as she neared the riverbank.

"Almost there," she said, panting.

As they waded out of the water, Yurubi let go of Ma's waist. She placed her hands on Ma's back, pushing hard to help her up the low riverbank.

"Run now, Yurubi," said Ma. "You're fast. I'll catch up later. Run."

Yurubi ran around in front of Ma and looked at her in shock. "No, Ma. I'm not going without you."

Ma's eyes rolled in the direction of the mountain, and she passed a wet hand over her ash-coated face. Her cheeks puffed out as she tried to catch her breath. Yurubi got behind her again and pushed.

"Let's go," said Yurubi. "You'll be fast again soon."

She tipped her head back and whistled twice into the sky. Somewhere behind, the pewee whistle answered.

FINDING SHELTER

The sun was sinking behind the hills when Yurubi and her mother made their weary way into a campsite on the sprawling flatlands near the mouth of the Jambou River.

All day, as they slogged up and down hills and across rivers, Ma had been talking about this place. It was far enough south to be as safe as possible from the angry mountain, she said. Not only that, it was very beautiful, she kept repeating. As Ma related stories of her previous visits to the area, Yurubi had been picturing flower-strewn hills rising gently from a wide green apron decorated with a shimmering silver stream and a huge frill of blue-and-white ocean.

But as they walked slowly toward a handful of rough shelters scattered around a small village, all Yurubi could see in every direction was grey, except for a smear of dull orange as the sun wiped its tired face on the edge of the far hills.

At least the acrid smell was not as strong here, and the rumbling of the mountain had become more like a distant thunder. Also, there were no pebble showers, although the ash showers had not let up.

A few people were moving about, trying to erect shelters, while others were sitting or lying in the open spaces, apparently too exhausted to move.

"Why aren't they taking shelter under the trees, Ma?" said Yurubi, looking longingly at the wide spreading almond trees near the river.

"Too dangerous. The branches might break under the weight of the ash and come crashing down on them."

Yurubi's shoulders slumped. She wanted so much to just lie down and close her eyes.

"Where will we sleep?" she said, grimacing as her exhaustion leaked into her voice.

"I don't know, child." Ma's voice sounded heavy and raspy. "Let's see if we can find some of the others first."

The smell of roasting crabs wafted across the campsite, making Yurubi's mouth water. Quite a way back, she and Ma had cracked open a few dried coconuts and pried out the meat, which they had been chewing on for most of the day. They had also managed to find some fruit without going too far off the trail, and they had drunk lots of water from the rivers and streams. But Yurubi's stomach was growling at the smell of the crabs.

Dragging her weary feet through the ankle-deep ash, she held onto Ma's arm and plodded toward a little group clustered under an ajoupa. It was a simple shelter made from coconut branches propped against a cross branch that was resting on two upright forked sticks.

Not many people from Warigara had made it this far. Many of them had stopped further back at Byabou, saying they would catch up later. Some had also decided to remain there, camping near a small village on a gentle slope overlooking the sea.

Yurubi knew Aloo was not among those who had stopped off along the way because she had heard his bird whistles just before she and Ma crossed this last river. She wanted very much to go find him and try to bring him into the camp but didn't think her feet could carry her much longer. Right now, they felt like two soggy logs.

She hoped Aloo would find a safe place in the surrounding hills where he could spend the night. She'd go looking for him early tomorrow and see if she could convince him to join the camp. There were so many people here from several different villages, no one would notice him, especially as everyone was coated in grey ash from head to toe.

"Erona, Yurubi, over here."

Yurubi turned to see Waasha waving at them from under a lopsided ajoupa.

"Look, we have a shelter," said Yurubi, squeezing her mother's arm in excitement. "We don't have to sleep in the open."

She waved back at Waasha and tugged Ma toward the little shelter as the last of the dull light disappeared.

FRIENDS ON THE PLAIN

Aloo crept slowly toward the camp, his eyes flicking nervously from one group to the next. Despite Yurubi's promise earlier in the day that he would be safe, Aloo's heart was pounding as he slipped out of the shadow of the trees near the river and edged toward the bustling camp. He had spent the night in the hills, wedged under a low overhanging rock that gave him a little protection from the constantly falling ash. He was up before dawn to drink from the river and forage for some fruit on the hillsides. Then he had climbed a dense tree and sat there munching on his guavas and watching the camp come awake. When Yurubi came looking for him, tweeting their bird calls, he had reluctantly agreed to join the camp. But not in broad daylight.

Now it was near dusk and everyone seemed busy, trying to get some task done before nightfall. The shouts and chatter reached him from all across the campsite.

"We need more water."

"… gather firewood."

"Our hut can fit two more people."

"The baby needs a wash."

"… set up a cooking area."

"Lots of crabs on the beach …"

"Bad cut … find the shaman."

"… coconut branches for the shelter."

Walking slowly, Aloo tried to spot the shelter that Yurubi said was hers. His heart jolted. A group of boys. Running toward him.

He turned his face away and squatted, pretending to be digging at something in the ash. The boys ran past. But one of them near the back of the group stopped.

Aloo's whole body tensed. He poked his fingers into the thick ash.

"No use looking for crabs now," a fast-talking voice said above Aloo's bent head. "We'll catch some on the beach tomorrow. Come on, we need to pick the coconuts before dark."

From under his brow, Aloo saw two short legs running off.

Drawing a quivering breath, Aloo stood and was about to turn toward the camp when the boy stopped again.

"Hurry," the boy called, waving at Aloo.

Aloo hesitated, his heart pounding. Perhaps he would draw less attention if he hung around the group of boys. He walked quickly toward the boy, who was grinning at him through a mask of ash.

"Guess you don't like picking coconuts in the dark," the boy said. "Me neither. But the chiefs said we'd better stock up on some tonight."

He was a stocky little figure with a round face and dancing eyes. "My name's Pipo. What's yours?"

"Ah-Aloo."

"Let's go, Aloo."

Pipo ran off again, glancing back a couple times to make sure Aloo was following.

By the time they reached the stand of coconut trees, the light had almost faded. The other boys were squinting up at the tall slender trees, trying to decide which ones to climb.

Pipo stood close, his head barely reaching Aloo's shoulder.

"Let's hurry before he starts giving orders," Pipo muttered, pointing his chin at a boy with long hair who looked like Garu.

"I'll take this one," said Pipo, running over to one of the shorter curved trees.

Aloo eyed a tall, straight tree that looked like it might be heavily laden with coconuts.

He grabbed the trunk and began climbing. He was almost at the top when he realized that the chatter and banter among the boys had stopped. It was deathly quiet, except for the chirring of a few early crickets. Aloo stopped climbing and looked down. The boys were all staring up at him with open mouths.

Aloo's heart started thumping. He'd done something wrong.

What was it?

Clinging to the base of the shortest tree, the boy called Pipo broke the silence.

"Did you see that? He ran up the tree! That's my friend Aloo. He's faster than anyone here."

Aloo's fingers dug into the tree trunk. With a weak smile at Pipo, he clambered slowly into the crown of the tree.

The chatter erupted again.

"... never seen that."

"Like an iguana ..."

"... race him one day."

"No way!"

"Need to practice more ..."

Aloo sat in the gently swaying bow of the tree, sweat pouring off him. Foolish. Foolish. Foolish. Why didn't he wait and see what the others would do? He'd had to learn early to climb fast. To hide. To escape. But other boys were not like that. What if they told everyone in the camp about him? Aloo passed a hand over his sweating face. He'd have to go hide in the hills again. If he felt threatened.

A light breeze from the sea fanned across his face, drying the sweat. Aloo turned to look out over the darkening ocean. Somewhere on the other side of that vast expanse of water, there had been a home. A family. A man. A woman. And a little boy who loved his mother more than anything.

But the memories of that place had grown so faint he was no longer sure if they were real or just dreams. All that was left was this deep yearning, this feeling of great loss and apprehension whenever he looked out over the ocean.

Below him, a steady thudding sound had started. Aloo peered out from among the branches to see the other boys pushing nuts off the trees with their feet. Good thing he had not started before them because he usually used his knife to cut off a whole bunch of coconuts, then he'd lower them to the ground on a rope so as not to make any noise.

Aloo followed their lead, working his way around the treetop. It was a silly way to pick coconuts because some of them would crack open when they hit the ground, despite the thick bed of ash.

"Ok, that's enough," someone called out. "Let's go."

The boys slid down the tree trunks, but Aloo remained on his perch, watching as they gathered the nuts and piled them in a heap.

Some of the boys were drinking from the cracked nuts then bashing open the shells on a rock to get at the sweet coconut meat.

The boys wandered off in twos and threes, each carrying three or four coconuts in their arms. Aloo leaned back in the tree and looked up at the sky. Except for a few stars that were struggling through the clouds, it was a dull cover of grey. It might be better to sleep under the rock ledge again tonight and—

"Aloo!"

Aloo jerked upright.

"Come on, Aloo, time to go. It's getting very dark."

Aloo peered down through the coconut branches. The squat figure of Pipo was standing under the tree, his round face tilted up, his eyes scrunched up against the falling ash.

"Everyone's gone already," said Pipo. "Let's go."

Aloo couldn't help smiling. Being alone in the dark was the least of his worries. But he climbed out of the tree bow and slid down the trunk, being careful this time not to go too fast.

"Can you carry four coconuts?" said Pipo. "You have long arms."

Pipo bent and picked up two from the heap, hugging them in the crook of his arms.

"If you put one more here," he said, gesturing at his chest, "I'll carry three."

Aloo looked from Pipo to the heap of coconuts on the ground.

"Hmm ... wait," said Aloo.

He ran about under the trees, gathering some fallen coconut branches.

"Oh, you don't have a shelter, huh?" Pipo said. He set down the coconuts and joined Aloo in gathering branches. "My family did this as soon as we got here. We're used to it because we move around a lot."

"Mmm," said Aloo, hurrying to lay out the branches on the ground. When he had enough, he began plaiting the fronds, his fingers flying.

"We can do that back at the camp where there's firelight," said Pipo. He looked around the stand of trees. "It's a bit dark here now."

Aloo's fingers flew faster. He ran off again and pulled at a thick vine hanging from a locust tree.

"We really should go," Pipo called after him.

Aloo cut off a few lengths of the vine and dashed back to the coconut heap.

He began piling nuts into the huge boat-shaped basket he had made.

"Are you this fast at everything?" Pipo said as he tossed some nuts into the basket.

Aloo didn't answer. When the basket was full, he tied it up with the vines, making two loops on one side.

He gripped one loop and gestured to Pipo to grab the other.

"You're a strange boy, you know," said Pipo, shaking his head. He glanced back at the basket they were dragging with about twenty coconuts inside. "In my village, only girls learn to weave and plait. Better not let Garu and his friends see you do that. They like to mock people."

"Hmmm." Being taunted was not his big concern. Aloo was more worried that Garu and the other boys from Warigara would come chasing after him again with weapons. Like they did that time, led by Buaba. Good thing Aloo had been fast enough to run up a tree.

"You're not much of a talker, are you?" said Pipo. "Me? My father says I talk like a hurricane." He laughed. "But I think it's because he's kind of quiet, like you."

Aloo smiled again. He felt somewhat at ease with this boy. Almost as if he could trust him.

"Where are we taking these?" said Aloo, jerking his thumb at the coconuts as he and Pipo drew closer to the camp.

"We'll put them in the centre of the camp. The chiefs said we should have some on hand for the babies and small children at night and early in the morning."

Aloo could see small groups of people milling around, mostly near the fires that dotted the plain. He wasn't sure he could do this.

"Er, can you pull the basket from here on?" he said.

Pipo stopped and looked up at him.

"You're worried about Garu and the others? They won't know you made this basket. And I won't be telling them, for sure," Pipo said with a little laugh. "There's my father," he said, pointing at a man who seemed to be wandering around in circles near a small fire on the edge of the camp.

Aloo's mouth went dry. He stood still, staring at the short broad-shouldered figure that appeared to be glowing orange each time he passed near the fire. This was a man, a grown man.

"I-is he—"

"He's alright," said Pipo swiftly. "He's just uncomfortable on land. He prefers to be at sea."

"At sea?" Aloo's head was reeling with Yurubi's stories about raiders and how they were always chafing to go to sea, even after they'd just come home.

"Yes, he's a great boatman and fisherman," said Pipo.

He sounded upset, like Yurubi did that time when Aloo had asked about her father. Aloo looked from Pipo to the thickset man near the fire. This was a bad idea. He'd better slip back into the darkness and try again tomorrow. He'd wait for Yurubi and go with her. He dropped the loop of rope he was holding.

"Y-you can drag them fr-from here," said Aloo, pointing at the coconuts.

"What? Why? Where are you going?" said Pipo, as Aloo began edging away.

Pipo dropped his rope and ran after Aloo.

"Look, there's nothing wrong with him," said Pipo in a strange sounding voice. "He was injured as a boy and couldn't become a warrior, but he's the best fisherman in the world, and he knows more about boats than even the warriors."

Aloo stopped.

"H-he's n-not a wa-warrior?"

"No, but ..."

Pipo looked over his shoulder at his father then turned to Aloo again.

"Aloo, I know you're not like the other boys," Pipo said, lowering his voice.

Aloo's stomach clenched. Pipo had spotted him already as different.

"Some of the boys ... well, they mock me and my father because he's not a fighter. And because he never seems to find his legs on land. But you're not like them, I can tell."

Aloo swallowed on the dryness in his throat.

"N-no, I'm not," he said, rubbing his big toe in the ash. "But I-I'm uneasy about meeting people. New people."

Pipo's round face relaxed.

"Oh, yes, I noticed," he said. "That's why you don't talk much."

He reached up and gripped Aloo's shoulder.

"You can stick with me. I'm not afraid to talk to anyone. My father says I talk—" He broke into a grin. "I told you that already."

Aloo smiled at him and ran back to the coconuts. Side by side, he and Pipo dragged the huge basket of coconuts into the camp. Aloo lowered his head, glancing rapidly under his brows at the little groups of people clustered around fires. Men and women in separate groups. No sign of Yurubi. Like him, almost everyone was caked in mud and ash. No one seemed to be looking at him.

He and Pipo left the nuts in the centre of the camp where there was a small stack of fruits and other supplies. Keeping his head down, Aloo followed Pipo out to the edge of camp. Pipo's father was still strolling around aimlessly, looking up at the sky.

"Father, this here's my friend Aloo," said Pipo, planting himself in front of the lost-looking man. "Aloo can climb faster than an iguana and knows how to pl— carry many coconuts at a time."

Pipo grinned at Aloo and winked.

"Good, good," said Pipo's father, absently patting his son's shoulder.

"Your mother left some food … She's sitting over there," he said, pointing vaguely across the camp. "There's fish. You boys should eat."

Pipo's head whipped around.

"Fish? Did you go—"

"No, no, from the river," his father said.

Pipo turned to Aloo with a smile and raised his brows. He tipped his chin, signalling to Aloo to sit with him near the fire. Aloo looked around again. He still could not spot Yurubi. Everyone seemed tired and worried. Pipo's father was strolling in the direction of the ocean.

Aloo sat next to Pipo, who was busy pulling some bundles of leaves from the edge of the fire. He pushed one close to Aloo and began stripping the charred leaves off another. The smell of roasted fish wafted up Aloo's nose, making his mouth water. But he waited, watching closely as Pipo unwrapped the thick fish and kept the last layer of leaves under it like a plate. Pipo bit into the steaming fish, chomping swiftly from the tail to the head.

"Wash are you waishing for?" said Pipo, his mouth full. "It's mullet. Alwash delishoush."

Aloo picked up his fish and unwrapped it, following Pipo's actions as best he could. It burned his mouth a little eating it that fast, but it was quite tasty. His eyes fluttered shut as he savoured the moist, slightly leaf-flavoured flesh.

"What are these leaves?" he asked Pipo.

"Huh?" Pipo tossed the bones and leaves into the fire and pulled another fish from the embers.

"This wrapping, what kind of leaves?" Aloo said, holding up a roundish blackened leaf.

"Seaside grape. My mother gathers them on every beach, whether here in Hiroon or on some other island. Here, have some more fish."

Aloo unwrapped the fish, more slowly this time, allowing it to cool a little and sniffing the aroma of the grape leaves mingled with the fish. He'd have to try this sometime, although it would mean going down to the beach to find the leaves.

"She goes to other islands?" he said after a while.

"Who?" Pipo was devouring his fish in quick bites.

"Your mother."

"Uh huh, the three of us go everywhere in our boat. But sometimes my father and I take a long fishing trip and Mother stays at home to—to do things women do."

An ominous rearing wave flashed before Aloo eyes. A boat upending. Heads bobbing wildly. Disappearing. Father sinking. Mother clawing—

"You can sleep here tonight if you like." Pipo's voice cut through the rushing sound in Aloo's ears.

Pipo wiped his hands on the grass and flopped back, shielding his eyes from the falling ash.

"We'll have to sleep on our sides close to the shelter, though. Or we might wake up blind."

Aloo looked at him in alarm but Pipo was grinning up at the sky. A joke. Like when Yurubi says it's going to rain frogs. Aloo laughed softly.

He wasn't sure he could sleep here, within sight of all these people. But he had made a friend. All on his own. And his friend was offering him a place to sleep. Aloo glanced at Pipo, who was now on his feet and was eyeing his family's lean-to.

"I think this side, away from the sea breeze, would be best," said Pipo. He threw himself on the ground close to the shelter and turned on his side, bringing up one hand to cover his ear from the falling ash.

"What are you waiting for?" He smiled up at Aloo and beat one hand on the ground, raising a cloud of ash.

Aloo couldn't help laughing as Pipo broke into a fit of coughing. With one last look around, Aloo lay down gingerly next to his new friend.

"First thing tomorrow, going for a swim," Pipo mumbled.

Aloo's head shot up. "Wha—Where?"

But Pipo did not answer. He seemed to have fallen asleep already.

Aloo turned on his side away from the camp. With all the fires in the camp, the area was very bright and there was a glow even when he closed his eyes.

After a while, he got up and crept away. Further away from the glow of the fires. He curled up tightly in the shadow of a black rock and covered his ear with one hand. Like Pipo.

UNDER THE ASH

Aloo's eyes flew open at the sound of an owl hooting. He lay still and listened. There it was again. And again. He smiled and rose to his knees. Cupping his hands around his mouth, he gave three answering calls then peeked out from behind the rock, trying to spot Yurubi. It was still dark, the fires had died down, and the camp was quiet except for an occasional cough from within some of the shelters. Near the lean-to closest to him, he could see Pipo's feet sticking out from behind the coconut branches.

Aloo brushed the ash from his eyes and peered across the plain. Still no sign of Yurubi. She must've woken up briefly and decided to call to him. He shook his head vigorously, sending ash flying in all directions. Now that he was awake, he might as well go find some food. He slipped away toward the river, heading for a cluster of guava trees he had spotted from the hilltop yesterday.

He wandered among the trees, munching on his favourite fruit and filling a small makeshift basket for Pipo. The grass underfoot was covered in a grey slippery mush of ash, dew and sea mist. In the distance, the Great Mountain grumbled every now and then, but it did not sound as threatening as the day before. A light sprinkle of ash continued to fall. Aloo did not mind this. He felt protected by the thick muck covering him from head to toe. If he stood perfectly still, he'd blend easily into the landscape, like the grey trees around him. But perhaps there was no need for that today. Perhaps no one would notice him as a stranger.

Aloo walked slowly back to the camp, thinking of what Pipo had said last night. Something about catching crabs. Then just before Pipo fell asleep, he had talked about going for a swim. Aloo felt a familiar tightening in his stomach as he thought about plunging into the ocean waves that he could hear crashing in the distance. As excited as he was about his new friendship with Pipo, he might have to slip away into the hills today.

An early morning bird broke into song and was soon joined by honking seagulls. A baby's cry quavered briefly. A woman spoke in a low voice. The camp was coming awake.

Aloo crept back to where he'd slept the night before and crouched behind the rock. Pipo seemed to be still asleep, and no one else was stirring in this part of the camp. Across the plain, a few people were moving about in the semi-dark, mostly women tending babies and small children.

Aloo slipped out from behind the rock, gently placed the basket of guavas near Pipo's head and walked away swiftly toward the hills.

"Aloo, wait!" Pipo came running after him, a guava clutched in each hand. "Where'd you get these? They're the best. You've been exploring already? We're going for a swim today, remember?"

Aloo's mouth went dry.

"Er … I was …er …" He glanced at the ocean, which was slowly picking up the dull reddish light of the sunrise. "I-I w-was go-going t-to the ri-river."

"Good idea." Pipo bit into one of the guavas. "We can swim and catch crayfish."

Aloo's jaw unclenched and he cleared his throat.

"Ye-yes."

'Heard there's a good swimming hole up there," said Pipo, gesturing vaguely. He trotted toward the river, crunching on the guavas.

Pipo and Aloo sloshed through the ash and mud along the riverbank, each carrying a string of crayfish hanging from their hips. As they came to another slow-running part of the river, Aloo squatted and began gently shifting the small rocks on the riverbed. He had learned this type of fishing from Yurubi when they were both very young. He lifted the stones one by one, his fingers curling underneath, feeling for crayfish. Each time he felt a movement he'd reach under the rock with his thumb and forefinger and grab the crayfish just behind the head. A quick pinch and the crayfish would stop snapping its pincers. Aloo would then thread it on the thin reed hanging from his waist.

"Good spot," said Pipo with a grin, holding aloft a big striped crayfish with wildly waving pincers. He leaned over and pointed at a school of little fish darting downstream. "Want some of those, too?"

Aloo smiled, remembering the mouthwatering mullets from the night before.

"They're a bit sm—"

Someone was coming. Running feet pounding on the dirt. In two swift leaps, Aloo splashed into the shadow of an overhanging clump of reeds and crouched low, his back pressed tight against the rough riverbank. He picked up a rock, gripping it tight.

Pipo leaned forward, his round face scrunched up as he peered at Aloo in the shadows.

"What's under there? Why are you—"

"Talking to yourself again, Pipo?" The voice above sounded like one of the boys in the coconut grove yesterday. Laughter from the others.

Pipo straightened up, his eyes flashing. "No, I'm not. I'm talking—"

"Yeah, yeah. Come on, we're going to play water hide-and-seek in the swimming hole."

Running feet again. Going further away this time.

Pipo puffed out his cheeks. "I guess we should go. We were heading there, anyway. No need to be afraid. I won't let them bother you."

Aloo let go of the rock clenched in his hand and slid out from under the reeds.

"I-I—"

"Don't worry, I can beat them at any water games," said Pipo. His eyes crinkled. "Bet you didn't know I was born in the sea."

"The s-sea?" A shiver ran through Aloo's body. He waded out of the water behind Pipo, whose short legs were moving like a bird about to take flight.

"Tell you about it later. Let's go." Pipo began running and Aloo loped after him.

Following the shouts and squeals coming from the riverside, they veered toward a row of almond trees and ran down a steep slope. The swimming hole was wide and shadowy, shaded by two huge almond trees.

Pipo dropped his string of crayfish on a rock, waded into the pool and dived out of sight.

"Let's get Pipo," shouted the boy who looked like Garu.

Aloo sat on a big jutting rock under the trees and watched the five boys frolicking like dolphins in the dark green water. One boy would dive under the water, disappearing for a while, then come up again, apparently when one of the others found him.

"Aloo, come on. What are you waiting for?" Pipo was treading water, his hair plastered all over his grinning face. "It's deep with lots of hiding places."

Pipo disappeared again as two boys swam rapidly toward him.

So, this was water hide-and-seek. He could do this. He had scared Yurubi once by hiding under a rock in the river for a long time while she splashed around frantically, looking for him. He smiled as he remembered how she'd pummelled his chest when he'd finally run out of breath and surfaced.

Aloo looked over his shoulder at the early light struggling through the fog of ash. His heart started a crazy rhythm as he untied the string of crayfish and jumped down from the rock. He waited until all the boys were underwater, then he slipped into the pool. It was cool and bracing yet calming. Aloo swam a little way upstream, enjoying the feel of the slow current pushing against his body. It had been days since he'd had a real bath.

"There's Aloo!"

Someone had spotted him. Time to hide. He took a deep breath and dived deep. He swam around a rock, then another and another, until he found one with an overhang. He slid under it and lay on the riverbed, digging his fingers into the coarse sand. He wriggled his toes as something nipped at them. If you stayed still in the river for any time, little fish, crayfish and lobsters would come nipping. It was even worse at night when he usually bathed and fished.

Above the rush of the current in his ears, Aloo could hear the boys shouting to each other, but he couldn't make out what they were saying. It was clear, though, that they couldn't find him. He smiled to himself. He liked this game. The nipping started again, and Aloo pulled his legs up under him. He turned his body around slowly, just in time to see a big claw withdrawing under the rock. A lobster.

Aloo was running out of breath, but this was too good to leave. He spread his arms wide then bent his elbows and reached under the rock from both sides. The lobster flipped toward his face. Fast as lightning, he grabbed the lobster behind its head and pinned it to the riverbed. No time to pull off the pincers. Chest burning, Aloo kicked to the surface.

"There he is!" someone shouted.

A sudden thunder rumbled as the mountain awoke from its overnight slumber.

Aloo sucked in a breath and swam rapidly to the riverbank, holding the struggling lobster aloft. Smiling broadly, he leapt onto the high rock where the other boys were standing, and he held out the live lobster. Its pincers, one much bigger than the other, were writhing frantically.

The boys stared at Aloo, their mouths hanging open. Pipo was the first to break the stunned silence.

"Woooh! Good one, Aloo!" he said with a laugh. "How did you do that?"

"It was under the rock where I was hiding," said Aloo, his eyes on the snapping claws. "Kept nipping my feet."

Pipo reached out and touched Aloo's arm.

"What's it made from?"

"It's—What? It's a—"

Suddenly, everyone started talking at once.

"Where did you get that paint?"

"We couldn't find you."

"Your mother makes it?"

"Even your toes!"

"It doesn't wash off?"

"Your hair, too?"

Aloo froze. They weren't looking at the big lobster. They were all looking at him. He flinched as a boy reached out and rubbed his shoulder. He should run. Now. He could outrun them. Drop the lobster and run for the hills. They would never find him. But what if they sent the big warriors after him?

"… didn't miss a single spot. Show us how you did that."

"Shut up, shut up, all of you," Garu shouted. "Can't you see? It's not paint!"

The other boys laughed, ignoring Garu. They jostled closer to Aloo, peering into his face, rubbing his arms, touching his hair.

"Of course, it's paint," said Pipo. "Best I've ever seen."

Aloo dropped the lobster and backed away.

He caught Pipo's eye, and the laughter drained out of Pipo's face. He jumped in front of Aloo and stood legs apart, facing the other four boys.

"Stop it," said Pipo. "You're making him uneasy. Leave him alone. He doesn't want to talk about his paint."

"It's not paint, you fool," said Garu, his lips curling. He tossed his head, flipping his long, wet hair away from his face. Look at him. He's … he's—"

"He's my friend," said Pipo. "I won't let anyone bother him."

A flood of warmth coursed through Aloo's body. Pipo was ready to fight for him. Pipo, whose head came up only to Aloo's chin.

Aloo unstuck his tongue from the roof of his mouth. "I-it's n-not pa-paint."

Pipo swung around. His mouth opened and closed again.

Garu shouldered the others aside and stood squarely in front of Aloo, looking him up and down. Aloo looked back at him with unblinking eyes.

"What happened to you?" Garu said.

"N-nothing. I-I don't know," said Aloo. He held himself as rigid as a bamboo stalk, slowly curling his fingers at his side. He would fight if he had to. He could not allow little Pipo to fight for him.

The other boys were silent, looking from Aloo to Garu and back again.

Another rumble of thunder broke the silence.

"We're going to see a shaman," said Pipo, elbowing Garu aside. "He would know what to do."

Pipo grabbed the flopping lobster, broke off its pincers in two swift twists and picked up the two strings of crayfish. He gave Aloo a slight nod and tramped up the slope.

MORNING MIRAGE

Ikupo lifted his head wearily as a shadow darkened the opening of his makeshift hut. He waited for the person to enter, but the shadow wavered and then disappeared. With a sigh of relief, Ikupo closed his eyes and dropped his chin to his chest again. He'd been up most of the night tending to some new arrivals. People with broken bones, gushing cuts and all sorts of terrible pains.

Then there were the frantic mothers with babies struggling to breathe. Those were the easy ones, though. Ikupo simply told the mothers to immerse the babies again and again in the river until their breathing improved and to dampen the floor of their shelters to keep down the ash.

It was the steady stream of badly injured people that was wearing him down. Apparently, he was the only shaman here, apart from a young one in the tiny village nearby. It didn't help that the two boys he'd been training in Warigara had not showed up at this camp. He didn't have many of the herbs needed to stop bleeding, ease pain or help close wounds. And his half-hearted mumbled chants were more for the benefit of the sick than the spirits.

Ikupo shifted his buttocks, trying to find a more comfortable position on the coarse grass. There was some kind of scuffling outside his hut, and he could hear whispering, but he didn't budge.

"He's our shaman," a voice said clearly above the others. It was Garu.

Ikupo sighed. He was in no mood to deal with that boy today.

More scuffling and the opening of the hut darkened again. Ikupo looked up to see a tight cluster of boys jostling outside. Ikupo squinted against the rising sun.

"Great One ..."

Shoving and hissing at each other, the boys squeezed into the small hut in a jumble.

"What's the matter?" In his own ears, his voice sounded gruffer than he'd intended.

"Go on, show him," someone whispered.

More pushing and jostling then the group broke apart.

Ikupo's breath stopped. He could feel his eyes stretching, stretching.

Against the orange light of the rising sun, the figure looked like a shard of rock flung from the deep heart of the Great Mountain. Except that no piece of rock could ever be that alive. Ikupo could almost feel the tension emanating from the boy who stood like an arrow quivering in its mark. The sleek line of his body was broken only by a dark breechcloth. A mass of tight locks brushed his shoulders.

Ikupo squeezed his eyes shut and opened them again.

"No, no, no, not now," he whispered, his breath rasping in his throat. "Leave me alone. I said no more."

The tall boy turned like a startled agouti and tried to bolt through the opening, but one of the others grabbed his arm and hung on.

"Please, Great One," the short boy said, looking over his shoulder at Ikupo with pleading eyes as he tried to tug his friend back inside.

"No, no ... didn't mean you," said Ikupo, fighting to catch his breath.

The two boys quietened, and the short one spoke swiftly.

"We were playing in the river. He was hiding under a rock. We couldn't find him. He came out of the water. The mountain rumbled and ... and ..." He pulled his friend gently forward. "Show him, Aloo," he said, his voice soft.

The tall boy was looking at Ikupo with terrified eyes. His mouth opened and closed again but no sound came out.

"He went all black, and it's not paint," Garu said loudly.

Ikupo creaked to his feet and shuffled toward the boy, who looked like a jittery, freshly painted warrior about to go on his first raid. Reaching out a trembling hand, Ikupo touched his shoulder. The boy flinched and Ikupo could feel him quivering like a trapped manicou.

"Aloo's your name?"

The boy nodded, staring at Ikupo with wide eyes, his high

forehead and cheekbones glistening with sweat. Ikupo dropped his hand from Aloo's shoulder but couldn't drag his gaze away from the boy.

"Tell me again what happened."

Ikupo saw Aloo's throat move as he swallowed.

The short boy stepped forward. "It's when he got out of the water, see. We glanced up at the sky when the mountain growled and when we looked back at Aloo, he was ... was like this."

"Pipo said it was paint," Garu broke in, flicking a disdainful glance at the short boy. "But I could tell it wasn't."

"We all thought it was paint," said Ranan.

"Shut up, I didn't," said Garu, rounding on Ranan, who dropped his head.

"Enough," said Ikupo. He wanted to chase off the four of them but knew he needed them here.

"Tell me yourself, Aloo. What happened?"

"I-I don't ... Th-this is h-how I-I am."

Ikupo drew a deep breath and lifted his chin.

"Yes, I see." He cleared his throat. "Where's your family?"

The boy started again. "L-lost ..."

"Like so many others," said Ikupo, staring into Aloo's panicked eyes. "Scattered by the wrath of the Great Mountain." He beckoned to Aloo. "Come, sit here."

Aloo's body tensed and his eyes flicked to Pipo, who gave him a slight nod. Aloo hesitated. Then he stepped forward and, in one fluid motion, sank to the ground in front of Ikupo.

A rush of a long-forgotten emotion flooded Ikupo's chest. His hand fluttered to his throat, his fingers fumbling among the beads there. Breathe, breathe, breathe.

"You boys can sit over there," he said, pointing at a low space under the slanting sides of the hut.

"And be quiet," he warned, as they started elbowing each other and whispering.

On shaking legs, Ikupo shuffled to the other side of the hut and carefully reached down a small gourd that was hanging from a hooked stick near the low roof. Using two fingers, he stirred the dark brew that a young shaman from the nearby village had given him the day before. His back to the boys, Ikupo took a strong draught of the bitter drink. His mind was reeling, but he had to find a way to deal with this.

He turned and began circling Aloo slowly, sipping from the gourd at intervals. Better not drink all of it now until he could find the plants to make a fresh brew. When the buzzing started in Ikupo's ears and the noises of the camp began to fade, he replaced the gourd on the hooked stick and positioned himself directly in front of Aloo, legs apart, facing the opening of the hut.

Ikupo closed his eyes and raised his arms above his head.

"Spirit of the mountain, spirit of the sea, speak to me," he chanted softly. "Spirit of the wind, spirit of the sky, speak to me."

The buzzing in his head grew louder. Behind his closed eyelids, he could see a whorl of colours. His tongue was filling up his mouth, but he kept up his chant.

"Spirit of the mountain, spirit of the sea, speak to me. Spirit of the wind, spirit of the sky, speak to me."

Ikupo placed his hands on the boy's head. The tremors of the boy's body ran up Ikupo's arms and entered his chest. The colours behind Ikupo's eyes morphed into a brief flash of his perplexing dream then melted away. He waited. Nothing more. The buzzing began to subside, gradually drowned out by the squeals of children playing outside, the chatter of women, the deeper timbre of men's voices.

Ikupo dropped his arms to his sides and opened his eyes. Aloo was looking up at him like a choking frog. As were the four boys sitting with their backs against the coconut weave.

Ikupo drew himself up and cleared his throat, feeling for his voice. "Stand, Aloo."

Again, there was that almost boneless movement as Aloo got to his feet. Ikupo placed a hand on Aloo's shoulder.

"This boy has been touched by the Great Mountain spirit and now bears the colour of its heart."

Aloo went still under Ikupo's hand. Out of the corner of his eye, Ikupo saw the other boys staring at him and Aloo with bulging eyes, their jaws slack. Pipo was the first to recover.

"When will he get back his own colour?"

"Never," said Ikupo. "He's now the kindred of the Great Mountain and must wear its colour for the rest of his life."

He could feel Aloo breathing again.

Over in the corner, Caloon sniggered. "He's going to look like that all the time?

"Yes, stupid," Garu said. "Don't you see? It can't wash off."

"You'll be the best warrior, Aloo," said Pipo, his face lighting up. He jumped to his feet. "You won't need paint ever."

"What if he can't fight?" said Caloon, a hint of envy in his voice. "It's not just about camouflage, you know. My father says—"

"Enough," said Ikupo, dropping his arm and rounding on the quibbling boys. "Aloo will need paint. He'll need it every day, like you all do."

He turned to Aloo. "You've been chosen to wear the colour of the Great Mountain's heart. Protect it well. Make sure you're always painted with roucou to keep off insects and to temper the touch of the sun spirit."

Ikupo reached out and fingered one of Aloo's tight locks. "The Great Mountain spirit has seared you from head to toe. This is your fate."

Aloo looked back at him with wide solemn eyes but said nothing.

"Go now," said Ikupo.

The boys scrambled out of the hut, jabbering among themselves as they ran off.

Ikupo followed them outside, his eyes fixed on Aloo, who seemed to be skimming across the plain like a low-flying heron. All too soon, he became a blur in the distance. Ikupo turned to face the Great Mountain, his mouth twisting in a faint smile.

"Seems like we're not done with each other after all," he murmured.

WATER WOES

The high melodious call of a sparrow broke through the chirping of morning birds and the murmur of the river. Yurubi looked up from the shallow pool near the sandy riverbank where she was sitting, lathering a wriggling baby with a handful of *bouleua*. Through her tangle of wet hair, she saw Aloo crouched in the shadow of an almond tree, half hidden by a clump of grass. After almost one moon of living in the camp, he was still very cautious about approaching anyone directly, even though no one was looking at him curiously anymore. The story of the boy seared by the Great Mountain was just one of many about the mountain's fearful rage.

Yurubi pushed back her hair and waved, beckoning Aloo to come over. He hesitated for a moment then bounded across the clearing and down the riverbank.

"Where are the other girls?" he said, looking quickly up and down the river.

"In there, somewhere, trying to find guavas," Yurubi said, pointing at a thicket further upstream. She and four other girls had been given the task today to mind some of the babies while the women went further inland to forage for edible roots and herbs.

"Not many guavas left around here now," said Aloo.

He squatted in the sand and reached out a finger to touch the baby's hair, which was sticking up like cactus spines. The child was slithering about on Yurubi's lap, splashing furiously with both hands.

"Strong little boy," said Aloo, with a soft laugh. "Going to be a great swimmer." He bent his head and ruffled the baby's hair. "Like Pipo."

Yurubi looked sideways at Aloo. His face was hidden behind his mass of locks, but she could see his mouth tightening.

"Where's Pipo today?" she said.

"Fishing."

"At the beach?"

"Uh-huh."

It was not like Pipo to go anywhere without Aloo these days. At first, Yurubi had been taken aback at how quickly they'd become friends, and she'd been somewhat envious when they returned to the camp on evenings with whatever they had caught that day— iguana, agouti, manicou, crabs or a string of river fish. But those feelings had soon given way to delight at seeing Aloo moving around in the camp, eating at her family's campfire sometimes and sleeping in Pipo's shelter.

If Pipo had gone fishing alone today, it was because Aloo had slipped away from him. And Yurubi knew why. She scooped up two handfuls of water and poured them over Aloo's fingers, which were still toying with the baby's hair.

"It's not so hard, you know," she said. "I can show you if you like."

Aloo bent his head even further. "I-it's not th-that. It's t-the waves and … the s-salt … and …"

He turned his gaze in the direction of the ocean, his face tight.

"I-if Pipo finds out—"

"He'd still be your friend."

Wrapping one arm around the wriggling baby, Yurubi leaned forward and tilted her head so she could look Aloo in the eye.

"Remember when I couldn't climb a coconut tree and you showed me how?"

Aloo nodded, a smile twitching at his lips.

"Every time I slipped, you'd catch me before I hit the ground and make me try again. Know what it felt like when I skinned my sweaty arms and legs on those rough tree trunks?" Yurubi grinned and slapped Aloo's arm. "Felt like a bee attack."

Aloo lifted his head and smiled back at her. "But now you can pick coconuts anytime you want."

"Yes, and now there's something I can show you how to do," said Yurubi, watching Aloo's face carefully. "We can slip away before dawn, just like we used to."

Aloo said nothing, but his eyes were pensive as he watched the baby slide off Yurubi's lap and begin sloshing around in the shallow water, gurgling and spitting in delight.

"Tomorrow," said Yurubi, "listen for my warbler call."

Aloo cocked his head. "Your friends are coming back."

He tousled the baby's hair one last time and ran off, disappearing into the bushes as swiftly as a moth.

Yurubi sighed. Back when she and Aloo were little, and he was learning Kalina words from her, he had told her a garbled tale about a boat at sea, big waves, he and his mother in the water. It didn't sound much different from the many stories Yurubi had heard around the campfire in her village, except it was being told by a captive. It seemed Aloo had been captured on some far island and had managed to escape from one of the villages near Warigara.

Yurubi had never asked him about his village because when she was small, she'd learned that it made captives sad to talk about their home. One time, when Minda was first brought to Warigara, Taima had started asking her about where she came from, but Waasha had grabbed Taima and dragged her away, scolding her in a low voice. *You're never again to ask Minda about her village or island. You'll only make her cry.*

So Yurubi had never tried to question Aloo about his home, and he'd soon stopped talking about the sea voyage. But he never went near the beach if he could help it, and he never went into the sea. Yurubi had paid no mind because that's just the way Aloo was about any wide open space. The first time she'd seen him walking calmly across the plain here, in broad daylight, with Pipo at his side, she'd gone as taut as a bowstring. Then her heart had soared. Aloo was losing his fear of open spaces, and he was making friends. She'd do anything to make sure that he would never want to go into hiding again.

It was still dark when Aloo rose silently from his spot in the lee of the rock near Pipo's shelter and slipped away from the camp. A stiff breeze lifted his locks off his shoulders as he ran along the river. Already, he could taste the salty spray on his lips and feel it sticking to the layer of ash on his skin. As he ran, the crash of waves on the shore grew louder, filling his head. Aloo began shivering. He broke through the row of sea grape trees along the shoreline and skidded to a stop. A wave curled and rolled to the shore, ran up the black sand and stretched toward Aloo as if to taunt him. He cringed. Behind that, another wave swelled. And another.

From where he was standing, Aloo could feel the pounding of the ocean in his chest. This was a very bad idea. There was no way he could go into that water.

A pale waning moon hanging over the horizon grinned sickly at him. Aloo groped for a low branch on the grape tree behind him and rested his buttocks against it, not trusting his suddenly weak legs. The smell of the ocean clogged his throat, bringing acrid tears to his eyes. He had been so careful not to ever get too close to the sea. He'd be mad to get in there and try to fight those waves again.

The call of a warbler broke through the rushing sound that was rising in Aloo's ears. He moved his tongue in his dry mouth, shuddering at the taste of the salt, and returned the call. He'd tell Yurubi he couldn't do this. He'd just have to keep dodging Pipo some days. Or go back into hiding. His stomach clenched at the thought. No more nights around family fires. No more days of hunting with Pipo. Worse of all, no more seeing Yurubi any time he wanted.

Her call floated toward him, closer this time. He answered with a quavering whistle, his gaze fixed on the rollers crashing on the beach.

"You're so early, seems like you slept here," said Yurubi, coming up behind him.

Aloo brushed a hand over his watering eyes and cleared his throat.

"I-I don't th-think I can g-go in," he said.

Yurubi came around in front of him and peered into his face. In the weak moonlight she looked like the water spirit he had once imagined her to be.

She reached out and took his hand.

"Come on, we'll just paddle near the shore," she said, her voice soft.

She tugged his hand gently. He stood and followed her, his heart crashing against his ribs like the ocean itself. The roaring in his head was growing louder, and a cluster of black spots began dancing in front of his eyes. He tightened his grip on Yurubi's hand and squeezed his eyes shut. A gasp rose in his throat as he felt the waves swirling around his ankles.

"Remember the coconut tree?" said Yurubi, a smile in her voice.

He squeezed her fingers, not trusting his voice. He waded into the sea, feeling the coarse sand sucking away from under his feet. A sharp, sour taste rose in his throat. The waves were bashing against his thighs and tugging at him with a persistence he remembered all too well. He dug his toes into the sand, his knees stiff.

'Let's paddle here for a bit,' said Yurubi, as if from a distance.

She sank down into the water, still holding his hand. A stronger wave slapped against Aloo, bouncing him slightly off his feet. He bent his knees and squatted quickly next to Yurubi, his fingers gripping hers. The water swirled around his chest and shoulders, cooling the sudden heat that had flared in his body.

"See? It's not so bad," said Yurubi.

Aloo could feel her bobbing up and down with the movement of the waves. He unlocked his knees and tried to do the same. It felt as if the waves were crashing right through his stomach and sloshing around inside him.

"It's different from playing in the river, isn't it?" said Yurubi. "A different kind of fun. It's also easier to swim here. You feel lighter in the sea."

Above the roaring in his ears, Aloo tried to focus on what she was saying. Lighter, yes. So light the waves could carry you—

"Kick your legs like this, you'll see," said Yurubi. "We won't go out. We'll just swim along the beach."

Swim. Yurubi wanted him to swim. Aloo kicked his feet off the bottom and tried to paddle with one arm as he clung to Yurubi's hand with the other. A wave slapped the side of his face, sending a sting of salt into his nose and throat. Aloo's chest tightened. He pressed his lips together hard and scrunched his eyes more tightly shut. But even behind his closed eyes, a mountain of foaming black water was rising.

"Look, Aloo, the sun's coming up."

His eyes flew open.

The whole world was tinged with pink. From the horizon to the lazy wave curling toward him. Aloo dropped his feet to the bottom and drew a ragged breath. A single seagull glided serenely across the pink sky.

"It's like being inside an enormous conch shell," said Yurubi in that breathy voice she got sometimes when she was looking at some-thing she really liked.

Her face was bathed in the glow of the sunrise, and her eyes were following the slow flight of the lone seagull. Aloo could feel the roiling inside his stomach gradually subsiding.

"Let's come back tomorrow," Yurubi said, turning to him with a wide smile.

Aloo curled his fingers more tightly around hers and waded with her toward the glistening pink shore.

CHIEFS' MEETING

Ikupo squinted up at the huge mushroom cloud hanging over the north of the island. Another shower of ash was about to start, but the village leaders sitting on the beach in the fading light seemed unaware of the bulging sky. They were gathered around a fire, drinking woku, smoking and bickering about food supplies, fishing, weapons, shelters and the like.

Ikupo shifted his behind on the coarse sand, sucked on his roll of herbs, and waited. This was going to take a while.

"Our crops are almost all gone," the Jambou village headman was saying, his wide forehead creased in a frown. "Too many people to feed. We'd only planted enough for the people in our village."

Oudou grunted and rubbed his chin.

"My hunters have been going inland, but they need better weapons," he said. "We left almost everything behind. It takes time to make good spears and knives."

"Our shelters keep collapsing," said another village chief. "When it's not the wind, it's the ash." He poked viciously at the fire, throwing up a shower of sparks.

The Jambou village headman spat into the fire. "You don't have to stay here," he said.

Oudou's eyes flicked from one chief to the other. "The ash falls everywhere on the island," he said.

They all fell silent.

Ikupo swallowed a mouthful of woku and cleared his throat. The village chiefs turned to look at him.

'Too much fighting all day, all night," said Ikupo. "Boys fighting, men fighting, women squabbling. They're angering the spirits."

Ikupo took a drag on his herbs and tilted his head back. The first drizzle of new ash plopped on his cheeks. The chiefs glanced up at the roiling mass of clouds overhead then fixed their gaze on Ikupo as the ash started to splatter him. Ikupo closed his eyes. Above the rush of the stiff breeze, he could hear the crackling of the fire, the crash and suck of the waves on the sand, and thin chirp of early crickets. Eyes still closed, Ikupo spoke slowly.

"The spirits are sending a message. Must listen carefully."

He spread his arms wide, palms upturned, allowing the ash to fall in his hands. After a while, he brought his hands together in front of him and opened his eyes. He peered at the splashes of ash in his palms, tilting his hands this way and that to catch the firelight. He was bent almost double, his hair hanging down on either side of his face. Ikupo blew lightly on his palms and watched as the ash rose in puffs and settled again. Fat blobs were pelting down now, pounding out a rhythm on the back of his head.

Ikupo could feel the chiefs' eyes on him. They, too, were being coated in ash, but they sat still, waiting.

"The boys …" Ikupo moved his fingers slightly, allowing some of the ash to trickle through. "Must start with the boys."

"The boys?" The Jambou village chief sounded like a trapped frog.

Under his brows, Ikupo saw Oudou place a bent finger on his lips. The Jambou chief opened his mouth and closed it again in a tight line.

"Their training … coming-of-age … why has it stopped?" Ikupo said. "The spirits are disturbed."

Oudou leaned forward, his ash-covered face like that of a beached manatee. He stared at Ikupo under knitted brows. "Training? They want us to restart the boys' training?"

Ikupo tilted his palms toward Oudou.

"So it seems," he said.

The chiefs stared at Ikupo's hands, their grey faces slack. Ikupo knew the swirls of ash on his palms would mean nothing to them but he let them look anyway.

"Yes, I see," said Oudou slowly.

Ikupo looked up at him in surprise. But Oudou was gazing into the sputtering fire, a hint of a smile on his face.

"Of course, that's what we have to do to stop the fighting and find more food," said Oudou, fingering his chin. "Break them into small groups to make weapons, build canoes, hunt and fish."

The Jambou headman brushed a hand across his eyes, his forehead unknotting for the first time.

"Yes, yes, they'd be away from the camp all day and come back only at night," he said.

"There are many warriors here to help train them," another chief said.

Oudou stretched out his arms toward Ikupo.

"Great One, as always, you are wise to the ways of the spirits," he said. "Tell them we have heard and will heed their wishes."

Ikupo nodded and rose to his feet, scattering the ash on his arms, shoulders and head. He could leave it to them now. He turned toward the camp, his mind already on the fresh batch of herbs he had asked Aloo to gather for him.

"We can start tomorrow, start them making tools and weapons," Ikupo heard one of the men say as he shuffled across the sand.

BOATS IN THE WOODS

The line of young boys followed a thin trail into the gorge, jog-
ging along behind Maruku and Kuriji. Dappled sunlight made
a moving pattern on the boys' painted bodies as they hurried along
under the trees, carrying axes, adzes and chisels made from stone
and conch-shells.

It was a bright morning unmarred by the dreaded mushroom ash
clouds or thunder. The woods were alive with bird calls, the rush
of sea breezes through the treetops, and the babble of the river as it
wound through the narrow gorge.

On the left, a wall of black rock covered by scrub and vines rose
almost vertically. On the other side, green hills folded steeply into
the distance.

At the back of the line, Aloo could tell this was new ground
for most of the boys. Not for him and Pipo, though. They had
ventured here once before, searching for fruit. Well, Pipo was the
one who'd been searching for fruit. Aloo had been more interested
in game. But they'd come away with nothing except stings from a
swarm of wasps that had chased them out of the gorge. Aloo smiled
wryly. He'd be keeping a sharp eye out for those wasps today.

Near the front of the line, Garu pointed to the left with his new axe.

"I've heard there are caves in that cliff," he said. "I'd like to climb
up there and look for iguanas."

Pipo, just ahead of Aloo, turned around and grinned.

"The red wasps and bats can't wait," he whispered, winking at Aloo.

"Seems like we'd have to pull ourselves up there on vines," said

Garu, still looking at the rock face. "Can't see any path."

"Jokoro would love that. He climbs like a manicou," said Ranan with a laugh, slapping the back of the boy in front and causing him to stumble a bit.

Jokoro turned around and raised his axe in a mock threat.

"Watch it, Ranan. Or I'll make a canoe out of you."

Ranan reared back, laughing. "You don't even know how to make a canoe."

Jokoro made a face and turned back to the front, waving his axe in the air.

"Let's try that climb later when we're done with the boats," said Garu.

"Errm, we'll finish the boats before nightfall?" said Pipo in a droll voice.

"Not if our axes are all as dull as yours," Caloon said with a snicker.

Some of the boys broke into laughter, twisting around to look at Pipo's axe, but he plodded along steadily, ignoring them.

Aloo reached out and touched Pipo's shoulder lightly. Garu and his friends obviously didn't know that Pipo and his family were boat people. Like Yurubi. She'd be on a canoe every day if she could.

Aloo's lips twitched at the memory of her paddling furiously to cross the river in a little lopsided canoe they'd built deep in the forest when they were small. The boat, made from a piece of light bafflow wood, had eventually keeled over and tipped Yurubi into the river. She was a strong swimmer even back then, and she'd splashed frantically after the runaway boat for a while before giving up and kicking her way to the shore. Aloo had stood on the riverbank, his arms folded tight across his stomach, unable to tear his eyes away from the upended boat bouncing downstream.

Since then, he had helped Yurubi build many other small canoes and sail them on the river. She was always coming up with ways of making them better, faster, lighter.

She should be here today. She could build a better canoe than any of these boys. Except Pipo, perhaps.

"This is it," Maruku called out from up ahead, as the group entered a little clearing on a knoll above the river. "You boys can run down to the river quickly for a drink then get back here and start felling trees."

The boys dropped their tools on the ground and ran to the river.

"Whoooo hooooo!" Garu shouted, dropping his gourd on the bank and jumping into the water. The others followed, leaping into the river and diving under the water to cool down. They splashed each other, stood on their hands underwater, and climbed onto rocks to do back flips in the river.

A hand clamped on Aloo's head from behind, pushing him under, and Aloo heard Pipo's gleeful laugh. Aloo spluttered a bit, but he stayed under. He curled into a tight ball, spun around, grabbed Pipo's legs and pulled him underwater. Puffing out his cheeks, Pipo made a face of mock rage and grabbed Aloo's hair. Aloo closed his eyes, went limp and sank to the riverbed. For a brief moment, he felt Pipo's hold on him slacken. With a grin, Aloo kicked away from Pipo and shot to the surface.

"Stop playing and get back here!" a voice roared from the stand of trees.

The boys scrambled out of the water, shaking their wet hair and laughing. They quickly filled their gourds and scampered back to the clearing.

Maruku and Kuriji were standing on either side of a thick gumbo tree, legs apart, axes held loosely. Aloo could see them counting with their eyes to make sure all the boys were there. Without a word, the two men gripped their axes, turned and began chopping near the base of the tree. With each whack of the axes, the notches on either side of the tree opened wider.

Aloo leaned forward, peering over the heads of the boys to get a better look. Arms moving in an easy rhythm, Maruku and Kuriji were turning their axes with each strike to make two different types of cuts, one slanting downward and the other slanting upward. Aloo also noticed that Kuriji was cutting a wider notch than Maruku.

"They're good," Pipo whispered to Aloo, although he didn't seem to be paying much attention to what the men were doing.

In fact, Aloo doubted Pipo could see anything much from where he was standing at the back of the tight cluster of boys. Aloo signalled to him to shift around to a better position, but before they could move, Maruku and Kuriji stopped chopping. The two men leaned on their axes and beckoned the boys closer.

Garu and Caloon rushed forward.

"We can do it now," Garu said. He gripped his axe in both hands and stepped up to the tree.

"Don't be foolish, boy," said Kuriji, his voice laced with laughter. "This is a solid gumbo-limbo tree. You're going to be cutting bafflow trees, like that one over there."

Kuriji pointed with his axe to a slender tree on his right. Someone giggled and Aloo could see Garu's ears turning red. Kuriji strode over to the bafflow tree and tapped the trunk with the back of his axe.

"You have to make sure they're not too old and rotting at the core," Kuriji said. "Tap them like this. If they sound hollow, they're no good for making boats."

Aloo cocked his head as Kuriji tapped the tree trunk again. It didn't sound hollow to Aloo, but he knew he'd have to try a few other trees to hear the difference. He glanced at the faces of the other boys. They looked tense and excited but not in the least amazed. For Aloo, though, it was so very strange being taught something by an adult. He usually just learned things on his own, sometimes painfully, or from Yurubi.

Kuriji had moved back to the gumbo tree and was beckoning to the group to come closer.

Shoving and sweating, the boys gathered around Kuriji and Maruku. As usual, Aloo stood at the back of the group, and Pipo stayed next to him.

"See here?" Maruku pointed the handle of his axe at the cut he'd made on the tree. "This is narrower than the notch on the other side."

He walked around the tree.

"The tree will fall on this side because this is where we're making the wider cut. Choose where you want your tree to fall and make the wider cut on that side. When it's almost ready to fall, call me or Kuriji, so we can show you how to drop it safely. Now pick a partner and get going."

Aloo turned to Pipo, who tipped his chin, gesturing to the edge of the clearing. The two of them slipped over there quickly as the other boys jostled among themselves and split up into pairs.

"Already picked one out," Pipo said. "It's big but we can manage it. Done this many times before with my father. It's that one over there."

Aloo's eyes opened wide. The bafflow tree Pipo was pointing at had a thick straight trunk and its bow seemed to be reaching for a space above the tangle of branches in the woods. Aloo had never attempted to cut down anything that big. The trees he and Yurubi had felled in the forest near Warigara were young ones with slender trunks.

Pipo walked up to the tree and tapped it with his axe.

"Hear that?" he said with a wide grin. "Good for making boats."

Aloo hit the trunk a few times with the back of his axe. It gave back a somewhat solid sound, but Aloo knew that bafflow trees all had a very soft light core. He tilted his head back, squinting up at the bow of the tree.

"It's a tall one," he said.

He stepped back and looked around the grove, trying to gauge where to drop the tree, so that it wouldn't break.

"Stop fussing and come over here," said Pipo.

Using his chisel, Pipo etched two lines all the way around the tree, about an axe's head apart, just above where the trunk started narrowing from the root.

"Try not to cut above or below these lines," he said, his words tumbling over each other as usual. "I'll cut the narrower notch on this side. You'll cut the wider one because it's easier."

Aloo bit his lower lip, gripped his axe in both hands and shuffled a few paces to his right, trying to place himself exactly opposite Pipo. He glanced around quickly to see if anyone was noticing his jittery movements, but the other boys were all dashing about trying to find the right tree and picking their partners. Maruku and Kuriji were swinging at the gumbo-limbo tree again in a slow and easy rhythm, while keeping an eye on the boys.

"See that?" said Pipo, jerking a thumb toward the two men. "That's the way to do it."

He hitched up his breechcloth and gripped his axe.

Let's go," he said with a grin.

Aloo glanced at Maruku and Kuriji again, noticing that they weren't striking the tree at the same time. He braced his legs and swung at the tree, aiming between the lines Pipo had marked. After he'd made a few notches, Pipo joined in on the other side, timing his cuts so that they alternated with Aloo's.

They worked throughout the day, stopping occasionally to wipe the sweat out their eyes, sharpen their axes with small grinding stones, drink from their water gourds or munch on some fruit.

Kuriji and Maruku took frequent breaks from their own hewing and strolled through the woods, checking on the boys, teaching them the right way to hold the axes, how to angle the cuts and how to tell when a tree is almost ready to fall.

The first time Kuriji came over to Aloo and Pipo's tree, he glanced up at the height of it then stood there with his arms folded across his chest. Aloo kept his eyes on the tree, trying hard not to lose the rhythm that he and Pipo had going.

"Where did you boys get those axes?" Kuriji said after a while.

Pipo stopped cutting and wiped his face with one hand. Aloo stopped as well. He could feel his face burning. Was something wrong with his axe?

"My father gave me this," said Pipo, holding up his axe, which was made from a huge conch shell fixed to a wooden haft with a thong.

"Mmmm," said Kuriji. He walked around the tree to look more closely at the narrow cut Pipo was making. Then he turned to Aloo.

"And you, boy, where did you get your axe?"

"I- I ... My ... I-I m-made it w-with m-my fr-friend."

Kuriji's eyebrows flew upward. "You made it? Here, let me have a look."

Heart thumping, Aloo handed over the axe. Kuriji held the stone head flat in his broad palm, turning it this way and that and running his finger along the edge.

Aloo stood motionless, his arms hanging at his side. He and Yurubi had spent days knapping the axe and a few other tools like a chisel and an adze after they'd heard about the boat building training. Since they were small children, they'd been making knives, bows and arrows and whatever else they needed for their secret adventures. Aloo had never thought about having to show the tools to anyone else.

Kuriji hefted the axe slowly then handed it back to Aloo with a strange look in his eyes.

"Touched by the Great Mountain," said Kuriji under his breath as he walked away.

"Call one of us before you try to topple that tree," he said over his shoulder.

Aloo looked at Pipo in bewilderment, but Pipo just shrugged. Perhaps Pipo hadn't heard what Kuriji had muttered.

"At least he didn't have to show us how to hold our axes," said Pipo with a laugh. "Come on, let's finish this."

Aloo nodded and was raising his axe again when he heard a creaking sound behind him. He spun around to see a tree leaning slowly to the right. Kuriji, who was walking in the opposite direction whipped around and started running toward the tilting tree.

"Out of the way!" he shouted.

Without breaking stride, Kuriji scooped up two boys who were in the path of the falling tree and dived to his left. The tree crashed to the ground, missing them by an agouti's whisker.

For a moment there was complete silence. Even the birds seemed to have gone still.

Then there was a dry rustle as Kuriji rolled over and spat out a mouthful of dirt and leaves. Ranan and Jokoro, whom he had snatched out of harm's way, untangled themselves from his arms and sat up with a dazed look, their faces streaked with grime, twigs clinging to their hair.

From the other side of the fallen tree, someone snickered, and another boy joined in. Kuriji got to his feet and spat again.

"You think that's amusing?" he said, his voice like pebbles falling off a cliff. He walked slowly toward the sound of the snickering, his mouth tight.

The laughter dried up. Although Aloo couldn't see the culprits from where he was standing, he knew it could only be Garu and Caloon.

Aloo shifted a little to his right and Maruku came into view, standing like a rock in the middle of the grove. Maruku's eyes flicked from Kuriji to a thick cedar tree where the two boys apparently were huddled.

"Garu, Caloon, get over here, now," roared Maruku, his face set like a mountain in a thunderstorm.

"Oh oh, they're in bad trouble," Pipo whispered behind Aloo.

The other boys stood rooted throughout the grove as Garu and Caloon sidled out from behind the tree and slouched toward Maruku. In a few long strides, Kuriji caught up with the two boys, and his arms shot out, grabbing them by the hair.

"You little—"

"Let me," said Maruku, raising one hand to stop Kuriji.

Looking straight at Maruku, Kuriji kept his grip on the two boys.

Aloo wasn't sure what that look between the two men meant but after a while, Kuriji let go of Garu and Caloon and stepped back.

"Pity," Pipo muttered.

A roguish look crept over Garu's face. He bent his head almost to his chest and started speaking almost in a whisper.

"We didn't know—"

"A Kalina man never hangs his head," Maruku roared, his voice echoing off the rocks in the gorge. "Look me in the eye, boy."

Garu's head shot up and he met Maruku's fierce gaze.

"Your father is a great chief, but you are nothing until you prove yourself, understand? It's the Kalina way," Maruku said, his words dropping like stones in a waterhole.

His gaze swung to Caloon. "And you, boy. If you're going to be a follower, try to choose a canny leader. No one survives in this land by being stupid."

Aloo could see a bright red flush covering the ears and necks of the two boys as Maruku continued the scolding.

"No one was hurt here today, but that's only because of Kuriji's fast legs and strong arms."

Kuriji straightened his back and raised his chin as the older man nodded in his direction.

Maruku's gaze swivelled to Garu and Caloon.

"No more foolishness from you two or anyone else. You're training to be warriors, not buffoons."

His eyes raked the woods, swiftly checking on the rest of the group.

"Back to work," he said. "Let's drop the other trees then call it a day."

GIRLS IN THE GORGE

Yurubi could feel grit in her teeth as a stiff, damp breeze picked up the ash that lay thick on the ground and blew it into her face. Next to her, two baby boys were crawling around, giggling in delight as they tried to chase a lizard that was scurrying through the grey dust.

"Come back here," said Yurubi, grabbing at the babies' ankles to stop them from crawling too close to the cook fire where Ma was stirring a big pot of cassava, fish and chili peppers.

"They're already trying to hunt," said Ma with a laugh. "Minda, Galeba, your boys will be bringing you meat soon," she called to the two women squatting near their fires a short distance away. They laughed uproariously at the sight of the babies trying to wriggle out of Yurubi's grasp to go after the lizard.

"This pot could use some more meat right now," said Minda, fanning at the steam rising from a stew of crabs and roots.

Yurubi smiled as she pulled the babies close to her side and wrapped an arm around each of them.

"I know, hunting is fun, but you'll have to grow a bit taller and learn to do more than crawl," she whispered.

One of the babies looked at her with solemn eyes then gurgled and tried to squirm away again. Yurubi rolled her eyes and clutched the chubby little body closer. Today her task was to mind the two babies while the women were busy preparing food.

"I hope we'll be under cover before that rain starts tonight," said Ma, eyeing the dark clouds rolling in over the ocean. Her anxious gaze shifted to the group of men and boys milling about on the plain, and she muttered something under her breath.

Following her mother's gaze, Yurubi noticed that the new huts being put up were still only half done. For the past few days, the group had been piling up branches, wood posts, *mahoe* strips and other materials to build more sturdy shelters before the rains started. But the men seemed to be in no rush. They sat around smoking, talking about weapons and occasionally shouting orders to the boys who were struggling to erect the huts.

"I hope we don't get that one," Yurubi said just loud enough for her mother to hear.

She pointed her chin to a lopsided shelter being built by Tueke from her village and another boy whose name she didn't know.

"Hmmm, it *is* a bit crooked," said Ma.

"A *bit*, Ma? Perhaps you should go closer."

"Never mind, it'd be better than sleeping outside in the rain," said Ma. "Much better."

"Not if it collapses on us," said Yurubi, rolling her eyes again.

Ma placed one hand on her hip and stared at the crooked hut as she stirred the stew, but she said nothing.

Yurubi, Ma, Waasha and Grandma Lulou had been sleeping on the ground under a rough ajoupa that sheltered them from the wind at night but would be useless in a rainstorm.

Yurubi was sure she could put up a shelter better than those two boys, but no one would allow her to do things like that. Instead, she had to fetch water, gather firewood and watch the babies while the women cooked, weaved makeshift hammocks and made rough clay bowls and mugs.

What Yurubi was itching to do was go into the gorge with Aloo to build a canoe. On the nights when he and Pipo ate from her family's pot, she'd be all ears as they talked about felling trees, trimming them, shaping the wood and learning new skills from Maruku and Kuriji.

Yurubi loved playing with the babies but didn't know how much longer she could just sit around in the camp minding them. She stroked the babies' hair absently, trying to think of a way to join Aloo and Pipo. Her eyes drifted to Waasha, who was off to one side pounding some wild roots on a stone. Waasha could make a paste, grain or powder from almost anything she put her hands on. Yurubi looked from Waasha to Ma and back again, an idea forming in her mind.

"Ma, can I go into the gorge tomorrow to search for some roucou and more roots for Waasha?" said Yurubi softly.

Her mother gave her a strange look. "Yurubi, you hate digging."

Yurubi bent her head. "I know how to find ginger," she mumbled. She scratched at a spot on her leg where the red roucou paint had faded. "I'm also good at spotting roucou plants."

Ma was silent. Yurubi raised her head to see Ma looking at the darkening sky again with a frown.

"I guess when that rain starts the insects will go crazy," said Ma. She bent her gaze on Yurubi. "If it's not pouring, you can go tomorrow with the older girls who've been gathering food. But do not stray from the group, you hear me?"

"No, Ma. Yes, Ma." Yurubi scrambled after the two babies, her heart racing. She crawled swiftly on her hands and knees and rolled the babies over on the grass, tussling with them until they broke into squeals of laughter.

"I'm going to see the boats," she whispered to them, joining in their bubbly laughter.

The heavy overnight rain had washed the foliage clean but had created slush on the ground. Yurubi sloshed through the thick slippery ash and mud behind five older girls who were trekking through the woods, gathering fruit, herbs and wild roots.

A cloud of buzzing insects seemed to be following them under the damp trees, but the red roucou paint on the girls' bodies prevented actual bites. Ma was right. The rain had brought out the insects in full force. Although Yurubi had used the roucou as an excuse to go exploring, it really was going to be needed. The basket on her back, supported by a strap across her forehead, was laden with roucou pods. She'd also dug up some wild yams and ginger, picked lemons, guavas, bell apples, and mammee apples, and gathered lemon grass and mint. On top of that, she had a coconut shell full of gum she'd collected from a tree to burn in a lamp at night now that her family had a little hut.

"My basket is already full, and it's heavy." Welusi leaned forward under the weight of her basket of mostly yams. "Let's go back."

"Can we rest a little first?" said Yurubi. She was not as tired as she sounded, but she didn't want to go back until she'd found the boat builders.

"I suppose we can rest a bit, but let's look for a place where it's not so squishy," said Taima, who was leading the group.

The girls followed her, their feet dragging, sweat pouring off them in the humid midday heat. From somewhere up ahead, a faint rhythmic sound reached them.

Welusi stopped, cocking her head to listen. "That sounds like chopping," she said.

"It must be the boys," said Yurubi, her words tumbling over each other. "They're building boats."

"Let's go find them," said Taima. "That might be a good place to rest."

She parted the bushes on the right and set off in the direction of the sound. It wasn't long before the group reached the grove.

Yurubi strained forward, drinking in the sight of several logs sitting on crutches, waiting to be shaped into canoes. Hardly hearing the chatter that had broken out around her, she lowered her basket to the ground and walked slowly toward a thick log that two men were hewing. The bark had been stripped clean, and dapples of green light were capering on the pale log. The men, backs to her, were making crosscuts along the length of the wood about two axe handles apart.

Yurubi knew those cuts would make it easier to level off the wood to a flat surface. After that, the log would be turned upside down, and the keel, bow and stern would be carved with the finest stone and shell tools. Then it would be flipped over again and hollowed out, filled with hot sand and stones to widen the sides, braced with wood strips, and chiselled to a smooth finish. Finally, designs would be lovingly carved on the sides and painted with multi-coloured dyes. Like a sleek dolphin, the canoe would kiss the waves—

"Yurubi!"

She spun around to see Pipo waving at her from the far side of the grove.

"Over here," he called.

Aloo appeared next to Pipo, a smile spreading across his face. With a lingering look at the gumbo-limbo log, Yurubi picked up her basket again and weaved through the trees toward Pipo and Aloo.

The other girls had opened their baskets and were handing out fruit, while some of the boys were cutting open coconuts for the surprise visitors. Welusi was sitting on a low rock, fanning herself with a broad leaf and taking huge gulps from a coconut. None of the girls were even glancing at the canoes that Yurubi found so riveting.

It was the first time she was seeing so many boats being built at the same time, although they were just small bafflow canoes that would hold no more than two people when they were done. Looking from one log to another, she smiled at the sight of a few crudely carved ones that she knew would turn out no better than some of her first little boats.

It was all she could do not to drop the basket and pick up an adze. Of course, the men would stop her and scold her. And then Ma would kill her. She grinned to herself, shifted the basket in her arms and dodged around a tree as she made her way to where Pipo and Aloo were standing.

Yurubi stopped in her tracks. The log was sitting high off the ground on two trestles, long and straight like a piece of the horizon. It had been cut flat on one side, and the keel was turned upward.

Yurubi set down the basket and walked slowly toward the log.

"What's in the basket?" she heard Pipo say as from a distance.

"Herbs, fruit."

Yurubi reached out and ran her fingers over the log, marveling at the smooth cuts. She'd been listening to Aloo and Pipo, well Pipo mostly, talking at night about the boat, but she had not imagined anything like this.

She turned to Aloo, who had come up behind her.

"Aloo, how—"

"Iffs goovva be fa beff boaff effa," said Pipo, coming up alongside Aloo, his mouth stuffed with fruit.

He handed Aloo one of the guavas he'd fished out of Yurubi's basket and took another bite of his own.

"What?" Yurubi said with a laugh.

Pipo chewed rapidly, closed his eyes and gulped hard. "Going to be the best boat ever."

"It's beautiful," said Yurubi. "How did you learn to make such smooth cuts?"

"Pipo knew how," said Aloo. "They're boat people. He and his family."

"Been building boats since I was little," said Pipo with an off-hand wave at the canoe.

"Me too," said Yurubi softly as her fingers trailed along the log.

She looked up as Pipo made a choking sound. Her eyes flew to Aloo, who'd gone still, holding the guava pressed against his lips.

Pipo crammed the last of his guava into his mouth, his eyes flooding with laughter. "Girffs can'd bill boaffs."

Yurubi could feel a rush of heat rising from her chest to her face. She clenched her hands.

"I can," she said through her teeth.

Pipo stopped chewing, a slight frown creasing his forehead. "What's the matter with you today?"

Yurubi glared at him, her throat tight.

Pipo tilted his head, looking at her with baffled eyes. Then he broke into a smile.

"I know. You want to see. Come, I'll show you."

He picked up a small conch shell axe and walked to one end of the log.

"See, this is going to be the bow. First, we'll shave it with the axes then use the adzes to shape it and make it smooth. Aloo's stronger and good with the axe, but I'm better with the adze."

Yurubi felt a burning behind her eyes. That was how she and Aloo used to work on their boats. She looked sideways at Aloo, who lifted his brows as if waiting for her to say something. Yurubi bit her lip, trying hard not to let him and Pipo see how close she was to tears.

With a churning heart, Yurubi watched as Aloo followed Pipo over to the log. They placed themselves on either side and began shaving the wood. Pipo's arm moved swiftly as he chipped away easily at the log. Yes, he was very much used to doing this. Aloo's movements were slower, but he, too, looked very comfortable. Yurubi could see that he was being careful to make neater cuts than usual. That was Aloo. He learned things faster than anyone she knew.

Yurubi plumped down on the ground with a sigh. Just as well that

Pipo didn't believe her. She'd only get into trouble. She brushed the leaves off a patch of earth and picked up a small twig. She glanced over her shoulder, but the other girls were still sprawled under the trees, chatting lazily and eating fruit.

Yurubi stared for a moment at the boat that was taking shape in front of her, then she began drawing in the dirt. She could already picture how it was going to look. Long and slender, sharp bow straining proudly to the sky. Slick sides slipping through the waves like an eel. Thin, broad paddles dipping swiftly to the green depths and rising to flash at the sun, again and again.

Yurubi's head shot up as a shadow fell over her. Head tilted, Pipo was staring down at her drawing. Yurubi was tempted to sweep her hand over the dirt, but something in Pipo's face stopped her. He squatted next to Yurubi, shifting so he could look at the sketch from her side.

"Aloo, come here," Pipo called softly.

He lifted his head and looked at Yurubi with wide serious eyes.

"You really can make boats."

Yurubi could feel laughter bubbling up inside her. He thought that's what she meant? That she could draw boats?

"Look at this," Pipo said to Aloo, who had dropped to his haunches next to them.

Aloo met Yurubi's eyes over Pipo's head.

"She knows how to make boats," said Aloo slowly. "Show him, Yurubi."

But Yurubi shook her head at Aloo. As much as she was aching to carve that log, she'd better not start any trouble now. For one thing, Ma would not allow her to leave the camp again.

Pipo sat back on his heels, his eyes flicking from the drawing in the dirt to the half-finished boat resting on the trestles. A slow smile stretched across his face.

"Yurubi will make the drawings on the side of our canoe," he said in a whispery voice. "She'll draw them, we'll carve them. It's going to be the best, best boat ever."

Yurubi couldn't help laughing. She looked at Aloo and shrugged. It wasn't really boatbuilding, but it would be better than digging for roots.

GOING HOME

It had been five moons since the people of Warigara and the other villages in the north had fled their homes. During that time, some families had moved on to other areas, going further south to places like Ribishi or trekking across the mountains to Layou and other villages on the western side of the island. Some of them, like Pipo's parents, had left by sea in light boats or rafts, taking their chances against the occasional grumbling of the Great Mountain.

From time to time, new people would drift into the Jambou camp, but they rarely stayed long. The camp was beginning to thin out, making it easier for the remaining families to find food.

For Yurubi, life had fallen into a kind of lazy pattern that she enjoyed sometimes, but more and more she was yearning for her hillside village on the lip of the deep forest.

Today, she was strolling in the shade of a big rocky outcrop with Welusi and Taima, keeping an eye on four toddlers who were staggering along in front of them.

"They're stuffing their mouths with something again," said Welusi, running forward to see what the babies were trying to eat.

"Don't worry, it's just watergrass," said Yurubi with a giggle. "It won't harm them."

The three of them laughed as the babies grabbed fistfuls of the grass, chewing on it like food.

"You've been doing this for many moons," said Welusi. "You must love babies."

Yurubi smiled, her eyes following the toddlers who were now trying to clamber over a small rock.

89

"They make me laugh, and I like talking to them," she said.

What Welusi and Taima didn't know was that Yurubi often whispered things to the babies that she couldn't tell anyone else. Like how her outings with Aloo before sunrise had become so very exciting since they'd begun practicing quietly to shoot arrows while swimming. And how she'd followed the shaman around for days, looking furtively at his ornaments, as she tried to come up with some drawings for the sides of Pipo and Aloo's boat.

"I'd like to go home soon. Wouldn't you?" Welusi's voice broke into Yurubi's thoughts. "I'm so tired of sleeping in a rickety hut with the sea blast blowing through it all night."

"Yes, me too," said Yurubi.

"I don't know," said Taima. She turned to look out across the camp. "I like it here. There are always new people around, and I don't have to work all day in the sun planting corn and cassava. I much prefer looking after the babies."

"Yes, and you also like chatting with Batuli," said Welusi, elbowing her playfully.

Taima's face turned even redder under the roucou paint. "He'll return to his village when we go home," she said in a dull voice.

"Perhaps he'd like to go live in Warigara," said Welusi.

"I don't think so. He's about to become a warrior. He's preparing for his coming-of-age ceremony when he goes home," said Taima.

"Like Tueke and those others," said Welusi. She turned to look at Yurubi. "And Aloo? Where will he go?"

Yurubi opened her mouth and closed it again. It didn't matter what she said, the girls all thought she was eyeing Aloo. She couldn't very well tell them that she and Aloo had been playmates since they were little.

"He's coming back to our village," said Yurubi finally, as Welusi nudged her. "He and Pipo both. Pipo didn't want to go sailing with his parents, said he'd like to stay and finish his boat. And Aloo, well ..." She smiled, thinking of the look on Maruku's face as he watched Aloo bent over the canoe, chipping away at the wood with a sure and steady hand. "Seems like Maruku is taking Aloo under his wing."

"They'll be going home in the boats they built, that group," said Taima. "As part of their training."

Yurubi's feet slowed.

"When?"

"Don't know. That's all I heard when I went to take food for Batuli last night."

Yurubi's heart was singing. The boat she had painted was going to sea. All the way from Jambou to Warigara.

"I also overheard Galeba saying that the warriors were getting restless and were waiting for the shaman to give word," said Welusi. "But when I asked her if the men wanted to go home or on an expedition, she didn't answer." Welusi sighed. "She sent me off to fetch water like a little girl."

"They never tell us anything," said Taima with a shrug.

"Never mind," said Yurubi. "We have good ears."

She ran over to the babies and crouched down, hugging them to her.

"We're going home to Warigara soon," she whispered.

The little boats were perched on the black sand like seabirds looking out to sea. At the end of the row sat Aloo and Pipo's canoe, two new paddles crossed on its back like folded wings. Yurubi stood looking at it, thinking that the fine featherlike paintings along its side made it look as if it could fly.

With an excited giggle, she broke away from the group of women and girls and weaved through the crowd, looking for Pipo and Aloo. She'd had to wait back at the camp with the women until the Jambou shaman finished his send-off ceremony for the boats before she could come down here. And now the boys were about to leave.

It had been two days since the shamans and chiefs had given word that the villagers from the north could return home. Some had set off already on foot, while some of the elders and others had gone in boats belonging to the Jambou warriors.

As anxious as Yurubi was to get home, she was happy that, except for Grandma Lulou, her family had not yet left, because she didn't want to miss the launch of the new boats. Especially Aloo and Pipo's. Where were those two anyway? The other boys were already milling around the boats, throwing playful punches at each other and talking in loud excited voices, but there was no sign of either Aloo or Pipo.

Behind Yurubi, a crowd was growing as people wandered down from the camp and village to see off the little boats.

"That one looks like a basket," she heard someone say, drawing laughter.

"Good for carrying fish," said another voice.

More laughter.

"Where are the boys for that long one?"

That's what Yurubi wanted to know. She turned and burrowed back through the crowd, worry jabbing at her like a thorn.

"Yurubi!"

She spun around to see Pipo standing on tiptoe on a rock, his hair whipping in the breeze, his face scrunched up as he strained to see over the heads of the people who were drifting down to the beach.

"What's happening? Yurubi called out, running over to him.

"Have you seen Aloo?" he said.

"No, I thought he was with you."

Yurubi's heart sank into her feet. Not now, not today. Not after all those mornings she and Aloo had spent at the beach. She scrambled up the rock and looked back toward the camp. It should be easy to spot Aloo's tall figure and his gliding walk, but she could see no one in the distance that looked like him.

"Pipo, Aloo, time to go," Maruku's voice rang out across the beach.

Yurubi and Pipo looked at each other.

"Come," said Pipo. "I've got to tell him a story, hope he'll wait."

He grabbed Yurubi's hand and they jumped off the rock and weaved through the crowd to the waterline. The other boys had split into pairs and were pushing their boats over the sand toward the water. Yurubi hung back as Pipo ran toward the group.

"Where's Aloo?" said Maruku, his brows knitting when he spotted Pipo.

"Wish I knew," Pipo muttered under his breath.

"What?" Speak up, boy," said Maruku.

He and Kuriji were standing next to their gumbo-limbo canoe, getting ready to push it out to sea.

"Had to relieve himself," said Pipo, talking fast. "Can we wait a bit?"

Maruku put his hands on his hips and pursed his lips.

"Well, just for a little—"

"Message from the Great One," a voice shouted. A young boy

92

broke through the crowd and skidded to stop in front of Maruku.

"Shaman says Aloo's sick." The boy bent over trying to catch his breath. "Too sick to travel today. A bad spirit."

Yurubi started forward then stopped, her eyes flying to Pipo, who looked like he'd been struck by a club. Yurubi had never known Aloo to be too sick to do anything. Not even the time when he'd eaten the nasty purple berries from a mapou tree. He'd vomited twice then picked up his little bow and crept forward again after the agouti he was stalking.

"Must have the runs," Maruku muttered. Placing a finger on his chin, he looked from Pipo to the canoe and back again.

The other boys had stopped pushing their boats and some of them were whispering and snickering among themselves. The news of Aloo's illness was flitting through the crowd and Yurubi could hear people behind her talking about the danger of taking a bad spirit on a boat. She wanted to run back to the camp to see Aloo, but the shaman probably wouldn't let her near. She'd have to wait until he was done with Aloo. Yurubi bit her lip and fingered the shell pendant at her throat.

"You'll have to pick someone else to go with you," Maruku said finally to Pipo.

"Someone else?" Pipo stared at Maruku, his nostrils flaring. "But it's Aloo—"

"Hurry up, boy," said Kuriji, stepping closer to Pipo. "The sun's climbing. Pick someone or I'll pick for you."

Pipo's eyes roamed wildly, from the grinning boys near the canoes to the cluster of onlookers. Turning back to Maruku, he straightened his shoulders.

"I'll take Yurubi," Pipo said loudly.

Yurubi's breath clogged her throat. There was a rush of wind in her ears as everything else around her fell silent. Then the laughter hit her like a tumbling wave.

"He wants to take a girl," Garu shouted, staggering about on the beach and pointing at Pipo.

The voices rose around Yurubi like a flock of crows.

"What?"

"A girl."

"Who?"

"Yurubi."

"Her."

Yurubi felt as if her feet were sinking slowly into the sand. But in front of her, Pipo stood with his legs braced, his lips pressed tightly together, looking at no one but Maruku.

With a grin stretched across his face, Maruku raised his hands to the crowd.

"He always likes to make jokes, this one," he said, gesturing at Pipo.

"But I'm not joking now," said Pipo, clenching his fists at his sides.

"Pipo, son, she's a girl," said Maruku, still smiling. "This trip is a challenge for boys. Young warriors in the making."

Yurubi cringed as Garu and his friends howled in laugher again. But Pipo folded one arm across his chest and propped up his chin with his other fist.

"I remember the first time I saw a piragua at sea," he said slowly, looking out over the ocean. "I was just a little boy about this high." He held his open hand at the level of his hip. "I was out with my father, learning to bait fishing lines. The waves were slow and gentle, and the sun was just peeping up from the water."

Kuriji dropped his chin to his chest and make a sound like a groan. But behind Yurubi, the crowd was pressing closer to hear Pipo's story. Yurubi felt a pair of hands grip her shoulders and she swung around to see Ma standing behind her, looking confused. Not knowing what else to do at this time, Yurubi patted one of Ma's hands and turned back to listen to Pipo.

"The piragua swung around the point of Ayoa like a big old whale," he was saying. "'Papa, Papa, look!' I shouted. The bait fell from my fingers as I kneeled on the seat and leaned over the side of the canoe to watch the brave warriors rowing that huge piragua."

Pipo was talking faster now, gesturing to show the actions.

"But I soon saw that something was not right. I blinked hard and looked again. No doubt this time. I turned to my father in shock. 'Papa, there are girls in the boat,' I whispered. 'More girls than warriors.'"

Maruku threw back his head and laughed and the crowd joined in.

"That's exactly what my father did," said Pipo above the din.

Maruku shook his head, still chuckling.

"So, you want to practice carrying girls in your canoe," he said.

"Well, hurry up, get your girl and let's go before the day runs away."

Yurubi's heart leapt as Pipo turned to her, grinning from ear to ear. But she could feel Ma's fingers tightening on her shoulders. Yurubi swung around and faced her mother, who had not even a hint of a smile on her face.

"Ma, can I?"

"No, you're a girl. They're all boys."

Ma set her lips in that way that meant no use pleading, Yurubi could feel her throat tightening. She had spent an entire day in the woods drawing those feathers on the side of the canoe. She had helped make it beautiful.

"Ma, I—"

"Let her go, sister," said Waasha softly, coming up alongside Ma. She rested a hand on Ma's arm. "She'll be safe with Pipo. And Maruku has said she can go. It's no shame."

Yurubi flicked a grateful look at Waasha and held her breath, waiting for Ma to speak. Ma's eyes trailed from Yurubi to Pipo to the long canoe on the beach then back to Yurubi again.

"You will go directly to Grandma Lulou and stay with her until I get there," said Ma, fixing Yurubi with a flint-like gaze. "You must—" Yurubi flung her arms around Ma's neck.

"Yes, yes, yes, Ma." she whispered in her mother's ear. "I will not shame you."

Yurubi drew back and looked at Waasha, her heart thundering in her ears.

"Waasha—"

"Go, Yurubi," said Waasha, with a smile. "Pipo's waiting."

Yurubi held on to the sides of the canoe as Pipo guided it through the surf. She really was here, at sea, in a beautiful boat that was riding the waves as smoothly as a dolphin. It was such a different feeling than being on the river. She loved the motion of climbing to the crest of a wave and sliding down the other side. Yurubi was sitting in the bow, facing Pipo, watching closely how he was gauging the curling waves, his short arms moving the paddle easily from side to side.

"Look at the loudmouths," he said with a grin, pointing his chin at the boats ahead.

Twisting around, Yurubi saw Ranan and Jokoro shifting about, trying to balance their heavily listing boat as it lurched on the waves. She felt sorry for them even though they were often mean to Pipo and Aloo.

"What if it tips over?" she said, as Ranan and Jokoro's boat rocked wildly.

Pipo's grin widened. "They'll try to flip over and get back on. If they can't, they'll swim to Maruku and Kuriji's canoe or back to shore."

Yurubi twisted the other way to get a better look at the men's canoe, which was in the lead, already past the breakers and turning north, although Maruku and Kuriji seemed to be paddling slowly.

"See what they did?" said Pipo. "That's what we're going to do. We'll go out a ways then turn north because it's harder to manage the boat close to the shore."

He jerked his chin again toward the cluster of little boats.

"Look at those two. They're in so much trouble."

Yurubi turned again to see Ranan and Jokoro swiping their paddles this way and that. But the little boat seemed to have a mind of its own as it kept going around in circles.

Yurubi couldn't help laughing.

"They'll be fighting soon," she said, as the two boys started hollering at each other.

Most of the other boats were turning north to follow Maruku and Kuriji's canoe, but Pipo kept his bow pointed at the horizon. Yurubi was eager to pick up the other paddle but thought she'd better watch Pipo for a while longer. It was not like canoeing on the river. There were big curling waves and a tide tugging sideways at the boat.

Yurubi swivelled again at the sound of laughter drifting over the water. It was Garu and Caloon.

"Look, Pipo's taking his girl to a faraway land," Garu shouted, pointing with his paddle.

"Or into the belly of a shark," said Caloon, baring his teeth and laughing. "Farewell, Pipo, farewell Yurubi."

Yurubi grimaced. Those two—they never let up.

96

"Idiots," said Pipo, sounding unruffled. He steadied the boat as it took a wave head on, and he continued to paddle into the sunrise, his round face lit by the orange light.

Soon the people on the beach began to look like little sticks, and the boat settled down somewhat, although it was never going to be smooth sailing on this sea.

With a few practiced strokes, Pipo turned the bow northward, guiding the boat skilfully over the waves.

Yurubi looked over her shoulder at the boats strung out behind Maruku and Kuriji's canoe.

"Garu and Caloon seem to be doing well," she said grudgingly. "Their boat looks fast."

"You think that's fast?" Pipo said, leaning over on one side to get a better look. "If Aloo were here, they'd be eating our wake all the way home."

Yurubi's heart dropped. It should've been Aloo here with Pipo after all the work they'd put into building this beautiful boat. Yurubi bent her head and ran her hand along the side of canoe. The truth was Aloo didn't like the sea. He probably would not have enjoyed this trip, even if he weren't sick. Like her, he loved to make things, but now that she was thinking about it, she couldn't remember a single time when he'd tried to sail one of the little boats they'd made.

"Don't worry." Pipo's voice broke into her thoughts, "It's not a race. It's a trip to learn boating skills."

"But not for you," said Yurubi, raising her head and laughing a little. She picked up the paddle between her feet and poked him lightly in the stomach with the grip. "You're practicing to carry girls."

Pipo's face split into a grin. "Was a good story, wasn't it?"

Yurubi leaned forward, her mouth dropping open. "You mean it wasn't true?"

"Ermm, some of it was," he said in that innocent voice he got sometimes. "My father did take me to sea when I very little to teach me how to fish."

Yurubi poked him again with the paddle. "You're such a story-teller, Pipo. But you're also a very good boatman. Bet you can show me how to use this."

Pipo laughed as she waved the paddle above her head.

"It's easy. Look, you hold it with both hands like this, dip it into the water and stroke backwards. Lift it out of the water, swing it forward like this, then stroke again."

Keeping a straight face, Yurubi raised the paddle and copied Pipo's actions in the air.

"Like this?"

"Yes, yes, very good, Yurubi," said Pipo, his words running over each other like they did when he was excited. "But you have to turn around to face the bow. The front, I mean. I'll steer. So you can paddle on one side only. Paddle on the left side, it's easier. When we're on top of a wave don't dip the paddle in. Go on, swing around."

Biting her lip to hold back a smile, Yurubi turned on her seat. Right hand on the grip of the paddle, left hand on the shaft, she dipped the blade into the water. It felt like part of her had slid into the ocean, and she was cleaving the waves with her bare arms. Now the motion of the sea was hers too, their bosoms rising and falling, carrying the boat forward.

"Yes, that's it," said Pipo behind her. "Keep an eye on the waves. You'll have to paddle harder when we're in a trough and going up the face of a wave. When we're on the crest, stop paddling. Oh, I told you that already. Yes, but let the boat slide down the back of the waves. If there's a big roller, we'll have to sort of slide along inside it, then over the top. Don't worry, I'll steer."

Yurubi grinned to herself as Pipo rattled on, but she was gladly soaking up all of it. These were the things she couldn't learn from sailing her little boats on the river.

With a toss of her head, she flicked her hair out of her eyes and raised her paddle as the boat topped a wave. In that moment, the sky tilted and tipped some of its blue into the ocean, which swiftly wrapped up the new colour, only to unwrap it again like an unbelievable treasure.

"Whoaaa, that was a biggish one," said Pipo. "You did well there, Yurubi. You remembered to stop paddling. Hold on, I'll turn the boat a little, so it won't ride like that too much."

"That was exciting," said Yurubi with a laugh, licking at the salty water on her lips. She turned to watch Pipo as he worked the paddle like a stirring stick, making some forward strokes, some backward ones and some slicing motions. She watched in admiration as he brought the boat almost to a standstill, then pointed the bow slightly toward the horizon.

"This way, we can tack across the big waves when they come," he said.

"How did you learn so much about boats?"

Pipo's brows flew upward. "You don't remember? Never mind, I'll tell you again."

He cleared his throat. "When I was very little, my father took me out to sea to teach—"

"Not that story again, you fabler." Yurubi batted at him with her paddle.

Pipo reared back, a broad grin on his face.

"That's for paddling the boat, not for beating people," he said.

Yurubi shook her head and turned to the front again, dipping her paddle into the water with fluid strokes.

"I still want to hear the real story," she called over her shoulder.

There was silence for a while, except for the slap of the waves against the side of the boat, and the distant voices of the boys and the occasional screech of a seagull overhead.

"My father damaged his leg when he was a boy, and he couldn't become a warrior because he couldn't walk straight, far less run," Pipo said behind her, his usually lilting voice sounding flat.

"He started spending more and more time in the sea, swimming as far as he could, diving near the reefs and rocks and learning about the creatures under the water. He became so good at fishing that his family was eating better than those who had hunters to bring home meat. Wasn't long before he began making his own boats. And when he asked to take my mother as his wife, her family eagerly said yes."

Pipo gave a short laugh. "I bet they didn't think she'd end up spending almost all her time at sea with him. I was born at sea, somewhere between the isles of Becouya and Cannouan."

Yurubi twisted around to chide Pipo again for making up parts of his stories, but he was gazing unseeingly at the horizon with not even a hint of a smile on his face. Facing the bow again, Yurubi wondered why Pipo seemed so gloomy. His family's life sounded like her dream. Building boats and sailing off to other isles.

"They washed me in the ocean and kept going till they came to a tiny cay where the fishing was good and the waters were placid," said Pipo. "They stayed for three whole moons."

Yurubi turned again at the hint of sadness in Pipo's voice. He was still staring out to sea, his eyes brooding, his arms working the paddle rhythmically.

"Not that I was *on land* the whole time." Pipo laughed dryly. "They said I'd already learned to swim in those tranquil waters by the time they were ready to leave."

"But what about the birth ritual?" said Yurubi. "How could your father go into retreat and fast and all that?"

"My father … he doesn't bother about things like that. My mother either. She didn't even bother to shape my head when I was a baby. I don't feel so bad about it anymore, though. On our trips from one place to another I've seen other boys, like Aloo, with round foreheads. Some girls too. We've travelled up, down and around these islands like no other family I know. The three moons we spent on the little isle after I was born were the longest time I'd ever been on land." Pipo sounded morose. "Before this last stay in Jambou, I mean."

Yurubi looked out across the ocean, seeing in her mind the family camping by themselves on the beach, the tiny baby splashing in the water, the boat sitting on the sand, waiting to take them wherever they chose.

"Born in a boat, eh?" she said, trying to make Pipo smile. "I don't know anyone else like that. The water spirits must claim you as their own."

"Don't you start," said Pipo.

"I think—"

"Yurubi, put the paddle in the boat," said Pipo with an edge to his voice.

"Pipo—"

"Now, Yurubi."

Heat flaring in her face, Yurubi lifted the paddle out of the water and rested it between her feet. Staring straight ahead, she gripped the sides of the boat and tried to swallow the lump rising in her throat. What was wrong with Pipo today? Perhaps he was more upset than she'd realized about Aloo not showing up. Or he was missing his father and mother.

"Hands inside the boat as well," said Pipo, his voice tight.

Yurubi snatched her hands away from the sides and put them in her lap. This was a side of Pipo she hadn't seen in the five moons they'd been in the camp. He'd changed like a tree lizard. He'd picked her to sail with him today, and he'd seemed so excited about her paddling. Now he wasn't even paddling but seemed to be just sitting there, sulking in the middle of the ocean.

Yurubi brushed a hand across her eyes and swivelled on her seat to confront him.

"Careful, careful," he whispered.

But he was not looking at Yurubi. He was leaning over slightly to his left, his hands clenched around the paddle across his knees, his eyes searching the water.

"Pipo, what is it?" Yurubi whispered.

"Barracuda," he said softly. "It was right here up alongside the boat."

A cold claw gripped Yurubi's insides. The boat, bobbing on the waves with no guidance, suddenly seemed very small and fragile. Yurubi hunched over and wrapped her arms around her middle, staring into the water. The stories she'd heard about barracudas leaped into her mind. Try as she might, she couldn't push back the images of the large mouth and two rows of knife-sharp teeth that she'd heard about in tales told in hushed tones. She shuddered at the memory of one particular story about a single barracuda attacking a school of grouper near a reef. In her mind's eye, she could see the water turning red as the slender predator tore into the grouper with fearsome speed and power.

"Should we call for help?" she whispered, glancing back at the other boats that now seemed to be pulling further away.

But Pipo shook his head and lowered his paddle carefully into the water.

"I'll just move us along slowly so as not to attract its attention or provoke it," he said softly, paddling with slow and gentle strokes. "It's the best way to avoid trouble with a barracuda."

"They're worse than sharks, aren't they?"

"Only if they're in schools."

Yurubi stared hard at Pipo, her heart drumming against her ribs. She hoped he wasn't making up this story. It was difficult to tell with him.

"But a lone barracuda can sometimes follow a boat out of curiosity," he said after a while.

Yurubi swallowed. Glancing toward the shore, she realized they were still just somewhere off Byabou, a long way from home. What if the barracuda decided to follow them all the way to Warigara?

She looked over her shoulder at the other boats, which were stretched out along the coast, bobbing along happily behind Maruku and Kuriji's canoe. Perhaps they had made the wiser choice to stay close to the shore despite the choppier water there.

"Pipo, do you think—"

"Watch out!" Pipo said hoarsely.

Yurubi screamed as something bumped into the boat, causing it to rock wildly. She clapped a hand over her mouth as a long, slim, bluish shape streaked from under the stern and disappeared into a wave with hardly a ripple.

Pipo plunged his paddle in to the water, trying to steady the boat.

"Hold on!" he said as a wave hit sideways, drenching them and sending the boat staggering.

Yurubi grabbed onto the side of the tilting canoe with one hand and clawed with the other at the shroud of wet hair over her face. Where was the barracuda? She gasped as the bow reared clear of the water and slammed down again. Pipo's teeth were glinting through his lips, his eyes narrowed, his arms moving in a blur from side to side.

"Grab your paddle and let's go," he said, tossing back his wet hair.

"Where is it?" Yurubi said, forcing the words past the knot in her throat.

"There, between your feet. It slid back."

Yurubi's feet jerked off the bottom of the boat before she could help herself.

"Th-the barracuda, I mean," she said, letting out a gushing breath as she looked down at the flat little paddle.

"Gone, I think. Let's not wait to find out. Come on, paddle."

Yurubi bent and picked up the paddle with shaking hands then swung around and dipped it gingerly into the water. Up ahead, the other boats were rounding the Byabou point. No one seemed to have noticed her and Pipo's plight. On Yurubi's right, a flock of screaming gulls was diving into the waves.

No sign of the barracuda.

"I think it's gone after those fish," said Pipo, as if seeing into her mind. "Try to paddle harder."

"What ... fish?" said Yurubi, driving the paddle into the waves, her breath still ragged.

"The fish those seagulls are chasing."

Pipo was sounding more like himself now, although he continued to push the boat along at a pace.

"How can you tell?"

"Well, see, there was this time when I was near the isle of Myreau on my father's boat and—"

Yurubi groaned.

"Pipo, please, not now."

Yurubi rolled her eyes but the tightness in her chest was easing. Pipo wouldn't be trying to tell a story if he thought the barracuda was still close by, would he?

"You don't want to hear the story?" he said, a smile in his voice. "How about a song then? There's this one my mother used to sing when—Well, never mind."

He began humming, and Yurubi could feel the boat slowing down a little. She cocked her head to listen, trying all the while to match the pace and rhythm of Pipo's paddling.

They were moving more smoothly now, pulling further and further away from the diving seagulls.

"Does the song have words?" Yurubi said after a while.

"My home is on the land, my home is on the sea, my home is wherever this boat takes me," Pipo sang in his easy voice.

Still keeping her eyes peeled for the barracuda, Yurubi mouthed the words silently as Pipo sang.

"My home is on the land, my home is on the sea, my home is wherever this boat takes me."

Yurubi stretched her neck as a frisky breeze tickled her face, whispered past her ear and lifted her hair off her shoulders. On her left, the mountains were preening under the touch of the sunlight, flaunting yellow, purple and orange colours, while the waves untiringly wooed the rugged coastline, spreading their white edges again and again on the glistening black sand and rocks.

Yurubi threw back her head, drank in the salty smell of the morning and picked up Pipo's song.

"My home is on the land, my home is on the sea, my home is wherever this boat takes me."

FINDING THE MARK

Life in the village was slowly settling back to normal. When Aloo had first returned to Warigara, he'd been spending most of his days in the bush, helping to gather materials to rebuild the village. The taboui and most of the huts had been destroyed by rocks from the Great Mountain or had collapsed under the weight of the ash. The men needed lots of sturdy wood to make posts, cachibou leaves to cover the frames, and long strips of mahoe bark to make the rope to bind it all together.

The taboui called for stacks of tall river cane for the sides and high roof. Some of the men and boys, including Pipo, had stayed in the village, clearing away the debris, while others went out to collect the building materials.

The women, meanwhile, had set about replanting cassava, corn, sweet potatoes, yams, cotton, tobacco and other crops. Yurubi was always busy minding babies while the women worked, or she was helping to make baskets and bowls.

Every day, Aloo would set off alone before dawn and return at dusk with bundles of wood, leaves and cane. Strolling through the familiar forest in broad daylight, feasting on fruit and nuts whenever he liked, he felt as if he had grown wings and flown away from that dark hole he had called home for so long. Like the Great Mountain, which was covering itself swiftly in green again, Aloo felt as if something had shifted, not just around him, but inside him. Some days he'd sit on a rock, staring up at the changing face of the Great Mountain, wondering if it had indeed claimed him as its own.

The breezes from the mountains and the ocean were stiffening and turning cooler. Now that the cluster of huts and the tall taboui were finished, warrior training had started again.

Today, it was shooting practice.

Aloo held his bow lightly in one hand, an arrow in the other, as he ran along a shoreline path, his elbows tucked in close to his sides. In front of him, a straggly line of boys hurried after Kuriji. They were all trying to be quiet, as Kuriji had ordered. Even Pipo, who was just ahead of Aloo, had hardly said a word all day.

Earlier, they'd been learning how to poison arrow tips with the sap of the manchineel tree. That was something Aloo had never done before. He'd never thought he needed to poison his arrows, but Kuriji said that was what warriors often did when they were going on raids. One careless movement in handling those arrows and someone could die, Kuriji had said, warning them to be careful and quiet. When they were finished, they had to give the arrows to Kuriji, who hid them away somewhere.

Now they were practicing to shoot. But not with poisoned arrows.

Aloo slowed down as he saw Kuriji raise his hand. The boys in front of him skidded to a stop and fitted arrows into their bows. Aloo kept his arms at his side as Kuriji pointed at a seagull sitting on a grape bush then signalled to Caloon.

Caloon stepped forward, gripping his bow tightly. He took careful aim at the bird and let loose an arrow. But the gull took off at that very moment, flapping its wings and gliding out to sea. Caloon's shoulders slumped when he saw his arrow nick the bare branch.

Aloo thought it was a fairly good shot, just much too slow.

"You have to be quicker," said Kuriji. "A warrior must be swift and sure."

He waved the group forward again. The cooling breeze on Aloo's face slackened as Kuriji turned inland. The line soon broke up because there was no path here under the tall trees.

Aloo continued to hang back but was making sure he kept Kuriji in sight. There were many targets here in the woods, scurrying in the underbrush, running up and down the trees and flitting overhead, but the boys had to wait for Kuriji to choose. It wasn't long before Kuriji stopped again and looked around. He beckoned Pipo closer and pointed at a bumpy brown lizard that was creeping down a tree trunk.

Pipo lifted his bow and let fly an arrow that pierced the upper part of the lizard's tail. The creature squirmed frantically until it broke off its tail then leapt off the tree into the bushes. Aloo couldn't help but smile when he saw the tail, pinned to the tree, still wriggling.

Pipo pointed at the tail, his jaw dropping.

"Did you see—"

His mouth clamped shut when he saw Kuriji coming towards him.

Kuriji walked up to the tree, one arm folded across his middle, his hand covering his mouth. He bent and looked closely at the arrow then threw back his head and laughed. The whole group joined in the laughter, gathering around the tree to look at the lizard's tail. Still hanging back, Aloo smiled when Pipo's laughing eyes found him. Pipo shrugged and then turned and pulled his arrow from the tree trunk.

"Next time aim for just below the head," Kuriji said to Pipo, his voice still laced with laughter.

Kuriji put his hands on his hips and looked around.

"Come on, we'll have to go further into the woods," he said. "I think we just scared away everything around here."

He set off again, walking faster this time, and the boys hurried after him.

Aloo was beginning to sweat a little in the steamy afternoon heat. He pulled a thin vine from an overhead branch and tied back his thick mass of locks.

As the group approached a small clearing, Kuriji raised his hand and put a finger to his lips. Sitting on a rock, mottled by sunlight, was a big green frog. Kuriji turned and signalled to Garu.

Aloo's gaze flicked from the frog to Garu and back. It looked like an easy shot because the frog was not moving, but it was not that close.

Moving swiftly, Garu stepped to his left to get a better line of sight. Then he shot an arrow. The frog flopped off the rock onto its back, its legs waving slowly.

Garu jutted out his chin, a faint smile on his face.

"Good shot," Kuriji murmured.

"Get your arrow," he said, as the frog stopped moving.

They set off again, the boys sticking closer to Kuriji as he weaved through the thickening woods. They wouldn't want to miss his signal in the dim light under the trees. Still at the back of the group, all Aloo had to do was move like he was stalking Kuriji.

Suddenly, Kuriji stopped and tilted his head back. He swung around and signalled to Aloo. A hawk. High up in a treetop. Spreading its wings. Already lifting off. Aloo sent his arrow skyward. The hawk staggered in mid-flight and came crashing down through the branches. It landed on the forest floor with a thud, the arrow stuck through its chest. For a moment, no one moved. Then the boys rushed over to the bird, which was still flapping a bit.

Aloo stood where he was, his bow dangling from his left hand, his eyes fixed on Kuriji.

Kuriji had not moved either. He was staring at Aloo, his lips set in a straight line. Aloo's mouth went dry. Had he done something stupid again? Wasn't he supposed to kill the hawk? But Garu had killed the frog. Aloo looked at Pipo. No help there. Pipo was squatting near the bird, his back to Aloo. The other boys were all clustered around Pipo, staring down at the hawk, which was still now.

Aloo moved his gaze back to Kuriji, who gave him a slight nod, then set off again through the woods without even a glance at the hawk.

At sunset, Kuriji called a halt to the training and led the boys to a stream. The water, rushing over the stones, was cool and soothing. After taking a long drink and dousing his face and neck, Aloo went to sit under a tree, the dead hawk between his feet. The other boys were splashing about in the stream, their voices loud as they teased each other about their shooting earlier.

Aloo nudged the carcass of the hawk with his toe, turning it over to look again at the arrow hole through its chest. Reaching into his quiver, he pulled out the arrow with the bird's dried blood on it and ran his finger over the tip. It was unbroken and still very sharp. A river reed shaft tipped with fish bone. Aloo preferred fish bone for shooting small targets because it was lighter than stone and easier to sharpen.

What had he done wrong? He'd gauged the hawk's movement

and aimed for its heart. The same way he always did when he was hunting birds. Same way he'd done when he and Pipo went hunting in the Jambou gorge. Pipo had never said anything about his shooting. Except for that first time. They'd been chasing an agouti and Aloo had hit it on the run.

Aloo frowned. Now that he was thinking about it, Pipo had looked at him the same way Kuriji did. For a moment. But Pipo's face had soon split into its familiar grin, and he'd dashed forward to grab up the agouti. While Pipo was freeing the arrow, he'd glanced up and asked Aloo how he'd learned to shoot like that. Not knowing what to say, Aloo had stammered something about hunting since he was little.

If he got a chance later, he'd try to ask Pipo about what had happened today. Right now, Pipo was wading slowly upstream, away from the rowdy group, fishing for crayfish.

Aloo shifted his gaze to Kuriji, still trying to understand what that look had meant. Kuriji was standing in the stream, tossing his head, flinging water from his hair. Aloo tensed as Kuriji turned and bounded up the bank, walking straight toward him.

"Show me your bow," Kuriji said, dropping down onto the grass next to Aloo.

Aloo handed over the bow, his eyes fixed on Kuriji's face. Kuriji still was not smiling but his lips didn't look as tight as they did earlier. He ran his fingers over the curve of the bow.

"You made this yourself?"

"Y-yes,"

Kuriji tugged on the bowstring. "This too?"

"Ye—No," said Aloo as he remembered Pipo joking about his weaving. "A gi-girl d-did."

Aloo and Yurubi had made two bows from the same piece of guava wood, heating it to bend it then rubbing the bows smooth with a special stone she'd picked up on a riverbank when they were fleeing south. They'd made the strings from hemp fibre, using a reverse weave that Yurubi had taught him. It'd made the bowstrings stronger, she'd said. She was right. His bowstring had not broken once. Hers either. She hadn't used her bow much, though. It was hidden in his cave, which was still their secret place although Aloo was living in the village now.

Kuriji was plunking the bowstring, again and again, but was no longer looking at it. He was gazing out over the stream. Aloo followed his gaze, but Kuriji didn't seem to be looking at anything. Sometimes Yurubi would get that same look just before she started talking about some secret adventure.

"A nighttime hunt," Kuriji murmured.

Aloo went still. Was Kuriji planning an adventure?

Kuriji turned to Aloo, his eyes narrowing. "Just the two of us. Don't tell anyone else. I'll pick a night soon."

Aloo's mind was tumbling with questions as he searched Kuriji's face. But before Aloo could get a word past his lips, Kuriji jumped to his feet and went striding back to the stream, calling the boys to leave.

WHEN NICHT FALLS

Aloo swallowed the last of his fish and shifted his position on the ground, turning away from the firelight. He could not get used to this habit of gazing into the fire. Whenever he looked away from the fire into the darkness, he could not see clearly. Next to him, Tueke and Pipo seemed not at all bothered. Tueke was leaning forward, cramming the last of his barbeque fish and potatoes into his mouth. Pipo had finished eating and was lying on his side, facing the fire. He'd been talking all night about making arrowheads, saying a boy needs new weapons when he becomes a warrior.

"I'd prefer to use fishbone because it's lighter and easier to carve, but Kuriji thinks a stone head is needed sometimes to get the job done," said Pipo.

"Let's make some of each," said Tueke, licking his fingers.

Pipo flopped over onto his back with a groan. "I hate chipping stone."

"I can make some stone heads," said Aloo.

In fact, he and Yurubi had been knapping arrowheads recently, sneaking away whenever they could to his old cave so no one would see her making weapons. She was getting better and better at it, trying out different ways of doing things.

"Aloo, I'll exchange you some bone arrowheads for stone," said Pipo, rubbing his eyes. "I've been saving some fish bones."

"I'll give you the stone heads," said Aloo with a smile. "We can make some bone ones."

"Let's start soon," said Tueke. His mouth stretched open in a huge yawn. "But not tonight."

Pipo laughed and sat up, passing a hand over his face.

"Tonight, my only task is to find my hammock," he said.

They'd been climbing trees and rocks all day, practicing how to leap and attack from above. By sunset, everyone had seemed tired. But Aloo, Pipo and Tueke had stopped at the river on the way back to splash around for a while, trying to cool down. Then they'd stretched out on the big rock, talking lazily about their day. By the time they got back to the village almost everyone had gone to sleep. A few women were sitting in front of their huts, painting their men with red roucou dye and talking in low voices.

Aloo, Pipo and Tueke had torn into the fish and sweet potatoes they'd found wrapped in leaves near the fire. Aloo was sure it was Yurubi who had left them food. Now that they were full, Pipo and Tueke were almost asleep near the fire.

Tueke yawned again and got to his feet.

"We'll start the arrowheads tomorrow?" he said.

"I'll be ready tomorrow, for sure," said Pipo, standing slowly.

They both waved at Aloo and stumbled off toward the taboui.

Aloo smiled, feeling something like warm soup flooding his chest as he watched them go. Sometimes it was hard to believe that he now had friends. More than one. He had slowly grown to like Tueke, and also Siwako, but was still very watchful around the other boys in the training group. Especially Garu and his band. Every time they came near, Aloo could feel his scalp prickling. Same as when Buaba was close.

Aloo's gaze followed Pipo and Tueke until they ducked inside the taboui. Aloo was the only one who never slept there.

At first, when he'd returned from Jambou, he'd been sleeping in the open in a little hollow on the edge of the village. It was near the shaman's hut, which was the first to be rebuilt. Pipo had put up a rough shelter that he'd invited Aloo to share, but it was very close to many others.

Lying under the low roof that first night, hearing the breathing of the other males close by, Aloo had felt like a trapped agouti. He'd stayed there shivering until Pipo fell asleep then had slipped away to the hollow behind the shaman's hut. Even though most people seemed to avoid the shaman, Aloo felt no danger near him.

After the taboui was finished and the males moved in there, Aloo had built a little hut for himself in the hollow. The shaman, who'd been keeping an eye on Aloo the whole time, had given him a brief nod when the hut was finished. Pipo had said he didn't envy Aloo but understood why he had to be near the shaman. Aloo wasn't sure what Pipo meant but didn't bother to ask. All that mattered was that he didn't have to sleep or dwell in the taboui.

He had no hammock but had made a sleeping platform from wood and grass. It was high off the ground like the ledge he used to sleep on in his cave. On the side of the hut next to the platform, he had cut a small flap that he left open most nights, so he could see the sky. On moonless nights like this, the little opening would be filled with stars.

Aloo stood and kicked some dirt over the dying fire then skirted past the taboui, heading for his hut. He was almost there when he felt a prickling on the back of his neck. He slipped behind a tree and stood still, his eyes boring into the dark. Nothing, no movement, no rustling, no breathing. Only the usual nighttime din of crickets and frogs. Chest pressed up against the tree, Aloo waited. And waited.

"Aloo!"

It was no more than a whisper. From high up. Somewhere in a tree. Aloo's eyes combed the foliage. Still no sighting. He waited.

"Aloo! It's time!"

Kuriji leapt from a tree. Warrior on the move. Painted black from head to toe. Black breechcloth, no jewellery. Bow and arrows, two knives.

Aloo's throat tightened.

"We go tonight," said Kuriji, standing in the open, hands at his sides, legs apart. "Bring your bone arrows."

Kuriji was running like a forest creature in the dark. With hardly a break in his stride, he was leaping over logs, ducking under branches, scaling boulders and swerving around trees.

Keeping about a spear's length away, Aloo followed him deeper and deeper into the forest. Although Aloo was wary of this night-time adventure, he felt as if his feet were skimming over the ground, his body filled with the pulsing clamour of frogs, crickets and grasshoppers and owls. All around him, fireflies and the eyes of night creatures painted fleeting dots on the darkness.

Kuriji sprinted up a slope and disappeared down the other side. Fast behind him, Aloo crested the little hill.

Kuriji was gone.

Aloo skidded to a stop and cocked his head, listening for the sound of Kuriji's feet. Nothing. Was Kuriji hiding? Was this part of the training? Aloo's eyes searched the bottom of the slope. There! A slight movement behind a huge log. Man, or animal? There it was again. Kuriji was on his belly, behind the log, aiming an arrow. Aloo threw himself to the ground and rolled back down the hill. A bowstring twanged, and an arrow whizzed into the bushes on the hilltop.

Kuriji was shooting at him.

Aloo rolled faster. Big tree. Wide, thick branches. Aloo sprang to his feet, ran up the tree trunk and burrowed into the dense foliage. Not a moment too soon. Kuriji slithered up the slope, still holding his bow. Aloo crouched motionless, barely breathing, but he could not still the heavy thumping of his heart against the tree branch. It was so loud, he feared Kuriji would hear.

This was not a group of young boys stalking him. This was a Kalina warrior. All the stories Aloo had heard about the warriors on raids flitted through his mind. He clenched his teeth and tightened his grip on the branch, willing himself not to start shivering.

At the top of the hill, Kuriji slid out of sight behind a tree. Aloo knew Kuriji's eyes were probing every tree, every bush, every spot that looked darker than the surroundings, while his ears were pricked for the slightest noise. He would know Aloo could not have gone far without making a sound. Aloo blinked as a bead of sweat rolled down his forehead and into his eye.

Kuriji was coming down the hill now, darting from one tree to the next. Even if Aloo could make a guess on which way Kuriji would dash, he dared not move to reach for the bow slung over his shoulder, an arrow in the quiver strapped to his back, or the knife on his hip. Aloo wasn't even sure he could shoot at Kuriji. He'd never fired an arrow at anyone before. And what if he killed or wounded Kuriji? He wouldn't be able to go back to the village. Ever. He'd have to go into hiding again. His head reeled at the thought.

In a nearby tree, an owl flapped its wings and screeched. Kuriji stopped in his tracks and looked up. A trickle of sweat crawled down Aloo's face like an insect and plopped onto the branch below.

As if he'd heard that, Kuriji ducked behind a clump of ferns. Aloo lost sight of him but knew he was crouched behind the bushes, scanning the overhead branches. Aloo's whole body was slick with sweat. He had to clamp his jaws even more tightly to stop his teeth from chattering. He could stay in the tree all night if he had to. He'd done it before. But he didn't know how much longer he could keep his arms locked motionless around this branch or cling with his toes to the tree limb under him.

A thick vine hanging off the outer branches of the tree swayed gently in the breeze. On the ground below, Kuriji's head poked out from behind the ferns. He seemed to be staring into Aloo's tree. The breeze picked up slightly, swaying the vine—

Breeze? There was no breeze. Aloo blinked hard. The leaves on the tree were still. Only the vine was moving. Aloo's breath stopped. A snake. Swaying between him and Kuriji. Positioned to strike one or the other.

Aloo leapt from the branch, grabbing the snake near the tail. He twisted his body in mid-air, swinging the snake outward to bash its head against the tree trunk with all his might. Aloo flexed his knees as he landed on the forest floor and whipped around, flinging the snake far into the bushes. Before Aloo could catch his breath, Kuriji sprang forward and gripped his upper arms, pinning them to his sides. Heart tripping, Aloo stared into the warrior's wide eyes.

"Who are you, boy?" Kuriji whispered. "Where did you come from?"

Aloo could not get a sound past the rock in his throat, even if he knew how to answer. He was starting to shiver deep inside. What could he say that would save his life? That he'd come from the sea? His chest heaved and his lips quivered, but no sound came forth.

"You're going to cry now like a girl?" said Kuriji, his face twisting. "After all that?"

His fingers, like claws, dug into Aloo's arms. He leaned closer, his breath searing Aloo's face, his eyes burning with something that Aloo could not fathom.

"Spawn of the Great Mountain," he whispered. "Don't ever tell anyone about tonight."

Aloo shook his head rapidly, his eyes never leaving Kuriji's face.

Kuriji straightened up and cleared his throat.

"I'm going to release you now," he said out loud. "Tonight's training is over. Let's go home."

Slowly, he let go of Aloo's arms then stepped back.

"I'll lead the way," said Kuriji.

He stepped past Aloo and set off through the forest, not once looking back.

SEA TRAINING

The village of Warigara was in a state of excitement as the big day drew near. In less than one moon, the boys would be inducted as warriors. Their fathers were already fasting in preparation for the ceremony and could be seen huddling with the shaman every so often, when he wasn't away in the bushes on one of his now frequent secret missions.

Like all the girls in the village, Yurubi had to help the women with their many tasks at this busy time. But while her hands were busy weaving cotton for new loincloths or collecting shells and stones for jewellery and charms, her eyes were straining to catch the work of the men as they shaped wood, bone and flint into new weapons.

Sometimes at night, when the women were painting the men with roucou, Yurubi would offer to paint Aloo and Pipo. This gave her a chance to hear about their training and some of the things they were learning when they went off each day with Kuriji or Maruku.

Today, though, the challenge was taking place at the beach, and most of the villagers had come down to watch. Yurubi was sitting high in a tree on the fringe of the beach, soaking up the slowly blooming colours of the sunrise. From her perch, she hoped to catch all the action on the beach and at sea.

Some of the young boys were also climbing trees to get a bird's eye view. Below, children were romping on the sand, squealing at the top of their voices as they pretended to shoot arrows at each other. The women were far back under the trees, while the men were standing on rocks or pacing the beach near the line of boys who would be tested today.

The boys all had their hair tied back and their breechcloths tucked in. They were carrying their bows and quivers strapped either across their shoulders or chest. At the back of the line, Pipo was fiddling with his quiver, shifting it from one shoulder to the next. In front of him, Aloo stood almost motionless, like a heron poised for flight.

It was hard to tell with Aloo, but Yurubi thought he looked a bit nervous. He still always seemed uneasy whenever he was near the ocean.

Ranan was at the front of the line, swinging his arms and bouncing on his toes. No doubt, Garu had pushed him to go first, so Garu could see what to expect.

Out on the water, Kuriji was slowly paddling a small boat piled high with dried coconuts. Maruku was on the beach, walking up and down the line of boys as they prepared to start.

"All ready!"

Yurubi giggled as she saw the boys stiffen up at the sound of Maruku's booming voice.

Maruku climbed onto a rock and waved at Kuriji, who lifted his paddle in response. Maruku put his hands on his hips and turned to look at the boys, his face set in stern lines.

"Today, you'll be fighting enemies at sea," he said, speaking slowly. "They will look like floating coconuts. Don't be fooled. You must aim well and shoot fast before they get you. When I give the signal, you'll swim out there, one at a time, and shoot at the enemies. When you hear Kuriji's whistle, stop shooting and swim back here. Now go!"

A cheer went up as Ranan ran to into the water and dived into a breaking wave.

"There he is!" one of the young boys in the trees shouted as Ranan surfaced and began swimming with strong strokes toward the boat.

As Ranan approached, a wide grin broke over Kuriji's face. Teeth glinting in the early sunlight, Kuriji tossed a coconut over the side of the boat in one quick motion. Ranan veered toward the nut then stopped, treading water. It looked like he was struggling to get his bow off his shoulder and free an arrow from his quiver. Meanwhile, the coconut was bobbing further away on the waves. Before Ranan could get off a shot, Kuriji lobbed another coconut into the water.

Yurubi couldn't help laughing. She was sure she could do better than Ranan in this challenge. When he finally managed to fire an arrow, he missed by a wide mark.

Still grinning, Kuriji tossed two more coconuts into the water. Ranan chased after one of them and managed to hit it from close up, but when he turned to the other one, he dropped the arrow as he was pulling it from his quiver.

He was treading water now, seeming not to know whether to go after the other three coconuts. He turned to look at Kuriji, who whistled sharply and waved him off.

As Ranan began swimming back to shore, Kuriji raised his hand, showing one finger to tell Maruku that there was only one hit. Using a net on a long pole, Kuriji scooped up the coconuts within reach.

Yurubi shifted her position in the crook of the tree. This was going to take a while, but she didn't mind because it was her only chance to watch the training. And this might be the last challenge before the big day.

As the sun climbed higher, the boys took to the water one by one, some managing to hit two or three coconuts, some none at all. It was much harder than it looked because they had to battle the waves and tide while aiming at a bobbing coconut.

Leaning back against the tree trunk, Yurubi recalled how clumsy she'd been the first time she tried to fire an arrow in the sea in Jambou. And she hadn't even been aiming at anything in particular. She'd just been trying to stay afloat while fitting an arrow into her bow. It had taken a few days before she'd managed to shoot at something in the water. Even Aloo, who was so good with a bow and arrow, had struggled those first few mornings.

Yurubi straightened up as she saw him running down the beach now with his easy stride, his bow over his left shoulder, his quiver across his chest. He didn't dive into the surf as the others had done but rather waded in slowly. When he was chest deep, he kicked off and started swimming with overhand strokes, keeping his head above the water. As he drew near the boat, he slipped his bow off his shoulder and held it in his left hand. He was swimming with a kind of awkward one-handed paddling motion now, and Yurubi couldn't quite see what he was doing.

Kuriji, the grin gone from his face, threw a coconut into the water. Aloo kept swimming for a bit then turned sideways, lifting his body half out of water, and fired off an arrow. Yurubi clapped her hands as she saw the arrow stick in the coconut. Kuriji tossed another one overboard. Again, Aloo turned sideways and Yurubi laughed softly when she saw that he had a few arrows clenched in his teeth.

He reared up with his bow, but at that moment a wave slapped him in the face, and he missed the shot. As another two nuts landed in the water, Aloo swam a little further out then turned to fire, hitting them both.

Yurubi knew that each time he turned, what he was doing was trying to avoid shooting into the sun.

He was chasing another coconut when a big wave began curling toward him. Aloo stopped swimming and began treading water. The wave lifted him, carrying him backward while he paddled wildly. Then it was gone. But so was the coconut.

Kuriji's whistle floated across the water, ending Aloo's stint. He swam slowly back to shore and seemed a little unsteady as he waded out of the water and walked up the beach. This probably had been the most difficult challenge for him. Yurubi knew he still did not like the sea, even though he had overcome his discomfort enough to learn to swim in it. She wanted to run down to him but knew she would not be allowed near the boys until the challenge was finished.

Pipo was in the water now, gliding toward the boat like a fish, his head hardly appearing above the waves. When the first coconut appeared, Pipo launched himself out of the water like a dolphin and hit the nut with a powerful shot. Yurubi clapped again, her breath catching in her throat as she watched Pipo circling the boat. It was one thing to hear stories about Pipo's prowess at sea, it was another to see him in action. He was swimming under the clear water at great speed, hitting the coconuts from below. For him, this must be so much easier than shooting fish.

He struck every coconut that Kuriji tossed out then turned at the whistle and made his way quickly back to shore.

Yurubi slid down the tree and ran across the sand, hoping to catch Pipo and Aloo before they took off on some other task.

They were standing a little way back from the group of boys clustered around Maruku.

"… one last challenge before the big day," Maruku was saying. "Just for fun. Kuriji's idea."

"What will it be?" someone asked.

"Hrmphh. It's a surprise," said Maruku. "Go on now, pull up Kuriji's boat, and we'll be done for today."

The boys splashed into the water to meet the approaching canoe, but Aloo stood where he was, watching as they grabbed the sides of the boat and pulled it up onto the sand.

The women began drifting back to the village, keeping up a steady stream of chatter and shooing the small children ahead of them. Maruku, Kuriji and the other men huddled under a tree, talking in low voices.

Yurubi strolled down the beach, away from the men, bending occasionally to pick up a shell. The sun was almost straight overhead and was bouncing sparkles of light off the waves and the black sand beach.

Glancing back, Yurubi saw that Aloo was still standing in the same spot, gazing out at the ocean. Pipo was stuffing his mouth with something, probably sea grapes, while the other boys were milling about, talking in high excited voices. Above the sound of the surf, all Yurubi could hear were snatches of their usual bantering and boasting.

She kicked at a half-buried shell and turned away when she saw that it was broken on one side. She wished Aloo and Pipo would try to slip away from the group for a while. She was sure that even if no one else had noticed she was still hanging around, Aloo would have.

With a sigh, Yurubi dropped the few shells she had gathered and turned for home. She didn't want to go past the men again, so she crossed the beach quickly and went into the trees then began making her way along the shoreline toward the path up the hill.

"Yurubi, wait."

Pipo came running through the trees, his wet hair flapping on his shoulders.

"Aloo saw you hurrying across the beach," said Pipo. "He was sure you'd be watching today."

Aloo appeared behind Pipo, his face drawn and greyish in the harsh midday light. Yurubi rushed toward him.

"Aloo, what's wrong?"

Pipo swung around and clapped Aloo on the shoulder.

"He's still wondering what happened out there today," said Pipo with a laugh. "For the first time, he was bested in a challenge."

Aloo's eyes widened and his lips twitched slightly, but he said nothing.

Pipo flopped down in the shade of a tree and squinted up at Aloo and Yurubi.

"Aloo can run faster and quieter than any of us. He can climb and hide like a lizard, and he shoots like a seasoned warrior." Pipo's teeth flashed in a grin. "But today we had to shoot at some barely moving coconuts in the water, and he missed one or two."

With a quick sideways glance at Aloo, Yurubi dropped down next to Pipo.

"From my spot in a tree, it looked like you did better than most of the others," Yurubi said to Aloo.

He shook his head and jerked his thumb at Pipo.

"Yes, I saw him hit every one," said Yurubi. She nudged Pipo with her elbow. "You looked like a dolphin out there."

"Told you, I was born at sea, and my father dropped me overboard right away."

"Dr-dropped you overboard?" Aloo's face turned even greyer.

"Pipo." Yurubi slapped him lightly on the arm. "That's not the story you told me. You said they took you to a little isle, and you learned to swim there."

"Doesn't matter. I was swimming before I could walk."

"That's why he's like a shark in the water," said Yurubi, looking up at Aloo.

"Or a sleek barracuda," said Pipo.

Yurubi turned and stared into Pipo's dancing eyes. She had never told anyone about their scary encounter with the barracuda. Not even Aloo because he had been so downcast and jittery after his return on foot from Jambou. She sure didn't want to talk about it now. Anything but that. She clapped her hands, smiling at Pipo and Aloo.

"So, you're near the end of your training, and soon you'll be warriors, sailing away every so often in the big piraguas to other islands," she said. "And I'll have to wait and wait until you come back to hear about your adventures."

Aloo sank down next to her, drawing up his legs and resting his chin on his knees. Yurubi picked up a twig and began tracing his toes, like they used to do with each other when they were children.

"Perhaps if I had my own boat, I could go places too," she murmured.

"Girls don't own boats," said Pipo, his voice cracking with laughter.

"I could have one if you'd both help me make it," said Yurubi, her head still bent over Aloo's feet.

"Why do think so much about boats?" Pipo said. His laughter seemed to have dried up.

"Because I like them," said Yurubi. She tickled Aloo's toes with the twig and giggled when she saw them curling.

"But don't you think about things like weaving hammocks and making jewellery?" Pipo said.

Yurubi dropped the twig and straightened up to look at him. She could feel the heat rising in her face.

"Why do I have to think about things like that?" she said. "I do them every day, but while I'm doing them, I think about boats and weapons."

Pipo's mouth fell open. "Weapons, too?"

"Yes, weapons. Sharp ones. Arrows, knives, spears, axes." Yurubi's temples were throbbing now.

"But you're a girl," said Pipo, his voice rising. "What's going to happen when someone takes you as a wife?"

Yurubi saw Aloo start as she jumped to her feet. "Pipo, you ... I thought you understood. Your parents—"

"Don't mention my parents. I'm ashamed of them. Always, I have to be different because of them. Always." Pipo's jaw clenched. "That's why I didn't go with them last time."

Yurubi stared at his set face for a moment, then she swung away and began running. Out of the corner of her eye, she saw Aloo leap to his feet.

"Let her go," she heard Pipo say. "When women get angry, you have to leave them alone for a while."

Yurubi gritted her teeth and ran faster. A swarm of insects followed her, humming Pipo's words around her head. "But you're a girl, but you're a girl, but you're a girl ..."

"Go away," she shouted.

She clawed through a clump of bushes, hardly feeling the thorns raking her arms or the nettles clinging to her legs. She broke through to a small clearing and stood still, the sun beating down on her back and shoulders. Where was she?

Yurubi dashed a hand across her eyes and batted at a bee near her ear. She looked around at the tangle of bushes then up at the almost cloudless sky. The sun was on her left and leaning slightly toward the hills. That meant she had to go right to get home.

With a sigh, she turned and beat a path through the bushes until she came to a familiar track leading up the hill. She climbed slowly, her arms and legs stinging in the heat. Near the top, she veered away from the village and trudged down to the river. No sense going home with streaks of blood all over her arms. She'd only have to face another scolding from Ma. Yes, about not behaving like a girl.

Yurubi clenched her hands and pushed the thought away as she slipped into the water downstream from where the villagers usually came. Stretched out on the gravelly riverbed, her feet braced against a small rock, she let the bubbly chatter of the river wash over her. It was babbling something about mountain showers, splatters of almonds, startled fish and wayward lilies.

When Yurubi surfaced, the first thing she saw through her screen of hair was the finger-like shadow of a cloud tracing the face of the cliff. Yurubi flipped the hair off her face and waded out of the river. She climbed slowly to Aloo's cave, keeping her eyes on the cloud shadow, which now looked like a fat bow.

In the cool dimness of the cave, she reached down her basket from the shelf and set it on the floor between her knees. She felt around in the basket until her fingers brushed against a rough roundish stone. It was about the size of her palm and had a groove that she had carefully cut down the middle. Yurubi had first picked up a piece of the stone near one of the rivers during that mad flight to Jambou, and ever since, she'd been on the lookout for it. It was very soft and easy to carve but was so strong it never cracked, no matter how long it was heated. Its rough texture was perfect for smoothing wood, bone and other materials, but Yurubi wanted to try it for something else.

She lit a small fire and put the stone in it, then picked up one of the thin river reeds she'd left soaking in a small bamboo trough of water. Holding the slightly crooked reed high over the fire, she heated it gently, all the while keeping an eye on the stone.

When Yurubi thought the stone was hot enough, she pulled it from the fire with a stick and fitted the reed into the narrow groove. She rotated the reed rapidly in the groove again and again along its full length and held it up to the firelight.

She laughed softly. The kink was gone.

One by one, she straightened the other reeds in the same way, then tied them together and stacked them on a wide stone shelf near the back of the cave.

FINAL CHALLENGE

The smell of barbeque fish wafted across the beach on clouds of smoke, following Aloo down to the waterline. He fanned the smoke away from his face as he picked his way through a tangle of small children rolling about on the sand. Usually, Aloo loved barbeque fish, but this morning he felt as if any kind of food would stick in his throat.

Today was the final challenge, and he still did not know what it was. Neither did Pipo or any of the other boys. All they'd been told was to come down to the beach without their weapons. Everyone else in the village was here too, as it was supposed to be a fun challenge.

Perhaps it'd be sand wrestling, since weapons weren't needed. The group had done wrestling before but that was in the hills. In the first match that day, Aloo had been pitted against Jokoro, who'd promptly flung his thick wide body at Aloo and pinned him to the ground. It had been Aloo's first hand-to-hand tussle with anyone other than Yurubi, and he wasn't sure how rough he was supposed to fight. He wouldn't mind having another chance today. Except for the queasy feeling in his stomach.

A line of young boys careened past him in a hand-over-foot race, shouting as they went.

Aloo walked to the water's edge, his eyes following a flock of boobies screaming and swooning at the glints of silver fish among the waves.

"Aloo, over here."

He turned to see Pipo waving at him from under the trees, where the boys were gathering around Maruku and Kuriji.

"… boys and girls will be taking part," Maruku was saying as Aloo ran over to join the group.

Hands on his hips, Maruku was smiling from ear to ear. "Kuriji's idea. He wants you all to have some fun."

The boys nudged each other, chortling and whispering until Kuriji stepped forward and held up his hands.

"You'll all go out to sea in that piragua there," he said, pointing at one of the medium sized canoes under the trees. "Maruku and I will follow in a small boat. You can each pick a girl to take with you."

"Whooo, whooo, whooo!"

The ground under Aloo's feet shuddered as the cheering broke out, and the boys started talking all at once.

"Listen," said Kuriji, raising his voice above the jabbering. "When we're far enough out, the girls will jump overboard and swim away. You'll wait for our signal then go after them and bring them back to the piragua. Now go get your girls and come back here to push out the piragua."

Aloo stood like a bamboo stalk wreathed in fog as the boys began running in all directions.

"I'll go get Yurubi and Taima." Pipo's grinning face floated into sight.

A jumble of voices drifted across the beach. Someone began beating out a rhythm on a dried log, echoing the pounding inside Aloo's chest. Bursts of laughter, shouts, squeals, arguments, orders churned around him. People jostled him on all sides.

"Let's go, let's go."

Aloo dragged his feet over the sand, following the boys as they pushed the piragua down to the water.

A familiar giggle whizzed past his ear.

"I'm going to sea in a piragua." Eyes flashing like sunbursts, Yurubi tucked in her loincloth and climbed into the canoe.

A swarm of girls clambered after her, squealing as the piragua lurched on the waves. The boys vaulted into the boat after them and grabbed the paddles.

All except Aloo.

He stood in the water up to his chest, the waves washing around him, the breeze smearing the wet salty smell all over his face.

"Aloo, come on," Pipo shouted.

Aloo shook his head, trying to clear the black dots dancing in front of his eyes.

"What's the matter, boy?" Kuriji shouted. "Get on board."

Aloo reached with one hand for the boat but staggered as a hot coal flared in his gut.

"He's sick again." Garu leaned over the side of the piragua, his lips pulled back from his teeth. "Just like last time. He's afraid."

"Come on, boy." Maruku's gruff voice. "Every warrior has to know how to rescue people at sea. Especially women trying to escape."

Laughter floated around Aloo.

"Here, grab my hand." Pipo and Yurubi's faces tilted toward him.

The pounding of the drums filled his head. He grabbed the side of the rocking piragua, catching his breath as the flame seared through his stomach. He squeezed his eyes shut and tightened his grip. The boat pitched, wrenching his arms, tipping him off his feet. A wave broke over his head.

He was clinging to his mother with all his might, gasping, sputtering, choking as she clawed at the snarling waves.

"Aloo! Aloo!"

Aloo! Alooooooogggg! Mother screamed, clutching him to her chest, crushing his ribs. The mountain of water smashed into them, tearing him from her grasp. He was sliding, sliding, sliding into the bottomless darkness, his chest on fire.

"Aloo! Aloo!"

He flailed with his arms and legs, his insides melting. The fire erupted, spewing from his throat in an acrid plume.

"Aloo! Aloo!"

Warped faces shimmered through black dots, lips moving. Waves washed silently against him. A pair of arms circled his chest, towing him backward through the surf. His head bounced lightly against a soft bosom.

Aloo closed his eyes.

The voices came rushing back.

"Not sure what happened ... not such a warrior after all ... always strange ... see him vomit ... shut up... just sick ... must've eaten something bad ... don't be stupid ... nothing but a coward ... can take you down any day ... shut up ... paddle the boat."

"Go on, Yurubi. I've got him." Waasha's voice under his ear.

She hoisted him by the armpits onto the beach. Aloo scrabbled about on the sand, trying to find his legs, but they felt boneless. Like an octopus' tentacles. He flopped back, closing his eyes again, surrendering to the relentless black dots.

UNDER THE SHAMAN'S EYE

The sharp whistle of an osprey bored into the darkness. Aloo's eyes flew open, and he stared dazedly at the jumble of bags, baskets, gourds, twigs, shoots and vines swaying above him. He moved his tongue, unsticking it from the roof of his mouth.

"Ready to come back?"

Aloo twisted his head, wincing as two rocks seemed to roll loose behind his eyes.

The shaman was sitting cross-legged just inside the opening of his hut, holding a large bamboo mug. Aloo's gaze followed the mug as the shaman raised it to his lips.

"Not this," said the shaman after taking a swig. He gestured with his chin. "Next to you."

Aloo turned his head and saw a mug near the mat on which he was lying. He propped himself up on one elbow and drained the mug, hardly catching the slightly bitter taste until he was done. He sank back onto the mat, sweat running down his sides, waiting for the rocking hut to settle down.

The osprey's call pecked at his temples. Still, it was quiet here. Except for the dull rasp of the shaman's breathing. No voices. Just like in the forest. Like that gorge between two steep hills, where no one ever went. He could build a hut there near the little stream. He'd leave one side completely open. Or weave a big flap that could be closed when it rained a lot. Perhaps Yurubi—

"When I was a boy, I thought I'd become a warrior." The shaman was squinting at Aloo through a wreath of smoke.

"I was a wily boy." He dragged on his pipe and blew out the smoke in big puffs. "Maybe that's why the spirits chose me."

Aloo stared at the shaman. Hard to imagine him as a boy. Or as a warrior. Small wrinkled face almost obscured by the bone ornaments in his nose, lower lip and ears. Shrivelled neck weighted by strings of beads and charms. Thin arms and lower legs encircled by bands and beads of every colour. Faded watery eyes peering through straggly strands of white hair.

How did the spirits choose someone, though? What was the shaman trying to say? Aloo was always happy to go foraging for special herbs and roots for the shaman, but that was all he knew how to do. He didn't know any chants, and he didn't like bone jewellery or the clattering sound they made with every movement.

He shifted on the mat, coughing as the cloying smell of the shaman's smoke filled the hut.

"Here." The shaman shuffled over to Aloo's side with a small gourd and refilled the mug. "Finish it."

Aloo raised his head and gulped the bitter drink, liking it less and less. The hut had stopped moving, but Aloo wasn't about to trust it just yet. He dropped back, his eyes fluttering shut.

"It's never wise to fight too hard against the spirits," said the shaman.

What did he mean? Aloo forced his eyes open to look at the shaman's face, trying to understand, but the smoke was getting thicker, clouding everything.

"A young man must bend his ears to the voices of the wind, the mountains, the sea ..."

Ikupo walked around the sleeping boy, dropping white pebbles on the floor as he went. When the circle of stones was complete, Ikupo squatted near Aloo's head and blew a few puffs of smoke into his face. That should keep him out for the rest of the day. That and the two mugs of mimosa brew.

Before pulling the flap closed on his hut, Ikupo took one last look inside. Even if anyone ventured out here and dared to enter his dwelling place, they would be afraid to cross that circle of stones. He sucked the last of the smoke from his pipe and hobbled to the village centre. He stopped near the banked fire, rummaging in his bag for a new wad of leaves. He lit his pipe again and sent up a few smoke rings toward the Great Mountain before turning and entering the taboui.

"Great One." Oudou rose from his stool and gestured to a mat on the floor. Ikupo nodded and took his seat in the middle of the taboui, his back to the opening. Oudou, Maruku and Kuriji pushed away their stools and sat on the floor facing him. Just the three of them? Better make sure.

"Buaba?" Ikupo asked. He drew on his pipe and passed it to Oudou.

"He's out on a mission for me," said Oudou. "But I can send for him, if you wish."

"No, no," said Ikupo.

"How's the boy?" said Maruku, reaching for the pipe.

"He's back from his journey into the darkness," said Ikupo. "Resting now."

"Good," said Maruku. "We can hold the final ceremony soon, as planned."

"A warrior must be able to fight at sea," said Oudou, his tone mild.

"Aloo's not a warrior," said Kuriji in a flat voice.

Maruku's hand hung in the air, holding the pipe. "But you've said yourself many times that he's by far the best in the group."

Kuriji's mouth tightened. "He has skills. Skills like no other boy I've ever seen. But he doesn't have the heart of a warrior. I tested him once. He doesn't like to fight. He will run and hide from the enemy."

Ikupo searched the young warrior's face, which was set in hard lines. "You tested him once? Not every day?"

"It was a special test," Kuriji muttered, his eyes straying to the opening of the taboui. He took the pipe from Maruku and drew lightly on it before handing it to Ikupo.

"In the wrestling matches, Aloo was beaten by Jokoro," said Kuriji, with a laugh that sounded like a snarl.

"No shame in that," said Maruku. "Jokoro's a big, strong boy."

"A big, clumsy boy. Aloo could easily topple him." Kuriji's voice was full of scorn. "But Aloo lacks the heart of a warrior."

Ikupo handed the pipe to Oudou again and waited while the chief took a deep drag. "Chief Oudou can see the heart of a warrior," Ikupo murmured.

"Mmmm." Oudou tipped his head back and blew the smoke toward the roof. "Can the boy fight at sea, though?"

Kuriji opened his mouth then snapped it shut again as Maruku leaned forward.

"Great One, is the boy fit enough to fight at sea?"

Ikupo sighed and shook his head slowly. "No."

They all fixed their eyes on him now, Kuriji looking like a stunned fish. The pipe was smouldering in Oudou's fingers.

"Aloo was marked by the spirit of the Great Mountain," said Ikupo, speaking each word slowly. "It has bound him to the land."

A distant hawk tossed a single screech into the silence. Ikupo dropped his chin to his chest and fingered his black stone charm. A piece of the Great Mountain's heart.

"What does it mean?" Maruku whispered, his voice hoarse.

Ikupo lifted his head and looked at the three men in turn. Their faces were slack, their eyes wide.

"The mountain spirit will not let the boy go to sea. It does not want the ocean spirits to claim him. It will suck out his strength and drag him back any time he tries to leave the land."

Silence fell again.

"But—but he swam out to the boat last time," said Kuriji finally, a deep frown creasing his forehead. "He even managed to hit some of the coconuts."

"Quiet," said Maruku, resting a hand on Kuriji's arm. "Listen to the Great One."

"It was just a little way from shore," said Ikupo. "Aloo was not seeking the help of a boat to take him away from the land. He was not about to enter the arms of the ocean spirits."

"How will he live?" said Kuriji, almost in a wail. "The ocean is our life."

Not so hard-shelled as he'd liked to think, this young one. But then, they never are. Ikupo shifted his gaze from Kuriji to Oudou, who was puffing on the pipe again.

"Well, Aloo cannot become a warrior, that's clear," Oudou said through a mouthful of smoke.

"But, Chief, he's the best of all the boys," said Kuriji, his nostrils flaring.

Oudou lifted his eyebrows. "Kuriji, you just said the boy's a coward."

"He's not a coward. He's—He's timid. That's it. That's his problem. He's timid. I was hoping one of you would—"

"Whatever it is, he can't be a warrior," said Oudou, waving the pipe. "You know a warrior must go to sea. Often. And for many days at a time."

Kuriji's throat moved, but he said nothing more.

"What should we do with him, Chief?" said Maruku. "The ceremony's soon."

Oudou turned and stretched his hands toward Ikupo.

"Great One, only you can discern the whims of the spirits. Only you can tell why they've marked this boy. He is now yours. Do as you wish."

INITIATION CEREMONY

The day of the initiation ceremony dawned dull and overcast. By midday, the rain was beating down in torrents. Lightning sizzled over the mountains followed by claps of thunder that shook the huts. On the men's side of the village, most of the warriors were squatting on the floor of the taboui, playing a game of kalah with small stones. The leaders and elders lay in their hammocks, smoking and chatting idly. In the cluster of huts on the other side, the women were huddled indoors, doing their best to prepare food for the ceremony later.

Aloo slipped past the huts and ran to the river, crossing quickly to the other side. It didn't take him long to find the group, which was sloshing through the mud after Kuriji.

Like Aloo, they were all drenched, their hair dripping down their backs, water running into their eyes, their breechcloths plastered to their bodies.

Flitting from tree to tree, Aloo trailed them through the forest, his ears pricked above the unrelenting rush of the rain through the foliage. The boys were hunting birds that they needed for the initiation ceremony, but they didn't seem to be enjoying the outing. Their faces were glum, their heads bent against the rain. Even Pipo looked downcast today.

The boys had been out since early morning, and they all had a bird slung over their slumped shoulders. All except Ranan and Jokoro.

Looking more ferocious than ever, Kuriji was upbraiding the two boys at every turn.

135

"We're not dry-weather fighters," he said, as Ranan missed an easy target for the third time. "Kalina warriors fight and hunt in every kind of weather."

Kuriji's head turned, his lips curling, as Jokoro lost his footing and sprawled in the mud with a thud.

"And *he* can be a warrior," Aloo heard Kuriji mutter under his breath as he strode away.

Aloo stood rooted behind a big tree, shame washing over him again.

You cannot be a warrior, the shaman had said to him a few days ago, after Aloo had woken up at dawn to find himself still on the floor of the shaman's hut.

Aloo had leapt to his feet, his entire body flaming with humiliation. He was ready to run deep into the forest and stay there. But the shaman's next words had stopped him.

You can be a great hunter. Erona and her family have no man to hunt for them.

As Aloo stood there quivering, the shaman had told him a rambling story about how the spirits guided the hands of hunters, builders and craftsmen. Aloo could not grasp all of it. But at the end of the story, he'd gathered that he was supposed to hunt, help build and repair dwellings, and make weapons. No need to go to sea. Despite his deep shame, Aloo had felt a boulder shake loose and roll off his chest. He didn't have to go back into hiding. And he didn't have to return to the ocean. He'd do whatever the shaman wanted. Once it wasn't anything like chanting, talking to spirits, or carving eerie drawings on rocks.

Since that day, Aloo had been either staying in the shaman's hut, where no one would bother him, or going off into the forest alone.

Today, his feet had tugged him to find the boys and follow them on their bird hunt. Kuriji was leading them now into a little hollow. He beckoned to Jokoro and Ranan and pointed to the bottom of the hollow. Craning his neck from behind his tree, Aloo saw a flock of doves bathing in a shallow pool of rainwater.

Kuriji signalled to the two boys to shoot at the same time. The doves flapped skyward, leaving two behind. Jokoro and Ranan ran down the slope, trussed up the birds and slung them over their shoulders.

Kuriji placed his hands on his hips and tilted his head back, allowing the rain to wash over his face.

"Let's go home," he said.

Aloo turned and slipped away through the trees.

The ground was still wet, but the rain had stopped, and the sky had cleared. A full moon cast a bright light over the village as the women hurried back and forth, laying out a feast of crabs, fish, cassava bread, yams and sweet potatoes.

Jars of woku and honey-sweetened water were brought out and lined up next to the food. Excited children ran and crawled underfoot, trying to pick at the food or dip into the drinks.

Taima and Welusi had been helping Yurubi herd the small children together for a while, but then the two girls drifted off, leaving Yurubi alone with the little ones.

From his hiding place in a big almond tree overlooking the village, Aloo's eyes lingered on Yurubi's bent head and hunched shoulders. That's how she'd looked that time when he'd been bitten by a snake and was sweating and throwing up in his cave.

When all this was over, and he could face people again, he would tell her not to be sad for him. They could still make weapons together in secret. And he was going to be a hunter for her family. And for any others that had no man to bring them meat. Her family would be the best fed in the village.

Aloo shifted his gaze to the taboui as the leaders and warriors emerged. Their faces and bodies were decorated with intricate black designs drawn in paint made from charcoal and gum tree sap. Their brightly coloured feathered headdresses stood out against the black sheen of the freshly oiled hair hanging down their backs.

Leading the men, Chief Oudou was resplendent in a headdress of brilliant parrot feathers. Jewellery of bone, coral and seashells adorned his neck, ears, arms and legs.

"Bring them out!" he said, as he led the warriors toward a row of stools set back from a big fire.

Wearing only breechcloths, the boys came running out of the taboui and stood facing the warriors. The boys were carrying the birds they had caught earlier, slung from cords around their hips.

The shaman shuffled out of the taboui, his face heavily painted, his mass of jewellery clacking with every step. At his signal, the father of each boy stepped forward and stood in front of his son. Maruku stood in front of Pipo, who had no family in the village.

Chief Oudou was the only father who had not yet taken his place. He was near Garu but was looking down the line of the boys.

"Tonight, you will be named warriors in the village of Warigara and the nation of Kalina people," the chief said, his voice ringing over the square. "You will defend your village and your island from raiders. You will hunt and fish to feed the village and to stock goods for trade. At the command of the warrior chief, you will take to the seas, seeking bounty for your people. You will also become builders, constructing boats to keep your people mobile and huts to shelter them from the sun, wind and rain."

Although Aloo was not in that line, he could feel the mixture of excitement and dread among the boys.

"If any of you cannot carry out these duties, this is the time to say. Your father will withdraw you from the line." The chief folded his arms across his chest, closed his eyes and waited.

After a long moment of silence, he opened his eyes and looked down the line again. No one had moved.

"Now, you will show to everyone here that you indeed have the courage and strength of body to be warriors," he said.

Aloo shivered. He was strong in body, but some part of his courage was broken. He could not get on a boat.

As a slow drumming started, the shaman shuffled up to the line of boys. Reaching into one of the small bags strung about him, he withdrew a strange looking bone. Aloo couldn't be sure, but it looked like the lower jaw of an agouti with the two sharp front teeth intact.

The shaman moved closer to Garu, who was on one end of the line. Oudou stepped back to give the shaman room. With slow movements that seemed to be in time with the drumming, the shaman dragged the agouti teeth again and again across Garu's chest, scoring crisscross lines.

Aloo's teeth clenched when he saw the blood welling from the scratches. This was truly a special challenge. Just like the chief said.

Garu's shoulders were tense but he did not flinch or utter a sound as the agouti teeth raked his chest. At a signal from the shaman, he turned and presented his back. Again, the shaman scored Garu's skin, drawing blood.

Nodding to Oudou, the shaman moved on down the line. When it was Pipo's turn, he lifted his chin and pushed out his chest. Aloo smiled. Pipo was the shortest in the line, but he was by far the bravest.

If Aloo had been in that line, he would've been standing right next to his friend. He'd stay still, holding his breath, while the shaman marked him. As still and quiet as that day when he had to hide from two hunters in the forest. He'd been sitting on one of the lower branches of a marmmee apple tree, swinging his legs and munching on the sweet fruit, when he heard the voices. Trying to scramble higher up the tree, he'd fallen and landed on his belly in a deep patch of thorny bushes. He had lain still under the bushes, holding his breath and not making a sound, even though the thorns were like fire in his face, chest, arms, belly and legs. The two hunters had walked right past the bushes, never knowing he was in there. And he was still very little back then.

If he were down there on the ground right now, he'd be much braver than Ranan, who was flinching under the shaman's hand.

When the shaman reached the end of the line, he nodded to Oudou again and went to sit near the fire.

There was a flurry of movement among the women who were gathered on the edge of the compound. Galeba and Waasha came forward, carrying a huge steaming pot between them. They set it down near Oudou and ran back to their place.

Standing in front of Garu, the chief stretched out his hand. Garu untied the bird from his waist and handed it to his father.

Oudou held the bird by its legs and dipped it into the big pot. When he pulled it out again it was dripping with a red sauce that looked like pepperpot.

Were they going to eat it with the feathers? It won't be very good. Aloo had tried that once when a sudden downpour had put out his little fire near a stream in the forest. He'd been so hungry he'd eaten the barely singed bird anyway but had to keep spitting out feathers with every bite.

Oudou slowly raised the dripping bird high above his head then brought it down lightly first on Garu's left shoulder, then on the right.

Oudou dipped the bird in the pot again. This time there was no pause. He slapped the dripping bird against Garu's chest and back again and again, moving swiftly like a striking snake.

Pepper in those fresh scratches. That must be stinging so badly.

Garu held himself rigid as a tree trunk, blinking rapidly, while his father beat him about the body with the steaming peppery bird.

When Oudou was done, he handed the bird to Garu and stepped back, keeping his eyes fixed on his son's face.

Moving quickly, the other fathers followed Oudou's actions but weren't bothering to take turns. Someone stifled a yelp, but Aloo couldn't tell who it was because the boys were all being peppered at the same time.

When the beatings stopped, Aloo could see sweat pouring down the boys' faces. Some tears, too. Pepper in their eyes would do that. The men stood in front of their sons, looking steadily at them with stern faces.

The women had been very quiet the whole time, but as the shaman rose to his feet, they began stirring and whispering among themselves. Shooing the young girls ahead of them, the women returned to their side of the village. Yurubi looked up at them with a gloomy face. She had not bothered to move from her spot under a tree, where she was sitting with the small children. She'd told Aloo a long time ago that terrible things could happen if females dared to watch a shaman's ritual. So that's probably what was about to start now.

The drumming picked up and the men moved back, leaving the boys to form a circle around the fire. The shaman began dancing slowly around the boys, shaking two brightly coloured rattles.

"Spirit of the Moon, Spirit of the Moon, light the dark way," he chanted as he hopped from one foot to the other.

After he completed the circle, he made the boys sit on the ground facing the fire. Dancing inside the circle now, the shaman was dropping what looked like small pieces of wood into the boys' cupped hands.

At a signal from the shaman, the boys tossed the wood into the fire, one by one. When they were done, the shaman sprinkled something in the fire. The flames shot higher and the smoke thickened.

"Spirit of the Earth, Spirit of the Sky, Spirit of the Water," the shaman chanted, fanning the smoke toward the boys with a palm leaf.

The boys stretched their arms into the thick curling smoke.

"Bear them up on your back, cover them with your breath, carry them quickly on your shoulders," the shaman chanted.

He reached into one of his bags again and pulled out a handful of charms. One by one, he tied them around the necks of the boys.

The charms looked like they were made of wood. Different from the one the shaman had given Aloo last night. Aloo looked down at the stone carving hanging from his neck by a cotton string. It was black and shaped something like between a lizard and a frog.

It was Aloo's own charm to protect him from sickness, danger and evil, the shaman had said. He'd tied the charm around Aloo's neck and tapped him on the head with his rattles. Just like he was doing now with the boys.

Aloo rubbed the charm between his fingers.

He was never going to be a warrior. He couldn't get back on a boat. Ever. He moved his hand over his chest. At least he didn't have to endure the scratching and peppering tonight. And he could eat. Unlike the new warriors down there, who'd have to fast for the next few days.

He slid down the tree and slipped away from the village. Tonight, he'd go to the forest to find food. Tomorrow, he'd be ready.

FIRELIGHT ON THE BEACH

Yurubi drifted away from her family's hut, head back, drinking in the soft light of the half moon. She wanted to run, but that would draw too much attention. Although Ma was turning a blind eye to a lot of things these days, it would do no good to cause her shame. So Yurubi strolled, stopping occasionally to pluck a blade of fragrant grass or listen to the raucous voices of the night creatures.

When she was well past the huts, she hooted softly twice like an owl. She cocked her head and waited. There it was. An answering call far below. She turned her languid footsteps in the direction of the beach path.

Sometimes on nights like these, when the moon was out and almost everyone was outdoors, Ma would pretend not to notice when Yurubi slipped away to meet Aloo and Pipo.

Not that there hadn't been talk.

When it wasn't Taima and Welusi prodding her, it was the women whispering behind her back. They all thought that now she had entered her fifteenth hurricane season, both Aloo and Pipo wanted to take her as a wife but she was having a hard time deciding which one she liked best.

As if she was ready for a mate. Yurubi laughed softly and flipped her hair away from her face.

The women would nudge each other and smile whenever they saw Aloo bringing her family not just meat but baskets of luscious fruit from deep in the forest. And their eyes would follow her as she trailed him all over the village when the warriors were away on expeditions and he was repairing huts or knapping stone.

The women thought those were clear signs of a brewing match. But some of them were rooting for Pipo because he was a warrior and a great fisherman.

Yurubi giggled as she recalled the look on Welusi's face when she was passing on that piece of gossip. Like a manicou sniffing for food.

They'd all be stunned if they knew that Yurubi was also sneaking away to the cave with Aloo to help craft the tools and weapons that he took to other villages to trade. Or that when she went out with Pipo on his boat, the strings of thick fish she brought back weren't all his catch. She'd learned to ignore Pipo whenever he tried to remind her that her mate might not let her do things like go fishing at sea. No matter what he said, he'd take her out sometimes and regale her with stories all day while she baited the fishing lines or helped paddle the boat. They'd return at dusk, laughing and caked with salt, often carrying enough fish to share among all the families.

Yurubi flicked away the grass stems and ran down the path to the beach. She gave her owl's call again and swerved toward the answering sound.

Aloo and Pipo were sprawled on the sand near a small fire that was spitting sparks in the breeze. Further along the beach, a few other fires dotted the sand. Mostly twosomes sitting in the moonlight, roasting crabs.

"You took your time tonight," said Pipo, as Yurubi sank down on the sand.

"Doesn't look like there was any need for me to hurry," said Yurubi, pretending to slowly count the three crabs trussed up near the fire.

Aloo smiled and sat up, his long locks swinging forward. He picked up one of the crabs, speared it on a stick and held it over the fire.

With a groan, Pipo jerked upright and did the same. He grinned at Yurubi.

"If you don't want that one ..."

She slapped his hand away from the last crab and skewered it. As she held it over the fire, Pipo cracked his against it, starting a silly childhood game of fighting crabs.

Aloo kept his crab out of the fray, turning it slowly, watching as the colour changed from black to red.

"I'm a fighter, not a runner," Pipo squeaked, scrunching his crab against hers.

Yurubi quickly untangled her crab's legs from Pipo's and bashed the heads together. "I'm a fighter *and* a runner," she said with a laugh.

"What do you suppose is out there?"

Yurubi glanced up to see Aloo waving at the horizon with his skewered crab.

"Nothing to hurt you, Aloo," said Pipo swiftly. He flipped his crab over and cracked it down on Yurubi's.

"That's not—What I mean is, if you paddled a boat way out there where the moon rises, what would you find?" said Aloo, breaking off a crab leg and crunching on it.

Yurubi pulled her crab from the fire, stopping the game. Aloo had that brooding look that he got sometimes when he was near the sea.

Pipo glanced at him then swivelled on the sand to face the ocean, waving the stick about to cool the crab.

"First, you'd find that your arms have fallen off from all that paddling," he said with a grin. "Then you'd find yourself falling off the edge of the world."

"But what if there's a whole other world over there, where the sun and moon come from?" Aloo's tone was stubborn now. He still was not much of a talker, especially compared with Pipo, but when he got hold of something, he didn't let go easily.

"Our boats always go that way or that way," said Aloo, pointing with his crab to the north and south. "They never go that way, into the doorway of the sun and the moon."

"The elders say there are legends of boats traveling across the ocean from an unknown place beyond the horizon, carrying a strange looking people," said Pipo.

"Strange looking?" Yurubi said. "How so?"

"Don't know, they're just stories," said Pipo, his voice light. "Don't know anyone who's actually seen the strange people."

Yurubi met Aloo's eyes and grinned.

"One of his stories, I think," she said in a loud whisper.

Aloo's lips twitched, but his eyes remained pensive. He pulled up his legs and rested his chin on his knees.

"Pipo, if you knew for sure that there was a land out there, would you try to go?"

His question sounded idle, but Yurubi could hear a tinge of something heavy in his voice.

"I'd like to try," said Pipo, picking at the crab meat as he looked out over the ocean. "Can you imagine the massive amounts of supplies it'd need though? And the number of men? Because we'd have to take turns paddling. We'd need at least two piraguas."

He sucked on his crab and licked the juice running over his fingers. "Maybe even three. Because if it's a land of many beautiful women, we'd need extra space for them."

"Wo-women? You'd want to bring back women?" Aloo said almost in a whisper.

Yurubi looked up sharply from the crab pincer she was cracking open. These days, Aloo hardly stuttered anymore. Yurubi's gaze flicked between him and Pipo, who was grinning from ear to ear.

"Aloo, Aloo, my friend, you're ready," said Pipo, his voice laced with laughter. "Told you already, you just need to say. No need to find a faraway land. I can bring you back a Taino woman next time we go on an expedition up the islands. Feisty or quiet, whichever you prefer."

"N-No," said Aloo, his eyes dropping to the half-eaten crab balanced on his knees. "No, I'm not ready."

Pipo laughed and flopped back on the sand, putting his hands under his head. "Me neither."

This was news to Yurubi. She didn't know they'd been talking about Taino women. She tossed her bits of crab shell into the fire. "We should try to catch some more crabs."

"Too lazy," said Pipo, closing his eyes. "Perhaps we can lure some to walk over this way."

Aloo's face broke into a smile. He stretched out his legs and started eating his crab again.

Yurubi threw a handful of sand at Pipo. "Tell us, Great One, how do we do that."

"By offering them live Kalina bait," Pipo said, shooting out an arm to grab at Yurubi.

She slid away easily, laughing at him.

"You'll have to try harder than that," she said, tossing some more sand at him.

He rolled over and made another grab at her but still couldn't reach her. Rising to his knees, he gripped Aloo's ankles.

"This one will do," he said, dragging Aloo away from the fire.

The two of them went into a tussle, tumbling head over heels across the beach. Yurubi rolled her eyes as they grappled with each other, rolling further and further away from the fire, neither one gaining the upper hand for long.

When she could stand it no more, she ran over and grabbed the hair of the first one she could lay her hands on, trying to drag him away. It turned out to be Aloo. He swiped at her legs with his, trying to bring her down, but he was a shade too slow. Yurubi jumped back with a laugh. Taking advantage of the break, Pipo untangled himself from Aloo and sat up with a grin.

"I'll take that as a surrender," said Pipo, brushing sand out of his eyes.

But Yurubi was paying him no attention. Her eyes were fixed on Aloo, who had flipped to his feet like a grasshopper. He spun around, his hair wild about his face, his teeth a slash of white in the moonlight.

When he leapt over Pipo's shoulder at her, she was ready.

She dived to her left and curled tight like a caterpillar, rolling away from him.

"Aloo, she's a girl," Pipo shouted.

Yurubi bounced to her feet and went into a crouch. She straightened up quickly as Aloo jumped on her. He grunted as her head caught him in the chest, but his arms shot out, trying to grab her. She dropped to the sand and rolled away.

She couldn't let him get hold of her because he was so much stronger than her. But she was an eel. Using her hands, feet, knees, elbows and head, she struck at him again and again, evading his grasp each time. Strike, dodge and roll. That's how she'd learned to fight Aloo.

He crouched, his arms curled in front of him, his eyes narrowed. Out of the corner of her eye, Yurubi saw Pipo watching them with his mouth open.

Yurubi feinted to the right then ducked left, throwing a fist at Aloo. This time, he didn't fall for the feint. He leapt forward and grabbed her arm. He swung her around swiftly, tossed her down on the sand and fell on her, pinning her with his upper body.

No use trying to throw him now. He was too strong. She remembered that, even though they hadn't sparred in a long time.

"You got lucky," she said, looking up into his laughing face.

He shook his head, his locks brushing her cheeks and neck.

"No, you got careless."

"You're crushing me," she said, shoving at his shoulders, but she couldn't budge him. "Aloo, I said—"

Yurubi went still as she watched the laughter drain from his eyes. She could feel his heart drumming against her breasts, his breath ragged on her face, his fingers burning near her temples.

"Yurubi, how did you learn to fight like that?" Pipo's voice reached her through the sound of crashing waves filling her head.

Aloo jumped to his feet, scattering a fine spray of sand over her. Yurubi sat up and shivered in the suddenly cool night air.

"Ask Aloo," she said, her voice snagging on something in her throat.

"Aloo, you taught her to fight like a warrior?"

"No, she taught me," said Aloo softly, his eyes fixed on her.

Pipo looked from one to the other, his face slack.

"I've never seen a girl fight like that," he said, shaking his head as if to clear it.

He seemed about to say something more but instead reached for Yurubi's hand and pulled her to her feet.

"Perhaps next time you can try to take me on," he said with a dry laugh, looking her up and down. "Now let's go find some of those man-eating crabs."

UNWELCOME VISITOR

Yurubi's fingers moved swiftly, knotting the long cords of cotton into the shape of a hammock. From time to time she lifted her head, making sure that the two babies under the flame tree with her weren't straying too far. Their gurgles and garbled chatter were the only voices around this morning.

Across the yard, Grandma Lulou was sitting in the doorway of the hut, her toothless jaws working steadily on a wad of leaves while her hands twisted strands of cotton into threads.

The men had left the day before on a fishing trip, after which they planned to visit two villages on the other side of the island to trade their fish and exchange news.

The young boys were down on the beach, supposedly hunting crabs but most likely playing water games.

Only Buaba and a couple of elders were over in the men's compound. At this time of morning, they'd be puffing on their pipes and droning on about the weather and fishing.

The women had left at daybreak to put in a new crop of potatoes on a hillside just outside the village. The young girls had gone with them, happy to be out in the open fields where they could pick flowers and romp on the grass when they were not learning to plant vines or carrying drinking water to the women.

Yurubi was relieved that she didn't have to go out there anymore. Planting was such dull work. Not that she hadn't tried. But she couldn't get excited about loosening the soil on an entire hillside with a digging stick. Or burying handful after handful of seeds, vines and sticks in the tilled soil. The women had grown weary of her poor attempts, which was why she'd been given tasks like making hammocks and watching the babies when the women were in the fields. She didn't mind, although she'd much rather go hunting in the forest. Like Aloo was doing today.

By sunrise, he'd have shot one or two animals already, and now he'd be running toward some laden fruit tree that only he knew about. He'd be soaring over logs and bushes like a rush of wind, his locks streaming out behind him, his shoulders glistening with sweat, his legs—

Yurubi snapped her mouth shut and snatched up the length of cord that had slipped from her fingers.

This was just silly. Daydreaming about Aloo. She tugged on the cotton, drawing a tight knot. *Aloo.* Never mind he'd been renamed *Coylaya* in the villages on the other side of the mountains where he went to trade. He was still Aloo. Her childhood playmate. Her sparring partner. Except that ever since that night on the beach he'd been popping up in front of her eyes at odd moments. Like a spirit.

Yurubi leaned over and grabbed the baby boy, who was crawling away at full speed.

"Come back here in the shade," she said, tickling his feet.

The other one was rolling around in the dried leaves under the tree, playing with a small, brightly coloured gourd that Yurubi had made for them. She'd cut a small opening in the top of the gourd, scooped it out and dried it. When it was dry enough, she had poured some seeds inside, sealed the top back with gum tree sap and painted it in bright zigzagging colours.

The baby girl picked it up with both hands and shook it then started licking it.

"It's not food," Yurubi said for the umpteenth time, taking it away.

She rolled the gourd behind the tree and grinned as the two babies scrambled after it on hands and knees.

"Just like you, when you were little," Grandma Lulou called to Yurubi.

"I wouldn't have tried to eat a gourd, no matter how pretty it was," Yurubi said with laugh.

"Oh yes, you would. You used to stuff everything in your mouth. Just like them."

Grandma Lulou squinted at Yurubi. "What's that?" she said, pointing with a gnarled finger.

Yurubi looked over her shoulder. The babies were crawling from behind the tree, Umari rolling the gourd in front of him and gurgling in delight, and Nupu giving chase.

"It's the babies playing," she said, turning back to Grandma Lulou.

"No, look, Yurubi," Grandma Lulou whispered, her pointing finger shaking.

Yurubi whipped around. Her heart jumped into her throat. Standing in the shadow of a torch wood tree near the top of the river path was a huge feral pig, its mean little eyes fixed on the two children.

Stretching her arms slowly so as not to startle the animal, Yurubi tried to grab hold of the babies, but they were just out of reach.

"Come back here," she whispered to them, her mouth dry.

They'd stopped playing and were sitting on the ground, staring with round eyes at the big black creature with the coarse bristles on its back and sharp tusks on either side of its snout.

Yurubi began to edge toward the babies, using her feet to pull herself along the ground on her buttocks. If she could hide the children behind the tree, she might be able to chase off the pig. Out of the corner of her eye, she saw Grandma Lulou hobbling toward the men's compound. She'd know not to shout in case she startled the boar into attacking.

Yurubi reached out to grab the babies, but Umari squirmed away, picked up the gourd and threw it with both hands at the pig.

"No, no, no," Yurubi whispered as the gourd rattled across the hard dirt.

The boar grunted and tossed its head on its thick neck. Eyes locked on the beast, Yurubi felt around frantically on the ground near her for something to use as a weapon, but all she came up with was a dried almond. Her bows and arrows were hidden far away in the cave. Even if she had them, the arrows would probably be useless against the thick, tough hide of a boar this size. There was only one thing to do.

Yurubi jumped in front of the two children and went into a crouch. She stared into the red eyes of the enraged animal, sweat pouring down her body, the blood pounding in her ears. Her breath stopped as the boar lowered its head and charged.

Yurubi turned and dived for the children, sweeping them to the right of the tree and rolling with them. The pig tried to swerve on its short legs but missed them by a hair's breadth and slammed into the tree trunk with a thud. It steadied itself, snorting fiercely as it swung around. Yurubi leapt to her feet, clutching the two screaming children to her. The boar lowered its head and rushed toward her again. She rolled to her left this time, tumbling with the children as far away from the animal as she could. As she sprang to her feet, the pig staggered and fell over on its side.

Clutching the babies tight, Yurubi turned to flee. She screamed as she smacked into a wet body. A pair of arms closed around her like tentacles, squashing the babies against her chest.

"It's dead," a voice rasped against her hair.

Yurubi reared back. Aloo was looking down at her with wide eyes, sweat streaming down his face.

"Aloo! What …? How …?" She looked from him to the twitching boar and back.

He dropped his arms and gave her a shaky smile.

Yurubi took a few steps on trembling legs toward the pig and saw with amazement that Aloo had shot it cleanly through the eye.

"What's happening here?" Buaba came running, holding a huge spear in his good hand.

"There was a pig," Yurubi said pointing with her chin at the animal as she fumbled for words. "It wanted to eat the babies. But Aloo killed it."

Slowing his pace, Buaba jogged over to the pig and poked it with the tip of his spear.

"It's dead alright," he said, bending to look more closely at the arrow sticking out of the boar's eye.

"How far away were you?" he said, glancing at Aloo.

"Over there." Aloo pointed to a spot about four bamboo lengths away, where two iguanas lay trussed up on the grass under a sapodilla tree. "I was coming up from the river when …" His voice faltered and his throat moved convulsively.

"You got him, Aloo," Grandma Lulou called out in a quavering voice as she came hurrying back. "Was a mean one, that pig. Had his eye on the babies."

"Yurubi saved them," Aloo said softly, something strange

burning in his eyes as he looked at Yurubi and the two children she still was holding.

"You got him good," Grandma Lulou said with a cackle, patting Aloo on the arm as she peered at the boar.

Buaba prodded it again with his spear.

"Must've crossed the river before that heavy rain two days ago and couldn't get back," he said. "When the women come in from the fields, they'll take care of this. The meat must be smoked well, so that it'll keep until the warriors' next trip. With this much meat, they'll be able to do some good trade."

"Yes, those Tainos in the islands up north love smoked pork," said Grandma Lulou, the corners of her mouth turning down as she made her way back to the hut.

Buaba stood looking at Aloo for a long moment. Then he nodded briefly and lumbered off to the men's compound, dragging his spear behind him.

As she watched him walk away, Yurubi suddenly felt as if her knees could not hold her up any more. She set down the babies and sank to the ground.

"Even if I had my bow and arrows, I couldn't have killed it," she muttered, bending her head to hide the tears that were starting behind her eyes.

"It's dead now," said Aloo, squatting in front of her.

"If you hadn't been there …" Yurubi gulped at the lump in her throat.

"Buaba would've killed it or chased it off," said Aloo. "You saved the babies. You gave that old boar a fight."

Yurubi shook her head, her eyes overflowing. Aloo parted her screen of hair and peered into her face.

"You're a woman warrior."

Yurubi's head jerked up. She searched Aloo's face but saw no hint of laughter. He was looking back at her with eyes like pebbles on a moonlit beach.

"What are you saying, Aloo?" she whispered. A ball of heat was spreading through her chest, threatening to consume her. "Why would you say that?"

Aloo reached out with one finger and touched a teardrop on her cheek.

"You're a woman." His voice sounded like it was clogged with smoke. "And you're a brave warrior."

He touched her lightly on the cheek again then ran off in the direction of his hut.

By nightfall, the story of the boar's attack was on everyone's lips. At first it was all about Aloo's remarkable shooting. But later, as the women were cooking dinner and preparing the pig's meat for smoking, a few of them went looking for Aloo to give him the boar's teeth and tusks and when they came back, they started talking about how Yurubi had faced down the fierce animal to protect the babies. It wasn't long before that part of the story was also being told and retold around the village.

Yurubi was turning the two iguanas on a spit when Minda came up to her, lips quivering.

"Go sit, Yurubi," she said, taking the rod from Yurubi's hands. "I'll bring the food when it's done."

"Where's Umari?"

"With his father."

Yurubi looked at her in surprise. Chief Oudou never seemed to have much time for Minda or their baby.

"He's showing Umari how to hold a bow," said Minda with a shaky chuckle, her face reddening in the firelight.

"Umari's going to be a fearless hunter," Yurubi said with a laugh. "You should've seen him throw the play gourd at that old boar."

Minda shook her head, a wry smile lighting her face.

Yurubi went to sit in the opening of her hut, Aloo's words still echoing in her head.

You're a woman warrior.

Woman warrior. What did it mean? Yes, she knew how to fight and hunt. And she loved boats. But a *warrior*? Warriors were men who went on raids and captured—

"Yurubi!"

Taima and Welusi came running, their eyes glinting with excitement, their hair swinging behind them.

"We heard you saved the babies from the pig," said Welusi, dropping a chain of flowers over Yurubi's head.

"And then Aloo saved you all," said Taima. "Minda and Galeba are going to make him a hammock. They went to his hut to take him gifts and noticed that he had no hammock."

"But Aloo doesn't like sleeping—" Yurubi bit back the words. Better not to say too much about Aloo.

Taima frowned at her. "He doesn't like sleeping?"

"It was a joke," said Yurubi tilting her head back to smile at the two of them. She reached out and grabbed their hands, pulling them down to sit next to her.

"These flowers are like a morning rainbow," she said, touching the brightly coloured garland resting on her breasts.

"We wanted to make you a coral necklace, but that would've taken too long," said Taima with a grin.

"This is more beautiful," said Yurubi, squeezing their hands as she swallowed a lump in her throat.

"You don't have to do any more work for the rest of the night," said Welusi.

"And when the food's done, you'll be the first to eat after we carry the men's," said Taima, beaming at Yurubi.

"That's too much," said Yurubi with a tremulous laugh. "I'm not a warr—a man, you know."

"But you fought like one today," said Taima with a grin, nudging Yurubi playfully.

"Not you, too," Yurubi muttered, covering her eyes with her hands.

IN THE HEART OF THE FOREST

The afternoon sunlight poked through the thick canopy, drawing shifting patterns in the small clearing deep in the forest. An occasional breeze ruffled the tree branches, stirring the birds to outbursts of song. On the ground, small green lizards scuttled about, making their own music as they chased each other through the dried leaves. At the centre of the clearing, Yurubi and Aloo were bent over a log.

"I'd like to make the sides as thin as possible," Yurubi said, drawing a line along the flat top of the log with a stick of charcoal to mark where they'd hollow it out. "It should be light and fast in the water."

"Like every boat you've ever made," said Aloo, glancing sideways at Yurubi.

"But those were small river craft," she said. "This canoe here has got to be sturdy enough to ride the waves at sea—"

"Yet light enough that it's easy to paddle," said Aloo in a droll voice.

"Just keep repeating that," Yurubi said with a grin, elbowing him in the ribs.

Aloo grimaced and staggered away. "Now I can't work anymore today," he groaned, bending over and holding his side. "I'm wounded."

"Oh, too bad you're hurt," said Yurubi, holding back her laughter. "You won't be able to manage the cassava bread and fish I have in my basket."

"You brought cassava bread?" Aloo said, straightening up.

"Not for you," Yurubi said with a grin, moving to the other side of the log. "You're in too much pain to chew that."

"But I can hear the bread and fish calling me," said Aloo, cupping his hand to his ear and leaning down over Yurubi's basket.

Yurubi couldn't help laughing. When Aloo was in a playful mood, he was like a little boy again. He still could go from quiet and watchful to frolicsome in a flash.

"Time for a break, I guess," she said, laying down her stick of charcoal.

Licking his lips, Aloo handed her the basket.

"What, you're an iguana now?" Yurubi said with a laugh. She delved into the basket and passed him some fish and bread.

"Yes, a very hungry one," he said, tearing into the cassava bread.

Yurubi sat on the ground and leaned back against the log, eating hers more slowly. High overhead, a parrot squawked hoarsely as if to say it was hungry too.

"Remember the first time we tried to make cassava bread?" Aloo said, looking down at the flat bread in his hand with a wry expression.

Yurubi laughed and shook her head. "It looked so easy when I was watching Waasha grate cassava and wring it dry in her sieve. I think our hands were just too small for that task."

"And then there was that grater we'd made."

"Yes, yes, I remember," said Yurubi with a giggle. "The stone chips kept falling out of the wood and into the meal."

"After you went home, I pounded the cassava root flat and roasted it."

"How did it taste?"

"Not as good as this." Aloo stuffed the last bit of bread into his mouth and squatted next to her, his face growing serious.

"I want to show you something," he said, his voice soft. "A special place."

"You mean there's a place more special than this?" said Yurubi, waving her arm around at the thick cluster of trees festooned with vines of every kind.

"You'll see," said Aloo, tilting his head.

A greenish slash of sunlight reached down through the trees, burnishing his cheekbones and splashing over his chest.

Yurubi got to her feet and brushed the crumbs off her legs, wondering at a strange tightness in her stomach. Perhaps she'd eaten too fast.

"If we don't make the best use of the time when the warriors are away, we'll never get this boat built," she said.

"We'll finish it, don't worry," said Aloo, standing now too.

"I guess we can call it a day." Yurubi stepped away and began packing up the tools.

Moving quickly, Aloo tossed armfuls of branches and vines over the log to conceal it then slung his bow and quiver over his back.

"Let's go exploring," he said, his voice buoyant.

Yurubi stopped in her tracks. "We're going exploring? I thought you knew where this place was."

"I do know where it is. I just need to remember how to get there."

Looking into his laughing eyes, Yurubi felt her stomach clenching again.

"Alright then, let's see how lost we'll get before we find this place," she said, giving him a shove.

They set off through the forest, beating their way through the thick undergrowth on what seemed like a haphazard route.

Despite her teasing, Yurubi knew there was no need to worry. Aloo was at home in the forest and could find his way even in the dark, like a bat. This was no different from the many hikes they had taken through the forest since they were children. Except for the strange discomfort she now felt in her stomach every time she looked into Aloo's face.

She pushed the thought away, keeping her eyes on his quickly moving feet. Before long, they came to a stream and began following its winding path. But after a while, it disappeared under a tall cluster of rocks.

"What now?" Yurubi leaned against the rocks and wiped her forehead.

"Now we climb," said Aloo, pointing upward.

Yurubi rolled her eyes and followed him as he clambered up the rock face. When he got to the top, he stretched out on his stomach and reached over the edge to give Yurubi a hand up.

"I think we should—" Yurubi's breath caught in her throat as she swung to the top. It was as if every colour in the forest had washed itself clean and come to dance in the gully below.

Bursting from its hiding place under the rocks, the stream skipped giddily down the narrow ravine, tumbling with abandon over a ledge and twirling flamboyantly in the pool below before slipping away into the greenery.

"How did you find this place?" she whispered, pressing Aloo's fingers, which were still wrapped around hers.

"I was chasing an agouti. It scampered over these rocks and disappeared."

Yurubi stood motionless, drinking it all in. The fine mist from the waterfall as it splashed over the rocky ledge, the reflection of the trees in the clear pool, and the small beach of coarse brown sand, the birds flitting among the patches of flowers.

The heat from the rock seemed to be seeping into her feet and rising through her body.

"Let's go down," she said, finding her voice again.

With Aloo leading the way, they climbed down into the ravine, going around the side of the waterfall until they came to the little beach.

Yurubi dropped her basket and splashed into the pool, while Aloo squatted on a flat rock, following her with his eyes. Yurubi gulped down some water then ducked under the surface, welcoming the cool flow of the stream against her body.

"You're not thirsty?" she called to Aloo above the rushing of the waterfall when she bobbed up again.

He shook his head, his locks swaying around his face like jungle vines.

"I'm going under there," she mouthed, pointing to the little waterfall.

She curled her toes over the smooth stones on the bed of the stream as she waded against the mild current. Aloo knew her so well he'd been in no doubt that she'd love this place. Seemed like he was content to stay on that rock and watch as she enjoyed it all.

Yurubi braced her legs, sucked in her breath and stepped under the cascade. In an instant, she was knocked off her feet and went sprawling back into the pool. Laughing and spluttering, she scrambled to regain her footing. There was a blur of movement and she found herself upright again, with Aloo's arms curled around her. For a moment, neither of them moved. Over Aloo's shoulder, a wayward finger of sunlight was drawing smiling rainbows in the mist near the waterfall.

Yurubi brought her hands up to push Aloo away but they crept under his neck, like lost children finding shelter.

Behind him, the little birds twittered into the quivering ears of the flowers while the butterflies flirted with every plant in sight, dropping brief kisses on their flustered leaves.

Yurubi glanced up to find Aloo's eyes steady with the same look that had been there for most of her life, waiting to be claimed. When his mouth touched hers, the gushing waterfall moved to a place inside her. She clung to Aloo and sank below the surface of the pool, knowing there was no need to breathe.

Behind her closed eyes, the artful rainbows swirled into new blends of colour and the wildflowers danced to the soaring music of the stream.

COOKING PRACTICE

Yurubi carefully placed two handfuls of corn kernels on the broad, slightly hollowed stone in front of her and picked up the oblong one next to it. She rolled the oblong stone over the corn, but the kernels skidded out from under it and scattered on the ground.

With a sigh of frustration, she dipped into the basket of fresh corn and put some more on the basin-like stone. No matter how long it took, she was going to learn to do this. And all the other tasks that the women did in the village.

Welusi and Taima could giggle as much as they liked, Yurubi was going to do everything she could to learn how to be a good wife. Even if it meant spending half of her day on dull chores like this.

Not that she'd told anyone yet about her and Aloo. But of late, she'd seen Ma and Waasha exchanging amused looks whenever she offered to do something like cook or grate cassava. Perhaps they knew that Aloo was going to ask permission soon to take her as his wife. Yurubi's heart tripped at the thought. Soon, soon, soon.

When the warriors returned, Aloo would tell Pipo, go talk to the shaman, and then ask Yurubi's family to take her as a wife.

With a smile, Yurubi began crushing the slippery corn. She and Aloo both wanted Pipo to be part of the celebration. She could already imagine the mischievousness in Pipo's eyes and the stories he would tell about her and Aloo.

While they were waiting, she and Aloo were working on the boat as fast they could and slipping off to their secret place at the waterfall every chance they got. It was like finding a whole new island that was just theirs.

On days like today when Yurubi was struggling with women's tasks, Aloo was in the forest, hunting and gathering materials to build a hut for her. When it was done and she became his wife, they'd share that hut every night, he'd said. Except when she was in her moon cycle, she'd reminded him, with a playful punch on the shoulder. He'd grabbed her hand and pulled her to him, moulding her back to his chest.

No matter what, I won't be like the warriors, he'd said gruffly in her ear, wrapping an arm around her waist.

He said he'd noticed that even when the warriors weren't away on expeditions, they rarely spent a full night in their wives' huts. He'd also promised that he'd never take a second wife like some of them did. Which was a relief because even the thought of him—

"Dreaming over the corn?" With a wide smile, Waasha knelt next to Yurubi and took the oblong stone from her.

"You need to roll your wrists more, like this," she said, grinding the handful of corn in a few quick motions. "Once you get the movement right, it's easy. Here, try now."

Waasha passed the rolling stone to Yurubi, scooped the ground corn into a bowl and put out some more kernels.

Yurubi nodded and tried to follow Waasha's movements, but the kernels seemed to have a life of their own, and they skittered off the stone into the dirt. Yurubi could feel the heat rising in her face, but Waasha seemed not to notice.

She placed her hands over Yurubi's, moving the rolling stone slowly. "Crush it a bit first, then roll your wrists like this."

Sweat pouring down her face, chest and back, Yurubi smashed the corn kernels with the rolling stone then ground them slowly, trying to roll her wrists like Waasha.

"That's it," said Waasha, her face lighting up. "Next thing I know you'll be out in the fields planting cassava."

Yurubi rolled her eyes. "I don't think so," she muttered, recalling how badly that went last time she tried.

Waasha's mouth opened as if to say something, but she seemed to change her mind. Her beads tinkled their special music as she rose to her feet.

"Perhaps you can do some cooking tonight if Aloo brings back a nice fat iguana," she said.

Yurubi grimaced. She hated skinning those huge lizards with their sharp tails and spines, but she nodded and reached up to press Waasha's hand in gratitude.

Later in the day, as the sun was slipping behind the hills, a young boy came running with the news that the warriors' boats had been spotted.

Yurubi's hand stilled over the small pot of corn soup she was stirring. Her eyes followed the boy's flying feet as he pelted down the hill to the beach with his friends. Her heart was flying too, but up into the sky, like a nightingale. The secret life that she and Aloo had been leading since they were children, first as playmates, then as adventurers and now as lovebirds, was about to change. They would still be all those things but no longer in secret. She'd be Aloo's wife, living in her very own hut that he'd built for her.

It was all she could do to stand still and stir the soup.

Around her, the women were scrambling to prepare a homecoming feast, which meant cooking more food and bringing out jars of woku. The young wives ran back and forth, oiling their hair, painting their faces and draping themselves in jewellery as they tended the pots.

While they chattered excitedly and cast eager glances at the seaside path, Yurubi's gaze kept straying in the other direction. Aloo had not yet returned from the forest. By the time he got back, there'd be no need to even share the news with him. Being Aloo, he'd take one look at the frantic activity in the village and know immediately that the warriors were back.

He'd better not be bringing an iguana this late because that would mean going down to the river to skin and gut it. A couple of birds would be good. Those were not too difficult to prepare.

Yurubi peered into the pot of gently bubbling soup. It must be done by now. She set down the ladle and picked up two clumps of coconut fibre. Holding the steaming pot carefully, she carried it over to the ajoupa near her family hut. It was too small to be shared at the feast tonight.

As she set down the soup, something brushed her shoulder. She spun around to see Aloo standing there with a broad grin on his face, holding two big iguanas. He dropped them into a large clay bowl at her feet and reached out quickly to touch her shoulder again.

"Pipo's back," he said, his eyes shining. "I'd better go help him up the hill."

Yurubi grabbed his hand and pressed his fingers briefly. "Yes, go."

As he turned and hurried across the yard, her eyes followed him, lingering on the tight locks bouncing on his back, the smooth stride that made him look like he was flying, and the straight lines of his body. She had to fight the urge to leave the iguanas and run with him hand in hand down the hill.

The iguanas.

Yurubi bent over the bowl, peering at them in the dim light. Laughing softly, she picked up the bowl and strolled back to her little fire.

"It's good to have some extra meat tonight," Ma said, looking into the bowl as Yurubi went by. "Already cleaned, too."

"Yes, Aloo did that," said Yurubi, her feeling of pride bubbling up into her voice. "And I'm going to cut them up and cook them now."

"You're going to—?" Ma placed her hands on her hips and leaned forward, peering into Yurubi's face. "Ah—Umm—Are you feeling well?

"Yes, Ma, I'm fine," said Yurubi, with a laugh. "All I need is a pot."

"I'll get it." Shaking her head, Ma went over to the ajoupa where the cooking utensils were kept.

Usually, iguanas were grilled whole over the fire, but Yurubi preferred the meat the way her mother her cooked it—cut into small pieces and stewed in a clay pot until it was tender.

Yurubi set about cutting up the iguana meat with one of her own thin, sharp knives. Now that she was doing all this cooking, a few more of these knives would be useful. Perhaps when she had her own hut, she could make small tools in there without attracting too much attention.

"If you put this in with the meat, it will give it a nice flavour," said Ma, setting down a small jar next to Yurubi.

"What's in there?"

"Herbs and spices. Lots of pepper."

"How much should I put in?"

"All of it, if you like. I usually chop a fresh lot every day."

Yurubi emptied the jar of spices over the meat, while Ma placed the pot on the fire and shoved more wood under it.

"The men are here, I think," said Ma, gesturing with her chin to the line of warriors cresting the hill. "We'll serve them whatever food we have ready, and we can have the iguana with some sweet potatoes later when it's done."

"This won't take long," said Yurubi, tipping the chopped meat and spices into the pot.

"Remember to add a little water," Ma called over her shoulder as she walked away smiling.

ALOO GETS A GIFT

Everyone had eaten and was gathered around the fire for the homecoming celebration. Puffing on rolls of tobacco and swilling mugs of woku, the men were boasting loudly about their latest expedition. The women were sitting together in a semicircle on the other side of the fire, talking among themselves, hardly listening to the tales. Like Aloo, they'd heard similar stories after every trip.

Aloo was more interested in exchanging silent words with Yurubi across the fire and watching the glow of excitement on her face. With a grin, she cut a look at Pipo, who was sitting next to Aloo telling funny stories. Aloo smiled back and shrugged slightly. As soon as he could get in a word, he'd share his and Yurubi's big plans with Pipo. Right now, Pipo was relating a story about his battle at sea with a huge stingray.

"Every time he flipped his tail over his head, I'd have to dodge his poison arrows, then I'd try to shoot one at him, but he was more agile than me in the water," said Pipo, his voice full of disgust.

Aloo bent over in laughter. Only Pipo could get into an exchange of fire with a deadly sea creature.

"So, what have you been doing, my friend?" said Pipo, clapping Aloo on the back.

Aloo straightened up and turned to look Pipo in the eye.

"Pipo, there's something—"

"People of Warigara, hear me now." Oudou's voice boomed out over the gathering.

The conversations around the fire died down, and all eyes turned to the chief. Decked out in one of his smaller headdresses and his bone jewellery, he was sitting between Maruku and Buaba, his pipe in one hand, a mug in the other.

"Guided by the mighty spirits, our brave warriors plied the seas far north of Hiroon, amassing great bounty along the way to bring back home. We also did good trade with the smoked pig. And from the fruits of that trade, I've brought a gift for the shooter."

With a jolt of surprise, Aloo realized that the chief was talking about him. At a nudge from Pipo, he rose to his feet. He could feel everyone's eyes on him. Except the chief's. Oudou was looking over Aloo's shoulder, signalling to someone. Aloo resisted the urge to glance back and instead held himself still, his gaze fixed on the chief's face.

"Your gift," said Chief Oudou, stretching out both arms as Kuriji came and stood next to Aloo.

For a moment, Aloo was confused. Then Kuriji moved and a young woman stumbled forward.

"I give you this Taino woman as a wife, to serve you well and bear you many brave sons and fruitful daughters," Oudou said.

The whooping, clapping and drumming that erupted seemed to be coming from a great distance as Aloo's eyes flew to Yurubi's stricken face.

"Woohooo! I didn't know she was for you." Pipo was on his feet, clapping wildly and stomping as Kuriji pressed the woman's hand into Aloo's.

Aloo dropped her hand like a hot coal, but she clutched at his fingers, sending tremors up his arm. His gaze flitted wildly from Yurubi to Pipo to the chief. "I-I don't—I can't—"

"Shhh, quiet, boy." The shaman's hands closed over Aloo's shoulders. Aloo swung around. "B-but I—"

"Not now, not here," the shaman whispered, staring up into Aloo's eyes.

"He's so overcome, his words have fled," the shaman said loudly, stepping forward with a dry laugh.

Everyone joined in the laughter, some of them clapping and stomping.

The chief puffed on his pipe, beaming at Aloo through the smoke. "Big moment for a young man. Give him a drink."

Aloo felt like the fire was licking at his face and chest. Trying to swallow the heat in his throat, he backed away, dragging the clinging woman with him.

"Here, here, take this." Pipo pushed a mug into Aloo's hand.

Aloo downed the liquid, hardly noticing its fiery burn. Someone finally pried the Taino woman loose and led her away. The drumming grew louder and the voices more raucous as the women began passing around more woku. Aloo's eyes searched frantically for Yurubi, but she seemed to have disappeared. When Pipo turned to accept a mug from Welusi, Aloo slipped away and ran to the women's compound.

It was dark and quiet on this side of the village. He crouched near Yurubi's family hut, listening for any sounds inside.

"Yurubi, are you there?" he called softly.

No answer.

He slipped around to the opening and peered inside. The lamp had not been lit, and there was no one in there. Aloo ran off into the shadows then stood still for a moment, trying to think of where Yurubi might be hiding. There was only one place. His feet sped down the familiar path toward the river then up the side of the bluff. He pushed aside the thick curtain of vines and vaulted silently into the dark cave. She was sitting in the corner where she kept her tools.

"Yurubi!" he said, springing forward.

"Aloo, go away," Yurubi said in a muffled voice.

"I don't want her," he said, reaching out to take Yurubi in his arms.

Her fist struck him in the stomach, and he stumbled. She leapt at him like an enraged iguana, pummelling his chest, shoulders and face. Aloo dropped to the floor, curled up in a ball and rolled away from her to the back of the cave. She stood there, breathing hard, her shoulders heaving. Aloo slithered on his stomach to a spot just behind her then jumped up and pinned her arms to her side.

"Yurubi, listen to me," he whispered in her ear as she struggled against him. "I don't want that woman. I'm going to tell the chief that."

"Are you crazy?" Her voice was choked with tears and anger. "You can't do that. You can't reject a gift from the chief."

"Why not?"

"Let... go... of... me," she said, trying to wrench out of his grip. "Why not? Why not? I'll tell you why not. For the same reason I'm not supposed to build boats or make weapons. It's not the Kalina way."

"But you *are* building boats and making weapons."

"In secret, Aloo. In secret. You know that." She sounded like her teeth were clenched. "Can you refuse the chief's gift in secret?"

He didn't understand what she was trying to tell him. But it didn't matter. He was not going to take any other wife. He released Yurubi cautiously, hoping she wouldn't fly at him again. She stood quietly, her shoulders slumped, her arms hanging at her sides. Aloo almost wished she'd try to fight him again.

Holding her shoulders gently, he turned her around to face him. He took both of her hands in his and placed them over his heart.

"Yurubi, I'll go to the shaman for help. I'll tell him I want only one wife. You."

Yurubi's chest heaved and she leaned her forehead on his shoulder, raining tears onto his chest.

"Oh, Aloo, you truly don't understand." There was something in her broken voice that he'd never heard before. "Not even the shaman can help this time."

THE PATH OF A BEETLE

Ikupo held himself completely still as a small brown beetle crawled over his left ankle. Up one side, down the other, its spiny legs scratching his skin. Landing on the ground between his outstretched legs, it faltered for a moment then burrowed under his right ankle. Ikupo waited for the insect to emerge on the other side but it seemed to be in no hurry. Still, he didn't move. After a while, the beetle crawled back out from under his leg. Ikupo stared as the beetle climbed up the inside of his right ankle, scrabbled across his instep and dropped down the other side. It scurried across the floor of the hut and disappeared.

Ikupo fingered his shark bone necklace as he pondered the beetle's message.

"The longer, harder way?" he muttered.

He looked up as a shadow flitted across the opening of his hut. With a sigh, Ikupo reached for a firestick and lit the tight roll of leaves he was holding. He sucked in the smoke and waited.

He had smoked half of the roll when the shadow appeared again. This time, it hovered at the opening. A basket spilling over with herbs slid inside the hut. Ikupo's lips twitched.

"Now the spirits are sending me walking herbs," he said out loud.

Aloo's head poked through the opening, his eyes flicking around the hut. In one swift movement, he bounded across the floor and flung himself at Ikupo's feet.

"Gr-Great One, pl-please, n-not her," he said in a strangled voice.

A cloud of weariness descended on Ikupo as he looked at Aloo's pleading face. Ikupo closed his eyes and drew the smoke deep into his chest. A wisp of fog swirled in his head, slowly forming the shape of the figure in his recurring dream. Aloo's hair brushed Ikupo's feet, tracing the path of the beetle. *The longer, harder way.*

Ikupo opened his eyes, squinting through the smoke at Aloo, who was still crouched on all fours like an agouti sensing danger.

"Chief Oudou has lifted you high, Aloo. Almost as high as a warrior."

Aloo shook his head violently, his locks whipping across his shoulders.

"I-I only want Yurubi," he said. "I-I was go-going to ask f-for her. Was ju-just waiting for Pi-Pipo to come back."

"You can have them both."

Aloo's eyes stretched wide and his mouth opened and closed like a fish on a line.

Stifling a sigh, Ikupo pointed over Aloo's shoulder. "Bring me that jar."

Aloo spun around, grabbed the squat jar and placed it close to Ikupo's right hand.

"I'll need a mug too," said Ikupo, avoiding Aloo's bewildered gaze. "Two mugs."

Aloo set down the mugs swiftly and squatted next to Ikupo, sweat forming on his high forehead. Ikupo filled the two mugs from the jar and handed one to Aloo, who gulped it down like water.

Good. That should help unstick the words from the boy's throat. Watching Aloo out of the corner of his eye, Ikupo took a sip of the slightly sharp brew. Aloo himself had been bringing large clumps of the plant with the shy little leaves. Not that he knew anything about its many powers, its magic on wounds inside and outside the body. He was leaning forward now, his mouth no longer tight as a bow.

"Great One, please, I don't want two wives. Just Yurubi."

Ikupo felt something stirring in his chest. He pushed it down hard and lifted the jar, filling Aloo's mug again. "You ever watched a beetle crawl across the ground?"

"What?" Aloo looked even more confused.

"A beetle. It climbs up and over things even when it can go around or under them."

Aloo's gaze trailed over the floor of the hut, as if he was trying to spot an insect.

"Great One, I—"

"You cannot refuse the chief's gift, Aloo. You must accept her. As you continue to rise in the eyes of the chief and on the wings of the spirits, you can ask for Yurubi later. It's a longer, harder path but the one you must take."

Aloo's face went grey. He looked as if he was about to throw up. "Why?"

"If you anger the chief, where will you flee to? You cannot cross the sea to another land. And no other village chief on this island will welcome you. They all respect Oudou too much. Word will spread."

"I can go ba—go into the forest."

"And take Yurubi with you?" Ikupo spoke as gently as he could. "That's what you'll give her? A life in hiding?"

Aloo went still. A distant look came over his face as he turned his head, gazing unseeingly at a shaft of sunlight outside.

"I have everything ready to build a hut for her," he whispered in a cracked voice.

"Build it for the Taino woman. Yurubi will understand. She'll wait."

LEARNING FROM THE EARTH

Yurubi stood inside the opening of her family hut, watching as the women packed their baskets. Soon they'd be gone to the fields, leaving her to watch the toddlers who were now either trying to climb into the baskets or clinging to their mothers' legs. Another day of wiping noses, washing bottoms and stuffing food into wailing mouths. Another day of trying not to notice the woman moving around in the hut Aloo had built. Another day of struggling to hold up her head and keep the pain at bay.

If only she could escape to the forest to work on her boat. But if she ventured out there, Aloo would show up, and she didn't have the strength right now for that. To be alone with him would mean looking into his tortured eyes and fighting the urge to slip her arms around his waist, to lean against his back and inhale the wild smell of the forest that always clung to him.

Yurubi squeezed her eyes shut and tamped down on that memory.

When the quivering inside stopped, she tilted her head back, her eyes tracing the rugged line of the mountains against the blue sky. She waited, listening to the song of the birds in the surrounding trees, the buzz of insects, the garbled chatter of the children, the rustle of Ma's packing behind her. Nothing. No magic. Perhaps it all stopped when one grew up. No one else had ever seemed to see or hear it anyway. Except maybe Aloo sometimes. Not that he'd ever said anything. But occasionally she'd caught that look in his eyes—

With a sigh, Yurubi snuffed out that image too. Time to get to her tasks. Turning to pick up her basket of weaving, she almost bumped into Ma.

For a long moment, they stood looking at each other, the story passing between them silently. Ma's face was soft and the look in her eyes reached all the way down through Yurubi, breaking the shield she'd been guarding so carefully this past moon.

"Ma, don't ..." The whisper seared Yurubi's throat. With a strangled cry, she folded forward and buried her face in the familiar refuge of Ma's neck. As Ma's arms closed around her, the pain in Yurubi's chest spilled over into tears.

"I know, I know," Ma whispered, stroking Yurubi's hair. "It's hard now, but it will pass, child. It will pass." She tightened her arms around Yurubi.

"The wind from the mountain runs cool through your hair, sometimes it goes roaming, whistling without care, but always returns, to run cool through your hair," Ma sang softly, rocking Yurubi from side to side.

Yurubi's chest heaved and sobs ripped through her body as Ma sang that old song she used to sing when Yurubi was a child.

"Erona, you're coming?" Waasha's voice came through the opening of the hut.

"Go on, I'll catch up," Ma called out, pressing Yurubi's wet face into her shoulder.

"Take your time," Waasha said softly behind Yurubi.

Yurubi caught her breath. What if all the other women out there saw her crying like this, like a silly little girl? With a shudder, she straightened up and covered her face with her hands. What had come over her?

"Come with me today," said Ma, rubbing Yurubi's upper arm. "Come help me plant the corn."

Yurubi dropped her hands and stared at Ma through her tears.

"You know I'm no good at planting anything, Ma."

"Doesn't matter. Come away from—from the village for a while." Ma smiled coaxingly and brushed a strand of hair away from Yurubi's face. "You don't have to stay in the fields all day. You can slip off to the river for a nice cool swim when you get tired."

Yurubi scrubbed at her wet face. Perhaps just for one day—

Her head jerked up.

"What about the babies?"

"Don't worry, Nimita can watch them."

Yurubi cringed inside at the mention of that name, even though its bearer had been looming here in the hut the whole time.

Nimita, Aloo's wife.

Yurubi swallowed the lump that rose in her throat again as those words scalded through her mind. Perhaps if she said them out loud sometimes, they wouldn't hurt so much.

Nimita, the weaver. She was so good at weaving, that's all anyone wanted her to do. She spent her days weaving fine cotton cloth for everyone and cooking for Aloo.

"Yurubi?" Ma was looking at her with a worried frown.

Shaking her head to clear the piercing images, Yurubi looped her arm through Ma's.

"Let's go plant some corn," she said, forcing her lips into a smile.

Ma smiled back and patted Yurubi's arm. "Good girl. I have a nice sharp digging stick for you."

Yurubi couldn't help rolling her eyes. "Can't wait to see it," she said, with a tremulous laugh.

As the path to the fields narrowed, Yurubi unhooked her arm from Ma's and fell back, walking with her head down. One foot after the other. Away from Nimita. Away from Aloo's wife. Aloo's wife, Aloo's wife, Aloo's wife.

Yurubi wiped a hand over the back of her neck, which was already growing hot under the morning sun.

Nimita was firmly Aloo's wife now. Yurubi had tried to tell him from the start that he could not reject the chief's gift, but it had taken the shaman to convince him. Not that Aloo had given in easily. After his first talk with the shaman, Aloo had disappeared into the forest for two whole days. When he returned, Yurubi had watched with burning eyes as he headed directly to the shaman's hut carrying a huge basket of herbs. Whatever happened there that night had prompted Aloo to take off for the forest again. This time, it was several days before he'd returned.

He'd found her at the river when he emerged from the trees at dawn. In a halting voice that speared Yurubi with each word, he'd told her he was not being allowed to reject the chief's gift. Even though she'd known that, part of her had been hoping the shaman would find a way out. She could hardly bear to look at Aloo as he promised in a choked whisper that one day, he'd take her as his wife. The river of tears flowing down her face seemed to be also running through Aloo's voice, but she could not bear to raise her eyes to his. Her body had slumped like an empty bag when he touched her fleetingly on the shoulder and ran up the path to the village.

Since then, they'd hardly spoken a word to each other. He still brought her family meat but now it was Ma who usually greeted him, patting his arm as he quickly handed her the cleaned and skinned animals, a sad smile twisting his lips.

Whenever Yurubi saw his tall, lean figure approaching, the dull ache in her chest would sharpen into a blade that ripped jaggedly at her breath, and she'd turn away, finding something to keep her occupied until he left.

Yet, her eyes would search for him whenever he went off into the forest, where he was spending more and more time, or when he was away on one of his frequent trips to other villages.

It was harder to avoid Nimita, though, because she lived in the women's compound. The sight of that woman sitting in the doorway of her new hut, her fingers deftly weaving strands of cotton, sometimes spurred an urge in Yurubi to tear down the hut with her bare hands.

Yurubi set her teeth as she plodded along behind Ma. Today was supposed to be an escape from all that. She was going to learn to plant corn, no matter what it took.

After that first day when Yurubi returned home too exhausted to even eat, she decided to go back out there the next day, and the next. Slowly, she learned how to dig holes to plant corn, yams, potatoes, cassava and cotton, how to pull weeds before they choked the young plants and how to loosen the root crops from the earth without damaging them.

Moon after moon, she stuck to the same routine. She'd rise early, pack some food and go to the fields for the entire day, escaping from the village, from the sight of Nimita. Even when the crops were in and the women began rotating to other tasks, Yurubi continued to go to the fields every day. Out there, with the sun and the rain beating down on her back, with the quiet steady look in Ma's eyes picking her up every time she flagged, her bruised insides were starting to feel less raw.

There were still those days when she dripped tears onto the shiny green buds that had poked up through the dirt from some very drab looking seeds, or when she ripped at the earth ferociously, trying to bury the rage that kept ambushing her at odd moments. But mostly, she worked stoically, allowing the idle chatter of the women to wash over her. Except for that time a few moons ago when Taima had started talking about when Nimita might have a baby. The words had seared Yurubi like a flame, and it felt like her hands were melting the digging stick she was clenching. She'd glanced up to see Taima quailing under a knife-like look from Ma, and the conversation had died. Yurubi had dropped her eyes again to the cassava root in front of her, fixing her gaze on her white knuckles until they began to unlock and turn brown again.

For a long time after, Taima's words continued to burn in Yurubi's mind like a hot coal. But as the crop seasons changed from planting to reaping and back again and there was no sign of a baby, Yurubi managed to push that thought to the back of her mind.

As a matter of fact, she hardly even glanced at Nimita anymore. On evenings like this, it was all Yurubi could do to finish her food before withdrawing to the quiet dimness of her family hut and curling up in her hammock. She usually fell asleep long before everyone else.

"Yurubi!"

She lifted her head wearily from her bowl of soup and turned to see Pipo beckoning at her from the edge of the women's compound.

With a sigh, she set the bowl aside and got to her feet. She'd managed to avoid Pipo for a long time as he was away more often than not. And even when he was at home, their paths rarely crossed anymore. Now, here he was, his head cocked in the usual jocular way, a slight smile playing over his round face. Yurubi tried to straighten her shoulders and lift her head as she walked toward him in the fading light.

"Yurubi." His voice faltered as she stood in front of him, but his wavering smile soon widened.

"Look, there's a big moon rising," he said, pointing over the sea. "A perfect night for roasting crabs."

Yurubi shook her head. "Not tonight, Pipo. I'm very tired. I was just about to get into my hammock."

Pipo leaned forward and cupped a hand around his ear, his smile stretching into a grin.

"Did I hear right? Yurubi's saying she's tired?"

Still the same playful Pipo. Yurubi gave him a weak smile.

"I work in the fields now, you know."

"Must be the hardest work in the world then. Never thought I'd hear you say you're too tired for anything."

A wave of desolation washed over Yurubi. No use trying to tell Pipo that exhaustion was her goal every day, so she wouldn't stay awake at night to hear the sinister spirits whispering in her ear about Aloo and Nimita in the hut across the yard. Yurubi bent her head.

"I'm going now, Pipo. Time to sleep."

"You're going to lie in the dark while all this moonlight goes to waste?" He flung his arm out, gesturing at the rising moon on the horizon. His voice was still teasing, but there was a thread of sadness in there. With a small wave of her hand, Yurubi turned and began walking back to her hut.

"Yurubi, wait."

Pipo ran after her and touched her on the shoulder.

"Listen, I'm going on a fishing trip on the other side of the island soon. Come with me."

Yurubi shook her head again. "I don't—"

"Just for a day. We'll leave at dawn and return at dusk. You can help me paddle or bait the lines." His teeth flashed in a grin. "Or do nothing except listen to my stories."

Yurubi was too weary to argue with him.

"I'll think about it," she said, raising her hand to stop him from saying anything else.

He cocked his head, giving her a whimsical look. Then he nodded, touched her shoulder again and ran off.

Yurubi eyes followed him until he disappeared down the hill to the beach then she returned to the hut, dragging her feet. As usual, she shut out the buzz of voices around her and ducked inside. With a weary sigh, she climbed into her hammock and pulled her knees up to her chin.

What had come over Pipo? Why would he invite her to the beach tonight? He'd never said anything to her about what had happened with Aloo, but he must've known why she was avoiding them both, why her life had changed so drastically.

Yurubi shifted in her hammock, turning on her back and crossing her arms over her chest.

No doubt, Pipo would've heard the talk about how she'd been invaded by a *maybouya*. If he ever learned the details of her visits to the shaman, he'd probably make a spellbinding story of it, but she was not about to talk about that with anyone. Not even Ma, who had pleaded with the shaman for help and was still plying him with gifts of food, herbs and pottery.

Yurubi smiled wryly. If Ma were a man, she'd probably be a shaman. *No maybouya's going to take my only child*, she'd said, her face set in grim lines as she gripped Yurubi's arm and tugged her along to the shaman's hut.

The pain was so bad at the time it was easy for Yurubi to believe there was some maybouya churning around inside her. Not that the shaman had ever said those words. In, fact, he hardly spoke to her at all.

On that first visit, he had peered at her with watery eyes, nodded at Ma then shuffled back into his hut. Looking at his stooped shoulders and bony back, Yurubi had rolled her eyes, wondering why everyone thought this frail old man could fix everything. But she'd followed him into the dim hut after Ma let go of her arm and gave her a push.

Without a word, the shaman had pointed to a mat in the middle of the floor and stood over her silently after she sat down. Willing herself to stay still, she'd folded her hands in her lap and bent her head.

After what seemed like a long time, he'd begun walking around her, using a stick to draw a circle as he went.

Despite herself, Yurubi had looked up from under her brows in curiosity as he set about lighting several small fires just outside the circle. Using a small palm leaf, the shaman had fanned the smoke toward her, mumbling something in a low scratchy voice as he circled her slowly.

At some point, she must've dozed off because that was all she remembered. When she drowsily opened her eyes and lifted her chin off her chest, the shaman was sitting in the far corner of the hut smoking, and he'd signalled to her that she could go.

That night, she'd slept deeply, without Aloo entering her dreams. There'd been no visions of the long straight line of Aloo's back as he dove into their stream in the forest, the light in his eyes as she showed him a new tool she'd made, or the look of intense concentration on his face as she described to him the voices of the river.

That one night of dreamless sleep was enough to impel Yurubi to return to the shaman's hut whenever he sent word for her to come. It had become a place where she didn't have to do or say anything, where she didn't have to worry about what anyone might be whispering behind her back, where there were no painful thoughts swirling around in her head.

Inside the circle that the shaman always drew around her, it seemed no maybouya could reach her, whether or not the shaman lit the fires. Sometimes he gave Yurubi a slightly bitter drink, at other times it was a thick black herb soup. Each time, she'd return to her hut and sleep without dreaming. Pity she hadn't gone to his hut tonight. She twisted in the hammock and slapped at a mosquito buzzing around her ear.

Perhaps the shaman's spells were beginning to work. Lately, she'd found herself scanning the riverbanks for reeds that would make good arrow shafts. Two days ago, while she was bathing, she'd found an unusual looking rock on the riverbed and had held it up, twisting it this way and that, thinking of what she could make with it.

These past few nights, her mind had been drifting to her abandoned canoe in the forest, although it had probably rotted by now. It would be no good for anything except firewood.

With a deep sigh, Yurubi turned onto her side again and scrunched her eyes shut, trying to dispel the image of her canoe going up in flames. If she was going to be hankering after boats again, she might as well go fishing with Pipo.

ABOVE AND BELOW

Yurubi sat drowsily in Pipo's gently rocking boat, holding a cotton line that was dangling over the side with a bone hook on the end. Occasionally, she twitched the line without even bothering to look at it.

She was enjoying the touch of the early morning sun on her shoulders, the soft breeze brushing her face, the interplay of blue and white through her half-closed eyelids.

The boat was just inside the wide bay at Larikai, drifting lazily on the tranquil waters in the shelter of the Great Mountain. The rhythmic slap of the gentle waves against the side of the canoe was broken every now and then by a splash near the rocks on her right. Pipo was over there fishing underwater with a small spear attached to his wrist by a long thin cord. From time to time, he'd surface and thread another squirming fish onto the hooked stick he'd wedged between two rocks. In contrast, the basket at Yurubi's feet held only small fry that she was using for bait. Not that she was in the least bit perturbed. Pipo had come here on this side of the island to fish. She'd come along just to keep him company. And to be in a boat again.

She shifted the line to her left hand and lay back in the canoe, her eyes idly following the graceful seagulls swaying in thin hammocks of clouds. She smiled as a late-coming gull daintily picked up a fine thread of pale orange light and delicately edged his white hammock. From somewhere inland, a parrot sent up a spatter of applause at the fine work—

Yurubi's eyes flew wide open, and she sat up with a start. What was happening? She twisted around in the boat, hardly daring to breathe as she gazed out over the water at the incoming waves. As they neared the shore, they slipped off their silver headdresses and donned the green and purple colours lavished on them by the sprawling mountain.

Yurubi dropped the fishing line and scrambled to her feet.

"Woooooohooooooooo!" she cried, raising her face to the sky.

Like a startled dolphin, Pipo erupted out of the water.

"Yurubi, what's the matter?" he shouted.

"Look, it's still there," she called back, flinging her arms wide.

She leapt onto the cross board in the canoe, hopping from one foot to the other.

"Yurubi, be care..."

The rest of Pipo's words were lost as the canoe rocked wildly, and Yurubi toppled overboard with a huge splash.

It was like falling into an upside-down rainbow. As the colours engulfed her, Yurubi kicked her legs and dived deeper.

"Uhhhhloooooooo!" she gurgled, sending a string of bubbles to cheer up a pale yellow fish wearing black eyepatches.

Laughing inside, Yurubi reached down to touch fingers with some orange seaweed straining against its tether on the speckled sand below. A school of fish, painted black and white like warriors, fanned out from behind a clump of blue coral and went chasing after a slender fast-moving creature. Yurubi was about to follow them when a powerful arm curled around her waist and hauled her to the surface.

"What happened?" Pipo flipped his hair off his face, staring at her with anxious eyes.

Yurubi gulped a mouthful of air.

"Oh, Pipo!" she gasped, throwing her arms around his neck. "It's come back!"

"What?" He peeled her arms away and leaned back, frowning. "Yurubi, what are you talking about? You toppled overboard, and I didn't see you come up."

"Pipo, the magic. It's come back," she said, her words tumbling over each other. "I was doing the happy dance. And I fell. But it's underwater, too."

Treading water slowly, Pipo gave her a strange look.

"Yurubi, did you hit your head when you fell?" He reached out to touch her head. "I remember one time when I tumbled off—"

"No, I didn't," she said, batting his hand away. "What's the matter with you? Can't you see—"

Of course, he couldn't. No one else could.

"Never mind," Yurubi muttered. "I was just playing a silly game with myself. I got bored waiting for the fish to bite."

A look of relief passed over Pipo's face.

"I told you, it's more exciting spearing them," he said, with a smile. "Come on, let's get back in the boat and eat some of that cassava bread you brought. I'm starving."

"What about your fish?" Yurubi pointed at the long string of fish dangling from the rocks on the far side.

"They're fine, they don't need to eat," said Pipo with a grin.

"Idiot," said Yurubi, splashing water at him as he hoisted himself into the canoe in one quick motion.

As Pipo turned and reached down for her hand, Yurubi tilted her head back. Over the land, a persistent breeze was knapping away at the clouds on the mountaintops, carving perfect arrowheads in the sky.

A DEEPLY HIDDEN SECRET

Yurubi woke with a smile on her lips. She lay still, trying to catch the tail of the dream that had made her smile, but it was gone. She stretched languidly and opened her eyes. It was coal dark and quiet, except for the usual chorus of snoring inside the hut.

Even in their sleep, Ma, Waasha and Grandma Lulou could scare off any raider.

Yurubi hopped out of her hammock and tiptoed outside to relieve herself. It was that quiet time just before dawn when the crickets, frogs and owls had given up quarrelling, but the early birds had not yet started singing.

Overhead, the stars were shimmering in perfect rhythm to some music only they could hear. Occasionally, an exuberant one would break away and slide spectacularly across the wide expanse of sky. It took Yurubi back to her childhood when she'd try to mimic that move and end up sprawled on her back over and over. They made it look so easy up there.

With a wry grin, she slipped back inside the hut and went over to Ma's hammock.

"Ma, Ma," she said softly, shaking her mother's shoulder gently.

Ma's eyes fluttered open and she started when she saw Yurubi.

"Yurubi, what's wrong?" she whispered, raising herself onto one elbow.

"I'm not going to the fields today," said Yurubi, keeping her voice low.

Ma rubbed her eyes and yawned. "Alright. That's alright." She patted Yurubi's arm and lay down again, closing her eyes.

Yurubi gripped the side of the hammock. "I'm going into the forest, Ma."

"Uh—good, good." Ma reached out and pressed Yurubi's hand. "Take Welusi with you. Bring me back some ginger."

Yurubi cleared her throat. This was going to be the hard part.

"I want to go alone."

Ma struggled upright and passed a hand over her face. "Yurubi, you know that's not safe," she said in a tired voice. "We never go into the forest alone, you know that."

"The men do."

"They're hunters and warriors, Yurubi. They're men."

"What's happening?" Waasha's sleepy voice called from her hammock.

"Nothing," said Yurubi quickly. "Just talking about what we're doing today."

"Too early," said Waasha with a yawn. She turned on her side and began snoring again.

"Ma, please, I'd like to be on my own today," Yurubi whispered.

A frown creased Ma's forehead as she leaned forward, peering at Yurubi in the dark.

"Be careful, Yurubi. The maybouya ..."

"But it's gone, Ma. Look." Smiling broadly, Yurubi straightened up and flung her arms wide.

Ma chuckled softly and reached up to lay her broad palm against Yurubi's cheek. "I don't know if the maybouya's still lurking. I truly don't. But right now, you do look somewhat like my bright-eyed girl of old." Her eyes swivelled to Waasha and Grandma Lulou's hammocks and back to Yurubi.

"Be careful out there," she said, dropping her voice. "Be very careful. Don't go too far. Try to leave soon before everyone else starts stirring."

Yurubi flung her arms around Ma. "Don't worry, I'll be gone before sunrise. And I'll be careful."

Ma patted Yurubi's cheek then flopped back in the hammock and closed her eyes.

Trying to contain her growing excitement, Yurubi crept around the hut, packing a small basket.

Better to leave now, although it was still dark. Otherwise, as Ma had been trying to say, people were going to start whispering about how the maybouya was making Yurubi do crazy things like going off into the forest alone.

Yurubi slipped out of the hut and walked swiftly toward the river as if hurrying to do her morning ablutions. At the riverbank, she put down her basket, untied her loincloth and stepped gingerly into the cool water. Slowly, she immersed herself up to the neck, shivering a little in the early morning chill. Above her, the faintest brush of light was beginning to smudge the sky.

Yurubi sank under the water and stretched out, bracing her feet against a rock so the current wouldn't carry her downstream. Eyes closed, she listened to the chatter of the tiny pebbles bouncing on the riverbed, the voice of the river filling her head. At first, it was only a rush of bubbly laughter, but slowly it became a song. Yurubi held herself still, straining to hear the words.

"Waiting for you, waiting for you …"

"Trees, reeds and rocks are waiting for you, waiting for you …"

"Warrior, warrior, warrior woman, they are waiting for you, waiting for you …"

Yurubi surfaced and gulped a mouthful of mountain air lightly flavoured with an ocean tang. As her feet found the bottom, she stretched out her arms, skimming her fingers over the river's silver ripples.

"I can hear you again," she whispered.

She splashed her way to the riverbank and tied on her loincloth. Grabbing her basket, she took a quick look around and raced up the bluff to the cave.

Warrior, warrior, warrior woman, her heart sang as she climbed. Every warrior needed arrows and a bow. And a knife or two. She slipped behind the tangle of vines and vaulted into the dark mouth of the cave.

In the many moons since Yurubi was last in the forest, nothing had changed. Except that today, the thick mat of leaves spread under her feet, the dark green light draped over her shoulders, and the feathers of whispers down her back felt like homage to a returning warrior.

Why had she stayed away so long? To avoid being alone with Aloo, to avoid any blatant reminders of their magical times in here together? Much good that had done her.

Anyway, she wasn't going to dwell on any of that today. She was going to practice her shooting, find Ma's ginger and some cooking herbs, and revel in this feeling of homecoming. And take her time while she was at it. She had all day.

She plucked a guava from a low branch and bit into it as she meandered along, stopping occasionally to drink in the sight of a riotous patch of new flowers, a formidable growth of thick vines running up a tree trunk, a chirpy bird calling to its friends, a pair of shiny eyes glinting behind a bush.

Rays of sunlight had started playing on the forest floor when Yurubi found herself on the edge of a familiar grove. She looked around in astonishment. How had this happened? Her feet had brought her here even though she hadn't planned to come this way. With a rueful shake of her head, Yurubi set down her bow and basket. Her heart quickened as she stared at the dense tangle of vines and brier that had grown over the place where her half-finished canoe once stood. It would take a lot of work to cut through that growth. Not worth the trouble just to find a rotting log.

Still, she untied her quiver and dropped it next to her bow then slowly began to circle the grove. There were some small trees here that she could fell on her own if she worked hard for many days. No need to bother about an old log that was nothing more than firewood. She tapped a couple of gumbo-limbo trunks with her knuckles and bent to examine the base of a slender one that looked promising. She was about to straighten up when she noticed a small gap in the dense vegetation over the site of the old canoe. Using a stick to avoid touching the web of nettles, she poked at the little space and discovered to her surprise that the growth was not as firmly rooted as it appeared.

Yurubi grabbed a bigger stick and broke off the twigs on the end to create a hook. She pushed it into the gap, snagged some of the brambles and pulled hard. She almost fell on her behind as the whole tangle of growth came swinging outward. But she lost her grip on the stick as she stumbled backward, and the mass of brambles dropped back into place.

Intrigued, she picked up the stick and tugged at the tangle of briars and vines, more cautiously this time. As it swung out again, she quickly propped it up with one hand, and slipped underneath. Her left arm and shoulder were beginning to sting from the brush with the nettles, but she was hardly aware of that as she crouched in the dim light, her mouth falling open.

In the centre of a tight space was a perfectly shaped canoe resting on wooden supports. It was the exact design she had drawn and redrawn so many times. Not a rotting log, but her dream canoe. Suddenly come to life. How was this possible? Her eyes must be playing tricks on her.

Head reeling, Yurubi took a step forward and reached out to touch the boat. She ran her fingers slowly over the smooth sides, the perfect curves to the keel, the sharply pointed bow, the sloping back.

She lifted the two long slender paddles, gazing in wonder at the blades, which were thinner along the edges than in the middle. The handles, slimmer than usual, had a little head on the end to prevent them from slipping out of the paddler's hands. Just as she had drawn them.

In a daze, she gently placed the paddles back into the boat and leaned over to look inside, noting how thinly the wood had been stretched. Everything was exactly as she had envisioned it when she'd started trimming the log. This was a sleek lightweight canoe built for speed and easy navigation.

Yurubi's heart was flapping like a hummingbird. Her legs were trembling so hard, she feared she would collapse. She sank to the ground and leaned her forehead against the keel of the boat.

Aloo, Aloo, Aloo …

While she had been punching the earth in anger with a digging stick, trying to bury her dreams, he'd been here working to give them life. She turned her head and rested her wet cheek against the smooth wood.

Aloo, Aloo …

It was no use trying to pry him loose. Like two liana vines, they'd been growing entwined since they were small. And how well he knew that. Without words, he'd done this, made something that was theirs and theirs alone.

For the first time, Yurubi allowed her eyes to wander around the small enclosure. It was a tiny makeshift hut lined with branches and mud to keep out the rain. It had been built cleverly to look like natural growth on the outside. The flap Yurubi had pulled open was tied to a crosspiece in such a way that it could be moved to allow passage in and out without breaking the covering of vines, nettles and brambles on the outside.

Yurubi drew a quivering breath and rose to her knees. She spread her arms along the length of the boat and laid her head against the hull, tears dripping onto her breasts.

She probably would've stayed like that all day if it weren't for the little thorns of light that started pricking at her eyelids. She stood slowly, her hands still on the boat. Trying to think now was like poking at a nest of crazy ants. But one thing was clear. This beautiful canoe must not remain sitting here in the dark, hidden in a forest.

CRACKS IN THE COVER

Word had spread that Aloo was about to launch a boat he had built secretly in the forest. Since everyone knew he couldn't go to sea, there was a lot of talk about whether it was a usable craft or something he'd made as an offering to the ocean spirits.

Faced with a rash of questions about his boat, his only answer was a smile. Some of the young men had even gone searching for the canoe in the forest, but Aloo knew they didn't stand a chance because they'd be looking along the river.

Then Garu and his friends had started taunting Aloo about the boat. Not that they'd ever stopped hassling him. Pipo said they'd never gotten over the fact that Aloo had appeared out of nowhere and had bested them in almost every challenge in their warrior training. Even though Aloo was no longer in competition with them and was not even a warrior, the honour he had gained after killing that ferocious pig had infuriated them, Pipo thought. Whatever it was, they'd been pestering Aloo at every turn. Now they were mocking him for building a boat he could never sail.

"He's going to tie a rope on his canoe and play with it like a little boy," Garu jeered, as Aloo went by carrying a bundle of grass.

Ranan and Caloon hooted in derision, slapping their thighs.

"No, wait, wait, I know," said Ranan, holding up a hand. "He's going to push it out to sea and hope some fish will jump aboard and row it back."

As his three tormenters doubled over in laughter, Aloo's grip on the bundle of grass tightened, but he refused to even glance at them.

They had nothing better to do than sit around throwing knives at every little lizard that ran by. And trying to find ways of pestering him. He didn't have to bother about them though.

All that mattered was that Yurubi had started looking at him again. Almost like before. Almost.

A few days ago, when he'd stopped at her hut to drop off some iguana meat, she'd broken away from the small group of women near the cooking fire and hurried across the yard to take the meat from him, her face alight with a look he had not seen in a long time. As she reached out to take the skinned and gutted iguana from him, she had gripped his hands, sending his heart racing.

"It's time to launch the boat," she'd said in choked voice.

Aloo's heart had leapt. She'd found the canoe. Her canoe. His canoe. Their canoe.

Pressing her hands in his, he'd felt the familiar frizzle of lightning passing between them.

"Yurubi—"

"Aloo, please, don't say anything," she had said, looking up at him with soft swimming eyes. "Just launch the canoe. For us."

He had nodded, his feet almost lifting off the ground as he watched her walk back to the fire, carrying the iguana like a prize.

That same night he'd cornered Pipo and told him all about the boat. Well, not everything. Just that he'd built a small canoe in the forest and would like to launch it soon.

After a lot of back slapping and friendly joshing, Pipo had offered to help carry the boat to the beach. They'd agreed they could not float it all the way down the river because of the shallows and falls downstream. But with the help of Siwako and Tueke, they could carry it to the river, float it part of the way, then lift it to the beach.

Garu and his clique could laugh all they liked, that canoe was going to sea. The dilemma for Aloo right now was how to make that happen without shaming himself in front of everyone again.

He tossed the bundle of grass and leaves on the ground near the shaman's hut and went over to his own place to get a ladder and some cord. The shaman was away for the day, gathering herbs. The leaks in his roof could be fixed before he returned. It was a simple matter of finding the bad spots and patching them.

Aloo slipped his bow and quiver off his shoulders and dropped them inside the opening of the shaman's hut. He propped the ladder against the side of the hut and climbed quickly to the roof. Balancing himself lightly on the steep slant, he pulled a big knife from a sheath on his hip and cut the thin mahoe rope that was holding the rotting thatch in place.

The shaman probably hadn't even noticed the leaks. And even if he had, he wouldn't care. He was looking frailer as the moons went by, but that wasn't stopping him from going into the bushes to talk to the Great Mountain or search for his special plants. The only difference these days was that he'd take of couple of young helpers with him whenever he was going to dig for roots or find climbing plants.

What would he say about the boat launch? Aloo hadn't spoken to him about it yet, but that didn't mean the shaman didn't know. He always seemed to be aware of everything. Sometimes even before it happened.

Aloo pulled the damp thatch loose and tossed it to the ground. Then he slithered down the ladder, bundled some of the dried grass into a tight flat stack, tied it with a length of mahoe rope and trimmed both ends of the stack. He picked up a stack of hardy cachibou leaves to make a good waterproof lining and clambered up the ladder again. Crouched on the steep slope of the roof, he lifted the thatch near the peak and began sliding the cachibou leaves underneath. This was the most important part. Once the leaves were put down properly, it was just a matter of layering the new thatch.

Something like a wasp zinged past his ear.

Aloo's head snapped up.

Two more buzzes.

Arrows!

Aloo dropped to his stomach, reaching for his knife. Arrows in broad daylight? Raiders?

Aloo flattened his forehead against the thatch as another arrow whizzed over his head. He had to get off the roof. But the arrows were coming from behind him. He couldn't jump off on this side. Bracing his arms, he slithered over the peak and down the other side of the roof. He was about to drop to the ground when he caught the glint of another arrow. At the last moment he flung himself sideways and the arrow winged past his ear. He hit the ground with a thud, landing on his side. Ignoring the pain knifing through his body, he scrambled to his feet and ducked into the shaman's hut.

Sweat pouring into his eyes, he grabbed his bow and fitted an arrow into it. He crouched low, listening for any sound that would help him locate the attackers. Why were they all the way out here on the edge of the village? They must've come through the forest. But in daylight? He raised the bow and crept to his right as his ears caught a slight rustling on that side. A whisper. Stifled laughter.

With a sigh, Aloo slumped to the ground and leaned back against one of the shaman's tall clay jars.

Garu and his friends. Whispering as they slunk away.

"Did you see him jump?"

"Yes, that was hilarious, especially when he fell like a girl."

"Did you hit him with that last arrow?"

"No, I said we weren't going to hit him, remember?"

"Think Buaba saw us?"

"Even if he did, he wouldn't care."

Aloo closed his eyes and raised his hand to his throbbing left shoulder. It felt like a sea sponge. A sponge about to catch fire. He eased himself into a lying position, holding his bow and arrows close to his side. There was nothing to do but wait for the shaman's return.

Aloo snapped awake.

Footsteps. Somewhere outside. He jerked upright, gritting his teeth as the pain pounded at him. Grabbing his bow, he edged around the tall jar. Fire seared down his left side as he fitted an arrow into the bow. He sucked in his breath, braced his back against the jar and raised the bow. The footsteps drew nearer. Sweat dripped off him as he tried to hold the bow steady through the pain, his eyes fixed on the opening of the hut. Scuffling footsteps. Some lighter ones. Clinking music.

Aloo dropped the bow and leaned his head back against the jar.

"Put it down there." The shaman's voice. Talking to his helpers. "Come back tomorrow, early in the morning."

"Yes, Great One." Light footsteps moving away.

The shaman shuffled into the hut, his eyes searching slowly until they found Aloo.

"Aloo, what happened to you?"

"Uhhhhh... I fell off the roof," Aloo muttered. The shaman would've seen the ladder and grass bundles outside. He'd know Aloo had been working on the roof.

He shuffled over to Aloo and leaned down, hands on knees. His white eyebrows knotted, and his mouth tightened as his eyes moved from Aloo's limp left arm to the bow in his right hand and the loose arrow lying nearby.

He reached out and began prodding Aloo's swollen shoulder and arm, sending darts of pain shooting through his chest, back and neck. Aloo clenched his jaw, clamping down on a groan. He could feel the prickle of sweat breaking out on his forehead.

Without a word, the shaman turned and hurried outside.

"Parwu, Tiki," he called, clapping his hands. "Come back here now."

As the two boys came running, the shaman fingered one of the charms on his chest.

He must be worried about something. What if he could not heal this injury? Aloo turned his head, looking at one arm then the other. The left one looked crooked and was now twice the size of the right. Aloo shuddered inside as an image of Buaba rose in his mind.

The shaman had moved out of sight with Tiki and Parwu and was talking to them in a low voice.

"Remember that custard apple tree you didn't want to leave today? Well you must run back there now, quickly as you can. Cut some strips of bark from the tree about this long and this wide. Bring them back here right away. No idling to pick any more fruit. I also need some cassava roots. Dig up the biggest ones you can find and bring them, too. About five. Run now."

Aloo eased down flat again and closed his eyes as a wave of pain washed over him. This was worse than when he'd eaten the fruit from a manchineel tree in the forest. He was just a small boy then and didn't know the little yellowish apple was deadly. He'd finished one, enjoying the sweetish taste, and was about to bite into another when he began to feel a burning in his throat. He'd sloshed down a soggy bank to a little stream below for a drink but could hardly swallow as a great fiery lump began filling his throat.

He'd barely forced some water down when he started spewing up. Weak and dizzy, he'd managed to crawl under a clump of bushes near the stream. He'd curled up there for two days, cramps racking his body, fire raging in his throat.

At least he wasn't vomiting now. But he might start soon if he had to drink that foul-smelling brew the shaman was pouring from a small jar in the corner of the hut.

"You can take your time, like a dove at a puddle," the shaman said, setting down a mug next to Aloo's right hand. "But you must finish it because later you'll want to float like a moth into the night."

Aloo nodded and lifted the mug cautiously. He still found it hard sometimes to follow what the shaman was saying. What did he mean about floating like a moth?

Aloo suppressed a shudder as he raised his head and brought the mug slowly to his lips. The brew was thick, black and nasty smelling. It hit his throat with a bitterness that made him want to gag. This was going to take a while. Like a dove at a puddle. A little bit at a time. Yurubi talked like that sometimes, too. She'd have no trouble understanding the shaman. If only she were here. It wouldn't matter if he had to swallow five mugs of this horrible drink. Her soft eyes would calm him. Her gentle hands would soothe his pain. Her delicate lips would make him forget …

"… fell off the roof. Same way an eagle falls off a tree. Bring that bowl over here."

Aloo forced his eyes open.

The shaman was squatting in the middle of the floor, rummaging around in one of his baskets, muttering to himself and giving orders to Tiki and Parwu.

Aloo shifted his position slightly, wincing with the movement. How long had he been asleep? It was already dark outside.

"Drain that mug now, Aloo," the shaman said, without raising his head. "Time to float."

Holding his breath, Aloo downed the thick brew. Through bleary eyes, he watched as the two boys flitted around the hut, fetching bowls, stones and baskets for the shaman.

"Cassava paste ready?" The shaman peered into a big bowl that Parwu set down near him.

"Yes, it's thick like you said to make it."

The shaman grunted and looked around. "Build up the fire and bring the two lamps."

One at a time, he lifted some strips of bark from a big bowl of water and placed them carefully on a flat stone then trimmed and pounded them till they looked soft. Must be the custard apple bark ...

Something brushed Aloo's face. He tried to lift his heavy eyelids.

"You have to sit up now, Aloo," the shaman said, squatting near him. "Move the lamp here, Tiki."

Aloo struggled upright, the hut swimming around him.

"Get behind him, Parwu. Hold him steady."

Parwu's arms clenched around Aloo's ribs from behind.

"Now, Tiki, grip his arm here, near the shoulder." Aloo winced as the shaman placed Tiki's hands on his spongy arm. "Keep it close to his side. Hold tight."

Aloo's head snapped back against Parwu's chest as the shaman took hold of his arm above the elbow.

"Float, Aloo, float. Float like a moth," the shaman muttered, moving Aloo's arm this way and that.

Aloo dug his right fingers into his thigh, his breath rasping out of his throat, as the pain slashed at him. He squeezed his eyes shut, rivers of sweat running down his face and chest. *Stop, stop,* he screamed inside, but the only sound that escaped was his harsh breathing.

"Ah, that's it." The shaman's voice penetrated the cloud of pain.

The tugging stopped. Aloo's dry mouth snapped shut, and he swallowed hard. His eyes fluttered open as something wet touched his shoulder.

"Still as a rock now. Don't move." The shaman was slowly wrapping the softened strips of bark around Aloo's arm, from shoulder to wrist.

After the torture a moment ago, the wet bark felt cool and soothing. Aloo's head lolled back.

The shaman dipped into another big bowl. Using both hands, he began pasting the thick cassava poultice over the bark. The pain gnawed at Aloo as his arm grew heavier and heavier. Now the shaman was pulling long strips of cotton from a basket.

"Bring the lamp closer," he said to Tiki.

Slowly, the shaman bent Aloo's arm at the elbow, setting off darts of pain.

He nodded at Tiki. "Hold it like this. Steady."

Aloo felt like his whole body was melting. As the shaman began wrapping the cotton strips around his arm, Aloo slumped against Parwu.

He must've drifted off because when he forced his eyes open, he was lying flat again. His gaze flew to his arm. It was fat and white, bound tightly to his body with cords, the lower part strapped across his stomach.

The hut was dark and quiet. The boys had gone. The shaman was lying in his hammock, smoking a pipe.

"You must not move, Aloo," he said, still looking up at the roof. "There's water and cassava bread near you."

Aloo glanced at the small basket near him. Nimita had sent it, no doubt. She would not have come out here. She was terrified of the shaman. Someone had brought the food. But hunger was not the problem right now.

"I-I only want to go—"

"A caterpillar crawls on its belly, hiding from hungry beetles."

Aloo groaned inside. Not now, not when he was still groggy from the brew and needed to go outside.

The shaman blew a stream of smoke up at the roof.

"The caterpillar is patient because it has a secret. It wraps itself in a cocoon and stays still until the time is right. When it breaks out of its cocoon, it's a new creature. With wings. It can laugh as it soars above the beetles."

"Great One, I—"

"If you stay still inside your cocoon, Aloo, you will fly again. But if you try to crawl out too soon ... Well, think about Buaba."

The image of Buaba with his floppy arm, uneven gait and constant frown flared before Aloo again. Biting his lip, Aloo looked longingly at the opening of the hut. His face flamed as he urinated on the floor.

ON A ROCK

Aloo sat up as he felt a tug on his big toe. He had a bite. He gripped the line with one hand and gave it a quick jerk. As it grew taut, he let out a few of the coils tied around his toe. The line ran through his fingers swiftly then slowed. He jerked it again and began reeling it in, twisting his wrist to wrap it around his lower arm. A fat silver mullet squirmed on the hook as he hoisted the line from the water. He swung the fish up onto the high rock where he was sitting and tried to grip it between his feet. He freed the hook and was reaching for his sharpened stick to string the mullet when it flipped out from between his feet and slid down the rock. Aloo made a grab, but the mullet splashed back into the river and disappeared with a flick of its tail.

Aloo leaned over, staring at the churning water. Then he sat back and laughed. No one-handed fisherman could catch that one. Shaking his head, Aloo dipped his fingers into a crevice in the rock and pulled a wriggling worm from his stash there. At least he could thread a worm on a hook without too much trouble. He dropped the line in the water again and made a loop around his big toe.

Not that he was trying too hard to catch fish. He had come upstream today to one of his old haunts to escape the constant baiting of Garu and his clique. It was getting harder and harder to bear when he saw them flapping one arm and pretending to fall like an injured bird.

He must've taken a big swig of woku before climbing onto that roof, Aloo had heard Garu saying one night as the men sat around the fire drinking.

Aloo hardly ever drinks woku, Pipo had said, giving Garu a fierce look.

Ah, maybe that's why it toppled him so easily, Garu had said with a smirk and a laugh.

Let it be, Aloo had said under his breath to Pipo, who was sitting next to him.

Aloo had never told anyone what had happened. Not even Pipo, even though Pipo probably suspected it had something to do with Garu.

Getting Pipo worked up would only start one of those fights that lasted for moons as more and more men began taking sides. Most times, fights like that would break out when the men were at home for a long stretch. Garu and his bunch would back off once they started preparing for another expedition. Right now, Aloo had a bigger problem.

He drew up one leg and rested his chin on his knee, looking out over the bouncing river at the solid line of trees on the other side. The canoe was still over there in the heart of the forest. And he couldn't think of a way to launch it. Particularly now that he could use only one arm.

He glanced down at the dirty wrappings around his chest. He had to stay in this cocoon for another whole moon. It didn't matter that the cotton bandages and hardened cassava paste were now brown and stained, that the cords around his body were frayed, or that the entire thing was smelly and often felt like an ants' nest. The shaman would not allow Aloo to even shift it a little. And each time Aloo was tempted to rip it off, he'd think of Buaba.

So, Aloo was well and truly trapped. In a cocoon. And in a quandary.

Yes, he and Pipo had already worked out how to get the boat to the beach. But then after that, what? Who would take it out to sea? He could ask Pipo. But Yurubi had said *launch the canoe. For us.* Those words kept echoing in Aloo's head. Over and over. *For us. For us.* Did that mean they could be together again after he'd launched the canoe? He could hear his heart pounding in his ears, as it did every time he allowed himself to dream about her. Since that day when Yurubi had asked him to launch the boat, she hadn't spoken to him again. But the softness was still in her eyes. Except for when she'd first seen him with his broken arm. Her whole face had turned bleak and hard. At first, Aloo had been confused, but then he'd caught a glint of tears and he understood. She was angry because she thought someone had hurt him. He'd taken a step toward her, but she'd turned away. He'd stood there, looking at her rigid back, his heart hammering against his ribs, hope fluttering to life in his chest.

A few days ago, he'd tried talking to the shaman about all of it. Yurubi, the boat, Nimita. But he'd picked a bad time. The shaman had been smoking one of those cloying mixtures of herbs and seemed to be having trouble seeing straight. Looking at Aloo with bleary eyes, he'd gone off on a rambling story about some kind of predator dolphin. Then the shaman had tottered over to his hammock and fallen asleep. All Aloo had gathered was that the dolphins were some big, fierce, black and white creatures. Was he supposed to look out for them before launching the canoe?

With a deep sigh, Aloo absently twitched the fishing line.

Yurubi was the person who had explained things to him when he was confused. Since she'd stopped talking to him, it felt like he had dropped off a cliff and hit his head on the way down. He'd been talking to Nimita a little recently, but that was different. Nimita with the timid voice, the shaky smile, and anxious eyes half hidden behind her hair.

At first, he hadn't been going to her hut at all. It was only after the shaman said Aloo was shaming her that he started going there sometimes. When he did, he'd lie on a mat on the floor while Nimita curled up in her hammock. Mostly, Aloo would ask her about her life before she came to Hiroon.

It seemed that her people lived very much like the Kalina. Except that the Taino farmed more and did not go on boat excursions as often. One of the first questions he had asked her was whether she had ever seen anyone else that looked like him. She had said no. The only people she knew other than her own were the Kalina. The fearful Kalina, she'd called them. Since she was a little girl, she and her friends had been hearing scary stories about Kalina warriors, she'd said.

Aloo's mouth twisted wryly. At least, there was one thing he and Nimita had in common. But he'd never told her that he, too, had spent most of his childhood in fear of Kalina men. And now both he and Nimita were living among them. He as a Kalina claimed by the Great Mountain, she as a Taino wife traded for the meat of a pig. Neither of them ever weaving smoothly into the life here. The least Aloo could do was try not to terrify her. So, he let her paint his body with roucou, oil his hair, bring him food every day. As all the other wives in the village did with their men.

On the nights when he slept in her hut, sometimes she'd come to him in the dark, after she'd blown out the lamp. Her gentle hands and soft body soothed him. Especially after a day of ribbing by Garu and those others. After a day of failing to catch even a glance from Yurubi.

Aloo anchored the fishing line under his heel and ran his hand over his head.

Yurubi.

He had finished the boat for her. Even though it hadn't started out like that. He'd begun working on the canoe right after he was forced to accept Nimita. During those days when all he wanted to do was tear down the forest with his bare hands. Instead, he'd curl his fingers around his tools and carve the log as carefully as he could, keeping his mind fixed on Yurubi's drawings. As the boat took shape, he began to dream of giving it to Yurubi the day she became his wife. And now she had found it. But Aloo still didn't know if he was any closer to making her his wife.

He lay back on the rock, gazing up at the thin tautly stretched clouds. All he knew was that he had to put the canoe out to sea. *For us.*

THE LAUNCH OF A BOAT

The morning dawned bright and clear, with a few wisps of clouds lingering on the horizon to greet the sun. A swarm of orange and black butterflies danced on a light breeze to the music of the morning birds. A jovial mood pervaded the whole village as this was a day for festivities, not work.

The women bustled about, gathering up their cooking utensils and food supplies for the young girls to carry to the beach.

"So much to carry," one of the girls whined, looking at the growing stack of packed baskets.

"Yes, yes, Sanani, we have many people to cook for today," said Carika. "Come over here."

Carika heaved one of the laden baskets onto Sanini's back and strapped it to her forehead.

"Go on now," Carika said. "Put everything under the big almond tree. Grandma Lulou and Nimita are there. Hurry now. No dawdling to pick grapes or cocoplums. You can get those later. Come back right away for another load."

"But Ma—"

"But nothing, get going." Carika turned away and began packing another basket.

As Sanini grimaced and set off down the hill with two of her friends, Aloo reminded himself that he too needed to get down there. Most of the men were already on the beach, probably starting in on the woku. But Aloo was here, lingering behind a tree on the edge of the women's compound, hoping to catch a glimpse of

Yurubi. There was no sign of her this morning, which was making him jittery.

Today was the big day. But Yurubi still had not said another word to him since she'd asked him to launch the boat. He knew that she'd gone back to the forest and painted the canoe in bright colours. Up to three days ago, she'd still been putting finishing touches on the boat.

This morning, Aloo had proudly pointed out to Pipo, Siwako and Tueke the delicate dolphin designs that Yurubi had etched on the sides of the canoe. Now, it was sitting on the beach under a covering of coconut branches, waiting for the big ceremony. With the help of his three friends, Aloo had taken it down to the bay at daybreak. The day before, they'd floated it down the river as far as they could and hidden it in the bushes near the riverbank.

When Aloo returned from the beach this morning, he'd found Nimita waiting to fuss over him with her paints and oils and a basket full of other things.

Now he was all ready, wearing a new multi-coloured breechcloth, a necklace of agouti teeth, a red cotton band on his upper right arm, and bracelets and anklets of coral. Two bright parrot feathers were stuck in his hair, which hung in oiled locks down his back. His left arm was strapped to his chest with a length of red cotton that was hardly noticeable against his freshly painted body.

If only he could see Yurubi for a moment, he'd feel less jittery about going down to the bay. As he stood there waiting and fiddling with the boat paddles, Sanini came running back up the hill, her friends close on her heels.

"There're boats coming!" Sanini shouted, panting hard. "They're coming around the headland!"

At the top of the path, she ran smack into Garu, who gripped her by the arms.

"Slow down," Garu said with a grin. "They're our friends from Wallibou and Troumaka coming to join the festivities." He raised his voice, pretending not to see Aloo. "They've heard all about the crazy land-bound Coylaya who's going to launch his boat. With one arm."

"Oh, alright," said Sanini in a fluster, wriggling out of Garu's grasp. "I'd better go before Ma starts calling."

Chased by Garu's mocking laughter, Sanini sped back to her mother.

"What took you so long?" said Carika as Sanini came running. "Playing on the beach, I bet. Here, take this basket. I'll be right behind you this time."

"Ma, there're boats coming!" said Sanini, still breathless as she shouldered the basket. "Garu said they're from Wallibou and Troumaka."

"Yes, yes, there'll be others coming from Byabou and Jambou as well," said Carika, hoisting a basket onto her own back. "We've got to start cooking soon."

Exchanging excited grins, Sanini and her friends trudged down the hill again, followed by the women. With one last worried glance at Yurubi's hut, Aloo followed more slowly, carrying the paddles on his right shoulder. He was soon overtaken by a group of fleet-footed young boys racing each other to the beach before the boats landed.

Just before Aloo got to the bottom of the hill, he pushed the paddles under some bushes and swung up into a tree. He needed a moment to steady himself for what was ahead. Wedging himself into a crook, he parted the branches and looked out over the bay. The sun was above the horizon now, and the entire shoreline was suffused with a delicate orange light. Gulls and boobies swooped across the sky, dipping and diving into the water among schools of fish, their screams mingling with those of the boys chasing each other up and down the beach. The smell of meat, fish, spices and woku wafted through the trees, carried on the salty ocean breeze.

Out on the water, the three boats Sanini and her friends had spotted were slowly nearing the shore, laden with men, women and children from two villages on the other side of the island. Shouts went up as two more boats appeared, rounding the bay on the south side. The brash sound of conch shells blared across the water from the approaching boats. People in groups of three and four trickled in from nearby villages on foot. The launch of the little canoe was just an excuse for villagers from all over to get together for a day of revelry. And despite Garu's mockery, he was right. Up and down the island, people had heard the strange story of the young man who had built a canoe way up in the forest but couldn't go to sea.

Aloo raised his hand to hold his head but stopped himself. He'd better not dislodge his feathers. No matter what, he had to stand up straight and strong today. For Yurubi. *For us.*

As the boats pulled into shore, the villagers on the beach began shouting, whooping, laughing and raising mugs of woku in welcome. They splashed into the shallows, helping to unload and pull up the canoes as grinning, hollering men, women and children jumped off into the water.

"Be careful, don't get that wet!"

"Where's my basket?"

"I'll take the baby."

"We caught a manatee on the way."

"Look how tall he's grown!"

"Is that a new bow? What wood did you use?"

The excited chatter continued as the men and women made their way up the beach and settled themselves in the shade of the trees, while the children romped on the sand. The women passed around fruit, woku and various juices, while some of the boys attacked a huge pile of fresh coconuts.

"So, where's this boat we're celebrating?" said Akawa, after downing two mugs of woku and lighting a roll of tobacco. He was a tall, slightly built warrior who was always eager to trade whenever Aloo took weapons to Wallibou.

"There," said Maruku, pointing at the brightly painted canoe in the shade of a tree, partly covered with coconut branches.

Akawa squinted through the smoke. "Hmmm, yes, I can see Coylaya's fine workmanship. What's he going to do with it, though?"

"At the moment, only he and the shaman know that," said Maruku with a laugh. "But we'll all find out soon enough."

"Where's Coylaya anyway? I heard he broke his arm."

"He's around somewhere," said Maruku, puffing on his tobacco roll. "Here, have another drink." He passed a jar to Akawa, ignoring the question about Aloo's arm.

"Good stuff," said Akawa, refilling his mug.

Aloo couldn't help smiling. Those two, they could probably drink woku all day if it lasted.

Aloo craned his neck at the sound of a familiar jangling up the hill. The shaman was coming.

It was time.

The hubbub on the beach slowly died down as the shaman reached the foot of the hill and emerged from the trees. He was wearing a ceremonial headdress made of woven cotton and an array of feathers. His face was painted in an intricate design of black, yellow, green and bright red. His entire chest was covered with strings of coral, animal teeth, seeds and shells. Polished bone ornaments hung from his nose and ears, glistening in the morning sunlight. The clinking sounds that usually accompanied him were louder today as he was also wearing several coils of shell jewellery around his waist, arms and legs.

Behind him came Tiki and Parwu, also heavily strung with ornaments and each carrying a drum. The three of them walked slowly across the sand toward the water.

Drawing a deep breath, Aloo slid down from the tree as Pipo, Siwako and Tueke came running down the hill. Like Aloo, they were all decked out for the occasion, but their faces were painted with streaks of black to show their status as warriors.

Pipo skidded to a stop, a grin splitting his face.

"Nimita turned you out well," he said, looking Aloo up and down. "Come on, let's put this boat in the water."

Siwako and Tueke slapped Aloo on the back, their eyes glinting with excitement.

"You look like a warrior today, Aloo," said Tueke.

Heart pounding, Aloo managed to give them a shaky smile as he picked up the boat paddles.

"Don't worry about anything," Pipo whispered out of the corner of his mouth, nudging Aloo as the four of them walked out of the shadow of the trees. "Remember, I'll jump on the boat if the Great Mountain takes hold of you. The shaman will know what to say and do."

"Here comes Aloo." Maruku's voice boomed out across the beach.

"Nice looking boat, Coylaya," shouted Akawa, before downing another drink.

"Good work, Aloo," called Kuriji, a wide grin on his face.

Aloo nodded and smiled but his legs were trembling as he ran over to the canoe with Pipo, Tueke and Siwako.

Pipo gripped the rope tied to the bow and pulled the canoe gently off the coconut shell chocks, while Tueke and Siwako tossed aside the covering branches. The villagers gathered around, clapping and cheering, many of them already quite merry from the freely flowing woku.

"It's so pretty."

"Look at the dolphins."

"It's very small."

"Good for fishing."

"The paddles look rather slight."

"Looks like it will be fast."

Placing the paddles gently inside the boat, Aloo bent and held onto the side near the bow. Under his brows, he quickly scanned the crowd. Nimita, eyes shining, mouth curved in a rare smile. Waasha, throwing laughing glances at Kuriji. Erona, arms akimbo, beaming at Aloo. Welusi and Taima, nudging each other, gazes fixed on Tueke and Siwako.

Yurubi, nowhere to be seen.

"Ready?" Pipo said, looking across the bow at Aloo.

Aloo swallowed hard and nodded.

"Ready," Tueke and Siwako said in unison.

With the four of them pushing, the little boat slid easily over the sand to the water's edge, where the shaman and his two helpers were waiting.

As the shaman raised his maracas to begin the ceremony, Aloo glanced back quickly. Maruku, Kuriji, Akawa, Chief Oudou and most of the other men were strolling closer. Only the women and a few elders remained in the shade of the trees.

Still no sign of Yurubi.

The rattle of the shaman's maracas began, and the drums joined in.

"Spirit of the ocean, spirits of the warriors lying beneath, accept these offerings," the shaman intoned.

Reaching into a small basket at his feet, he tossed handfuls of food into the water. A school of little fish appeared, jostling close to the surface to nibble at the cassava bread, corn and chunks of roasted meat floating on the waves.

"Touch this new vessel, spirit of the ocean, bear its weight lightly on your bosom each time it comes to you," the shaman chanted.

This time he emptied a jar of woku into the water. Then he turned and nodded at Aloo.

With a wildly beating heart, Aloo bent again and took hold of the canoe. It hit the waves with a slap as he and his friends slid it into the water. Pipo quickly wrapped the rope around his hand to prevent the boat from plunging away.

Aloo was now thigh-deep in the water with the waves hitting his chest. His feet felt like rocks on the seabed.

The maracas and the drumming picked up, and the shaman's voice rose above a buzzing noise that was starting in Aloo's head. Not again, not now. Aloo swiped his wet hand over his face.

"Aloo, son of the Mountain Spirit, sends this canoe forth and gives it into the care of ..."

The rest was lost as the buzzing grew louder. Now there were shouts. And screams.

The rhythm of the drums and maracas grew frantic.

Eyes blurring, Aloo turned to Pipo. But Pipo was not looking at him. Neither were Tueke and Siwako. They were all gazing back over their shoulders, their faces slack. With a jolt, Aloo realized the screams and shouts were coming from behind him.

As he twisted around, a figure streaked past him and vaulted onto the boat.

Like a waking seagull, Aloo's heart flapped in befuddlement then took wing.

Yurubi stood lightly balanced on the rocking canoe, her body awash with the sprawling colours of the sunrise in front of her.

The orange light glinted off the bright feathers in her hair, the bow and arrows slung across her back, the knives hanging from her hips.

Then she turned.

The commotion behind Aloo faded into a distant roar. He could only touch her with his eyes, but he felt as if his lips were tracing the slashes of black paint across her smooth cheeks, the coral necklace nestled between her proud breasts, the shell ornaments encircling her slender waist, arms, wrists and ankles.

"For us," he whispered, as her eyes blazed down into his.

"Aloo, you kept this a close secret!" Pipo's voice penetrated the daze. "But, yes, she's the right one to take out the boat. She loves fishing. Why did she dress up like a warrior, though? Did you know I taught her to paddle? It was when ..."

The uproar came rushing back, drowning out Pipo's voice.

"She's carrying weapons!"

"What happened to her?"

"She's gone completely crazy!"

"Aloo gives this boat into the care of Yurubi!" The shaman's thin voice rose above the ruckus.

At those words, Yurubi's lips curved like a new moon. With one last glance that melted through Aloo, she swung around and picked up a paddle. Her long hair swaying across her back, her arms moving as rhythmically as the waves themselves, she paddled the canoe away from the shore.

The shouts became even more frenzied.

"Get her back here!"

"She's a woman!"

"We can't allow that!"

"I'll go get her."

Aloo tore his gaze away from Yurubi and spun around.

Garu was weaving across the sand, strands of hair plastered across his leering face.

Aloo clenched his teeth, every muscle in his body going taut. Drunk as Garu was, there was no telling what he'd try to do, even if he couldn't swim fast enough to catch Yurubi's boat.

"If he comes down here, I'll have to drown him," Pipo said under his breath.

"We'll help you," Siwako murmured.

"Then feed him to the fish," Tueke grunted.

Grinning like a frog going after a fly, Garu staggered down the beach but lurched to a standstill as the shaman stepped in front of him.

"Leave her alone," the shaman said, his voice like a cold splash of water dousing Garu's grin.

"Great One." Garu hiccupped and pointed unsteadily at Aloo. "He gave his boat to a wom'n." Garu's arm swept wide. "Look, a woman p'tending to be a warrior. Sh-she has arrows and a bow and—and ev'thing."

"She can't be a warrior," a man yelled. "She's a *woman*."

The shaman drew himself up, the curved bone ornament in his nose quivering.

"*All* Kalina are warriors," he said, baring his sparse yellow teeth.

Garu reared back and stumbled a few steps away.

A stunned silence fell over the crowd, and all eyes turned from the little boat out in the bay to the shaman. Standing there glaring at the men, the feathers in his hair askew, he looked like a ruffled hawk.

"All creatures of the Earth fight every day for survival," he said. "Some on land, some at sea, some on far shores. All fighters. Until one claims the other. Or until the spirits claim their own. The spirits have called to me, saying, 'We've marked this woman as ours.'"

A strangled cry like that of a dying parrot rose from somewhere on the beach. Aloo's eyes flicked over the crowd. Erona. Half hidden among a cluster of women who had drawn near after the commotion erupted. She clapped a hand over her mouth, her wide eyes pooling with tears. But the shaman seemed not to have noticed her. His gaze raked the crowd of sweating men, lingering on Garu.

"Who will dare defy the call of the spirits? Who will dare to touch her?"

The crash of the waves and squeals of children at play further up the beach seemed thunderous in the silence, as people looked in dismay from the shrinking figure in the boat to the shaman and back.

"Never heard of a woman warrior, though," someone mumbled after a while.

"Hush." Chief Oudou's voice, very soft. "The Great One has spoken. Let it be."

But the shaman wasn't done.

"Oh, you've never seen this, you've never heard that." He leaned forward, setting off a clatter of jewellery. "Have you looked over all the lands? Have you looked into all the depths of the sea? The ocean is wider than the land and holds great wisdom deep in her bosom."

Aloo's mouth twitched. This was going to take some time. With a jerk of his head at his friends, Aloo waded ashore and slipped around the back of the crowd. He found Erona and Waasha with their arms around each other's waists, their faces drawn in distress.

"Aloo," Erona mouthed, clutching his good arm, her eyes swimming in tears.

Not sure what to say, Aloo pressed her hand against his side and nodded toward the shaman, who was pointing with his maracas out to sea.

"Out there, under the waves, lurk some of the fiercest hunters and warriors," the shaman said. "Have you seen the killer dolphins? Beautiful to the eye, painted black and white by the ocean spirit, roaming in pods. Sometimes arcing above the waves, sometimes lurking below."

Some of the men nodded but they looked a bit puzzled. Aloo smiled. He knew what this story was about because the shaman had explained it carefully to him two nights ago.

The shaman turned his head, staring at the little boat riding the waves out in the bay.

"The leaders of the pod, the deadliest dolphins, are the females," he said, almost to himself.

As the men stood there dumbstruck, the shaman gestured to his two helpers, and they set off down the beach, sloshing through the frothy edges of the waves. Shaking his maracas and chanting under his breath, the shaman sprinkled handfuls of powder on the sand and into the water as he went.

Erona turned to Aloo, her lips trembling.

"He said the spirits have marked Yurubi," she whispered. She covered her mouth again, her shoulders heaving. "The maybouya. It's the maybouya again. I thought—"

"No, no, Erona," said Waasha softly. "That's not what he said." She pulled her sister close and steered her clear of the throng of people drifting back under the trees, talking in low voices about what just happened.

"... been plagued by a maybouya for a long time."

"Always a strange girl that ..."

"... spirits will take her soon."

"Don't listen to them," said Waasha, hugging Erona tighter.

Aloo wanted to help calm Erona's fears, tell her all that the shaman had said to him. But Aloo was not sure he could explain everything without giving away his steadfast burning desire to take Yurubi as his wife. *Leave it alone*, the shaman had said two nights ago, after Aloo had spilled all his uncertainty about his arm, the boat, and when he could ask for Yurubi as his wife.

She'll know when the fruit is ripe, the shaman had said. *Some women are chosen by the spirits.*

That's when he had explained about the predator dolphins. Afterward he had questioned Aloo about the boat, drawing from him the story of its building.

You finished the canoe for her? Then she must be the one to carry it forth to the ocean spirits. Leave it to me.

Even so, it had not crossed Aloo's mind that Yurubi would appear in full warrior garb. But he should've guessed that once she had the shaman on her side, there'd be no holding her back. He grinned wryly as he followed Erona and Waasha, who were walking closer to the water.

"Look, look at Yurubi paddle that boat," said Waasha, shaking Erona's arm gently. "I think what the shaman was saying is that she's marked as a hunter. Right, Aloo?"

Aloo nodded. "No one will bother Yurubi now. The shaman has spoken. He told me about the fierce dolphins, too. He talks strange sometimes. He means to say that Yurubi can be a woman warrior."

"See, that's what he means," said Waasha. She curled an arm around Erona's shoulders, lifting her chin as she gazed at the dwindling figure in the boat. "A woman warrior."

A TOUGH TASK

The sound of stone on stone rang out in the tiny hut on the edge of the women's compound. Sitting on the floor, Yurubi chipped away at a stone adze, trying to make the edge as thin as possible without weakening it. A breeze from the sea blew through the opening of the hut, ruffling her hair, which was kept off her face by a thin cotton cord tied around her forehead.

Yurubi smiled as she ran her finger over the edge of the stone adze. It was almost done. She needed to chip it just a little more, rub it with a chunk of pumice rock to make it nice and smooth, then grind the edge to a fine finish.

As she worked, a trickle of sweat ran down her chest, pooling under the zemi necklace the shaman had given to her. Despite the breeze, it was warm in the hut because of the small fire she always kept going to heat pieces of wood, bone and other materials.

The adze she was making was for Aloo. Not that he couldn't make his own. But Yurubi wished to give him something after all the trouble he'd taken to build this hut for her just the way she wanted it—on the far end of the women's compound, with the opening facing the sea.

Yurubi's hands stilled, and she tilted her head. Now that she was thinking about it, perhaps she simply wanted to give Aloo something that no one else would. Smiling at her whimsical thoughts, she picked up the pumice stone and began rubbing the adze. At least, Aloo would appreciate the careful work she was putting into this special tool. He and Pipo were the only two men in the village who would even touch any of the knives, axes, bows, arrows or spears that Yurubi made. Even Siwako and Tueke were reluctant because of the belief that it would bring bad luck to a man to touch a weapon made by a woman.

But Yurubi didn't care. The women loved her implements. They were all eager to get her thin-edged bone knives, small shell axes for chopping wood, fine-pointed digging sticks, boards dotted with sharp chips of stone for grating cassava, and light bone-tipped spears for river fishing.

Not that it had happened overnight.

Once again, she'd had to endure shocked stares, smiles of pity, glances of raw fear, and whispers about the maybouya. Then there were the grumbles about her knapping stone instead of tending the crops or helping with the women's other tasks. But as Ma, Waasha and Grandma Lulou began using Yurubi's tools, the other women soon grew curious. They'd drift over to Yurubi's new hut in twos and threes to watch her work, their faces agog, their eyes roving over the neatly stacked baskets of flint, stones, pieces of wood, reeds, bones, cords and other materials lining the hut. After a while, the women became bolder and started fingering Yurubi's knives.

Yurubi grinned, remembering the astounded look on Carika's face when she realized the knives were sharper, lighter and easier to use than those made by the men. After that, Yurubi couldn't make cutting tools for the women fast enough.

If she finished Aloo's adze today, she'd start on an axe for Welusi. Among the supplies in the baskets, there was bound to be a conch shell that would be perfect. Welusi had been hinting that she needed a new axe because she'd accidentally broken her old one. Whether or not Welusi had broken it by accident, Yurubi would make her a new one.

Yurubi put down the pumice stone and reached for her water mug, resting her gaze for a moment on the ocean, which was snarling at an indifferent sky.

A shadow bounced in front of the hut then went still. It was a woman's outline.

Yurubi chuckled.

"Welusi, I haven't started your axe yet," she called out.

The shadow remained motionless. Welusi was being coy, perhaps still a bit embarrassed because of the cowardly way she and Taima had distanced themselves from Yurubi after the boat launch. They'd get that petrified look on their faces every time she came near. But Yurubi wasn't holding that against them because she understood how the shaman's words could've scared many people. Even the men, brave warriors most of them, avoided looking at her or when they did, glanced at her out of the corner of their eyes in fear of the maybouya they thought had possessed her. Never mind that she could hunt and fish as well as any of them, or that she helped feed their families when the warriors were away on long expeditions. She was still treated like an outcast. But that was fine because the less attention the men paid her, the more freedom she had.

Yurubi shook her head and laughed softly.

"You'd better come in and help choose a shell," she called to the unmoving shadow outside her hut.

Slowly the shadow began to shorten, and a head poked around the opening of the hut.

Yurubi's back stiffened.

"It's me," said Nimita in a low voice, edging into the hut. "I—I came to see you."

Swallowing back the bitterness rising in her throat, Yurubi lifted her chin.

"Need a new knife?" she said, her voice sounding brittle to her own ears.

"No ... no," said Nimita, clenching her hands in front of her chest.

She hesitated for a moment, her eyes swivelling around the hut. Then her mouth thinned, and she darted forward. Yurubi went rigid, her fingers tightening around the pumice stone.

But Nimita dropped to her knees, her hair swinging across her face. "Help me, please," she whispered, her chin quivering.

With a jolt of surprise, Yurubi met Nimita's round eyes, which were clouded with anguish like a downed bird.

"Why, what's the matter?" Yurubi heard herself whisper.

"It's Aloo," said Nimita, covering her face with her hands.

A cold claw gripped Yurubi's insides. Aloo had left the day before on a trading trip to Wallibou, taking a route over the Great Mountain. *Up one side, down the other,* he'd said. *Back in four days.* Had something happened to—

"He doesn't come to my hut anymore," Nimita mumbled through her fingers. "Even though his arm has long healed."

Yurubi's breath gushed out of her mouth. Had she heard right? Heart drumming, she stared at Nimita's bent head.

"I'm so ashamed," Nimita sobbed. "I'm no good ... haven't given Aloo any sons ... I'm a bad wife and ... and that's why he ... he doesn't want to sleep in my hut any... more."

Slowly, Yurubi's fingers uncurled and the pumice stone dropped on the floor. She brought a hand to her chest, trying to quiet the clamouring in there. Aloo was safe. He was unhurt. That thought resounded above everything else. But like ants after a long rain, Nimita's words swarmed to the surface. Aloo had stopped sleeping in her hut.

Yurubi lifted her face to the breeze, allowing its tinge of lavender and lime blossoms to wash over her. She felt as if her feet were flying, her hair rippling behind her like a stream, as if she were in the forest chasing nothing but the promise of a pomegranate's sweet kisses—

"I want to go home." Nimita's anguished whisper broke through Yurubi's euphoria. "Please help me."

Yurubi blinked and leaned forward, searching Nimita's wet crumpled face. "What do you mean?"

Wiping her nose on the end of her loincloth, Nimita scooted closer. "You have a boat," she said, talking swiftly in a low voice. "You can go wherever you want. If you take me fishing with you one day, you can tell everyone I drowned. Or that we were attacked, and I was stolen."

Yurubi looked at her in disbelief. "What are you saying?"

"Please, help me get back to my island," said Nimita, gripping Yurubi's hands.

For the space of a heartbeat, Yurubi allowed herself to think about what that would mean. She saw again the trees breathing in great rushes, the yellow sunlight bouncing about like new butterflies, as Aloo bent his head close to hers, his shoulder brushing against her back, his breath feathering her neck.

But the next moment she fell back to earth as she met Nimita's tearful gaze. Drawing a tremulous breath, Yurubi disentangled her hands from Nimita's.

"I can't do that," Yurubi said half to herself.

"Oh, please," Nimita cried softly. "I'll give you anything." She looked around wildly, her eyes flitting over the frayed little hammock hanging across one corner of the hut. "I'll make you a new hammock. I'll make you loincloths, head bands, arm bands, leg bands, anything you want." She flung herself down onto her stomach and clutched Yurubi's feet. "Please, please, help me."

Yurubi's head jerked around as the distant sound of children's laughter floated into the hut.

"Nimita, get up before someone comes and sees you like this," said Yurubi, drawing her feet away.

Nimita didn't know what she was saying. She really was just a young girl, barely old enough to be a wife. It was no use explaining to her that the canoe was just a little fishing boat not made for long trips, or that two women alone on the open seas would soon be attacked by raiders.

"Listen, you cannot go back home," Yurubi said, as Nimita sat up and covered her wet face again with her hands. "You were brought here as... as a wife for Aloo. You were traded, not captured. You can't go back. You'll shame your people."

"I don't care!" cried Nimita, tears leaking through her fingers. "I'll do something outrageous when I get there, and everyone will think a bad spirit has taken hold of me. Then they'll leave me alone, and I'll do whatever I want—"

Nimita's hands slipped down over her open mouth, and she stared at Yurubi with bulging eyes.

"Yurubi, I-I'm so-sorry, I di-didn't mean ..."

As Nimita's voice trailed off, Yurubi shook her head and picked up the pumice stone. She bent over the adze again, rubbing it with force.

"Why don't you go see the shaman?" she ground out between her teeth. "Perhaps he can help you. Just like he helped me."

"But I'm afraid of him," Nimita whispered, her mouth trembling. She crept closer to Yurubi. "Will you go with me?"

Yurubi's hands paused, and she closed her eyes.

Nimita was so exasperating it was no use even getting angry at her. And she had no idea what she was asking. But she was not the smug wife Yurubi always thought her to be. She was a timid little creature who seemed lost and ashamed. She didn't know that Aloo had stopped going to her hut because he and Yurubi had tentatively become friends again, and he was hoping—

Quashing that thought, Yurubi opened her eyes to find Nimita slumped over, head between her knees, her shoulders shaking.

"Alright," Yurubi said with a sigh, "I'll go with you."

EARLY MORNING QUEST

Yurubi walked quickly in the semi-dark, glancing back over her shoulder occasionally to make sure Nimita was following. Although the sun was not yet up, Yurubi could feel rivulets of sweat trickling down her back as the thick air pulsed against her like a huge animal.

As she neared the shaman's hut, she broke into a jog, hoping to get this over with before the whole village came awake.

"Yurubi, wait!"

She swung around to see Nimita standing still, arms wrapped around her middle. Letting out a sigh, Yurubi ran back to her.

"I'm afraid," whispered Nimita, her eyes gleaming white in the darkness. "What if he—"

"No need to be frightened," Yurubi repeated for about the fifth time since they set off. "He's a kind shaman. He'll try to help you, but we've got to hurry before he goes into the hills. He likes to leave early."

She grabbed Nimita's cold hand and started walking again. When the shaman's hut came into view, Yurubi slowed down and tightened her grip on Nimita's fingers.

"Great One," she called softly, creeping forward. "It's Yurubi."

She had to call from a distance whenever she was visiting the shaman because she didn't want to upset him by getting too close when he was performing his rituals.

There was no answer. Yurubi edged closer, tugging a shivering Nimita along.

"Great One!" Yurubi called again, a bit louder this time.

Still no sound from the hut, only the faint smell of a pungent herb the shaman usually smoked.

"He must've left already," Yurubi said to Nimita after a while. "We'll have to come back another day."

As they turned away, Nimita's shoulders sagged, probably in relief, but she continued to clutch Yurubi's fingers.

"Yurubi!"

Yurubi spun around at the raspy voice, wincing as Nimita's nails dug into her hand.

The shaman was standing in the opening of the hut, his hair straggled about his face, his ornaments and charms askew on his shrivelled chest.

"What's wrong? Is someone hurt?" he said in a sharp tone.

"No ... no ..." said Yurubi, taken aback by his abruptness. "It's Nimita—she came to ask for your help because ... because she hasn't been able to have any babies."

The shaman's eyes flicked from Yurubi to Nimita and back, his mouth tightening.

"No time for this now," he snapped. "The spirits are gathering. I must hurry."

He turned back inside the dark hut, muttering to himself.

A wave of heat washed over Yurubi. "Don't know what's wrong with him today," she said under her breath, her throat thick with humiliation.

"Let's just go," Nimita whispered, cowering behind Yurubi. "He's scary."

"He's not sca—"

Yurubi bit back the words, not sure how to explain the shaman's crabbiness today. "Sometimes he's busy with spirits and things like that. We can try again another day."

They set off again, Nimita practically running ahead this time. She truly was terrified of the shaman. It might be best if Aloo brought her next time because the shaman tended to treat him like a son and wouldn't bite his head off. Yurubi looked back over her shoulder, still confused about the shaman's behaviour. Since she had openly become a hunter and boatwoman, she'd been going to him at least twice in every moon for special protection because she couldn't join the regular rituals that were held for the men. He was sometimes grumpy or distracted but had never snapped at her like that. What bug had bitten him this morning? Was it because she had taken Nimita to see him?

Yurubi daubed at the sweat prickling her forehead and slowed her pace, allowing Nimita to hurry back to the village ahead of her.

Aloo could easily accompany Nimita next time. Except that Nimita hadn't told him anything about what was troubling her. She probably didn't realize that Aloo was different from most other men, that he would listen to her. Perhaps when Aloo returned from Wallibou today with presents for Nimita, she'd pour out her heart to him. He'd hold himself still, listening quietly, his eyes moving over her face, searching beyond her words.

Yurubi kicked at a snail's shell in her path. She would not allow those stinging tentacles to writhe to life inside her today. She skirted the women's dwellings, where there were sounds of people coming awake, and ducked inside her work hut. She quickly gathered up her bow and arrows, strapped a hunting knife on each hip and grabbed a small basket.

With a brief glance at the muddled sky, she strode through the opening of her hut and turned toward the river.

"Yurubi, you're going hunting today?" Waasha sounded somewhat anxious as Yurubi hurried past.

With a quick nod, Yurubi waved and began running. The voices of some early risers followed her down the path.

"Bring back a nice plump agouti!"

"Or an iguana!"

"…some parrots!"

A faint smile cracked Yurubi's lips as she caught that last bit. It was nothing more than good-natured teasing because everyone knew she refused to kill parrots, although the meat was a great favourite among the women. Yurubi simply could not bring herself to aim an arrow at the big birds that looked like they'd been dipping in every flower in the land and sometimes seemed to be talking to her when she was alone in the forest.

Leaping across the rocks, Yurubi crossed the river. She dropped her basket and weapons on the bank and slipped into the water, revelling in its cool rush against her body. When she emerged and began climbing the slope into the forest, she felt like she was shedding some of the worry about Aloo, Nimita and the shaman.

There was an unusual hush in the forest, as if all the creatures were holding their breath. But Yurubi could almost feel them pulsating around her.

Taking a familiar path, she walked slowly in the dim light, her gaze flicking from side to side, from the forest floor to the tree branches and back. Not that she was sensing any immediate danger. It was simply a survival instinct she had learned after she started venturing deeper and deeper into the forest on her own. Some creatures, especially snakes, were very clever at blending into their surroundings. Then there were those black boars that sometimes hid in the undergrowth, waiting for unsuspecting prey. And Yurubi could still remember the agony of treading on a fire ant nest.

She stopped to pick a handful of dew-misted berries and watch two brown lizards fighting at the base of a tree. Legs splayed, they snapped at each other, whipping their tails like weapons. But soon they went into a cinch that looked more like an embrace, and they stopped moving.

Yurubi tossed a berry at them and grinned as they broke apart and scuttled away into the undergrowth.

She stuffed the last of the berries into her mouth, plucked some leaves to wipe her hands, and shifted the small basket strap on her forehead. Should she keep going along the river or veer inland?

Although the sun had barely risen, the forest was already steamy, and sweat was trickling down between Yurubi's breasts again. On a day like this, it might be a bit cooler on the thickly wooded slopes further inland. Tightening her loincloth, Yurubi set off again.

Meandering up and down the hills, Yurubi could feel the forest enfolding her, absorbing her into its teeming milieu like one of its own.

She was scrabbling through the bushes at the foot of a slope when she caught a swift movement halfway up a huge beetwood tree. Wiping her brow with her upper arm, she reached back over her shoulder for an arrow. She stood perfectly still, her bow held ready, her eyes searching the different hues of green draped down the trunk of the tree.

There it was! A tongue flicked out from behind the vines, and Yurubi sent an arrow flying in its direction. There was a thud as the arrow struck the tree, and the next moment a ruckus broke loose.

The creepers shook violently, and leaves began flying everywhere as a rapid thumping erupted.

Yurubi fitted another arrow into her bow and crept out of the bushes, keeping a distance from the tree because she still could not see what was behind the shuddering vines. She slid around to her right then stopped as she saw a gap in the creepers. She leaned forward, narrowing her eyes.

Behind the thick drape of vines, a long tail was beating frantically against the tree trunk. As Yurubi edged closer, she saw a huge iguana skewered head down on the tree by her heavy arrow, its body wrenching from side to side, its spines raised in anger.

Yurubi lowered her bow and let out her breath. She had to find a way to get the iguana down. But first …

She reached back into her quiver, her fingers searching for a special thin arrow. Moving to the base of the tree directly under the flailing iguana, she took slow and careful aim, trying to ignore its menacing blood-red eyes and the forked tongue darting from its open mouth. The slim sharp arrow caught the iguana under its neck, and its movements slowly subsided.

Yurubi set down her basket and bow and squatted under the massive tree, eyeing its straight trunk. She had learned to climb when she was a child and, unlike most other girls, had never lost interest. In fact, she had spent a lot of time in this very forest trying to compete with Aloo as he slithered up and down trees and rock faces like a lizard. But this beetwood tree was going to be a challenge. The iguana was pinned on the trunk at a point about four times Yurubi's height, and the branches didn't start until much higher up.

Shrugging off her quiver, she stood and grabbed some of the thick creepers on the tree trunk, but each time she tugged them, they either broke or came loose.

Walking slowly outward from the tree, Yurubi began testing the strength of the long vines hanging from the branches until she found one that seemed strong enough to bear her weight. She turned and folded her lips, eying the distance to the trunk. This was going to be tricky.

Reaching up high, Yurubi began climbing hand over hand on the thick vine, her legs wrapped around it.

When she got to eye level with the iguana, she straightened her body, gripping the vine tightly with her hands and feet and started swinging, trying to gain enough momentum to reach the tree. High above, a squawking flock of parrots seemed to be cheering her on.

As she swung closer to the tree, Yurubi leaned out and tried to grab the shaft of the arrow but could only brush it with her fingertips. On an outswing, she pulled herself higher on the vine, brought her knees up and kicked her legs hard.

As she whizzed toward the tree, she leaned out and managed to grab the arrow briefly but couldn't pull it free.

Yurubi gripped the vine with both hands again, swaying slowly as she tried to think of a better way. All this swinging high above the ground was exhilarating, and she could do it for the rest of the day, but she needed to get that iguana down.

She tipped her head back, squinting up at the parrots that were flapping about in the treetops, keeping up their raucous cheering.

"Why don't you all come down here and help me?" she said with a laugh.

Tensing her arms and legs, Yurubi began swinging again. Then she arched her body, gave a powerful kick and zoomed in toward the tree. Reaching out at full stretch, she grabbed the arrow and wrenched it sideways, snapping off the end with the fletching.

Yurubi smiled in triumph and dropped the broken bit to the ground.

"Got you noooow," she sang as she worked her legs again and hurtled toward the iguana, her hair lifting off her shoulders.

Holding on with one hand, she stretched her entire body, her right hand reaching for the iguana. Her fingers closed around the tip of the scaly tail and she yanked hard. The iguana came free of the broken arrow shaft and dropped to the ground with a thud.

Yurubi threw back her head and joined the cawing of the parrots. But as she swung away from the tree, she felt the vine slip. She clutched it tightly with both hands, its ripping sound reaching into the pit of her stomach as the leering face of the iguana rushed up to meet her.

OUT IN THE OPEN

The waterfall thundered against the rocks, its cold sharp spray raising bumps on her skin.

On the other side of the shimmering cascade, Aloo was frolicking in the pool, silver cascades streaming from his hair, shoulders and arms with every move. He turned and beckoned to her, his smile so wide she felt she could live in it forever.

"I'm coming to you," she mouthed at him silently through the rush of the waterfall.

As he arched again like an ecstatic dolphin, her breath snagged on the scent of new flowers, wet foliage, and damp earth. The smell of their special place.

She braced her body, preparing to slide under the waterfall and into the pool with Aloo, but her legs seemed stuck between the rocks. She twisted sideways, but the movement sent a burst of pain through her head, and she still couldn't free her legs.

"Aloo!" she shouted above the roaring in her ears. "There's something …" Her eyelids fluttered and a blurry canopy of green wavered above her.

"Aloo," she called weakly, beckoning to him with fingers that felt thick and sticky.

But he had disappeared.

The sound of the waterfall was pounding in her head, and she couldn't move away.

She started as a loud crack split the air. Wiping a hand across her eyes, she strained to see what was happening, but everything had become blurred. With a massive effort, she twisted to the side and almost jumped out of her skin when a huge lizard appeared in front of her.

Lifting her strangely heavy arms, she daubed at her eyes again and tried to fix her murky gaze on the grinning creature.

An iguana, it seemed. Why was it playing so close to her, though? She blinked hard, trying to clear her eyes, and looked around in befuddlement at the piles of green branches everywhere.

Shivering in the stinging cold spray, she turned her head again and stared at the iguana. Splayed on its stomach, it was sloshing about in a mud bath, its tongue hanging out.

The iguana!

She had shot it with a big arrow, skewered it to a tree. How did it get here—?

With a groan, Yurubi flung her arm over her eyes. This was not the waterfall. And Aloo was not here.

Not the waterfall. Still, there was that rushing sound in her ears and the splash of water on her body.

Water?

Slowly Yurubi lowered her arm, squinting through the deluge. Rain was pelting down through the wildly yawing treetops, stinging her face and chest. The roaring in her head was punctured by cracks and snaps as a fierce wind tore at the tree branches.

A sudden chill gripped Yurubi. How long had she been here? She scrabbled in the dirt, trying to raise herself, but her hands slipped in a trough of mud, and she fell back with a splat. She closed her eyes as a sharp pain seared through her head.

Moving more carefully this time, Yurubi sank her knuckles into the mud and slowly pushed herself into a sitting position. For a moment, the forest tilted crazily, and Yurubi's throat tightened in panic, but everything soon righted itself, and she let out a ragged breath. Perhaps too soon. Looking around, she felt as if she had landed in a completely different place when she fell.

She was sitting in a pool of mud, raindrops bouncing off her head like pebbles, gritty water streaming down her face and dripping off her chin. Near her, twigs, leaves and insects floated in a web of rivulets. The iguana, half submerged in the mud, looked soggy and bloated. Green branches were strewn all around, and foliage was flying everywhere, chased by a snarling wind.

Yurubi's head was throbbing so hard, it felt like a grinding stone. Moaning deep in her throat, she threaded her muddy fingers through her dripping hair and grimaced as she touched a bump the size of a turtle egg on the back of her head. She rubbed her fingers over her scalp gingerly and then looked at her hands. There was no blood, which was a relief. It was time to go home.

Holding her pounding head, Yurubi tried to stand but couldn't get her legs to move. She leaned forward and tossed aside some of the greenery strewn over her lower body. She tugged at one of the bigger branches near her legs, but it wouldn't budge. Glancing up into the trees, she saw the raw scar of a broken branch that looked frighteningly big. Fighting back a growing sense of alarm, Yurubi dug her heels into the dirt and wriggled her body, but when she tried to slide her legs out from under the foliage, her knees jammed painfully against the branch.

She bit her lip and leaned forward again, straining to lift the branch but couldn't get enough leverage. With a groan, she sat back, holding her head, which felt as heavy as a huge green calabash. As if that was not enough, her stomach was rumbling, and her throat felt parched. Yurubi plucked two big leaves from the fallen branches near her and stuck one in either side of her mouth, tilting them slightly upward to catch the raindrops.

As the cool rainwater trickled into her mouth, she tried to calm her breathing, to dull her ears to the roaring of the wind through the trees and quash any thoughts of crawling creatures converging on her in the fast approaching darkness.

Despite herself, her eyes were drawn to a furtive movement in the bushes near her. With a shudder, Yurubi looked away and bent double, peering instead at the thick branch resting on her legs just above the knees. She wriggled her toes, rotated her ankles and tensed her calves. Nothing hurt, but she wasn't sure if that was good or bad.

As best she could tell, the heavy branch was propped up on two protrusions that seemed to have sunk slowly into the earth as the torrential rain softened the ground over the course of the day. Now she was trapped under the branch, an easy target for any predator that might come along.

Yurubi glanced at the iguana, which seemed to be staring back at her with mocking eyes.

"What are you looking at?" she muttered. "It's not as if you're doing that well yourself." She wrinkled her nose. "You're dirty, smelly *and* bloated. Not to mention," she dropped her voice, "you're *dead.*"

The iguana continued to grin inanely at her. Rolling her eyes, Yurubi covered her face with her hands and flopped back on the wet ground, shutting out the sight of the iguana that had caused her so much trouble. What was wrong with her? A maybouya must have taken hold of her while she was knocked out. Why else would she be talking to a dead creature? She should be trying instead to listen for the voices of the spirits. She held herself still, listening hard, but all she could hear was the splatter of the rain and the roar of the wind.

Through her fingers, she could see the trees bending this way and that, giving glimpses of the darkening sky. Warm tears leaked out of the corners of her eyes, mingling with the cold raindrops.

Who would dare to cross the river in this storm and come looking for her in the dark? Who would even be able to find her in this forest at night? Aloo? Yes, Aloo. But what if he was still in Wallibou or didn't even know she had gone hunting today?

What had gotten into her anyway? Running off like that without even packing some cassava bread, thinking she could never go hungry in the forest once she had her bow and arrows and her knives.

The knives! Yurubi's hands flew to her sides. They were both still there. Heart leaping, she sat up and withdrew the knives from their wicker sheaths. She held them tightly, her mind racing as she looked at the long thin blades and sturdy handles she'd crafted herself.

Carefully, she returned the knives to their sheaths and wiped her face. Bending forward, she parted the leaves to look more closely at the thick branch. She'd never tried cutting or splitting a branch this size with a knife, but she didn't have a lot of choices right now. She ran her fingers over every part of the knobby bark she could reach, searching for cracks in the branch. Nothing.

Yurubi blew a puff of air through her mouth and leaned back, propping herself up on her hands.

It would take a long time to hack through that branch, even if the knives held up. How much longer could she sit here without being attacked by some creature? Then there was the very real danger of another branch or an entire tree crashing down on her in this vicious wind.

She shifted slightly as she felt her palms sinking deeper into the mud. The ground beneath her was fast turning into slush, not just from the rain but also the runoff from the nearby hill.

Yurubi straightened up with a start.

She held her hands in front of her, gazing at the thick mud on her palms. An idea was flitting through her mind, but would it work?

With a quick glance at the sky to see how much light she had left, Yurubi wiped her muddy hands on her thighs, on her soaked loincloth and then on some green leaves.

Closing her eyes, she tilted her head back and let the rain beat down on her face, washing away some of the dirt. Then she withdrew the knife on her right hip and leaned forward again, her heart thumping.

Gripping the knife tightly in her slippery fingers, she began digging away the soggy earth close to the outside of her right knee. When a small pile of dirt built up, she scooped it up with both hands and tossed it behind her. As she wiped her hands again and picked up the knife, she noticed a little rivulet off to her right. She swiftly dug a small drain to channel the water into the trench she was scooping out under her leg.

Bent almost double, with the rain beating down on her back, Yurubi deepened and lengthened the furrow, working toward her calf and straining to her heel. Sometimes she had to reach over the top of the branch, and at other times she had to squeeze her arm under it, digging on the outside of her leg, then on the inside, and back again.

The trickle of water she had diverted under her leg was softening the earth, but at times she had to dislodge stones and hack through strands of tough roots. Her biggest worry, apart from the danger of falling branches overhead and crawling creatures, was that she'd slash herself in the fading light or lose the knife as she stretched her arms to their limit. The other knife was still secure on her left hip, but she was hoping to save that, to keep it intact and sharp, for her trek home.

She could feel the sting of some nicks on her leg but had no time to worry about that.

Pausing for a moment to wet her dry throat, Yurubi wriggled her right leg and found that it was no longer pressed up tightly against the branch. There was not enough room, though, to bend her knee, which meant she'd have to free the other leg before she could slide out from under the fallen tree limb.

She wiped her hands again, this time on her wet hair, and leaned to the left, starting on another trench. As before, she made a shallow drain to bring in some water. Somewhere behind her, there was a cracking sound, and she whipped her head around.

"Ayye!" Yurubi yelped as the wet knife slipped in her mud-slick hands and slashed her knee.

The next instant, a huge branch crashed to the ground behind her, spattering dirt against her back. Yurubi's heart thundered in her ears, and she could feel warm blood running down the side of her knee from the cut.

She looked up fearfully into the thrashing treetops as the voice of the wind changed from a howl to a scream. This was no regular storm. A thought cut through her mind like a hot blade. Was this what the shaman was talking about when he said the spirits were gathering? Yurubi clutched the charm hanging between her breasts. The shaman had said it would give her protection both on land and at sea. She hoped with all her heart that he was right.

Moving swiftly, Yurubi scooped up a handful of mud and plastered it over the cut on her knee, trying to stem the flow of blood. Her hands came away covered in a gooey mess that she wiped quickly on the ends of her hair. She grabbed the knife and bent again to her task, this time digging with one hand and scooping with the other. She'd seen the women doing something similar with their digging sticks when they were planting certain crops, but she'd never quite mastered it. Her clumsy efforts would have to do today.

The knife clanged against a stone and fell from her hands. She blinked raindrops out of her eyes and groped around in the mud under her left leg, feeling for the stone. Using both hands, she worked it loose, and when she eventually lifted it out, she felt the pressure on her left leg ease somewhat. She loosened some more dirt around her knee with the knife, then scooped it out quickly and twisted her leg from side to side.

She jammed the knife back into its sheath and braced herself on her hands, trying to drag her lower body backward. Her left knee was still wedged.

Yurubi slid forward again and turned both legs inward, her big toes pressing down to the ground. Slowly, she eased her body back again. Her legs scraped roughly against the branch but slid all the way out. She was free!

Heart racing, Yurubi scrambled to her feet, but her legs folded under her and she collapsed again.

"What—?"

She couldn't feel her legs, she realized. They were cold and numb, except for some slight thorn pricks now starting in her feet. There was no time to wait this out. Dark was closing in on her. She'd have to do it the hard way. Rubbing her hands briskly together to warm them, she drew her legs up and began kneading the muscles, wincing as the thorn pricks spread like fire from her feet, up her calves to her thighs.

Yurubi slapped another handful of mud over the cut on her leg, flexed her knees and ankles, and stood up again. She was ready to move. She hesitated for a moment, eyeing the iguana, but shuddered at the thought of even touching that bloated carcass.

She rummaged through the pile of branches under the beetwood tree until she found her bow, arrows and basket then set off at a run through the writhing forest.

Long before she reached the river, Yurubi could hear its deep rumble above the roar of the wind and the incessant rush of the rain beating down through the trees. She was running like an agouti in full flight, dodging branches, bounding over fallen tree trunks, sliding down slopes, leaping over new streams. The wind tore at her, sometimes toppling her, but each time she'd spring up and set off again without a break.

"I'm a warrior, I'm a warrior," she chanted through her teeth as she raced against the fading light.

At one point, she lost her footing and tumbled down an embankment. She curled tightly into a ball and rolled to the bottom of the slope. With hardly a pause, she was up and running again, her entire body slick with mud.

Under all that mud, she was covered in scratches, cuts and bruises, but that was the least of her worries. Her foremost concern was how to get across the swollen river. She knew that when the river overflowed its banks, it sometimes washed out full-grown trees, which would move more slowly in the swift current than dried logs. If she could grab the branches of a floating tree, it might eventually carry her to the other bank. Or, she could try to ride it until it snagged somewhere in a deep bend of the river, and hopefully she could make her way to the other bank.

Spotting a break in the trees up ahead, she broke into a smile, giddy with relief that she had made it to the river before—

"Whaaaaaa!"

Yurubi skidded to halt, a ripple of shock coursing through her. Wrapping one arm around a small tree to steady herself in the fierce wind, she rubbed her hand over her face, shook her head and stared again. In front of her was a mountain of raging brown water, the likes of which she had never seen before. The river was foaming, kicking, spitting, roaring and rumbling like an enraged creature. It had climbed the near bank and was swirling through the trees, edging closer to where Yurubi stood rooted in awe. Logs, big trees, bunches of coconuts, and dead animals swept past like twigs, while huge boulders tumbled through the dark brown melee, bashing against each other in a ferocious non-stop battle.

Peering across the river through the slanting rain and kicking spray, Yurubi could see only a deepening grey haze on the far side. Clinging to the little tree, her hair whipping about her face, she felt a rock drop into her stomach. There was no way she could get across now. She'd have to spend the night here on this side of the river.

With a shiver, Yurubi looked back into the darkening forest. Not only would she have to find a place to hole up, she'd have to go deeper into the trees beyond the reach of the rising water.

With one more yearning glance at the foggy, darkening hillside across the river, she got down on her hands and knees and crept to the edge of the brown water that was lapping at the tree roots. Cupping her hands, she splashed her head and face then washed the rest of her body as best she could, using a handful of leaves to scrub away the caked mud. That would have to do for now. The rain would do the rest.

Yurubi staggered back into the forest, racking her brain to think of a place that would provide shelter from the wind and falling branches. The snapping overhead reminded her of the most imminent danger. If only she could find a cave. But the ones she knew of on this side of the river were deep in the forest along a steep rock face. A rock shelter of any kind would do.

She moved as fast as she could in the dark, heading north, trying to recall exactly where she had seen those two huge rocks leaning against each other, partly covered in moss and vines. She remembered clambering to the top of them one day when she was searching for some thin but strong fibres to secure an adze handle.

It would have been easy to find the place in the daytime when she could see the landmarks. But now, not only was the forest dark, everything was obscured by the pelting rain, and Yurubi was being battered by the increasingly ferocious wind snarling through the trees.

She staggered along in what she hoped was the right direction, trying to ignore her growling stomach. She had to get under cover as soon as possible if she was to survive the night. As she ran, her eyes swivelled from side to side at the fearful sound of branches cracking and crashing at intervals.

Using the rumbling of the river on her right as a guide, she veered slightly inland, still maintaining her northward trek. Bent almost double against the wind, she was tripping over roots and stones, slipping on wet leaves, and crashing into low bushes in her haste. The cut on her knee had opened up again, and she could feel the warm blood running down her leg.

"I'm a warrior, I'm a warrior," she gasped again, trying to drown out the ominous thought of treading on a snake. "I'm a war—uukk!" Yurubi smacked into an obstacle and fell on her back, but the fall was broken by her basket. With a groan, she jumped to her feet and put out both hands, feeling for whatever was blocking her path. A frantic hope raced through her as her fingers touched a rough rock surface. Could this be it? Yurubi scrabbled around in the dark, running her hands over the rock and realizing with growing excitement that it was tall and slanting. She leapt back as something long and wet slapped her in the face. She brought a hand up to her forehead, her heart thumping, her eyes boring into the darkness.

Another smack! This time on the side of her head.

Yurubi's hand shot out, instinctively grabbing at a swaying outline and flinging it violently away from her. She stood motionless for a moment then leaned her forehead against the rock, a shaky laugh bubbling up in her chest. It was only a string of thick vines blowing in the wind. Not a snake.

Drawing a shuddering breath, she worked her way around the tall rock and soon felt the surface of another one across a small gap. A wave of relief washed over her.

She crouched down, peering into the small coal black space between the rocks. She fumbled around on the ground until she found a long stick. Poking it into the crevice, she beat it from side then waited for a bit but could detect no movement in there. She unstrapped her basket and her quiver of arrows then squeezed into the space and pulled her things in behind her. There was just enough room for her to stand bent almost double or to sit with her legs stretched out.

Still apprehensive, Yurubi dragged the stick back and forth across the ground, clearing away what seemed to be twigs and leaves. Not taking any chances, she swept her hands over the space she had cleared. Gingerly, she sat on the wet ground. She could try to light a fire, but that might be futile because everything was soaked.

With the stick in one hand and a knife in the other, Yurubi rested her head wearily against the rock, listening to the storm raging overhead.

THE FIST OF THE STORM

The thin watery sunlight was already dribbling away when Yurubi limped up the path to the village. She spat out some grit and daubed at her face, wiping away some of the muddy water streaming from her hair. Her entire body felt like one massive bruise after yesterday's spills and the battering she had just endured during her terrible crossing.

Although the river had dropped considerably from the night before, it was still a swift muddy torrent. She'd spent most of the day foraging for fruit in the soggy bedraggled forest, waiting for the current to slow down. When she'd finally plucked up the courage to launch herself into the raging brown water far upstream, the current had picked her up like a twig, ripping away her tattered loincloth, pummelling and spitting at her, tossing her against logs and rocks and pulling her under at times.

With one of the knives clenched in her teeth, she had battled mightily, swimming hard for the other bank. She had made it to shore way downstream from the village and had clambered up the hill, naked and shivering, her hair plastered to her back and shoulders. The cut on her knee had turned puffy red and was throbbing with each step she took.

At the top of the path, she stopped suddenly as she saw Siwako standing there, holding an axe.

"Siwako!" Her voice came out in a croak, but her heart was leaping at the sight of another villager.

Siwako's eyes rested on her briefly then slid away.

"You made it," he said in a dull voice.

Taken aback by his listless greeting, Yurubi nodded and walked on. After her ordeal in the forest and the river, it would've been nice to see a welcoming smile, at least.

She entered the clearing to the women's compound and stopped dead in her tracks. Not a single structure was standing anywhere. A few women, some of them also naked, were slowly picking through a tangle of tree branches, sticks, wood, hammocks and utensils. The small children were slithering around in a mud hole where the big flame tree used to be.

In her desperate attempts to get home, Yurubi hadn't even considered that the terrible storm would've ravaged the village too, not just the forest. She hobbled toward the group of women, her eyes searching for Ma.

"Yurubi," said Carika, straightening up. She swept an arm around in a helpless gesture. "It was very bad. There was—"

Her voice faltered, and she rested a hand on Yurubi's shoulder.

Yurubi felt tears pricking at the back of her eyes. It had indeed been bad. But here was Carika of the sharp tongue being kind to her.

"Where's Ma?" Yurubi said, blinking hard as she looked across the piles of debris.

"Errm, over there," said Carika, pointing vaguely in the direction of the men's compound. Her eyes shifted to the left, and a look of relief washed over her face. "Oh, there's Waasha. She'll take you to—"

"Yurubi!"

At the sound of Waasha's voice, Yurubi turned and ran into her arms. Without a word, Waasha hugged her tight, which only caused Yurubi's tears to spill over.

"I have to go find Ma," Yurubi mumbled into Waasha's neck. "She must be so worried."

"Come, Yurubi, come with me," Waasha said softly, turning Yurubi in the direction of the men's compound and keeping an arm around her shoulders.

"The hurricane flattened everything," Waasha said, speaking fast as they picked their way across the yard. "We ran for the hills, going as deep into the trees as we could to find shelter from the wind but ... but ..."

Waasha's voice broke, and she passed a hand over her face.

"It … it was very dark … we lost some…"

Yurubi stopped and turned to look into Waasha's flooded eyes. A cold droplet of water trickled down Yurubi's spine.

"What are you saying, Waasha?"

Waasha shook her head, tears running down her face.

"We found her this afternoon … too late … It-it was a big tree…"

A clammy hand crept around Yurubi's heart.

"Who?" she whispered.

Waasha's mouth trembled.

"Nooooo!" Yurubi shrieked. "Noooooo!"

She doubled over, clutching her stomach as a white-hot pain knifed through her.

"Not Ma," she choked out. "Tell me not Ma."

Waasha's arms closed around her and raised her upright. Yurubi's knees crumpled and she sagged against Waasha, shuddering as wave after wave of dizziness washed over her.

"Come, I'll take you to her," Waasha whispered, half dragging, half carrying Yurubi to a small clearing beyond the flattened men's compound.

Through her blurred and streaming eyes, Yurubi spotted Ma lying on the wet grass next to two other people. With a visceral cry, Yurubi broke away from Waasha and flung herself on Ma's bosom.

"Maaaaa!" She pushed her head under her mother's chin like she used to do as a child when she'd wake up in the middle of the night.

But this time Ma's arms remained at her side and her bosom was cold and unyielding under Yurubi's cheek. A massive fish hook was tearing at Yurubi's insides, ripping away her breath in heaving gasps, dangling her over a dark precipice. She dug her fingers into Ma's stiff shoulders and screamed, over and over, until the gaping darkness finally swallowed her.

As from a great distance, she heard a voice calling her name.

"Ma," she whimpered.

"Shhh, shhhh, she's close by." Waasha's soft voice.

She held Yurubi close, rocking her gently. They were lying on the damp ground under a rough ajoupa that barely kept off the rain dripping from the dark sky.

"At daybreak, we'll go pick a spot for our new hut, and we'll put her there."

Yurubi's insides twisted at the thought of putting Ma under the ground. Her tears began to flow again, drenching Waasha's shoulder.

"I-I left her," Yurubi sobbed. "I-I ran off like a s-silly girl and left M-Ma to d-die."

"Shhh, shhhh. You didn't run off, Yurubi. You went hunting, like you always do, to bring us meat."

Yurubi groaned as the bloated iguana floated before her eyes again. "N-no, you d-don't un- understand." She gulped hard, forcing back the tears. "The shaman tried to warn me. He told me the spirits were gathering. But I was too silly, unable to bear the thought of Nimita giving Aloo—" She sat up with a start, bumping her head against the sloping cover of coconut branches. "Aloo! Where's Aloo?"

"With the shaman." Waasha took her hand.

Yurubi's breath stopped.

"He's injured?"

"No, no, but—"

"Why didn't he look out for Ma?"

"He was—He had some other things to do." Waasha stroked her hand. "Yurubi—"

"What could be more pressing than taking care of Ma?" Yurubi pulled her hand away. "She took him as a son."

"Yurubi—"

"Never mind, Waasha." Yurubi's shoulders slumped, and her tears started again.

It was easy to fan her anger at Aloo, but she was the one to blame. She should've been here to take care of Ma, instead of flitting off into the forest like a skittish butterfly.

Yurubi hung her head between her knees and sobbed. The pain in her chest was spreading through her entire body.

"Come, rest for a while, Yurubi. Soon, the sun will rise."

Unable to speak, Yurubi shook her head and cried even harder. Perhaps she'd die from this agony in her chest, and she'd go under the ground with Ma.

Waasha sat up and curled an arm around Yurubi's heaving shoulders.

"The wind from the mountain runs cool through your hair, sometimes it goes roaming, whistling without care, but always returns, to run cool through your hair," Waasha sang softly, leaning her head against Yurubi's.

"M-Ma's s-song," Yurubi moaned.

"When I was a little girl, she used to sing it to me too," said Waasha. "We lost our mother when we were young. The river took her. At the time, Grandma Lulou was visiting from Imayarou, and she came to stay in the hut with me and Erona after our mother was put under the floor. The days turned into moons, but Grandma Lulou was in no hurry to return to her village. She taught me and Erona to cook, to grind corn and cassava, and later to weave and plant. But it was Erona—" Waasha's voice cracked. "It was Erona who became my mother, who oiled my hair and made me pretty necklaces, held me to her bosom when I was frightened."

Yurubi clung to Waasha. "I didn't know," she sobbed. "I didn't know you and Ma lost your mother when you were little. I always thought Grandma Lulou—" Yurubi reared back, her lacerated heart rising into her throat. "Where is she?"

"She's safe. She's with Welusi. Pipo carried her into the hills when the shaman said we had to flee. Erona and I were with a small group of women. Then I twisted my ankle, and I fell behind. I think Erona—" Waasha's voice dropped to a shaky whisper. "I think she got separated from the others because she was hanging back. I think she was waiting for me to catch up."

Waasha was probably right because that's what Ma would do. But it wasn't Waasha's fault that a tree—

Yurubi squeezed her eyes shut, trying to close out that thought. The image of Ma lying stiff on the ground rose before her again. Ma and two others.

"Waasha, who were the others? The two near Ma?"

"Young boys from another village. We don't know where. Must've been playing in the wind and rain … A rockslide up in the hills last night … We found them on the way down."

Yurubi groaned. Two little ones. Snatched away by the spirits.

She and Waasha rocked each other, their tears mingling on their cheeks and chests.

"Erona wanted to stay behind, you know," Waasha whispered.

"She didn't want to go into the hills with us. Said she'd stay and wait for you."

Yurubi went still as those words sank in. Ma would've stayed back to wait for her. But that might've been even more dangerous. There would've been no place for Ma to take shelter when the wind came roaring in from the sea.

"I forced her to go." Waasha's voice dropped to a thin broken thread. "I—I told her she couldn't stay here alone. Told her over and over that you were a warrior and—and you'd know how to take cover."

"You did right," said Yurubi, patting Waasha's back. "Look at the village. You did right."

She buried her wet face in Waasha's neck as the wail of a child rang out in the dark, like an echo of her own anguish.

"I managed to take cover in the forest," Yurubi said after a while. "But I'm no warrior. I know that now."

"You *are* a warrior. Very brave and strong. You just survived a night in the forest. Alone. In a fierce storm."

Yurubi shook her head. "You don't know," she whispered. "I was afraid snakes would get me."

"Yurubi—"

"I'm no warrior, Waasha. I'm terrified of snakes. And barracudas." She wiped her nose with the back of her hand. "And I truly don't think I can bear to put Ma under the ground."

Waasha's arms tightened around Yurubi. "Do you think the men aren't afraid of anything?" she whispered against Yurubi's ear, her usually gentle voice sounding fierce. "Some of them are just as scared as you are of snakes and big killer fish, although they'd never admit it. Some are afraid of maybouya and all kinds of other things. They might not say the words, but the fear surfaces in their eyes at times. Don't be fooled."

Waasha stroked Yurubi's hair in silence for a while then drew back and took Yurubi's face in her hands.

"Yurubi, you're a warrior of great heart. I know of no one else, man or woman, who'd face down a boar without a weapon."

Again, Yurubi shook her head. Perhaps back then, when the pig showed up, she'd had some fire in her. But it was all gone now. Gone with the loss of Ma. Gone with the loss of all hope of a life with Aloo. Gone with the fear that had straddled her last night under those rocks in the forest.

"Gone," she whispered. "All gone."

"Erona was my mother, too," Waasha said softly, wiping Yurubi's tears with her thumbs. "We'll do what has to be done, together. Let's rest a little before the sun comes up."

FIGHTING TO RISE AGAIN

The sun beat down on Aloo's back as he bent over a thick stake, driving it into the ground with a stone sledge. He was working his way around the newly built taboui, putting in some stakes to reinforce the support posts.

He had this idea that if he could brace the main posts with some stakes, it would strengthen the structure. But most of the other men had no interest in any extra work, especially when there was still so much else to be done.

The only person willing to help was Pipo, who was squatting near one of the stakes, tying it to a post with a length of wet mahoe that would tighten as it dried.

"Uh ... how do you know for sure this will work?" Pipo grunted, his arms flexing as he pulled the ends of a mahoe strip into a tight knot.

"No way of telling until the next big wind comes," Aloo said, hunching his left shoulder to wipe the sweat from his face. "I used to build all kinds of play huts when—when I was small. I'd knock them down and put them up again. In different ways. That's when I started trying out the stakes to make them stronger."

Pipo rested his arms on his thighs and glanced sideways at Aloo.

"Play huts?" Pipo said, a wide grin spreading across his face. "You liked being with the girls, huh? Or they liked being around you?"

"Er ... no, I played by myself," Aloo fixed his eyes on the stake he was pounding into the ground. "I wanted to live in—I used to think a lot about building a real hut."

"Well, you've built a lot of them since then," Pipo said with a laugh. "Some very good ones too."

Aloo smiled briefly but did not raise his eyes even after he'd finished driving in the stake. He was thinking of the long lonely days he had spent in the dim cave, playing quietly with sticks, stones, leaves, seeds and bits of vines. Waiting for night to fall so he could venture outside. Then after the great venting of the mountain spirit, he'd slowly found a different life. Found almost everything a man could want. That was until—

"Listen, my friend," Pipo said, resting a hand on Aloo's shoulder. "If it would help, I'd bring you back a wife next time we go on an excursion. I can find one who—"

"No," Aloo said quickly. "I don't want—I'm not ..."

He drew a deep breath and turned to look at Pipo, whose smile had disappeared. "Don't do that, Pipo" he said, forcing the words past the tightness in his throat.

As Pipo looked at him in sombre silence, Aloo bent his head again, fumbling around in the tool basket.

"She's gone, you know," said Pipo after a while, his voice low. "And Yurubi, she's gone too, in a different way."

"I know," Aloo muttered, a sudden tiredness washing over him. "I'm—"

"Pipo! Aloo!"

Tueke was waving from the edge of the women's compound, his face and body glistening with sweat in the afternoon heat.

"Need a little help here," said Tueke, gesturing in the direction of a lopsided hut he was trying to build for Welusi. "Can you come for a while?"

"You want to do this right now, or should we tell him we'll help him later?" Pipo said under his breath.

"Take the sledge and go ahead," said Aloo, his voice sounding hollow in his own ears. "I-I'll pack up the rest of the tools."

Pipo hesitated for a moment then shouldered the sledge and strode off.

Aloo drew a ragged breath and slowly began gathering up the tools. As usual, Pipo was trying to be kind. He just didn't know that his words were like pepper on a fresh bruise. How could Pipo know about the yawning dark crater that always seemed to be waiting?

Or the snare of dreams that entangled Aloo every night. Mountains of raging water and silently screaming, drowning women. Some nights, there was no telling where their screams ended and his began. And always, always, there was the water. Snatching away the women in his life. His mother, Nimita, Yurubi.

That day of the storm, his heart had jumped into his throat when he'd spotted Nimita down on the beach. A tiny solitary figure standing in the pelting rain, facing the huge waves smashing ashore and the wind tearing in from the sea. While everyone else was running for shelter in the hills, Aloo had raced down to the beach. But by the time he got there, Nimita had disappeared. He'd shimmied up one of the crazily swaying coconut trees on the beach, clinging to the branches with all his might, trying to spot her. But she was nowhere to be seen, either on the beach or in the water. He had screamed her name over and over, the wind ripping away his voice. Then the tree next to his had snapped, and the coconut-laden top went sailing past his head. That's when he'd slid down to the ground and stood there, swaying like a reed. Gulping on the sand-laden wind, he'd wrapped his arms around the tree trunk, trying to ward off the dreaded black spots dancing over the ocean toward him. When he'd managed to find his legs again, he had stumbled back up the hill, his mind reeling with thoughts of Nimita swallowed by the sea and Yurubi stranded in the forest.

Back in the deserted village, he'd staggered around in the descending dusk, looking frantically to see if Yurubi had returned. Dodging flying chunks of wood, pots, hammocks, the entire side of a hut, he'd searched the whole village. Then he'd dashed to the river, only to be halted by the sight of a seething brown beast. It was tearing at everything in its path, gnawing its way up the banks with fearsome speed and ferocity.

Standing there, fists clenched, his eyes raking the far banks, he'd heard a sinister voice above the roar of the river and the unrelenting slaps of the rain.

If you try to go to her, she too might choose the water, the wind had snarled in his ear.

He'd turned and ran for the hills.

In the blinding rain and with the wind at his back threatening to lift him off his feet, he'd stumbled upon Waasha hobbling along by herself on a swollen ankle. Without a word, Aloo had hoisted her onto his back and set off running again. Bent almost double, he'd followed Waasha's pointing finger and the directions she was screaming in his ear to catch up with Erona.

They had no way of knowing that Erona had been struck a glancing blow on the head by a massive falling tree and was lying under its branches, not far from where Aloo had picked up Waasha.

When Aloo and Waasha had finally caught up with some other villagers, night had fallen, and the wind was tearing at everything in its path like a crazed creature. Most people were huddled in the lee of the hill, some of them frantically digging holes in the side of the slope, so they could curl up inside. Aloo had scooped out a hole and tucked Waasha inside, then flattened himself against the hillside near her, clinging to a prickly clump of shrubs.

Even then, with the wind and rain battering him, the torture had begun. The question that would torment him night after night was already tugging at him. If he'd spotted Nimita in the water, would the have launched himself into that foaming maelstrom to rescue her?

With a sigh, Aloo ran a hand over his head and hoisted the tool basket onto his back. He walked slowly over to Tueke and Pipo, who were pushing against the side of the hut. As soon as they shoved in one part, another section would bulge out.

In spite of himself, Aloo smiled.

"What's this?" he said.

"It's a fighting hut," said Pipo with a grin, straightening up.

Tueke continued to shove at the tangle of coconut weave, panting with exertion. "We ... just ... need ... to ... get ... this ... side ... in."

Aloo walked slowly around the tilted hut, taking in the crooked poles and sagging side covering. Tueke was a good hunter and warrior but building was not one of his strengths. The problem right now was finding a way to rebuild this hut without offending him.

Aloo circled the hut again then stopped in front of Tueke.

"I was just telling Pipo, I have this idea—"

"Not more stakes," Pipo said with a groan, covering his face with one hand.

Ignoring Pipo, Aloo looked straight at Tueke.

"I have this idea for building some stronger shelters. Would you let me try it out on this hut?"

A look of relief flared in Tueke's eyes, but his forehead knotted in frown. "Would it also be … er … straighter?"

Aloo suppressed a smile. "Yes. But we'd have to take down the whole thing and start over."

Tueke's face fell. "Take it down? After all the hard work—"

"Yes, it's about to fall over anyway," a voice shouted.

Garu, Caloon and Ranan strolled into view, sniggering and pointing at the hut.

"It looks like this," said Garu, raising his arms to form a roof shape over his head and bending his body sideways at the waist. Caloon and Ranan held their stomachs and staggered about, roaring in laughter.

Tueke's lips tightened, and his hands clenched into fists at his side. "I'll—"

"Don't listen to them," said Pipo, gripping Tueke's arm and turning him away from Garu and the others.

"If Welusi sneezes, it's sure to come crashing down on her," Garu shouted, to even more laughter.

"It's going to fall before that, as soon as Tueke starts snoring in there," said Ranan.

He snorted, puffed out his cheeks and blew a stream of air from his mouth.

"Look, it's swaying," he said, pointing at the hut.

Garu and Caloon hooted and pounded each other on the back as the side of the hut flapped slightly in the afternoon breeze.

"Stop it," said Aloo quietly, swivelling to face them. "Leave him alone. I'll help him fix the hut."

The laughter dried up as Garu and his friends looked at Aloo, their eyes widening.

Aloo had trained himself to never rise to their baiting, but now he could feel a tick starting in his jaw as he met Garu's mocking eyes.

"Well, now, master builder," said Garu, drawing out the words. "You're helping to look after other men's wives?"

Caloon and Ranan guffawed again, looking from Garu to Aloo in glee.

Aloo clenched his teeth, forcing down the heat rising in his chest.

Garu snapped his fingers and grinned. "Ah, yes, I forgot. Your wife ran off, into the arms of the ocean spirit. She chose him over—"

Aloo leapt forward, a blaze of fire searing through his body. His left fist caught Garu a glancing blow on the shoulder as Garu dodged at the last moment. Aloo swung around, going into a crouch, his eyes narrowed to slits. Garu barely had time to take up a similar stance, when Aloo sprang again, his fists flying at Garu's face, chest and stomach. Garu dodged and ducked, blocking some of the blows with his forearms. As Aloo pressed in closer, Garu brought up his elbows sharply, jabbing Aloo hard in the chest and belly.

Aloo flinched but did not utter a sound. He jumped away and ran backward, swiftly putting distance between himself and Garu until he was brought up short by the side of Tueke's flimsy hut.

With a triumphant gleam in his eyes, Garu strode forward, clenching his fists at waist height.

Aloo felt as if his entire body was being consumed by fire as his eyes fastened on Garu's mocking face. Aloo charged at a dead run. Garu's grin widened as he halted and swivelled slightly. He was about to stick his leg out. Aloo leapt into the air and drew his knees up.

The grin on Garu's face faltered, and he jumped sideways.

Aloo twisted his body in mid-air, and his legs shot out. His feet slammed into Garu's chest, knocking him to the ground with a thud. Aloo pounced on Garu and grabbed him by the throat. His head pounding, Aloo gritted his teeth and tightened his grip. Black dots jumped in front of his eyes. Interspersed with flashes. Flashes of his mother's face sinking under a massive wave. His coal-black cave. Nimita's tiny figure on a wild beach. Erona's crushed body. Yurubi's listless eyes. Buaba's baleful gaze. Garu's taunting grins ...

"... Aloo! Stop, you'll kill him!" The voice reached Aloo faintly through the roaring in his ears. He blinked rapidly and a blotchy, puffy face swam into view.

"... Aloo! Enough!" Two pairs of hands grabbed Aloo under his armpits and hauled him off Garu.

Aloo flung off the hands and jumped to his feet.

On the ground, Garu gave a great shudder, sucked in a ragged breath and began coughing and spluttering.

As if emerging from deep underwater, Aloo heard a rush of sound. He looked around dazedly. A laughing, babbling crowd. A cluster of young boys running around, gazing up at him with wide eyes. Pipo and Tueke grinning in glee.

As the roaring in Aloo's ears slowly subsided, he began to catch snatches of the excited chatter in the crowd.

"... great fighter... almost killed him ... see that flying kick ... never fights... should be a trainer..."

Out of the corner of his eye, Aloo saw Caloon and Ranan pulling a red-faced Garu to his feet.

Aloo turned toward Tueke and Pipo, his heart still slamming against his ribs.

"I-I'll help w-with the hut a-another day." Aloo muttered as he edged away.

Away from all the eyes. Into the forest. Dim light. Thick cover. Trees. Dark cave.

A STRANGE ENCOUNTER

Aloo felt as if the ground under his feet was no longer solid. Since the fight, he'd become almost as jittery as when he had first ventured among the villagers. Try as he might, he couldn't seem to find his footing anymore.

Whether he was working on Tueke's hut or skinning an iguana at the river, Aloo was always on the lookout for Garu and his followers. The fight had not ended with Garu's humiliation. It was not the Kalina way. And, as Pipo and Tueke kept reminding him, Garu was the chief's son. Still, there were times when Pipo would grumble that he should've let Aloo kill Garu.

Most of the other men seemed to be waiting and watching with eager eyes. Sometimes Aloo would catch Kuriji looking at him with a strange expression. Aloo didn't know what to make of it. All he knew was that if another big fight broke out, the only ones sure to back him would be Pipo, Tueke and Siwako.

Aloo smiled dryly. If the women were allowed to fight, they too might take his side.

Since his fight with Garu, he couldn't help but notice the jostling among the young women to bring him food at night. But Waasha, who had been cooking for him since Nimita's disappearance, often scattered them with a withering look.

If only Yurubi would come near sometimes. But these days she rarely left the hut where her mother was buried. And when Yurubi did come outside, she never really looked at anyone. Her shoulders were slumped, her face downcast, and her eyes dull. It didn't matter how many iguanas, agoutis or mullets Aloo brought her, she never raised her eyes or spoke to him.

Then there was the shaman. Every time he got ahold of Aloo, he'd talk about shifting winds and tides and clouds. As usual, Aloo could make no sense of it.

These days, Aloo was spending more and more time alone in the forest. But tonight, he was sitting with Pipo around the fire, listening to a babble of stories about raids. But Aloo was not listening too closely. The blow-by-blow telling of the chase and capture of villagers in other lands could still stir a sick feeling in his gut.

He took a quick mouthful of woku and looked around, trying to shut out the raucous voices. Across the flames, he caught the eye of Chief Oudou, who was sitting by himself, smoking a pipe.

Oudou raised a finger and beckoned.

Aloo went still. This was not good. The chief. Garu's father. Beckoning. Unsmiling.

Pipo nudged Aloo in the side. "Chief's summoning you. Be careful," he said, speaking fast out of the corner of his mouth. "Say nothing, listen only. Tell me everything after. Go quickly."

Aloo rose to his feet, his heart thumping against his ribs. He could feel eyes boring into him from all sides as he circled the fire and squatted next to the chief.

Oudou was a laconic chief who almost always looked unruffled. But in battle he was a cunning, fierce and unforgiving warrior, Pipo had told Aloo several times.

The chief turned his inscrutable gaze on Aloo then gestured to him to sit. Aloo sat crossed legged on the ground, his heart drumming against his ribs.

For what seemed like a long time, Oudou said nothing. Puffing placidly on his pipe, he gazed across the fire at the boasting young men on the other side.

"Young warriors," Oudou said after a while, pointing at them with his pipe, "they always talk about our expeditions. I wonder if any of them know about the time raiders came to our village."

With a jolt of surprise, Aloo glanced at the chief.

"H-here? Wh-when? W-who?" He hated it when the words got stuck in his throat like this.

Oudou's mouth curved in a faint smile. He lifted a huge mug of woku from the ground in front of him and drank deeply.

"Kalina from one of the islands in the north," he said, wiping his mouth. "It was Buaba who spotted them. He was just a young boy at the time. That night he was sleeping outside."

Oudou's teeth glinted in the firelight. "Buaba had the runs, probably from stuffing himself with too much pepperpot. He didn't want to keep dashing to the river. Didn't want to sleep down there either. So he lay down just outside the shaman's hut, where he'd be near the embankment. He was squatting on the cliff side, peering through the grass at an owl on the hunt, when he spotted a movement on the water far below. Didn't take him long to realize it was a boat. He scrambled up the bank and ran to wake the shaman."

Oudou sucked on his pipe. "That was the last raid on our village."

Aloo waited in silence for the chief to continue. But Oudou was taking long tokes on his pipe and seemed to not want to talk anymore. Surely, the story couldn't end there. Aloo swallowed, trying to unclog his throat.

"H-how d-did you f-fight them?"

Oudou dragged deeply on his pipe, tipped his head back and blew the smoke skyward. "We didn't fight them." He stuck the pipe in his mouth again and gripped it in his teeth. "We crushed 'em."

As sick as Aloo felt in the stomach from all the talk tonight about raids, he was curious about this one. How could a village hold off a stealth attack at night? All the stories he had ever heard had been told by the attackers.

Oudou took a swig of woku then set down the mug, belched and wiped his mouth with the back of his hand. He put some more tobacco leaves in his pipe, tamped them down and sucked on the pipe until he got it going to his satisfaction. His face wreathed in smoke, his eyes fixed on the flames in front of him, the chief picked up the story again.

"The Great One was not happy to be awakened from his dreams by a smelly young boy," Oudou said with a short laugh. "But he followed Buaba to the edge of the cliff and saw that indeed there was a big canoe edging into the bay. He signalled to Buaba to be very quiet, and they both ran to the taboui to wake us.

"Our chief at that time was a wily warrior called Yoloko. He was

Kuriji's father. While we were scrambling about for our weapons, Yoloko bade us be quiet, and he stood staring into the starlit sky. We, the young ones, were grabbing everything we could lay our hands on—knives, bows and arrows, clubs—but the chief picked up only his bow and arrows.

"He told us to follow him, warning us to be careful not to wake the women and children or to make any noise that would alert the raiders. He led us to the cliff further along from the shaman's hut. From there, we could see the boat pulling into the little cove under the cliff, carrying about thirty warriors.

"No one was allowed to speak. Yoloko was giving us orders by means of gestures. At his signal, we all set our feet and pushed at a massive boulder near the edge of the cliff. We had to rock it back and forth to work it loose. Then we clustered behind it and waited for Yoloko's signal. He was peering over the cliff with his arm raised. When he dropped his arm, we pushed with all our might, rolling the boulder forward. It pitched over the cliff with hardly a sound.

"For an endless moment, we were rooted there, drenched in sweat, our eyes fixed on our chief. He was standing motionless, head cocked. Then we heard a huge crack far below. We ran to the edge of the cliff, but all we could see was the top of the boulder.

"Yokolo spun around and sped toward the beach path. We grabbed up our weapons and followed fast on his heels.

"When we got down to the beach, the only sounds were the breaking of the waves on the shore and the soft hoot of an owl. We slithered over the rocks under the cliff as silently as eels until we got to where the boulder had fallen. We could barely see it below the surface of the water.

"There was no fight that night. The canoe and everyone in it were smashed to pieces. They'd been coming in over the rocks on the seabed when the boulder hit.

"We waited until the first light of dawn then jumped into the water to collect some keepsakes."

Oudou tapped his pipe gently against his right palm, gazing into the distance, his face glowing in the firelight. "I still have mine."

"W-what is it?" Aloo had heard about fight keepsakes, but he'd never asked to see them.

"You've seen it," Oudou said, still looking into the distance. "It's threaded through the ends of my hammock. I lost it in the hurricane but found it again snarled in the tatters of my hammock."

Aloo's mouth went dry. "T-that's f-from—?"

"Yes, from that night. The upper part was crushed. I took only the lower arm. Two bones."

Aloo's head was spinning. "A-all those b-bones in the t-taboui …"

"No, not all were from that night. They were from different fights. Some on land, some at sea."

Aloo could feel his entire body breaking out in a sweat. His stomach was starting to churn again. He rubbed a hand over his face, wiping the sweat that was now running into his eyes.

"G-great Chief, li-like Bu-Buaba that night …" Aloo clutched his arms across his stomach, his face flaming as the chief turned to look at him. "I-I—The p-pepperpot …"

Oudou's mouth twitched as his eyes moved over Aloo's drenched face. Then he erupted into a roar of laughter. "Run for it, boy," he said, throwing back his head.

Aloo stood swiftly, cringing inside at the many eyes fixed on him. He swivelled and fled to the river, chased by the chief's rolling guffaws.

TOUGH CHOICES

"Coylaya, where do you want these?"

Akawa heaved a huge bundle of wood onto one shoulder and reached down to pick up a smaller stack.

"In the women's compound," said Aloo. "On that little point that juts out over the sea."

Akawa raised his eyebrows. "You're going a build a hut there?"

Aloo nodded and shifted on his haunches, tugging a length of rope toward him.

"Doesn't seem like a good spot for a family shelter," Akawa said. "Too much wind."

"It's for Yurubi," Aloo said softly, wrenching the cord tight around four long poles. "She likes to work there."

"Ah, Yurubi. The maybouya's still got a hold on her, huh?"

"It's not—She's not—She's sad because … because the spirits took her mother," Aloo said through his teeth.

It was cool here under the thick cover of the forest, but it felt like the sun was blazing down on the back of Aloo's neck as he met Akawa's searching eyes.

Akawa cocked his head as if he'd caught some faint distant sound. Then he dropped the small stack of wood he was holding and lowered the bigger bundle to the ground.

"Listen, Coylaya," he said, squatting in front of Aloo. "When all this building work is done, a break would be good, huh?"

"Yes," said Aloo, dropping his eyes again to the rope he was tying around the poles.

"Come with me to Wallibou."

Aloo's hands stilled. "Er … what—? Yes, but—"

"Wait, listen." Akawa bounced closer on his toes. "A great hunter and fighter like you shouldn't be doing menial work. In my village, you won't have to fix crooked huts or skin dead animals. You'd be free to hunt and craft all the weapons you want. We can never have enough of your bows and arrows."

Akawa dropped his voice. "Coylaya, it doesn't matter that you can't go to sea, we want you to help train our boys to hunt and fight on land."

The heat on the back of Aloo's neck softened and slid down his chest into his belly.

"I-I … I'm—"

Akawa clapped him on the shoulder, grinning widely. "And, my friend, you'd have your pick of the women in the village. Or we could bring you a feisty wife from the northern islands."

Akawa rose to his feet and shouldered the bundle of wood again.

"In Wallibou, the Great Mountain protects us from the wrath of hurricanes. We don't have to keep building new huts. When we're done with the work here in Warigara, I can let someone else take the boat home, and I'll walk with you over the mountains to our village."

He hoisted the other stack of wood and set off through the forest, weaving as easily among the trees as if he was carrying a few sticks.

"It would be a better life, Coylaya," he called over his shoulder.

As soon Akawa's back disappeared, Aloo dropped the rope and sprang to his feet. His body was breaking out in a sweat from the heat that had now engulfed him. He wiped his hands over his face.

The people of Wallibou wanted him to be a trainer. Like Maruku. And Kuriji.

Akawa had just said it. Right here.

Aloo looked around at the silent tree trunks.

Akawa had come to help build huts. And to bring a message. From his village.

With a quick shake of his head, Aloo moved to a gnarled tree stump and sat down. He leaned over, elbows on knees, staring at his feet.

His feet. All he needed to travel to a new place. He didn't have to get in a boat.

In Wallibou, he wouldn't have to be always on the lookout for Garu and his pack. Or keep trying to slip past Buaba's bitter and baleful gaze. He'd be Coylaya. A black rock. A trainer of young warriors.

Aloo squeezed his eyes shut and covered his face with his hands.

If he moved to Wallibou, Pipo would come often in his boat to visit. Siwako and Tueke would come sometimes. Yurubi, never.

Yurubi. How could he bear to leave her?

His heart tripped as he recalled again his first glimpse of her after the hurricane. Head bent, tangled hair falling over her breasts, slim shoulders tightly braced as if for a fight. His breath had snagged in his throat, and the heavy coils around his heart had fallen away. It didn't even matter that when she looked up, she'd turned away from him with nothing but a cold, strange glance. He'd felt something inside him right itself and settle into place.

Never mind that she hardly bothered to look at him these days. Or when she did, it was with sad, distant eyes that made him feel as if a knife was ripping at his insides.

Aloo leaned over further and held his head.

After the hurricane, fighting through his torment, he'd set about rebuilding Yurubi's family hut straight away. Wanting to make her comfortable again. To shelter her mother's resting place.

Waasha had rewarded him with a wide smile, a huge calabash of crab stew, and a new necklace of agouti teeth. Yurubi had bent her head and hurried inside to carefully place a stool over the spot where Erona was buried.

Later in the day, Aloo had caught a glimpse of Yurubi sitting on the stool, her head resting on her knees, her hair touching the ground, her arms wrapped tightly around her legs, her shoulders heaving. He had started toward her, but a hand had gripped his shoulder, stopping him.

"Let her be," Waasha had said softy behind him. "She just wants to be with her Ma right now."

Aloo had nodded and turned away. Glancing back once at Yurubi huddled over her mother's resting place, he'd felt as if his feet could carry him no further. But under Waasha's watchful eye, he'd kept walking. And walking. Then he'd started running. And running. Till he'd ended up at his and Yurubi's special place. Under the falls. Where there were no tears. Only torrents of water.

Since then, he'd been doing everything he could to spark a light in Yurubi's eyes, to shield her from all the whispering again about the maybouya, to brighten her days.

From his early morning forays into the forest, he'd bring her plump berries, guavas, wild yams, wild peas, skinned and gutted animals, and bundles of firewood. Some days, he'd run far upriver and return with a string of silver fish or a basket of crayfish.

Whatever he brought, he'd set it down quietly in a big basket near the opening of her hut and slip away. One morning as he was filling the basket, he had sensed a movement inside the hut and had looked up to see Yurubi coming awake in her hammock. She had turned her head and looked at him, her eyes soft and untroubled. Something like a stream of honey had flooded Aloo's insides and he'd started forward.

Yurubi—

But then the coldness and gloom had clouded her eyes again, and Aloo had swung away, a rough rock forming in his throat.

As the memory of that morning assailed him, Aloo's throat tightened. He lifted his head and stared at the rough tree trunks in front of him. The truth was Yurubi didn't need him. She could hunt, fish, and fight as well as any warrior. *And* she could cook, weave and take care of babies.

Aloo's stomach knotted. He and Yurubi used to talk about babies. Way back. Before the chief decided to bring him a wife. Now, Yurubi wanted nothing. Except to be close to her mother. And who could blame her? If he had even a hair from his mother's head, he'd want to keep it close, too.

But he'd still want Yurubi as his wife.

That's what he should've told Chief Oudou and the shaman when they gave him Nimita.

I still want Yurubi as my wife.

Aloo propped his chin in his hands, his gaze following a brown trembler pecking among the leaves under a shrub.

At the time, he'd been so uneasy living among people, dwelling in a village. So fearful of taking a wrong step. Always worried that someone would find out he wasn't really a spawn of the Great Mountain. Constantly terrified that they'd toss him back into the ocean. And it would swallow him. It would never carry him to that land where everyone was black all over, without paint. If there was such a land anywhere but in his dreams.

Aloo jumped to his feet and began pacing among the trees.

He still wanted Yurubi as his wife. But she was gone. Just like Pipo said. Gone. The girl who'd climb a huge guayacan tree to pick a purple flower or lie on her stomach forever to watch a line of ants carry a dead grasshopper. Gone. The woman who'd fight a snake to stop it from eating a fledgling thrush, or who'd follow the river upstream for a whole day to find the right stone to sharpen her arrowheads. Gone.

She'd seeped into the earth where her mother lay. And she might never emerge again.

Aloo ran his fingers over his head and clasped them behind his neck. No use asking the shaman about this. He'd only mumble words that Aloo could not follow.

Tilting his head back, Aloo lifted his face to the single ray of sunlight poking through the treetops. Perhaps if—

Footsteps. Akawa. Returning.

Aloo dropped his arms and swivelled on his heel.

A smile flitted across Akawa's face as he appeared from behind a tree. "Ready, Coylaya?"

Aloo swallowed hard. "Yes." He raised his face to the fingers of sunlight reaching down through the treetops. "Yes, I'm ready. But first, we finish Yurubi's hut."

BEHIND THE CLOUDS

Yurubi pulled in the paddle and sat back with a sigh. She shivered a little, hunching her shoulders against the breeze, which suddenly felt cool now that she had stopped paddling. The little canoe bounced on the waves, sharpening the nagging pain in her head.

This was the hardest part of each day—trying to carry out at least one useful task despite the constant headache and the feeling of being slowly crippled by a huge rock sitting on her chest. She folded her hands on her lap, facing the horizon, which was slowly taking on a pale purple hue. A flock of seagulls swooped down just ahead of the boat, squabbling as they scooped up their food from the waves. The din reminded Yurubi of why she was here drifting on a slow tide just beyond the headland. She picked up her fishing lines and reached into her basket for the calabash of bait.

She was bent over, threading a slippery fry on a bone hook, when the canoe lurched suddenly. Yurubi swung around, her fingers convulsing on the hook.

Her shoulders sagged at the sight of Pipo sitting in his fishing canoe, smiling at her. Where did he come from? And why did he have to bump her canoe like that? He, of all people, should know she'd be scared it was a barracuda.

Pipo leaned forward, tethering his boat to hers with swift movements. Then he leaped lightly into Yurubi's canoe, grinning from ear to ear.

"What are you doing?" Yurubi's voice was thick from lack of use.

"I'm joining the er ... fishing excursion," Pipo said, his eyes flicking to the blood dripping from Yurubi's fingers onto the tangle of fishing lines.

Yurubi could feel her face flushing under his gaze. "Pipo, I don't want—"

"Here, let me do that." He bent down and took the lines from her.

"I rolled out of my hammock this morning, thinking I'd go diving for some lobsters," he said as he deftly unravelled the lines and baited the hooks.

"I run down to the beach and what do I see? Someone's already ahead of me. So, I give chase. Boat in front not moving very fast, then it stops near a flock of swooping gulls. Clever fisherman, I think. He's going to drag his net through that school of fish. A few moments later, I realize it's you. Smart fisherwoman, I think, but she won't be using a net or spear, so I better go help."

Yurubi leaned over the side of the boat and dipped her hands into the water, washing away the blood and hiding the unexpected prick of tears behind her eyes.

She thought she had emptied all her tears when Ma died, but here she was on the verge of crying again for some obscure reason. Perhaps it was Pipo's unexpected appearance and his familiar, blithe chatter.

"All done," he said behind her. "Now we can sit back and wait for the fish to bite."

Yurubi splashed some water on her face and turned around. Pipo was sprawled on the stern seat, his back against the side of the canoe, his legs stretched out on the board. He had wrapped the fishing lines around the cross board and was sitting with his arms folded, a smile stretched across his face, his hair loose about his shoulders. He indeed looked like he'd jumped out of his hammock and headed straight to the sea.

Yurubi opened her mouth to tell him again that she wanted to be alone, but she gulped instead as she felt her throat tightening. She turned away and pointed blindly at the horizon.

"It-it's very dull this morning, mostly grey," she said in a choked voice.

"Mmmm, yes. And I think I know why." Pipo's voice was lazy. "When I was a young boy living for days on end at sea on my father's boat, he used to tell me stories about the spirits of the ocean. There's this one spirit that lives below the horizon, and he's busy night and day, running to catch the sun and moon when they slip down one side and rushing to push them up again on the other side. Sometimes he's so tired from all the running back and forth, he shoves both the sun and moon up above the horizon at the same time. The harder the spirit pants, the deeper the colours bloom out there." Pipo chuckled. "He must be moving quite slowly this morning."

Yurubi felt her face twitching. She raised her hands to her cheeks, moving her fingers over her mouth in wonder. She was smiling. Something she didn't think she could do ever again. What was it about Pipo? He'd managed to make her panic, cry and smile, all in the time it would take for a crab to cross the beach. All before the spirit could push the sun above the horizon.

A smile cracked her face again. "I can almost believe that story," she said, still facing away from Pipo.

"I have another one to tell you." Pipo sounded strangely hesitant. "Would you like to hear it?"

"You'd tell me anyway," she said dryly, her eyes fixed on the muted colours slowly spreading across the sky.

Pipo cleared his throat. "I've been on a trip around the island this past moon, stopping at every village to ask about my father and mother."

Oh, that was it. Pipo always sounded strained whenever he was talking about his mother. Yurubi shivered. She'd become worse than him. She couldn't even think of the word mother without a sharp jab of pain.

"Not that I was trying to find them, just wanted to hear about them," Pipo said. "In almost every village, someone remembered them, talked about them as the boat people. So, after many stops and many stories along the way, I decided to take that name as well." Pipo's laughter sounded self-mocking to Yurubi's ears. "I'm now one of the boat people."

Not trusting herself to speak, Yurubi nodded. It had taken Pipo this long to realize that like his father and mother, he belonged more at sea than on land, that he was more at ease on a boat than anywhere else.

"I think you are too, Yurubi. I think you're one of the boat people," Pipo said.

Yurubi shook her head. "No, no, I'm not. It was all a silly dream."

"A dream? But here you are fishing at sea on your own boat. Seems very real to me. And now, look, we have a bite. You want to pull in this one?"

"No," said Yurubi, not even bothering to look. "You can get it."

"Alright, I'll get this. But the next one is yours."

The boat rocked as Pipo shifted about, pulling in the fish.

"It's a scrawny little grunt," he said with a chuckle. There was a plop as he tossed the fish into the basket. "That's what you're going to catch if you insist on fishing with these lines. Now, if you'd take a spear and dive in ..."

Yurubi closed her eyes and shut out Pipo's spiel. She turned her head slightly, allowing the breeze to riffle through her hair. Pipo and everyone else probably thought she was coming out here most days because she still enjoyed fishing and being on a boat. They didn't know it was so she could be alone. If she managed to catch enough fish to feed herself and Waasha, that was quite by chance. She was done with the childish dreams of being a hunter, a boat builder, a warrior. Done with the foolishness of thinking that magic happened sometimes at the touch of her gaze. She was not a frivolous young girl anymore. She had already reached twenty hurricane seasons. All she wanted to do now was watch over Ma's resting place and look after Waasha as best she could. It was just the two of them. Grandma Lulou had left, gone back to Imayarou. Right after Ma had been put under the floor. Grandma Lulou had packed a basket one morning and gotten on a boat with some fishermen from Imayarou, saying it was time to go back home. She never once—

"... and Aloo, as always, kept gazing at the horizon. It was like the old days, except that you weren't there."

Yurubi felt a jolt that had nothing to do with the canoe's bouncing on the waves.

"... we ate so much, we could hardly move after. So, we slept on the beach. There're only gentle waves on that side of the island. Aloo didn't seem worried that the ocean spirit would trouble him. He burrowed down behind a log and never stirred until dawn." Pipo laughed lightly. "Still no way to get him on a boat, though."

Yurubi swung around to meet Pipo's dancing eyes.

"Has he—" She swallowed and tried again to get the words out. "Has he—"

"Taken a wife?" Pipo raised his eyebrows. "No, but he seems happy anyway. He has an esteemed position in the village. He trains the young boys, teaches them how to shoot, climb, and fight hand-to-hand. Soon, Wallibou will have the best warriors in the world. Of course, he hunts and makes weapons too, though his arrows are still not as good as yours."

Yurubi let out her breath slowly under Pipo's amused but searching gaze.

She hadn't seen or heard from Aloo since that evening a few moons ago when he'd appeared, silently as always, and crouched next to her on a rock near the river where she'd been sitting staring unseeingly across the water. Although she hadn't turned her head to look at him, she'd felt the weight on her chest shift briefly as he took her hand. But then he'd said something about going away, and a lightning jag of pain had shot through her body then fizzled out, leaving her more benumbed than before. Somewhere in the fog of her mind she knew at the time that he, too, was in distress, tortured by the loss of her mother, by Nimita's disappearance, by the fallout from his fight with Garu. But Yurubi could not find the strength to even look at him then. Now, here she was snapping up every word about him like a starved sandpiper.

Pipo cocked his head, giving her a quirky look.

"Yurubi, why don't you go to him?"

Yurubi's arms shot out, and she grabbed the sides of the canoe as if it had rocked violently.

"What do you mean?" she said, even more unnerved by Pipo's unsmiling face.

"I mean move there, to Wallibou, so you can be with Aloo, so he can take you as a wife," Pipo said, speaking slowly.

Yurubi released her grip on the sides of the canoe and crossed her arms over her chest.

"My mother's bones are here," she said, forcing the words past the roughness in her throat. "This is where I belong, this is where I will remain."

"Well, then maybe I'll take you as a wife."

Yurubi's mouth tightened, and she stared at Pipo in stony silence as he slapped his thighs, his laughter bouncing over the water. Did he think she hadn't heard he had a wife somewhere on Wai'tukubuli island up north? Not that Yurubi cared. He could have as many wives as he liked, once he didn't start looking her way.

After a while, Pipo's merriment subsided to a grin, and he reached over and tugged Yurubi's hair.

"You don't laugh at my jokes anymore," he said. "You don't even strike back. What happened to the warrior woman, huh?"

"I don't want to be anyone's wife. And I don't want to be a warrior."

Pipo straightened up, a teasing smile still playing around his mouth.

"You don't want to be a warrior? After all the fight you put up?"

"It was nothing more than a childish tantrum." Yurubi swallowed the lump rising in her throat.

"I could've saved Ma if I had stayed near the village, like a normal woman, instead of traipsing about in the forest, trying to be a hunter," she said in a hollow voice.

Pipo's smile dried up, and his eyes narrowed. "Be careful, Yurubi," he said softly. "You don't know the ways of the spirits. Not even the Great One can always foresee their actions or tell why they get furious, why they strike down some and leave others. We shouldn't even dare to guess."

At those words, Yurubi felt something inside her splintering, and her eyes started to fill up again. Blinking hard, she raised her face to the grey sky. A lone hawk was circling high overhead, tilting this way and that in search of something to lure him back to earth. The excited voices of children playing on the beach carried over the water, reminding Yurubi that this was just another day.

She scooped up some water and splashed her face then sat back and straightened her shoulders.

"That one's taut," she said in a croaky voice, pointing at one of the three fishing lines tied around the cross board.

Pipo gave her a bemused look then moved over so she could tend the line.

"Your fish this time," he said, peering over the side of the boat into the water.

Relieved at the shift in Pipo's attention, Yurubi played the line in and out for a while, then she reeled in a small red snapper, freed it from the hook and tossed it in the basket. She bent over, baited the line again and threw it out.

"Not much of a catch so far," said Pipo, nudging the basket with his toe. "This way of fishing is so slow."

"I know, I know, you can catch many more with your spear," Yurubi said, trying to steady her voice.

"I can teach you how to do that, too, Yurubi, but not here in plain sight of everyone. I know a place, near a cluster of little isles, where you can almost scoop up the fish with your hands. There are so many of them, in so many colours, you can pick not only the size of fish you want to eat but also the colour."

"Another one of your stories, I think," Yurubi said, shrugging her shoulders.

"Woman, do I ever make things up?" Pipo grinned at her through the hair blowing across his face.

He couldn't be expecting an answer to that. Yurubi rolled her eyes and picked up the paddle, steering the drifting boat away from the headland.

"Alright, alright, so sometimes I tell fireside stories," Pipo said with an easy laugh. "But I promise you, this one's completely true. You'll see for yourself if you come with me. The waters are calm and clear, fishing is very easy. And there's not just fish but an abundance of crabs, conch, lobsters, birds."

"And where is this enchanted place?"

"No more than a day's trip from here."

A wave slapped the two boats together then tugged Pipo's away until it was brought up short on the end of the rope. Pipo reached back, running his fingers absently over the taut rope.

"Yurubi, do you remember I told you long ago that I was born at sea?"

"Yes, I believed you then. Not so sure now."

"It's true." There was no hint of a smile on Pipo's face. "And I was taken to a tiny isle, just like I said. Well, the place I'm telling you about is near there. Come with me, I'll teach you how to fish with a spear."

Yurubi knotted her brows, fighting through her fog of desolation to grasp what Pipo was saying. He was offering to teach her how to spear fish but wanted to do it near the place of his birth. He'd gone looking for his father and mother and had stopped to see Aloo, checking whether Aloo might venture on a boat.

Yurubi looked closely at Pipo, who was nibbling at his lower lip. It might be that what he really wanted was a trusted friend to go with him to this place he kept talking about, a place special to him. Perhaps he was still hoping to find his father and mother.

"I think I can go for a few days," Yurubi heard herself say as from a distance.

A STRING OF ISLES

The boat edged past a tall black cliff and swung into a deeply curved bay that was overshadowed by steep mountains turning purple in the evening sun.

Pointing at the half-circle of pale sand that fringed the bay, Yurubi opened her mouth to say she'd never seen a beach that colour, but at that moment a huge flock of terns swooped down from the mountains and settled on the beach, facing the boat.

Pipo glanced at Yurubi and grinned. "Just because no one lives here doesn't mean we don't get a warrior's welcome. Wait till you see the crabs."

"It's so different on this side," Yurubi said, as she and Pipo paddled the canoe easily across the calm crimson waves into Becouya bay. "All the way over, looking at the island from the other side, I kept thinking it was like a malevolent dark green lizard with a long tail. I was dreading landing here."

Pipo threw back his head and laughed. "That's what you were thinking? I couldn't tell, not from the way your head was swivelling from the flying fish to the dolphins."

Yurubi cracked a smile. Perhaps Pipo knew that if he'd told her before about fish that could fly, she would've jeered at that as one of his more outrageous tales. She couldn't believe her eyes when she'd spotted the flying fish for the first time. Mouth agape, she'd stopped paddling when she saw them rising out of the water, spreading their long fins and skimming over the waves.

Then came the dolphins, leaping in graceful arcs in front of the boat as if leading the way to the isle in the distance.

The crossing from Hiroon had taken all day, what with the choppy seas and a treacherous tide, but those unusual sights had made it worthwhile. Along the way, Yurubi's admiration for Pipo's seafaring prowess had rekindled as he showed her how to slide the small canoe along the belly of a high wave instead of going over the top and how to feel for the drift of a strong tide and ride it as far as possible.

But there was no need for any of those skills now that they were inside the deeply curved bay.

"We'll stay on this beach tonight and see what else we can find on the isle tomorrow," Pipo said, as the bow of the boat crunched on the sand.

He vaulted over the side and waited for Yurubi to follow. Then he pulled the canoe up the beach and tied it to a coconut tree. The flock of birds had taken flight, leaving the beach to scurrying crabs and bright-eyed lizards.

Yurubi stood calf-deep in the gentle surf, taking in the spreading almond trees that lined the bay, the sharply rising hills, and the bright flowers dotting the lower slopes. She bent and picked up a handful of sand, running the coarse, pale grains through her fingers. Pale yellow sand on a wide beach below green mountains. That's all it was.

With a small sigh, Yurubi turned to look at the sunset. She'd watched the sun emerge from the ocean almost every day of her life but had very rarely seen it slip below the horizon like this. The colours were more vivid than at sunrise. This was a beautiful island, surrounded by flying fish and dolphins, teeming with crabs, birds and lizards, full of colour everywhere. Beautiful, but not magical. Nothing will ever be magical again. Not for her anyway. Magic could be found only in the realm of shamans and perhaps behind the eyes of a fanciful child.

Yurubi brushed a hand over her eyes and waded ashore. She walked slowly across the sand to where Pipo was squatting under an almond tree, rummaging among their supplies.

"It's a small island, but there's a lot of food here," he said, making a sweeping gesture as she approached. "We'd hardly have to hunt for anything."

He handed Yurubi one end of a small hammock and stretched the other end to a nearby tree.

"Almond trees make good shelters," he rambled on, pointing up at the wide-spreading branches and shiny green and red leaves.

He tied his end of the hammock to one of the thick branches, shooing away a big brown lizard.

"Sometimes ants also invade these trees, but I'd rather cope with ants and lizards than crabs at night," he said with a laugh.

Yurubi knotted the cord on her end and tried to curve her lips into a smile

"Seems like your stories about the many crabs on this island really are true," she said, kicking at a red one scuttling near her toes.

Pipo grinned at her and reached for the other hammock. "Wait until tomorrow, you'll see what I mean."

"Can't resist stretching your story, can you?"

Yurubi ducked as Pipo threw an almond at her.

"Come on," he said, as they finished hanging the second hammock. "Let's go scoop up some of these crabs and roast them. I'll build a fire first."

"Go ahead," Yurubi said. "I'll empty one of the baskets and bring it to hold the crabs."

As Pipo strode across the sand, Yurubi bent her head and ran her fingers along the length of the hammock. She'd be sleeping here tonight. Her first night away from Ma since—since—

Yurubi swallowed and dropped her arms to her side as the heaviness in her chest began seeping into her limbs. Dragging her feet, she stumbled down to the water. The sun had disappeared and there was only the faintest smear of scarlet on the horizon. The waves lapping at Yurubi's feet felt surprisingly warm and smooth. She slid into the water, allowing the soft waves to wash over her. Eyes closed, she began swimming slowly underwater. After a while, she allowed herself to sink to the bottom.

Yurubi lay on the dark seabed, rocking with the lulling motion of the waves above her. She buried her fingers in the rough sand, moving them slowly, all thoughts ebbing from her mind.

In the fluid silence, the faintest of sounds reached her.

"Yurubi."

Her fingers stilled in the sand. Was that the voice of the ocean spirit? Yurubi's chest was beginning to burn a little, but she lay still, eyes closed, waiting.

"Yurubi."

There it was again, louder this time. The ocean spirit had never called to her before. Although she had no breath left, she must wait and listen closely.

"Yurubi!"

The waters around her churned and Pipo's face appeared, his eyes round, his lips streaming bubbles like a blowfish as he mouthed something at her.

Chest searing, Yurubi pushed off the seabed and kicked to the surface. Pipo shot up next to her and tossed his hair off his face, his mouth still moving.

"What's the matter? What were you doing down there?" he spluttered, his voice rough.

Gulping hard on the night air, Yurubi shook her head.

"You were gone for a long time, Yurubi. A very long time. Didn't you hear me calling? It's not that deep here. You must've heard me."

Treading water, Yurubi sucked in another mouthful of air. Her mind was fumbling with what had just happened, what it felt like down there on the dark and quiet seabed, the sense of belonging, as if she and the rock on her chest could slowly crumble and settle peacefully into the sand on the bottom of the ocean.

She spun in the water, turning away from the troubled look on Pipo's face.

"I was listening—I thought I heard—I *thought* I heard you calling," she said, still breathing hard.

Pipo swam in quick circles around her, making hardly a ripple.

"You can stay under for a long time," he said finally, slowing down to a crawl. "You'll do well when we go diving for lobsters and conch. And when we get to the tiny isle where I first set foot on land, you can dive all day, once you remember to come up sometimes for air."

"Yes," said Yurubi, drawing a breath of relief at his more jovial tone. "I think I'd like that."

She must try to remember that this was Pipo's journey to ponder his own story, to revisit the place where his life started.

"I might need some more diving practice before I go tackling lobsters, though," Yurubi said, striving hard to lighten her voice also.

Pipo chuckled and tipped his head toward the beach. "If you're all done with your practice for tonight, let's go ashore and build a fire, toss some of those crabs into it," he said, reaching for her hand under the water.

For a moment, Yurubi hesitated, but as he tugged her hand playfully, she curled her fingers around his, and they swam backwards on the placid waves to the beach.

Yurubi stirred in her hammock and turned on her side, scrunching her eyes shut more tightly against the morning light. Time to get up and take her place on the stool near Ma. In just a moment. She started as a bird whistled almost in her ear. Her eyes flew open to an expanse of blue water and sky.

Becouya.

Pipo.

She twisted around and glanced over at him. He was sprawled on his back, snoring heavily, one leg hanging out of his hammock.

They'd both been so exhausted last night, they'd dozed off on the beach near the fire after eating a pile of roast crabs. It had taken a nip on her toes by some creature to get Yurubi moving from her place on the soft sand and into her hammock. Lulled by the lapping of the waves on the beach, she'd fallen asleep again almost immediately. She had no idea when Pipo had made it to his hammock. For all she knew, it could've been this morning.

She hopped out of her hammock and strolled down the beach, sidestepping scurrying crabs and brown lizards. Except for the call of birds, it was quiet here. Yurubi waded into the soft warmth of the water. When it was up to her chest, she stood still looking down at her feet on the white sand. It seemed enticing down there, but it might be better not to go under today.

She swam a little way out then turned on her back and spread her arms. She was not going to listen for any voices today or try to find any place of solace. It was enough to lie here atop the gentle waves in the cool of the morning and watch the birds gliding across a cloudless sky.

She wasn't aware of how long she'd been floating or how far she had drifted until she caught a movement out of the corner of her eye and turned her head to see Pipo swimming toward her from quite a distance. When Pipo was in the water, he was like an ocean creature. Every line and movement of his body betrayed his love of the sea.

"It's floating practice today, I see," he said, as he drew near.

Yurubi turned her face to the sky again and closed her eyes. "Mmm, yes, I think I might stay here all day."

"Then I'd better go get the boat, so I can catch up with you in Cannouan," said Pipo, his voice laced with laughter. "Because that's where this tide will take you, as gentle as it is right now."

"I don't care," said Yurubi, her lips twitching. "Floating is easier than paddling a boat."

"You're right about that." Pipo laughed softly. "I liked doing this when I was a little boy, especially at night. Felt like I was swaying in a massive hammock hanging from the sky."

Yurubi opened one eye and squinted at Pipo, who was also floating on his back, his arms and legs spread wide. Perhaps he, too, used to see magic when he was a child.

"Did you ever—"

Yurubi bit her lip. How could she ask a grown man if he'd ever made magic happen with his gaze?

"Did I ever do what?" Pipo hooked his fingers on hers, a smile still in his voice.

"Did you ever fall asleep in your huge water hammock?" Yurubi said, pushing away her thoughts about magic.

"Many, many times. You should try it." Pipo's fingers tightened. "Don't worry, I won't let you sink. If you start going under, I'll catch you. Like this."

She felt Pipo slide under her, his body cupping hers, his chin resting on her shoulder.

"Like a live hammock," he said softly in her ear.

Somewhere inside, Yurubi could feel a smile starting. Without a doubt, Pipo was the most skilful talker in the world. As they swayed together on the waves, Yurubi peeked between her eyelids at the sky. Nothing up there but vast blue, streaked with white. Nothing around her but the swish of the waves and the soft rasp of Pipo's breath against her ear.

With a twinge of regret, Yurubi rolled away from him and began swimming ashore.

"Yurubi, wait!"

She kept going, knowing that Pipo could easily catch up with her if he wished. The smile she had felt inside a short while ago had shrivelled away. No matter how hard she tried to forget about the magic she'd seen in the world around her, to tell herself it had disappeared forever, she kept getting blindsided by these flashes of hope that it was still there. But the truth was, if she couldn't see the magic here, in a place this beautiful and serene, she'd never find it again anywhere else. Swallowing back her chagrin, she set her teeth and swam harder.

When she reached the shore, she dug out a piece of cassava bread from her basket and sat under the almond tree, chewing stoically.

Out in the bay, Pipo was swimming around, disappearing underwater for long intervals. When he finally came ashore, he stood looking back out to sea for a while before walking slowly up the sand. As he approached, Yurubi reached into her basket for another piece of bread and held it out to him, avoiding his eyes. Pipo stood over her, eating silently, his hair dripping water onto her legs.

She passed him the almost empty water gourd. "We'll need to find some drinking water soon," she said, looking up and down the unbroken curve of sand.

"Umm, there's a place up in the hills where water oozes from a rock," said Pipo, sounding a bit hoarse. "But for now, we can drink coconuts."

He cleared his throat and gestured with his chin toward the mountain. "I was thinking we'd go up there today, find some water, hunt some iguanas. I brought a couple of extra bows and lots of arrows."

Yurubi glanced up at him in surprise. "You'd like me to go hunting with you?"

"Yes, you're a hunter, aren't you?" There was a slightly rough note in his voice.

"I've already told you, that's all behind me. I'm not a hunter or a warrior."

Pipo tore at the cassava bread with his teeth. "But you don't want to be an ordinary woman, either."

"Pipo, it's not—"

"I'll get the coconuts," he said, stomping off down the beach, his shoulders rigid.

Yurubi bent her head, shredding the cassava bread between her fingers. Perhaps it would be better to go back home now, back to the safe shelter of her hut, back to her place near Ma. It was easier there to shut out the whispers about a maybouya, to avoid the pitying glances of the women, the mocking gaze of the men, the reproach of friends.

But you don't want to be an ordinary woman, either.

Those words were roiling in her stomach like a handful of crushed peppers.

Yurubi hugged her knees and leaned her forehead on her arms, pressing back the tears welling behind her eyes. Pipo's words echoed in her head, pounding against her temples with every thud of the coconuts falling on the sand down the beach. Lizards and crabs were scrabbling over her feet to get at the bread, while something that felt like ants were crawling up her back. Still, she didn't move.

"This one's for you."

She jerked her head up to see Pipo standing over her, holding a coconut.

"I picked a whole—"

Pipo's free hand flew out, swatting at Yurubi's shoulder. He kicked sand over her feet, chasing away the crabs and lizards. He dropped to his haunches, a deep frown between his eyes.

"Yurubi, you're covered in insects and all sorts of crawling things. Can't you feel them?" He set down the coconut in the sand near her and brushed his hands rapidly over her head, back, and legs. "What's happening? Why are you letting them run all over you like this?"

Yurubi met his perplexed stare briefly then lowered her head onto her arms again. Pipo no longer seemed miffed, but now he was fussing like Grandma Lulou.

"This trip … It's probably not a good idea," she muttered.

"What? It has hardly started." Pipo went quiet for a while.

From between her half-closed lids, Yurubi saw him reach for the coconut he'd propped upright in the sand.

"Here, you'd better have your coconut before a lizard drowns in it."

With a small sigh, Yurubi raised her head and took the coconut from him. As she drank in small sips, Pipo shifted around to squat directly in front of her. He leaned forward, his eyes intent.

"Listen, Yurubi, you've got to fight this. You're a warrior."

Yurubi swallowed and shook her head slowly. "No, Pipo, I'm not." She lowered the coconut and turned away to gaze out over the water. "I'm nothing. I'm just a body haunted by a maybouya, as everyone knows."

"I don't believe that." Pipo's voice was strong and firm. "You're a warrior. *All* Kalina are warriors, just like the shaman said. Maybe you didn't hear him because you were already on the boat, your and Aloo's boat, speeding off into the sunrise. But we all heard the Great One. He shouted it to everyone on the beach that day, to those men who were so outraged and wanted to stop you, to drunken Garu who wanted to go after you. *All Kalina are warriors.*"

Yurubi felt a pang of longing for the fire that had filled her back then, that had made her think she could do anything. If only she could find the embers of that mettle now.

Out of the corner of her eye, she could see Pipo watching her closely, fingering the large shell earring against his right cheek. After a while, he moved back and sat cross-legged on the sand.

"Way up north, along the string of islands, there's a land called Madinina," he said, his voice taking on a familiar lilt. "It very much resembles Hiroon. Tall mountains, swift rivers, and bountiful forests fringed with beaches, both black and white."

Yurubi took another sip of the coconut, set it down between her feet and turned to face Pipo. She'd always liked his stories about far off lands, places she used to yearn to see. Now, of course, she'd never see them, but this tale might help take her mind off her troubles, at least for a while.

Pipo's eyes took on a faraway look.

"On Madinina, there's also a mountain spirit that sometimes wakes from his slumber, roaring, spitting and belching, just like our Great Mountain. But Madinina is different from Hiroon or any other island in one very striking way." Pipo turned to look directly at Yurubi, his gaze steady. "Only women live there."

Yurubi could feel her eyes stretching.

"Yes, it's inhabited only by women. And. They. Are. All. Warriors," Pipo said, wagging his finger at her with each word.

Yurubi's breath caught in her throat.

"Warriors?" she whispered.

"All of them. They live in one big village. It is so cleverly located that it's almost impossible for even the most furtive raiders to sneak up there. It's protected on three sides by mountains and cliffs. And even on the open side, it cannot be seen from the sea. But the villagers can spot any approaching boats. There are no men on the island, and if anyone tries to land there without an invitation, they're picked off like flies."

Pipo held Yurubi's eyes. "The women on Madinina are some of the fiercest Kalina warriors in the world. They hunt and fish for their own food, build their own huts, and make their own tools and weapons. When they have need of a man, they bring him to the island. That's how they make babies. Once they're done with the man, they send him off again."

"They can get men to... to do whatever they want?" This was growing into the strangest tale Yurubi had ever heard.

Pipo grinned at her. "They can, and they do. When the baby boys are old enough, the women send them away, too. The boys are sent to other islands to live with men and to be trained as warriors. The little girls are also trained as warriors, but by the women on Madinina. The girls grow up to be fierce and deadly fighters."

Yurubi could not tear her gaze away from Pipo's face. She was well aware of his gift for spinning stories, but part of her very much wanted to believe this one.

"Have you ever seen any of them? The women?"

Pipo chuckled. "No, I've never seen them. But perhaps one day I'll be paddling along in my boat, enjoying the ocean breezes, and a summons will come."

"How do they—Oh, never mind, it's all a fireside story." Yurubi tried to smile. "You almost had me believing it, though."

"Almost?" Pipo chuckled. "You'd never heard about Madinina before?"

Yurubi shook her head. "Does it really exist?"

"Every warrior and fisherman in Hiroon knows about Madinina." Pipo sounded indignant, although he was laughing.

"I don't think it's the kind of story they'd want to talk about," said Yurubi, picturing in her mind a large band of women armed with bows and arrows, spears, clubs, knives.

Pipo tipped his head to one side, smiling at her. He pointed at the coconut between her feet. "If you're done warming that up, I'll cut it open for you. You're way behind. I've already had two."

Yurubi's mouth twitched as she handed him the nut.

No matter what, Pipo could always be counted on to make her smile.

He drew his knife and walked away to find a log on which to split the nut. Yurubi's eyes followed him, taking in his buoyant step, the straight line of his back, and the shiny black hair swishing from side to side across his broad shoulders. As he straddled a log and hacked at the coconut, he whistled softly, mimicking the call of a warbler nearby.

A lump rose in Yurubi's throat. Pipo was the only person, apart from Waasha and the shaman, who had not turned away from her since she'd become so burdened. Even Aloo had left. Not that she could blame him or any of the others. She had withdrawn from everyone because there was nothing left in her except this massively heavy rock. But Pipo had not given up on her. He'd steered around her for a while, like almost everyone else. But here he was now, telling her stories, trying to make her laugh, trying to stir her interest in something, anything, again. Yurubi got to her feet and went over to sit on the log near him.

Still whistling, he handed her the two halves of the nut and a small spoon shaved from the green husk.

"Are we leaving the supplies here when we go into the hills?" Yurubi said, as she scooped out the soft white jelly.

Pipo stopped whistling, his lips still puckered.

"Yes," he said after a slight pause, his eyes lighting up. "We'll have to bundle it all up and hang it on a tree, though. Otherwise, we'd have to go searching for it down the crab holes when we get back."

Yurubi chuckled softly as he strode away whistling to the call of a thrush this time. She finished the coconut and quickly sorted through the supplies, packing a small basket to take on the trek. Pipo was down the beach, pulling the boat further up the sand. Yurubi rolled up the rest of the supplies in one of the hammocks and tied it to a low branch on the almond tree.

"Let's hope the bees don't mistake that for a hive," Pipo said behind her.

"Then we'll have honey for the rest of the trip, and you'll be sleeping on the sand," she said, trying to join in his easy banter.

With a guffaw, Pipo strung his knives, bow and arrows about him.

"You'll have to carry that on your hips," he said, as Yurubi lifted her basket and wound the strap around her forehead.

"What? Why?" Yurubi turned to see him holding out a bow to her, his eyes steady on hers.

Yurubi's breath stopped. Slowly, she removed the basket strap and tied it around her waist. With an unsteady hand, she reached out and took the bow from Pipo. He handed her a quiver of arrows, and she took that also, her heart thumping as she looked from left to right at the weapons clenched in each hand.

"We're going this way," Pipo said, turning in the direction of the steepest hill.

Sucking in a slow breath, Yurubi slung the bow over one shoulder, the quiver over the other, and followed Pipo into the trees.

The climb up the mountain was steep and winding. Yurubi stayed close on Pipo's heels as he picked out a path to the top, meandering around rocks, big outcrops and fallen trees.

As the sun rose higher, she could feel rivulets of sweat running down her face, her back and between her breasts. It had been a while since she'd been on this kind of trek, and it was beginning to feel like a challenge.

She grabbed hold of a thick shrub and pulled herself up the face of a rock.

Ahead of her, Pipo's back was beaded with sweat, but he seemed unbothered by the steamy heat. He climbed with easy strides, stopping occasionally to pick a handful of juicy red plums or a few yellow guavas.

Yurubi steadied herself on the lip of a rock and passed a hand over her wet face. She fished two plums out of her basket, popped them into her mouth and began climbing again. As she edged past a clump of thorny bushes, she bumped into Pipo, who was standing still with one hand raised. He reached back with his other hand and drew Yurubi slowly forward, then pointed up into a tree ahead of them.

Yurubi blinked to clear the sweat from her eyes and followed the line of Pipo's pointing finger. A huge brownish iguana was lying motionless on a branch halfway up the tree.

Pipo jerked his head, signalling to Yurubi to take the shot. Yurubi's eyes opened wide. She shook her head quickly and flicked her thumb at Pipo, urging him to get the iguana. But Pipo folded his arms across his chest and turned his head away.

With a small sigh, Yurubi reached over her shoulder for her bow. She fitted an arrow and squinted at the iguana, taking careful aim. Yurubi held her breath and released the arrow. It flew wide of the creature, cutting through the leaves of the tree and landing harmlessly on the far side. Yurubi dropped her arms, her entire body flaming in mortification. It had looked like such an easy shot.

Sensing danger, the iguana lifted itself on its legs and tilted its head from side to side, its spines fully erect.

Pipo turned to Yurubi and nodded again.

She quickly reloaded the bow and fired off another arrow. This one nicked the spines of the iguana, which leapt from the branch and disappeared into the bushes on the far side of the tree.

"Told you I'm no longer a hunter," Yurubi muttered, fingering the string of the bow.

"You're out of practice, that's all." Pipo reached into her basket for a guava, took a big bite and set off again.

Yurubi rolled her eyes and made a face behind his back as she tramped after him.

As they climbed, Pipo turned his attention to the many birds in the trees. Going after some of the bigger ones, he shot down a few terns and pigeons and strung them over this shoulder. He kept urging Yurubi to try, but each time she shook her head. She'd suffered enough embarrassment for one day when she tried to hit that iguana.

The sun was leaning toward the horizon when Yurubi and Pipo came down the other side of the mountain. They worked their way around its base, across tracts of bright flowers, until they came to a coconut grove that stretched from the foothills to a rocky beach.

"This is what I wanted to show you," said Pipo, spreading his arms wide.

Yurubi placed a finger on her chin as she looked out over the stand of tall trees interspersed with stunted bushes growing from a reddish soil.

"Mmm, nice," she said. "Lots of coconuts. We won't go thirsty."

Grinning from ear to ear, Pipo took her hand and drew her forward. "Look closely, Yurubi."

As they got nearer to the trees, the earth seemed to be pulsing. Yurubi stopped abruptly, her gaze fixed on the ground ahead of her. "Crabs!"

"So many, you can scoop them up by the basketful," said Pipo with a triumphant laugh.

"It's real," Yurubi said, unable to take her eyes off the teeming mass of crabs under the trees.

"Like all my stories." Pipo waved his arm again over the plain. "Go on, woman, fill up your basket."

Yurubi hesitated. What would it feel like to walk into that huge colony of crabs? She shivered a little at the thought.

"You know, Pipo, we ate a lot of crabs last night. I think you'd prefer some barbequed meat tonight." She touched the string of birds hanging from his shoulder. "These all look plump and meaty. They'd be more filling than crabs after our long trek today."

Pipo cocked his head and raised an eyebrow. "You think I can't eat birds and crabs on the same night?"

"Oh, I know you can. And not only on the same night, but at the same time." Yurubi made a mock grimace. "A bird leg in one side of your mouth, a crab claw in the other."

"You should try it sometime. Chewy on one side, crunchy on the other." Pipo curled his fingers around his chin. "I remember hearing about a warrior who used to eat—"

Yurubi covered her ears and shook her head rapidly.

"Alright, alright, I'll save that story for another time," Pipo said with a laugh. "If you're not going to *gather* any crabs now, we'll head back to the beach." He pointed to his left. "Going that way, it's an easy walk on mostly flat terrain."

The days melted into each other and took on a lazy cadence as Pipo and Yurubi sailed south through a string of islands and cays. Along the way, the moon had waned and waxed again, becoming a thin yellow crescent that dipped below the horizon as soon as the sun disappeared.

Yurubi's plan to spend no more than a few days on this trip faded as she and Pipo fell into an easy daily rhythm that started with a swim in the clear waters at one of the white sand beaches where they'd made camp. After the swim, Yurubi would crush some of the roucou she'd been collecting along the way. She and Pipo would paint their bodies carefully, not just to protect their skin from the sun but also to ward off the mosquitoes and other insects that seemed bigger and more vicious on these islands.

While they daubed on the roucou and waited for it to dry, they'd talk about what they would like to do, although their activities didn't vary much from day to day.

Some days they'd venture into the green hills to pick fruits, dig for wild roots, and look for a spring at which to fill their water gourds. Sometimes Pipo would shoot a few birds or an iguana.

But mostly they stuck to the sea, catching thick groupers and red snappers, diving for conchs on the seabed, gathering whelks on the rocks, and spearing lobsters along the reefs.

With every passing day, it seemed that the sea was seeping into Yurubi's skin, that the calm soft waters were somehow bathing her on the inside, slowly eroding the stone lodged in her chest.

She and Pipo never spoke again about water hammocks, and he seemed to have forgotten about the uneasiness of that day.

On an overcast evening, when they paddled over a reef toward a cluster of cays off Myreau island, Yurubi knew it would be their last stop before they turned for home. Even before Pipo's chatter dried up, Yurubi knew that one of the cays inside the wide curving arms of the reef was where he'd first set foot on land, that the blue-green waters surrounding the islets were his first playground. When he dived over the side of the canoe and began swimming toward the largest of the cays, Yurubi understood his need to go first and alone.

After that first evening, which Pipo spent wandering over the islet, absently picking up bits of charred firesticks, broken seashells, shards of pottery and the like, he became himself again. He laughed in delight when Yurubi returned from a swim and told him she'd never seen so many sea creatures in one place, in so many colours. He taught her to catch fish and lobsters with her bare hands, how to find the best squid by following the hawksbill turtles, and which of the many types of seagrass along the reefs were good for eating.

When he handed her a bow and told her they were going bird hunting, she nonchalantly followed him into the canoe. She didn't know then that they'd be shooting at birds in flight, from a moving boat. Her aim was worse than it had ever been. But after a few more of those outings, with Pipo as her trainer, she learned how to bring down seabirds whether she was on the boat or in the water. On land, it all became easier than ever, and she often picked coconuts by severing the stem with an arrow.

Then one morning, without a word, she and Pipo loaded up the boat and paddled back across the reef into the heaving ocean. Pipo's chin was held high, his eyes fixed straight ahead. Yurubi stroked the bow and arrows between her feet with her toes. She knew they'd each shed some burden on this trip. They were also going home with something they had each found in these isles, in their own way.

A SULTRY NIGHT

Yurubi rubbed her eyes and flipped over in her hammock, trying to get comfortable. She was tired after a long day in the forest but was restless on this stifling hot night. Her body was bathed in sweat, and her eyes felt as if there was sand behind the lids. She wished the rain would hurry up and start, so the heat would abate.

She turned on her side, squeezed her eyes shut and brought her hands up over her ears to shut out the sound of some night creature rustling around in the roof of her hut. Very softly, she began humming a lullaby that she used to sing to the babies. She was in her work hut, so she didn't have to worry about disturbing anyone.

As she hummed, she tried to imagine that she was back in the southern islands, lying under a clear starry sky, listening to the rhythmic swish of the waves on the beach, her hammock swaying in a cool breeze.

That memory stirred a smile but brought her no closer to sleep. Yurubi rubbed a hand over her damp face and sat up with a sigh. She filled a bamboo mug from the water gourd hanging from the roof and went outside.

The air was so thick and heavy, she felt almost as if she were walking under water. All around her, the night was pulsing with the chirring of insects and the call of frogs. Yurubi sat on her favourite spot on the point of the abutment and drew a deep breath. The sharp tang of the sea was overpowered by a damp smell that signalled rain. Yurubi sipped some water, set down the mug and lay back on the grass.

Gazing up at the sky, she tried to find a star, but the only lights she could see were flickering fireflies. She stretched her arms above her head and closed her eyes, content to lie there at least until the rain started.

She was thinking of building a bigger canoe but was in no rush to begin. She was still going along at that relaxed, unhurried pace she'd found in the southern islands. She felt no obligation to follow the women's daily routine and no longer cared whether anyone thought she was still in the clutches of a maybouya.

Since her return from that trip with Pipo, she'd started hunting again, her mind fixed on the story of an island of women warriors. Some days, Yurubi worked in her hut, making bows, arrows and tools. At other times, she sketched boats on big pieces of bark that she'd brought back from the forest. Sometimes, she spent the day at the river, lazily fishing or gathering reeds.

In the village, she kept to herself, except for when she was helping Waasha with the cooking. Occasionally, she'd go fishing with Pipo or spend time on the beach with him at night, catching and roasting crabs. Recently, he'd been talking about making a trip to Wallibou. He never stopped trying to bring her and Aloo together again.

Yurubi shifted her position on the grass and sighed. How could she and Aloo ever get back to where they were? Everything around her had become all tangled since that night Chief Oudou had given Aloo a wife.

At times, Yurubi felt like she was trapped alone in a huge briar patch. Any movement she made only caused the thorns to rip into her more deeply. She couldn't escape, and no one could get to her. Even Aloo, who was bound to her in ways only the spirits understood, had given up and moved away. Yurubi bit her lip. It must've been terrible for him, though. Aloo who had lived most of his life in the dark, alone in the forest at night, and sleeping in a cave during the day.

Yurubi sat up and brushed away the tears that were beginning to leak from the corners of her eyes. What if she went along with Pipo on a trip to Wallibou one day? Just for a quick visit. Would Aloo's eyes light up with joy when he saw her, or would he give her that proud disdainful look he'd often directed at Garu and Caloon.

Jumping to her feet, Yurubi paced the small patch of grass outside her hut.

What if Aloo had already chosen a wife? Not that she'd be going there to be his wife. She only wanted to see him, to see how he was living on that side of the island.

Yurubi picked up her mug and drained it. This heat was making her crazy. She walked through the low shrubbery, toward the far point overlooking the sea. She found her usual spot on the edge of the cliff and plumped down on the grass, hugging her knees. A couple of frogs in the bushes near her fell silent for a while then started up their croaky song even more loudly than before. Yurubi tossed a pebble into the bushes, chasing them further away so she could hear herself think.

The idea of visiting Aloo was beginning to take hold, and Yurubi could feel her heart racing at the thought of seeing him again. She rested her chin on her knees, staring unseeingly at the dark ocean. In her mind, she could see Aloo waiting on Wallibou beach, his strong legs poised lithely as if to run, his broad cheekbones and narrow chin framed by the tight locks falling over his shoulders, his eyes wide in elated surprise, his teeth flashing in a delighted grin.

She'd run to him—

What was that? Yurubi leaned forward. Something was moving down there on the water. A boat? She frowned as her eyes moved over the roiling waves. Whatever it was had disappeared. A big fish, most likely. Yurubi laughed softly. She'd been so deeply caught up in her thoughts of a trip to see Aloo, she was already imagining the boat going north around Taraty point to Wallibou. She'd have to wait a while to make that trip, though. It might be many days before Pipo and the other warriors returned from their expedition up north.

Yurubi rubbed her eyes and yawned. If only this cloying heat would lift so she could sleep.

She yawned again and was about to lie back on the grass when she caught a movement again far below. Yurubi stared down at the dark water, seeing only the white crests of the waves breaking close to the shore. She squeezed her eyes tightly shut then opened them again. There it was. A long light-coloured shape, bobbing near the point of the bay to her right. Yurubi strained her eyes in the dark. That could not be a fish. A huge log, maybe. It disappeared again in the billowing waves. Yurubi kept her eyes fixed on the water close to the point, waiting to see if would appear again.

She sucked in a sharp breath. There it was, closer than where she'd seen it last. It seemed to be moving slowly but steadily, following the curve of the bay to her right. A boat. It could only be a boat. Yurubi dropped to her stomach and slithered as close to the edge of the cliff as she dared. She could hear the waves pounding against the rocks below, the racket of the frogs and crickets, the occasional hoot of an owl, but no voices.

Could it be the warriors returning? But why at this time of night and so quietly? And this boat was coming from the south. The warriors had gone north. Yurubi's heart was beginning to pound.

Wiping the sweat dripping into her eyes, she looked back over her shoulder at the village. Should she wake everyone? But what if it was a boatload of warriors from Imayarou or one of the other villages heading out on an excursion? Or warriors from a village further north returning home? Buaba and everyone else would laugh at her and whisper not so quietly about the maybouya that had made her crazy.

There was only one way to be sure. With a last look at the boat to fix its position in her mind, Yurubi slithered backward, jumped to her feet and ran into her hut.

She grabbed a bow and a full quiver of arrows, strapped on her knives, and sped silently around the edge of the village, down to the beach.

From his perch in the big almond tree, Aloo sighed in disappointment as Yurubi disappeared down the beach path. He had been sitting in his old spot in the almond tree, drinking in the sight of her after these many moons. It had taken every bit of his strength to remain where he was, watching her stretched out on the grass, her arms above her head. He'd had to cling to a branch to stop himself from leaping to the ground and running to her.

Pipo had said that Yurubi was now back from her dark place. Said he'd bring her to Wallibou one day soon. But Aloo wanted to see for himself. To be alone with her. To look into her eyes. Watch every movement of her body. Then he'd know for sure.

He had left Wallibou early in the morning and trekked over the mountains. It was sundown when he got to the forest near Warigara. He thought he'd go see the shaman first and then find Pipo and his other friends. No telling when he'd find Yurubi alone, but he could wait for as long as it took.

As he neared the edge of the forest, he'd caught a glimpse of a group of women cooling themselves in the river. He'd slipped back into the trees, his heart racing. What if Yurubi was among them? He wasn't ready to see her so soon. Especially not with other people around. Aloo had leaned back against a tree trunk and squeezed his eyes shut, sweat pouring down his face in the close heat.

Later, when the women left the river, he had crossed further downstream and climbed swiftly to his old cave. There was nothing in there except some bits of wood and stone. A few old dried reeds. Yurubi no longer went there, it seemed.

Aloo had stretched out on the ground, twisting one of the reeds in his fingers until he dozed off.

He'd awoken with a start, his throat dry, his body drenched in sweat. He'd gathered up his bow, arrows and water gourd, edged out of the cave and slipped down to the river for a drink.

As he'd done so many times as a boy, he'd crept through the bushes until he reached the big almond tree. From his familiar vantage point high up in the thick branches, he'd looked out at the sleeping village with a sense of sadness. After all, this was his first home in Hiroon. He missed it. Despite the tumult that always seemed to engulf him here.

As his eyes moved over the village, it hadn't taken him long to realize that the warriors were away, the women had banked the fires early, and everyone was under cover. Snug in their hammocks before the big rain they knew was coming.

Then his heart had jumped into his throat as Yurubi emerged from her hut. She seemed restless on this sweltering night. Watching her pace about in front of her work hut, flopping on the grass at times, Aloo wanted nothing so much as to hold her close to his chest until whatever was troubling her melted away. But before long, she'd ducked back into her hut and slipped away to the beach.

Alone. In the middle of the night.

Aloo couldn't help but smile. She was still the most fearless woman he knew.

But this was his chance. He swung down from the tree and ran to the point on the cliff where Yurubi had been lying. The flattened grass under his feet was still warm from her body. Aloo closed his eyes, imagining that he could still detect her special scent of crushed flowers and coconut oil.

What would he do when he got to the beach? Call out her name softly? Or play their old game of stealth? Sneak up on her and watch her eyes flare in surprise then narrow in concentration as she tried to topple him. They'd roll around on the sand, their bodies slick with sweat, her breasts pressed tight against his chest—

Aloo's eyes flew open. From somewhere far below, a faint sound had reached his ears. He squatted on the edge of the cliff, his eyes searching the beach. No sign of Yurubi. But if she was sitting near the bottom of the path, he wouldn't be able to see her from this spot.

Shrugging off his bow and arrows, Aloo stretched out on his stomach. He grabbed two sturdy shrubs and leaned the upper part of his body over the cliff. Now he could see a movement of some kind on the beach. Yurubi. Hard to tell what she was doing, though. Aloo leaned out further. Yurubi seemed to be slowly moving toward the water. She was dragging or pushing something—

She was pushing a canoe into the water.

Aloo slid back from the edge of the cliff and jumped to his feet. Where was she going? Fishing? In the dead of night? She never used to do that. Aloo brushed the sweat out of his eyes and stared in bewilderment at the little canoe now bouncing on the waves. He looked up at the sky and then out at the horizon as he felt a slight drizzle.

This was not a good time to be on the water. The drizzle would soon become a huge rainstorm. The waves were also kicking up. It would be rough out there in a little canoe. His stomach clenched at the sight of the big rollers bashing against the rocks on the right side of the bay. That huge log will soon be smashed to—

Aloo's heart lurched. That was no log. He dropped swiftly to his stomach again, his eyes fixed on the churning waves. It was a long canoe.

His mouth went dry as his gaze flicked from the canoe approaching the point on the right to Yurubi's little boat bouncing on the waves inside the bay.

No, no, no! He leaped up, grabbed his bow and arrows and raced to the beach, his legs at full stretch, his feet barely touching the ground.

TWO WARRIORS

Yurubi dug the paddle into the waves, steering her boat toward the northern end of the bay. The drizzle was steadily becoming a downpour, cooling her sweating body but blurring her sight.

As her boat lurched to the top of a big wave, she twisted around to see whether the big canoe had rounded the southern point. Nothing out there but whitecaps and spray hitting the rocks. Yurubi's boat dropped into a trough again, and the darkness seemed to deepen as the rain pelted down harder.

If she could get out of the bay on the northern end before the canoe came around the southern point, she'd slip into the water and hide behind her boat to see what the big canoe would do. If it kept going north without turning into the bay, she'd know it meant no harm. She'd try to stay out of sight until it went past. But if it swung stealthily toward the beach …

Yurubi bit down on her lip. She'd make it as hard as possible for those warriors to raid her village. Her bow and arrows were strapped tightly across her back in a pouch, and she had a sharp knife in a sheath on each hip.

She blinked the rain from her eyes, gripped the wet slippery paddle tighter and plunged it into the curling waves.

Standing on the beach with foam swirling around his feet, Aloo watched with a thundering heart as Yurubi's little boat slid out of sight behind a wave. He squinted through the pouring rain, gauging the distance to see if he could swim out there. But what if the big canoe came around the point before he could reach Yurubi? He shuddered inside. A boatload of raiders. A young woman. Alone. At night.

Aloo turned and ran back to the line of coconut trees. Bent almost double, he scooted among the boats pulled up there until he came to Pipo's small fishing canoe.

Swallowing hard to force back the nausea rising in his throat, Aloo pushed the boat as fast as he could to the water. It hit the waves with a small slap, tilted to one side then righted itself.

Aloo gripped the side of the boat, bracing himself to leap aboard. His stomach clenched. The black dots were back. Jumping wildly in front of his eyes.

Not now, not now, not now.

The familiar panic ripped through his chest. He doubled over and vomited in the water. The rain beat down on his back, and the waves slapped at his chin. Gasping for breath, Aloo heaved himself into the boat. He could hardly see anything. Only black spots swirling in the rain.

Stretching his eyes wide, he fought to push back the looming darkness. He fumbled for the paddle.

Must get to Yurubi. Must get to Yurubi fast.

Yurubi hunkered down in her little boat, gripping the sides tightly as it tossed about on the waves. The rain was falling so hard, the drops felt like gravel hitting her head and shoulders. She wiped her dripping face and peered intently through the thick grey downpour, waiting for the big canoe to appear. Once in a while, she picked up the paddle and nudged her boat away from the rocks on her right.

She strained her ears for any sound of voices but could hear nothing except the gushing of the rain and the crash of the waves against the rocks. The stealth of the big canoe was worrying. If it turned out to be a boatload of late-night travellers just passing by, she'd edge closer to the rocks, slip into the water and wait for them to go past. If the travellers managed to spot her little boat near the rocks, they'd most likely think it was moored there or had washed out to sea from the beach.

If the canoe—

It reared up out of the darkness on the crest of a wave, long and sleek.

Yurubi's breath caught in her throat. A piragua. Without a doubt.

It swung around the point, steering wide of the rocks. It dipped into the trough of a wave and rode easily to the top of another. Its bow was still pointed northeast as it slid silently past the long tip of the bay. Yurubi squinted through the downpour, her heart pounding, as she tried to see how many people were aboard. It didn't appear to be fully loaded, but in the dark and with the rain coming down in torrents it was hard to tell.

Brushing the rain quickly from her eyes, she breathed a bit easier as she saw the piragua moving further out to sea. A big wave lifted her canoe, carrying it closer to rocks. Yurubi grabbed her paddle and with a few swift strokes guided the boat away from the jagged black teeth under the cliff.

When she looked up again, the piragua was in a tight turn, its bow coming around toward the bay.

Yurubi's whole body stiffened. The stories she had been hearing about raids since she was little were coming to life in front of her eyes. A piragua of warriors making a stealthy approach to the shoreline. Next would come their rapid silent climb up the hill to the village, the raining of fire-arrows on the huts, the swift abduction of the young women running out of the huts, the deadly assaults on the men and boys trying to fight back.

Yurubi's heart slammed against her ribs as the piragua lined up on the centre of the bay. She could try shouting to warn Buaba and the shaman, but she doubted they would hear her above the pounding of the rain. Her shouting would also alert the approaching warriors that she was a woman alone out here on the water.

Her lips tightened. There was only one choice.

She reached around and drew her bow from its sling. Then she slid three arrows from the quiver and lay down in the bottom of the boat, resting her elbows firmly on the seat. The rain streamed off her body in rivulets, and her hair hung in wet vines around her face. She fitted one of the arrows into the bow and held the other two loosely between the third, fourth and fifth fingers of her left hand for quick reload. A trick Aloo had taught her.

She had never shot at anyone before, but this was no time to get queasy. These men were coming to destroy her village.

Yurubi closed her eyes briefly.

"It's an invasion of huge iguanas," she whispered under her breath, as her boat rocked up and down. "Just iguanas."

She opened her eyes and tightened her fingers resolutely on the bow and arrow, waiting for the next wave.

As the piragua rose on the crest of a wave, she released the arrow. Without a pause, she reloaded and fired off the other two in quick succession. There was a muffled shout from the piragua, and it slowed.

Yurubi grabbed another handful of arrows from the quiver. Blinking rapidly to clear her eyes, she shot three more arrows in quick succession. Again, she heard a stifled sound, and this time, a low babble of voices.

The piragua was turning in her direction.

Had they spotted her little boat? She ducked her head below the edge of the canoe as a hail of arrows whizzed past. The raiders were shooting to her right, which meant they hadn't seen her boat yet.

When she peeked up again, the piragua was closer. Straining her eyes through the downpour, she tried to quickly count the number of people onboard. Her heart sank. There were about fifteen raiders. What chance did she have of holding them off? The women in Pipo's story flashed through her mind. They were warriors, all of them. They would never yield to a boatload of raiders. Yurubi set her lips tightly.

The piragua was edging forward, though not directly toward her. The men had fallen silent again.

Yurubi shoved her bow back into the sling and tightened the strap. She lay still, waiting for the big wave she could see rolling in. She flattened herself in the bottom of the boat as the wave curled above her. The boat spun and staggered as the wave picked it up like a twig then dropped it behind into the trough. Yurubi leapt overboard. Staying underwater, she swam swiftly toward the rocks along the northern arm of the bay, going a bit further inland.

When her outstretched fingers brushed against a rock, she gripped it and slithered out of the water. Although the rain was still pounding, she could hear low voices carrying over the water.

Yurubi squatted behind a rock and smiled grimly as she saw the piragua turning toward her little boat. The raiders had spotted it. Careful not to make any sudden movements, Yurubi eased her bow from the sling and pulled a fistful of arrows from her waterlogged quiver. Her aim would be a lot better now that she was on solid ground.

She squinted along the length of the arrow, her heart racing. The waves hissed and gurgled among the rocks, and the rain beat down on her back. She let fly her arrow and quickly fitted another into the bow. Her hands moving like lightning, Yurubi let loose a string of shots at the piragua.

Again, she heard exclamations. Again, a hail of arrows flew in her direction. She ducked behind the rocks then slid into the sea and sank deep underwater, swimming back out along the arm of the bay. The last thing she wanted was for the raiders to go ashore.

She swam as close to the rocks as she dared, aiming for the out-stretched finger of the bay, close to where she'd left her boat. Her chest was beginning to burn, but she couldn't risk surfacing yet. She moved her body like an eel, keeping her eyes peeled for the end of the rock wall on her left.

When the rocks began to peter out, Yurubi knew she was near the point. She swam quickly around the point and rolled onto her back. Pushing her nose above the water, she sucked in the night air. When her chest stopped heaving, she surfaced cautiously. She swept her hair out of her eyes and swung her gaze toward the piragua. It was moving slowly, edging closer to the spot where Yurubi had last been. She looked around quickly, trying to spot her canoe. She caught a brief glimpse of something tossing about on the far side of the bay, but she couldn't see well enough through the rain to tell whether it was her canoe or a piece of flotsam.

Without a boat, Yurubi's movements were more limited. But she was not done yet.

Right now, she was both hunter and prey. She would have to keep relying on the black rocks and torrential rain for camouflage as she tried to confuse the raiders.

She eased in among the rocks. As she reached out to pull her herself up, a wave slammed into her, bashing her against the rocks. Yurubi bit down on her lip as pain seared through her. The immediate sting of the ocean told her that she'd hurt her right leg.

Fighting the pain, Yurubi clambered onto the rocks. She crouched behind a small outcrop, blood trickling down her leg, and reached for her bow and arrows. She'd have to be careful not to waste her arrows since her supply was thinning out.

Yurubi steadied herself against the rocks, lined up her sights on the torsos in the slow-moving piragua and fired off one, two, three arrows. She saw two men rear back but had no time to check whether they'd been hit or were dodging her arrows.

Quickly, she reloaded the bow. Her heart jumped as she saw three or four people dive overboard. They were spreading out now and coming at her in the water and on the piragua.

She ducked as an arrow zinged by her ear and another one hit a rock to her right. The raiders had spotted her. She was not wearing any face paint. Even through the rain, the sharp eyes of the raiders would've picked out the lighter spot among the black rocks.

Yurubi gritted her teeth against the pain in her leg and fitted another arrow into her bow. She couldn't risk any movement now. She would fight to the death here among the rocks, if she had to. She sent another three arrows speeding toward the piragua.

Getting back in the water was no longer a choice. Not with blood streaming down her leg. Death by an arrow, even a poisoned one, was preferable to a shark attack. She shuddered at the thought of those wide jaws and jagged rows of teeth.

Heads were popping up in the water now, and arrows were coming at her thick and fast. Yurubi ducked down further behind the rock, her heart pounding. Easing her hands out, she fired blindly at the piragua. Her lips cracked in a grim smile as she heard a muffled shout. She loaded the bow again and was edging the tip of the arrow around the side of the rock when she heard a shout.

"Ambush! Into the water!"

Yurubi risked a quick peek around the rock. She sucked in her breath at the sight of a raider toppling sideways as he attempted to dive over the side of the piragua. Immediately after, a man in the water let out a gurgling sound, and his head disappeared below the surface.

Yurubi's eyes widened, and her heart leapt as she spotted a canoe at the mouth of the bay. It was bigger than hers and appeared to be empty. But a deadly stream of arrows was coming from somewhere near it, picking off the raiders wherever they appeared.

Whether it was a warrior from a nearby village or an ocean spirit, Yurubi wasted no time trying to find out. The rain had eased off a little, and she could now see more clearly across the water. She held her bow and arrow ready, her eyes searching the waves. When she saw a figure rear up out of the water to shoot at the boat, she quickly fired off an arrow and had the satisfaction of hearing a loud gurgling sound that told her she had hit him.

As she slipped another arrow into her bow, a head appeared in the water closer to where she was crouched among the rocks. Before Yurubi could let fly, an arrow caught the raider in the side of the neck, and he floundered then sank out of sight.

Yurubi let out a ragged breath and glanced quickly at the canoe that had appeared so fortuitously. Whoever was out there had the night sight of an owl and the aim of a pelican on the hunt, no doubt about that.

The piragua was drifting about on the waves and seemed empty, which meant the surviving raiders were probably all in the sea. Yurubi's eyes swept the waters between the boat, the piragua and the rocks where she was perched. The raiders would not try to swim away. These were warriors. They'd fight to the end. And they'd be targeting her more readily than the other fighter out there because they had a better sense of her position. Like her, the raiders couldn't see the other fighter, it seemed. Arrows were flying wildly all over the bay.

Yurubi swallowed back a gasp as a head popped up in front of her, followed by two hands holding a bow. She shot him at close range. With a choking sound, he sank out of sight. Yurubi pressed her body into the rocks, her heart pounding in her ears as she waited to see if he would resurface.

After a while, Yurubi's shoulders slumped, and her grip on her bow slackened. She had fired many arrows tonight but hadn't seen them strike home. Except for that last one. She clenched her teeth. These men had set out to steal her life, to kill the people in her village. If the raiders realized it was a woman they were fighting right now, they would converge on her without pity.

She shifted her throbbing right leg, trying to ease her weight off it. She had no idea how many raiders were still in the water, but she

was not going to give up until they—

An arrow hit the rock near her face and ricocheted to her left. Yurubi ducked, her heart racing. Two more arrows flew over her head. She scrunched down tightly behind the rock, fearful of even a nick because the arrows were most likely poison-tipped.

Any movement now could be fatal. But she couldn't just crouch here until her attackers found her.

Aloo held lightly to the stern of the boat and paddled his legs in the water, bringing the canoe around slowly, so that it would appear to be moving on the tide. He was using the boat as a shield as his eyes bored through the rain, searching for the raiders. Their abandoned piragua rocked on the waves, drifting further out to sea on a strong tide. Aloo tensed. A darker shape. Near the piragua. Aloo let go of the boat and raised his bow. The shape disappeared. Slipped under the piragua, probably.

Kicking his legs, Aloo moved the boat in a southern direction, so he could see the other side of the piragua. He kept his head close to the waterline, letting the waves wash over him occasionally, trying not to vomit again. When the other side of the piragua came into view, Aloo stopped kicking. Four heads. The surviving raiders. Huddled close to the hull of the piragua. Planning their next move.

Aloo tugged at the bobbing canoe. He couldn't get a good shot from here. But before he could pull the boat around, the raiders all turned toward the northern point of the bay, swimming away quickly, disappearing under the waves.

A flood of panic swept over Aloo. They were heading to the rocks where Yurubi was hidden. They were much closer than he was. They could get there faster. He'd have to get back in the boat. No other choice now. But what if he passed out again?

It was sheer luck that he had even managed to get out here, past the mouth of the bay. Like a drunken man, he'd paddled the boat away from the beach, fighting the black dots, trying to intercept the piragua before the raiders could hurt Yurubi. Then a big wave had lifted his canoe. It tilted sickeningly. And the darkness swallowed him.

When he came to, his boat was way out at sea, drifting fast on a strong tide. Dizzy and nauseous, Aloo had paddled frantically in the rain, aiming for the piragua that was pointed straight at the beach. His heart had jumped into his mouth when he saw the men shooting arrows toward the rocks on the far side of the bay. He had quickly grabbed his bow, slipped over the side of the boat and fired off a string of arrows at them. His heart had swelled with pride when he realized Yurubi had taken out some of them on her own.

But now the remaining four raiders were swimming fast for the rocks where she was hiding. And he had little chance of finding all of them in the water before they reached her.

Aloo gulped at the lump in his throat.

"Look out, there are four of them!" he shouted at the top of his voice in a warning to Yurubi, hoping at the same time to draw the raiders back to him. But they were swimming deep underwater. They might not have heard him.

Aloo vaulted into the boat, clenching his jaw tight to stop from retching.

Yurubi's eyes flared wide and her breath stopped.

Aloo?

Here?

A wave of exultation flooded Yurubi's heart like a song. Aloo was here, Aloo was here.

Of course, it was Aloo. Who else could shoot like that in the dark?

But Aloo in a boat?

Yurubi flicked the hair out of her eyes. She was itching to peek out from behind the rock but couldn't take that chance. Four raiders were heading toward her, and she didn't know whether they were swimming or coming in the piragua.

As if Aloo had heard her thoughts, his voice rang out over the water.

"They're swimming!"

Yurubi bit her lip, her heart pounding. Four raiders against her and Aloo. There must be a way. Scrabbling between the rocks, Yurubi scooped up two handfuls of the wet black sand and plastered it over her face. It was coarse and didn't stick very well, but it would do for now. She grabbed up some more and slapped it on her shoulders and chest. Then she waited. Before long, a big wave crashed into the rocks, spewing spray high into the air. Yurubi popped her head up and glanced quickly over the water. She caught a glimpse of something that looked like a canoe staggering across the mouth of the bay. Her heart sank. If that was Aloo, he wasn't going to make it to the coastline before the raiders.

With a sick feeling in her stomach, Yurubi eased down behind the rock again. She knew Aloo had been shouting not just to warn her but also to distract the raiders. Or at least try to split up the attackers. But that was not working. They were coming after her first, then they'd lie in wait for Aloo.

Yurubi fingered the two remaining arrows in her quiver.

She had to move from this spot. The rain had petered out to a drizzle, allowing her to see more clearly around her, but it also meant the raiders would be able to spot her more easily.

She smeared some more sand over her face and torso and began crawling backward, her eyes raking the rocky shoreline in front her. She winced each time her right leg scraped against a rock but kept going as fast as she could. If she could get to the little cave-like overhang in the cliff behind her, she might be able to pick off at least two of the raiders.

When she backed onto a patch of coarse sand, she knew she was close. With her toes, she scoured the face of the cliff until she found the opening. Not a moment too soon. As she scooted under the overhang, she saw a head pop up briefly on the edge of the rocks.

Crouched low with her back pressed against the cliff, Yurubi loaded her bow and held the one other arrow loosely in the fingers of her left hand.

Her eyes flicked from left to right and back again. The men were most likely crawling on their bellies among the rocks, looking for her. She caught a blur way off to her right. Then as a wave crashed into the rocks, she saw another quick movement on the far left.

So that was their plan. They were spreading out to search for her. The waves hissed and sucked among the rocks, occasionally throwing plumes of spray into the air.

Suddenly, a shape slid from behind a rock slightly to Yurubi's right and lay there, looking around cautiously. Yurubi hesitated for a moment, straining her eyes to make quite sure it was not Aloo.

No, this was a broad squat man, with a thick neck. She shot him through the neck, reloaded her bow and swung it around as another man leapt from behind a rock on the left. Her arrow caught him in the chest. He staggered forward a few steps then toppled over with a thud.

Now Yurubi could see one of the raiders moving swiftly toward her hiding place. She was out of arrows. Very slowly, Yurubi put down her bow and eased the quiver off her shoulder. She crouched on all fours under the overhanging rock, the blood pounding in her ears.

An arrow whizzed into her hiding place and buried itself in the sand near her feet. Yurubi grunted and stomped her left foot in the sand, pretending to collapse. She remained crouched low, holding her breath.

Narrowing her eyes to prevent them from glinting in the dark, she watched as the raider edged out from behind a low rock and crept forward, his bow held ready. As he drew nearer to Yurubi's hiding place, he dropped his arms slightly and squatted lower to peer under the overhanging rock.

Yurubi dived at him like a killer dolphin. Her head caught him squarely in the chest, knocking him backward on the sand. His arrow flew harmlessly skyward, and his bow clattered onto the rocks behind him. Yurubi pounced on him, raising the knife in her right hand. But his arm shot out and caught her wrist, jerking her hard against him. The knife fell from Yurubi's hand. She felt the man's lean ropy body go still and his grip on her wrist slackened for a moment.

"A woman?" he said, his voice high in disbelief.

In that instant, Yurubi brought her left knee up and slammed it between his legs. His howl of pain echoed off the rocks as Yurubi rolled away rapidly.

Jumping to her feet, she caught sight of the fourth raider leaping over the rocks to her left, his long legs moving in a blur. He landed lightly near the other man who was writhing on the little patch of sand.

"A woman!" the tall raider said softly, looking from Yurubi to his friend on the ground.

Yurubi drew the knife on her left hip and went into a crouch, facing the two men.

"Tumusu, you've got a wild one here," the tall one said, a note of glee in his voice.

His eyes moved over Yurubi, from head to toe and back up again.

"Where's your man, little manicou?" he said with a laugh, swinging his bow and arrow from side to side almost playfully.

Yurubi's eyes flicked from him to the one called Tumusu, who was now staggering to his feet. A grim resolve settled in her chest. She might not be able to take down both men, but she'd get one.

"Get back, she's mine," said Tumusu, his voice like stone.

Yurubi's tongue felt stuck to the roof of her dry mouth, but she dared not swallow or lick her lips. That'd be a sign of fear.

Tumusu slipped a knife from the sheath on his right hip and braced his legs, his eyes fixed on Yurubi.

"Her man is lying dead or injured somewhere among these rocks or under that cave," he said to his friend, gesturing with his chin. "Go find him."

"In a while," said the taller man, with a broad grin. "I don't want to miss this. Besides, you might need my help to capture her."

Tumusu's face twisted in rage, and he spat in the sand between his feet. "Get out of my way, Roudou. I said she's mine."

The man called Roudou laughed under his breath and drew back. "Watch out for that knife, Tumusu. She probably knows how to use it."

Yurubi narrowed her eyes, focusing fully on Tumusu now. He was a short stringy man with a face like a hawksbill turtle. He and his friend might want to capture rather than kill her, but that didn't mean they would spare her any pain. She tightened her grip on the knife.

Tumusu sprang forward. Yurubi held her ground. At the last moment she twisted aside and slashed at Tumusu as he went flying past.

Roudou's laughter bounced off the cliff.

Yurubi pivoted to face Tumusu again. He had recovered quickly and was running at her. Yurubi nimbly sidestepped him again, but this time he swerved sharply, slamming into her left shoulder. She staggered and fell on her side in the sand.

Like a streak of lightning, Tumusu appeared over her. Yurubi's legs shot out. She swept one of Tumusu's ankles, gripped his other leg between hers and rolled hard. He toppled to the sand, his rancid breath whooshing against her face. In a flash, Yurubi plunged her knife into the side of his neck. Once, twice, three times. She sprang away from his flailing body and jumped to her feet. Gripping her bloody knife tightly, she spun around to face Roudou.

His laughter had dried up. He was holding his bow at full draw, the arrow aimed at Yurubi's chest.

"There's no man, is there?" he said in a hoarse whisper. "You're one of those warrior women ..."

Despite the deadly peril staring at her from the tip of Roudou's arrow, Yurubi felt a surge of elation.

It was true. It was all true. Pipo's story about the island, the fierce women warriors, their deadly skills.

The wonderment in this man's voice told all, although his face remained hard as wood.

Yurubi lifted her chin. No, she was not one of those mighty women, but she would die like a warrior here on the rocks of Hiroon.

She set her lips and tensed the muscles in her legs.

"You won't make it," Roudou said. His fingers tightened on the bow and something like regret flickered across his face.

Yurubi leapt at him, her knife held low. He twisted away awkwardly from her knife hand, his jaw slackening in surprise. His arrow flew far to her right. Yurubi brought the knife up swiftly, catching him under the ribs as he leaned toward her. She gritted her teeth and twisted the knife. That's when she saw the arrow sticking out of his back. She jumped away, her eyes frantically searching the rocks behind him.

The raider dropped to his knees and toppled onto his face.

"He's as dead as anyone could be."

Yurubi's breath snagged in her chest.

In a blur, Aloo rose like a shadow from behind an outcrop and bounded over the rocks.

"That was the last one," he said softly, as he landed on the sand in front of Yurubi.

For a heartbeat, the crashing of the ocean faded as his eyes met hers and moved over her face.

"Aloo—"

He reached out and pulled her tight against his wet chest. Yurubi closed her eyes, drinking in the familiar smell of his skin, the pounding of his heart under her cheek. She wrapped her arms around him as her legs began to tremble. His lips brushed the top of her head, her temple, her cheek, her mouth, and rested there.

Yurubi's eyelids fluttered as a smudge of light from the far horizon danced across her face. She tightened her arms around Aloo, threading her fingers through the mass of wet locks hanging down his back. A plume of spray spewed high off the rocks and showered over them. Yurubi felt the wave cascading through her limbs. Somewhere, high up on the cliff, a single bird note broke open the morning.

Aloo lifted his head and nuzzled Yurubi's hair, his breath fanning down the back of her neck. Over his shoulder, a bundle of grey clouds untangled drowsily and reached out thick fingers to lift a wisp of purple above the horizon. A pair of seagulls fussed in impatience, dipping their wingtips into the deep, then rising to swipe swathes of orange, red and silver across the sky.

Yurubi's smile soared into the mix, unfurling into a backdrop of the newest blue.

THREE MOONS LATER

"Even when she was little like you, she was never afraid of anything. Not forest animals, not fierce men, not maybouya."

The children clustered around Pipo were gazing at him with owl-like eyes, their rapt faces glowing in the firelight.

"I'm not afraid of animals, either," a little girl piped up. "I threw a stick at an agouti down by the river and chased it away."

One of the boys jeered at her. "An agouti? Pfff, that's not even—"

"You did well," Pipo said, tousling the top of the girl's head. "When Yurubi was a young girl, she used to practice hunting by going after agoutis."

The moonlight played like mischief on Pipo's face as he turned to glance at Yurubi.

She was sitting under a tree on the other side of the clearing, leaning back against Aloo, his arms curled loosely around her middle, his chin resting lightly on her head.

"Sometimes, when little Yurubi caught an agouti, she'd skin it with her teeth if she didn't have a knife," said Pipo, his voice rippling like an ocean wave.

The little girl clapped a hand over her mouth, while the boys snickered.

Yurubi cast a withering look at Pipo and rolled her eyes, but he only grinned and picked up his story again.

"On the night of the Big Fight, Yurubi tricked the raiders into thinking she was three or four people. She swam back and forth along the bay, shooting at them from different spots. With her bow and arrows, which she'd made herself, she fought alone against a boatload of warriors."

Pipo straightened his back and flung his arms wide.

"And then Aloo showed up." Pipo clenched his fists and worked his arms like two paddles. "He had to battle hard to get away from the Great Mountain spirit to make it out to sea."

"Why was the mountain spirit trying to capture him?" said the little girl, frowning hard.

"The Great Mountain spirit claims Aloo as its own and gets upset when he tries to go too far away," Pipo said. "That's why Aloo took a while to reach Yurubi on the rocks. As he raced toward her, paddling in my fishing boat part of the way, the mountain spirit tried to grab him back. But he jumped overboard and began swimming as fast as he could. Then two raiders who were hiding under Yurubi's upturned boat tried to ambush him. But they didn't know about Aloo's many special skills."

"What's 'sp-special skills?'" the little girl asked, glancing sideways at Aloo and Yurubi.

Pipo took a sip of his woku and shifted his position slightly. A smile tugged at his mouth as he looked around the circle of small upturned faces, into the spellbound eyes fixed on him. He set down his mug and propped his elbows on his thighs.

"Aloo was the first new friend I made when we both joined up with the people of Warigara, after we fled from the raging mountain. Aloo could climb a tree faster than a manicou, and he had better night eyes than an owl."

A boy in the circle stretched his eyes wide with his fingers and leaned toward Pipo. "Like this?"

Pipo laughed.

"Much, much better than that. And he didn't have to stretch his eyes either. In fact, he could see better like this." Pipo narrowed his eyes to a slit.

The children giggled and edged closer to him.

On the other side of the fire, near the taboui, Chief Oudou and his warriors lolled against their women, talking in lazy voices about a day of games for all the villagers. With gentle hands, the women smoothed oil into the men's hair, smiling as if at some secret only they knew.

Out on the edge of the clearing, Ikupo sucked on a thick roll of leaves and closed his eyes as Pipo's smooth voice wafted over him.

"Yurubi and Aloo fitted perfectly together as soon as they laid eyes on each other. They were like two bowls made from the same calabash. They were both fervent ..."

Ikupo sensed rather than saw Yurubi and Aloo rise from what had become their special spot under the small poui tree and stroll hand in hand toward their hut.

Ikupo pulled on the roll, feeling his body melding into the tree stump at his back. The firelight faded, and he was floating again into his old dream.

Wisps of smoke rose before him, gradually growing thicker, writhing and swirling.

Slowly, the shape emerged. A broad-chested warrior with thickly muscled arms and legs, head held high, a mass of curly black hair streaming behind him, his glistening body the colour of newly turned earth after a rain shower.

A wayward breeze whispered down Ikupo's back as the familiar words echoed in his head.

From the soil of Hiroon, this great warrior will grow, though long, long after your time, Ikupo. He will lead the people of Hiroon against a massive wave coming from afar. His enemies will quake at the sound of his name, which will echo from shore to shore.

Ikupo's head flopped back.

"I've done my part," he breathed, his face tilted to the Great Mountain. "I've prepared the ground and sifted the seeds. They're yours now. Grow our mighty warrior and grow him well, whether on your back or under your chin. My task is done."

Deep in his dream, Ikupo floated up the Great Mountain and nested like a sparrow in its green embrace.

THE END

AUTHOR'S NOTE

This story was inspired by my deep desire to know what life was like for the indigenous people of my home country, St. Vincent and the Grenadines (Hiroon), before the arrival of the Europeans.

Almost every account I had read of the Kalina was written by a European — a sailor, a soldier, a missionary or a settler — and in all likelihood would've been filtered through the lenses of their own cultural and societal norms. There was very little on record that reflected the perspective of the early Kalina people.

That led me to ponder the words of American author Toni Morrison: "If there's a book you want to read, but it hasn't been written yet, then you must write it."

So, I delved into the work of historians, archaeologists, palaeontologists, anthropologists and naturalists and pumped life into the dry facts and artefacts, drawing on my imagination to fill in the many gaps.

In writing an African character into the story, I leaned on the side of the argument that Africans had been crossing the Atlantic to the Americas for exploration and trade long before Columbus made it to the New World. In my research, I found archaeological reports and anecdotal evidence in support of that argument. Reports of physical oceanography studies indicated that ancient African boats, even as basic as a dugout canoe, would have been able to cross from the west coast of Africa to the Americas in a few weeks.

In the interest of storytelling, I may have taken license with some historical facts, mainly in cases where there was an absence of conclusive information. For example, I could not establish that St. Vincent and the Grenadines was one of the native habitats of the peccary, which I chose to refer to as a pig in the story, although its presence was recorded in nearby Trinidad and Tobago and in Central and South America.

I had no reservations about placing an eruption of the island's volcano in the 14th century, since the earliest historical record of such an event in that location goes back only as far as 1718.

The writing of this book has been an intriguing journey in tribute to the people who gave St. Vincent and the Grenadines a place in history as the last Caribbean territory to fall to European colonization.

ACKNOWLEDGEMENTS

I'm deeply indebted to many wonderful people who helped make this book possible.

I want to thank Ivenia Benjamin and the team at Emmanuel Publishing House for the hard work, patience and professionalism invested in giving wings to this book. Ivenia, your interest in this tale, even before you had seen the manuscript, was highly motivating. Thank you, Susan Sayre, for your keen eye and diligent editing.

Sarah Dronfield, I cannot thank you enough for your brilliant and detailed critique, which was invaluable in helping me to tighten the story and iron out the kinks. You were the perfect fit for this historical fiction novel, and you went the extra mile to offer guidance on navigating the path to publication.

Special thanks, my dear artist friend Veronica Peace, for your fine creative work on the maps and the beautiful cover illustration. Thank you for reading my first draft and responding with such excitement. Your unwavering support and encouragement throughout this writing project meant the world to me.

To my children, Nicky, Vashti and Nichole, you made this a family effort by jumping in right from the start, buying me books for my research and digging up articles, papers, maps, drawings, photographs and other relevant material. Vashti, your insights were phenomenal as you read and reread the manuscript. Nicky, thanks for taking the time to sound out my two imaginative grandchildren on the appeal of the story. Reka and Nya, you were the beacons on this adventure, and you made it all worthwhile. This story is a better one because of the immeasurable love and talents you all shared with me.

I want to thank my extended family and friends all over the globe for reaching out via text messages, emails and phone calls to let me know that you're always there for me. My childhood friend, Irwin Martin, thanks for going the distance with me on my journey over the years from scribbler to writer.

None of this would have been possible without my beloved mother, Leila Deane, to whom I owe everything. Mom, it would take an entire book to detail the ways in which you inspired, nurtured and helped give life to my dreams and aspirations, from as far back as I can remember. So, for now, I'll offer, with all my heart, a simple thank you.

ABOUT THE AUTHOR

Peggy Carr is a journalist, writer, poet, wanderer and storyteller. Her nomad spirit has taken her from her home country of St. Vincent and the Grenadines in the Caribbean to Taiwan on the other side of the world, where she works as a news editor.

Her love of storytelling spurred the creation of *SHAPE OF A WARRIOR*, her first novel.

Early in her writing career, Peggy won a prestigious BBC poetry prize, which motivated her to start publishing her poems. Her most popular collection, *HONEY AND LIME,* contains a section that speaks to the youth of her country in Vincentian dialect.

Her poems have also been published in anthologies around the world, from the Caribbean to the United Kingdom and as far as New Zealand. In 2014, she was selected by the BBC as her country's representative poet in the BBC Scotland's Poetry Postcard series for the Commonwealth Games.

Peggy is a Cultural Ambassador of St. Vincent and the Grenadines. She is deeply invested in helping young people find purpose, direction and self-awareness.

Apart from writing, Peggy loves going on various types of adventures with her three children, two granddaughters, and numerous other relatives and friends.

https://peggycarr.wixsite.com/website

Made in the USA
Monee, IL
31 October 2020